WHITE THR

SARAH THORNTON
WHITE THROAT

TEXT PUBLISHING MELBOURNE AUSTRALIA

textpublishing.com.au

The Text Publishing Company
Swann House, 22 William Street, Melbourne Victoria 3000, Australia

Published by The Text Publishing Company, 2020

Book design by Imogen Stubbs
Cover image by Max Rozen / Getty Images
Typeset in Sabon 11.5/16.5 by J&M Typesetting

Printed and bound in Australia by Griffin Press, part of Ovato, an accredited ISO/NZS 14001:2004 Environmental Management System printer.

ISBN: 9781922330031 (paperback)
ISBN: 9781925923476 (ebook)

A catalogue record for this book is available from the National Library of Australia.

This book is printed on paper certified against the Forest Stewardship Council® Standards. Griffin Press holds FSC chain-of-custody certification SGS-COC-005088. FSC promotes environmentally responsible, socially beneficial and economically viable management of the world's forests.

To Dad, for the gift of the sea and the love of boats.

Biological diversity is messy. It walks, it crawls, it swims, it swoops, it buzzes. But extinction is silent, and it has no voice other than our own.

Paul Hawken

The ute erupted into the clearing with a roar, floodlights shuddering and bouncing against the black of the rock face. The light drew a kamikaze rush of flying insects towards it while crawling creatures scurried into the scrub.

'Donut, man! Donut!' yelled the passenger over the thunder of the engine.

Foot flat to the boards, the driver swung the car into a wickedly tight circle, back wheels spinning through muddy puddles, skating across the gravel, plumes of filthy water rocketing towards the crescent moon. The floodlights swung back around over the base of the quarry.

A shout from the passenger: 'STOP! STOP!'

The driver slammed on the brakes. There was a hair-raising slide before the vehicle slumped to a stop, rocking once with the last of the momentum, a ripple of light wafting across the clearing.

'There!' he pointed. 'Shine the lights over there.'

'What are you on about?' said the driver.

But the passenger was already out of the car and walking quickly through the insect cloud. 'Bring the torch!'

The driver switched off the floodies and peered into the darkness as the other man walked outside the beam of the headlights. He grabbed the torch from the glove box and jumped down out of the vehicle, shoes crunching in the gravel. A swampy stench filled the clearing and there was a shimmer, a buzz in the air, as if the night

1

was struggling to reconstitute itself. His mate slowed, stepping carefully as he approached a dead tree at the base of the quarry, the driver watching him as he leaned forward to look, then stepped back abruptly with a stifled shout, bent over double and vomited into the shadows.

The driver's hand shook on the torch as his eyes adjusted. There was an odd shape silhouetted in the torch beam. He walked towards it.

The fallen tree lay across the ground, a long dark finger of black, over half a metre wide at its thickest. The shape was a body—a woman, lying on top of the tree, face up, her legs and arms straddling the trunk and hanging limp either side. Bare feet, one sandal on the ground at the edge of the ring of torchlight. Her eyes were open, staring, her head and face bloodied, hair flung back against the tree.

And what was holding her there, balanced on the trunk like that, was a branch about two finger widths in diameter, speared straight through her chest and pointing reproachfully into the night.

CHAPTER 1

Looking out over an ebb tide from the back verandah was like watching God paint stripes. Creamy tidal flats, milk-green shallows, then bands of ever-deepening jade and turquoise. And beyond, sparkling in the sun, the sapphire brilliance of the deep channel. Each colour as transient as her own streaky existence.

Clementine Jones shifted her position on the wooden deckchair, her feet resting on the verandah railing, laptop perched on a towel draped across her sweaty legs. She'd been working on the latest submission for the turtle campaign.

The house-sitting gig she'd landed here in this little coastal backwater paid bugger all but it had offered a cheap ticket out: a reason to leave Katinga. The owner, Noel, was travelling overseas. Noel's house, if you could call it that, was a faded pastel-yellow fibro shanty just out of town overlooking the Great Sandy Straits, with Fraser Island—K'gari to the Butchulla people since distant times—floating on the horizon.

The backyard ended where the beach began and the place was surrounded by an acre of bush each side, but the shack was completely run down—brown stains under the windows, mould under the eaves, rickety timber verandah. It was more about minding Noel's dog, Sergeant, a fifty-five kilogram bull-mastiff, than looking after this renovator's delight.

Piama was billed as a 'seaside resort village' but really it was more of an oversized tidal flat, and there were only so many 'beach' walks she could do. After repeat readings of the ten plaques along the boardwalk explaining the life-giving wonders of mangroves, she'd reached her boredom threshold. It was about the same time as she registered the rash of 'Save the Turtle' posters plastered around town. She'd called the number at the bottom. It had blown her away when Helen answered the phone. *Auntie* Helen—here in Piama, running the Wildlife Association of the Great Sandy Straits.

Clem watched as Pocket roused himself from under the pandanus and followed the shade around to the other side, flopping like a rag doll and stretching himself out next to Sergeant. Her little blue heeler looked about the size of a chihuahua next to the mastiff.

She shooed a march fly from her shin, watched it fly off into the lazy sheoak drooping over the guttering and let her thoughts wander to the phone call from Melbourne that morning. A follow-up on a job offer from Burns Crowther, a law firm wanting to expand its sports law division, looking for a solicitor with a profile.

Profile. She had one of those now. It was why she'd had to leave Katinga. But the managing partner didn't seem to care: 'You've got a name in sporting circles—all that publicity around the Cats' victory...oh and the little girl with the heart problem. How's she doing, anyway?'

This profile. This was the thing that hung inside her like a stone.

She had to admit, though, the offer was enticing. And as the afternoon sun reflected on the backs of a mass of soldier crabs, spreading like a purple blanket across the sand, she pictured the bustling streets, the exhilarating buzz of Melbourne...a slick inner-city apartment, champagne by the Yarra, coffee in a cobbled laneway.

Her screen flashed. Another email from the Cats' club President, John Wakely, wanting to know when she'd be starting pre-season training. There was a bit of a tone to this, his third message. Not

4

surprising since she hadn't replied to either of the previous two. The players were *champing at the bit* he wrote, *asking for training dates so they can mark their calendars.*

That was a laugh, the thought of Torrens or Devo or Maggot Maloney actually owning a calendar. Wakely must really be getting cranky now, though, because he mentioned her bonus. Paid on condition, he pointed out, that she coach again next season.

She felt a flush rise in her cheeks. She could return the money, but that wasn't what they wanted. They wanted her back, coaching, preferably to another premiership.

The march fly was back and getting stuck into her ankle. She didn't reach down to brush it away. She deserved the sting.

\\/

There was a reason Clementine had never set foot in the WAGSS headquarters and, as she stepped through the doorway of Helen's shed that Tuesday in October with the draft submission in her bag, she knew she'd been right.

A ladder and some gardening tools lined one side of the shed. Open bags of blood and bone provided the aromatic backdrop to the trestle table draped in a green bedsheet that commanded the central space. Hovering at one end of the table was a woman in blue harem pants, the crotch hanging somewhere near her knees. Beside her stood a dreadlocked man in a blousy hemp shirt and striped purple pants. There were two other women, middle-aged, one in a floral dress, the other in shorts—each cutting out letters from a sheet of gold cardboard. The man was in the process of gluing a giant T on the end of 'SAVE THE TUR' while the harem-pants woman worked carefully on an L.

It wasn't the clothing or any other one thing that did it. It was the whole scene. A picture—like a Renaissance frieze of the Last Supper or that Sidney Nolan painting of the Ned Kelly trial—telling the whole story in one panel. The feeling was something like a feral kindergarten.

She walked briskly towards the back of the shed where Helen sat at a desk staring at a monitor, her chin resting on her cupped hand. One finger was crooked across her lips as she read, eyes trawling left to right, expecting enlightenment at any moment.

'Ah!' she said, throwing her hands up in the air and springing from her chair, 'Clementine!'

Helen had insisted she bring the submission over in person so they could go through it together. She'd assured Clem it would be just the two of them. Now, as everyone at the tables looked up, Clem felt a barb of suspicion. Helen was going to try to get her involved in the protest this Thursday—a sit-in at a bank in Barnforth. On the list of things Clementine had expressly ruled out when she'd agreed to help Helen with the campaign, occupying business premises ranked high. Just above obstructing traffic but a few rungs below chanting and tambourines.

Helen wore the lightest of sundresses, thin straps across her tanned shoulders, her auburn hair piled high in a messy topknot. Though she was the same age as Clem's mother, she seemed younger. She had laughter lines around her eyes these days, but her skin was still amazing—she'd always worn hats despite allowing the rest of her body the full kiss of the sun.

'You must meet the team. Everybody, this is Clementine, the lawyer I told you about.'

Clem nodded at them and gave an awkward smile.

'Lovely to meet you,' said the woman in shorts, holding out her hand, 'I'm Gaylene.' She wore bifocals and had a magnificent head of thick wavy hair that brushed her shoulders like a mane.

'And this is Ariel,' said Helen, with her hand on Yoga Pants' shoulder, '...Mary,' she gestured at the smiling woman in the dress. 'And this is Brady.' His face looked older than his body, with deep lines and discoloured teeth. Clem wondered if he'd had some sort of addiction. They all smiled eagerly with what Clem suspected was recruiting fervour. Helen had worded them up, for sure. *Bloody hell, Helen.*

She was standing there grinning foolishly when Brady thrust out his hand and flashed his dirty pegs. 'G'day. Looking forward to sticking it up the banks on Thursday?'

\\/

Clem stood in Helen's living room looking out towards the paperbarks along the river's edge. Turtle Shores, with its beautiful old Queenslander homestead and three acres of untouched bushland by the river, was prized Piama real estate.

Helen had made the seachange to Piama three years ago, right after her retirement. It must have been about five years after Uncle Jim's death. The couple had been old family friends of Clementine's parents before they'd moved across town, then interstate and, finally, lost touch altogether.

A cooling breeze laced with eucalyptus rustled the wooden chimes at the back door and swept on through the louvred windows. Helen had created a real beachy feel—seascapes hanging on the walls, lots of shells and bits of driftwood alongside a black and white photo of Jim. She'd recently turned sixty and a greeting card was propped open with a sunbleached purple sea urchin. Clem glanced at it—roses on the cover, inside a handwritten joke about ageing and then *all my love* followed by a string of kisses.

She turned to watch as Helen made espresso, her blind cat, Fluffy, doing figure of eights around her legs. If nothing else, Clem thought, she would at least get her first decent coffee since she'd passed through Brisbane. And Helen baked, too.

'Sooooo, about Thursday,' said Helen, manhandling the portafilter on the coffee machine.

'There's no Thursday, Helen. In fact, I'm skipping from Wednesday straight to Friday this week.'

'But it would be good for the campaign if you could take on... you know...more of a leadership role. Having someone with your background there, at the coalface—it would give us so much more presence.' Helen had spent years in public relations. She had a keen eye for these things.

Clem didn't care. 'Um, Helen, remember when I said I'd provide legal support from my home office? And my very clear list of exclusions?'

'Yes, yes, of course, and I'm grateful, we all are. I would suggest it's more than legal support, though. The letters...the way you write...they're the only reason we got a meeting with the minister.'

The Federal Minister for the Environment and Energy was considering the environmental impact statement supporting Marakai Mining's proposal to build a new coalmine fifty kilometres inland from Piama. The project involved road and rail following the river right past Turtle Shores, then on to a planned two-berth deep shipping port with a dredged channel out to the ocean.

The development had a lot of local support, and only partly because of the new jobs that were promised. It would also be heaven-sent relief for a cluster of residents, mostly pensioners, whose houses would be acquired to make room for the port. A financial-planning scandal had ripped through Piama recently, wiping out nest eggs and just about everything else, leaving a trail of life-throttling mortgages. The prices the company was throwing around promised a way out.

WAGSS, on the other hand, was fighting for the survival of an endangered freshwater turtle, its habitat threatened by the development.

Clem had researched the legislation, scouring hundreds

of pages of the company's applications for approval, searching for weaknesses, any loose thread that could be unpicked. She'd drafted a letter to the minister and a hard-hitting submission to the department. But she'd done it all from the back verandah at the shanty. All except for that one meeting, which had, admittedly, gone well. Helen was still stoked at how they'd double-teamed the minister. But the big takeaway for Clem was the newspaper articles the next day—the photo captions as they left council chambers: *Clementine Jones...former lawyer...Manslaughter...young mother...nine months' prison.* It was a running commentary she couldn't seem to leave behind, popping up any time she stuck her head above the parapet.

Helen put the coffee mugs on the table, went back to the kitchen and returned with a plate of brownies.

'But what I don't understand is why you wouldn't want to participate more fully.'

Clem took a brownie and shook her head. 'I'm just shy, Helen.'

Helen nearly spurted her mouthful of coffee over the table. 'That's a good one. Shy? The coach of a men's footy team?' she said, snorting with laughter. 'Actually, you've never told me how that came about.'

'The footy?' said Clem, biting into the fudgy cake, stalling.

'Yes.'

'Wrong place, wrong time.'

'Come on Clem, I've known you since you were in nappies. You can give me more than that.'

Clem put down her mug, placed the brownie back on the saucer, slowly.

'Same reason I signed up with the turtle campaign, Helen— boredom, sheer boredom. There was a vacancy. I applied. Apparently coaching an under-sixteen team and playing women's footy for five years was more than enough experience,' she said. 'Well, given that I was the only applicant.'

'But what were you even doing there? I mean, you're a corporate lawyer...'

Would she ever get used to this? Helen had been so discreet for the last three weeks: not a single question. But now the fortress was under attack.

'You don't need to tell me about what happened in Sydney, Clem. I've read all that—I know what you've been through. It's just, I'm interested in how you came to take the next step.' She took a sip of coffee. Smiled again.

That smile. It was Helen's answer to everything, it was an invitation, a welcome, expressing delight or disapproval, joy or sorrow. And it brought back powerful memories.

The night Dad brought them all in to the hospital to see Mum—only she wasn't Mum anymore. She was this grey, ghostly, whispering thing.

Clem remembered standing there by the bed in the blue jumper Gran had knitted her. It was too small now and rode up, leaving her back exposed to the winter cold. Mum would have known she'd outgrown it. Dad didn't. He didn't seem to know the things Mum knew, and everything else was in the laundry basket. He was working, visiting Mum in hospital, caring for two kids, often cross, impatient with her little brother Josh...and, she realised now with a stab of pain, holding it together with strands of iron will and not much else.

That night, after saying goodbye to Mum, with her scary black-circled eyes and her cracked lips, Dad dropped Josh at Gran's and took ten-year-old Clementine to their old family friends Helen and Jim—bewildered, stunned and clutching a bag of dirty washing.

Auntie Helen had welcomed her with that smile, brighter than the light that shone over the back door. She'd washed Clem's school uniform and tucked her into bed with a hot milk and honey, the kind Mum made with the nutmeg sprinkled on top, then she'd kissed her forehead with lips like pillows. Clem spent five months at Auntie Helen and Uncle Jim's until Mum had recovered enough to come home.

'It can help sometimes to share stuff, you know,' said Helen.

Clem had told one person: Rowan, the guy who'd saved her life in the Arkuna National Park a couple of months ago. Had it helped to tell him? To look into another person's eyes and share her unspeakable shame? She remembered well the flood of relief the moment she'd finally had the courage to say the words—the knot clenched tight inside had loosened, just a bit. *Yes,* she thought, *it had helped.* A single connection with another human being. And yet, she'd still run—left him standing there in her driveway. As she'd said to him, telling a friend, one friend, was not the same as facing the whole town.

And now here she was with Helen, her childhood mum when Mum couldn't be Mum.

Clem took a deep breath and let it out in a sigh. 'I...yeah... well, I couldn't face Sydney.' The only thing she knew after her release from prison, the only certainty in the swirling eddy of her fractured life, was that she could not face her colleagues, her friends, her family, anything of her previous life.

Helen waited with patient eyes, both hands around her mug, saying nothing but speaking volumes with her stillness.

'And...well...this is not something I normally discuss,' said Clem, swivelling her mug around and around on the table.

Helen nodded, sipped her coffee.

'Yeah. So then I headed out west, and south...just drove around for a couple of weeks. Anywhere but Sydney. Ended up in Katinga.' Crushed by guilt, wanting nothing but anonymity.

She still had moments—in the middle of the night, usually—waking up in a sweat, seeing Sue Markham's head slumped on the steering wheel. A blood alcohol level of 0.095, so the charge sheet said. Significantly impaired, but not so drunk that she could forget that image. Thinking about it now, she felt the dry hollowness in her stomach again, did a silent count to settle herself—*three, four, five.*

'Then the team started winning, is that right? And you uncovered some sort of criminal conspiracy?'

Clem nodded, still staring down at the mug on the heavy wooden table.

'And then, wham, your past was all over the papers again.'

Clem cleared her throat. 'I think I better get going,' she said, standing up.

'No, no. Please, stay. It's my fault. I shouldn't have pressed you.'

Clem was already out the door and hurrying to the car.

\1/

Helen came over Thursday evening. She brought a bottle of sav blanc and filled Clem in on how the sit-in had gone. Ten of them in there for two hours, holding up the green bedsheets, letting every poor sucker in the queue know that *Elseya albagula*, the endangered white-throated snapping turtle—a turtle that could breath underwater through its bum, no less—was about to be extinguished in the Rivers region when construction began on the new port. The bank manager had been surprisingly tolerant until Brady brought out his handcrafted African bongo drums and the police were called to escort them out.

It was weird at first, drinking with Helen—navigating that cleft in time when grown-ups of your childhood cross over into your adult universe. The years collapse like a concertina as you find yourself in the same room—but thinking about the style of the furniture now, without regard to how it might come together as a cubby house.

Clem brought out another bottle from the fridge and as the evening wore on Helen began referring to her as Earless the Fearless on account of the fact a lowlife thug had sliced off the top of her ear in the Arkuna National Park. From anyone else it would've been bad taste, but with Helen it was welcome relief from the unbearable intensity of it all.

And then there was the turtle. They were onto the top-shelf stuff by then, falling on the floor giggling like schoolgirls.

'Oh God, how I love that turtle,' said Helen, slurring. 'Its little face and its bad breath. White-throated, arse-faced little darlings. Reminds me of all the butt-breathing arseholes who started sniffing around after Jim died.' She laughed so hard she knocked over a glass.

Police have released the name of the woman found dead at the base of Howard's Quarry on Sunday 13 November. Helen Westley, aged sixty, of Piama, was President of the Wildlife Association of the Great Sandy Straits. Four-wheel-drive enthusiasts made the gruesome discovery just after ten that evening. It is understood that Ms Westley's battered body was found impaled on a fallen tree at the bottom of the fifteen-metre drop. Investigations continue.

CHAPTER 2

Clem gripped the order of service tight and turned it over. She could barely look at the photograph on the cover: Helen with her hands clasped in her lap, wearing the necklace she loved, the one Jim had given her just before he died. On the back was a verse Clem recognised, adapted from Theodore Roosevelt's 'man in the arena' speech:

Helen Elizabeth Westley
The woman in the arena...she knew great enthusiasm,
She spent herself in a worthy cause, she dared greatly.

Clem had taken a seat in the fifth row, expecting the pews in front of her to fill up, but only a handful of people trickled in before the service started. Someone junior in a Queensland Parks and Wildlife uniform had been sent to pay their respects for Helen's years of volunteering in the national park, there was a guy in a suit she suspected was from the Galimore Foundation, the main source of funds for WAGSS, and about twenty of the local protesters. She picked out Ariel and Brady, Gaylene and Mary— the ones she'd met in the shed last week. Ariel kept her head bowed and wept throughout, Gaylene had her arm around her shoulder. Mary dabbed at her eyes and Brady looked stunned or stoned or both.

Was that really all? There had been no children for Jim and

Helen; they'd tried, but no dice. Helen's mother, stricken with dementia in a nursing home in Newcastle was the only family she had. The lump in Clem's throat was the size of an apple. So few people, for a woman who'd contributed so much.

And the police were making out it was suicide. Ridiculous. Disgraceful. Clem had told a pasty-faced constable as much, pointing out the long line of people who would be pleased that Helen, the wildlife warrior and thorn in the side of industry, was dead. Insisting that Helen was no more suicidal than her cat, Fluffy. When Clem demanded to know *where the fuck the suicide note was* the sergeant had come out to the counter: a short, wiry woman with a permanently fierce look on her face. Clem made the same points to her, with undiminished force, before storming out yelling, 'Bloody well do your job and find out who the hell pushed that good woman off the cliff!'

She found herself staring blankly now at the front of the chapel. An old friend of Helen's from Sydney had started on the eulogy. Maggie someone. Clem remembered the name. Helen had said Maggie was horrified when she left Sydney to live in the uncivilised backblocks of Piama, *Wouldn't you rather Noosa, darling?* They'd laughed about it, she and Helen, mimicking the Double Bay accent. It must have been the day after that night they'd got pissed together, a week ago now. Helen hadn't been right to drive. She'd slept in the spare room and woken up in her go-getter mood, apparently unaffected by the big night, a fact that had only made Clem's monster hangover even more loathsome.

Over breakfast Helen had resumed her pitch to get Clem more involved in the WAGSS activism.

'I get that you don't want the performance art stuff,' she'd said, nibbling at a slice of pawpaw, 'But we'd be a good double act at meetings—your hard-arse to my charm. And believe it or not, your profile helps too. You've got a public persona like a magnet,' she'd said. 'You're intriguing to people—smart city lawyer who stumbled...'

Clem had recoiled at that. 'Stumbled? Is that what you call it? I drove my boyfriend's Prado down the wrong side of the road, Helen, and I killed a person.' She gulped and lowered her eyes, 'A living person. A kid's mother.'

It was the hangover, she realised that now, but she regretted her petulance.

Helen had just nodded with a forgiving smile and made a perfect little sound, neither rebuke nor consolation. Then she'd asked what Clem planned to do next, whether she would return to her legal career.

She'd hit unerringly on the thing that scared Clem most: the uncertainty, the absence of any clue as to what she should do, where she should go, who she should be—it tangled her up in a web so thick she could barely see her hand in front of her.

'You were so successful. Do you miss it?'

'Which part?' Clem said, buying some time.

'Lifestyle, money, fancy digs, sporty car...oh, it was red, right? I bet the car was red,' she said, excitedly.

'Yes! A red Alfa Romeo.' They laughed and Helen admitted she missed it too—her old life as a media advisor in Sydney, married to Jim, the love of her life, living large on the northern beaches.

But Helen had known the truth of it without having to be told, without Clem opening her mouth, because then she said, 'I guess that's the hardest part...not knowing what you want, where you're headed?'

That was Helen. She seemed to know before you said anything, reaching out with effortless tenderness.

Clem's tears were streaming again now, as they had since she'd found out the dreadful news.

Maggie was still speaking, from under her perfect silver bob, mostly about the high jinx of university days before the two of them proceeded to their careers: 'Both ending up in media relations, would you believe! Helen for corporates and me handling matters of state for a spate of government ministers.' There followed a sequence of tales that gave ample opportunity for repeated name-dropping. Helen would have been pissing herself, thought Clementine. She'd left that world behind years ago.

The air conditioning in the chapel was too cold. Typical Queensland, steaming outside in strappy dresses and singlets, then goosebumps inside. Clem shivered as Maggie wiped away a tear, then composed herself to introduce Jonathon Galimore, the suit from the Galimore Foundation, the CEO in fact. He seemed rather young but it wouldn't be a big role, administering his great-aunt Glenys' multimillion-dollar fund for species survival—probably just him and an admin making payments, implementing whatever the board decided, attending a few functions. Nonetheless, Jonathon took the opportunity to big-note himself, each anecdote a thinly disguised reflection on his personal heroics. It was a relief when he moved on to the foundation's achievements in shoring up populations of endangered animals across Australia. Finally, he mentioned Helen's contribution, almost as an afterthought.

Clem didn't feel she could speak, but it seemed horribly wrong that these people knew so little of the woman Helen was. The love and comfort she'd freely given to her best friend's little girl; the courage she'd had to take on such an unpopular cause in Piama; her spirited leadership of the rag-tag group of locals caring for their endangered cohabitants on the Earth—the goshawk and the sedge frogs, the koalas and the curlews, and of course the white-throated snapping turtle, so exposed and friendless now. It was a life overlooked.

And everyone in the room believed it was suicide.

Clem couldn't disguise the puff of disgust that escaped from her mouth. A couple of heads turned.

18

Jonathon had finished. That was it then, thought Clem. No prayers or poems, just the civil celebrant winding things up. Clem stuffed her wet tissue into her pocket and stared at the pale wooden coffin, imagining Helen inside and blocking out the well-meaning platitudes issuing from the celebrant, a stranger to Helen. The curtains began to draw together. Helen. Lying there in the box, unable to move, her laughter brought to absolute stillness, her beautiful smile lifeless. Decomposing already.

The curtains closed, with a sigh, too fast: a jaunty swinging at the corners, a frivolous wave. Clem sat for a moment. She said a silent prayer, watched as the pews emptied, then followed everybody out.

\\\/

She'd been inside the chapel less than an hour but the weather had changed. The light breeze had dropped, leaving a dense, expectant heat that hung beneath a tower of storm clouds. The full height of the front was directly above, fifty storeys of outraged cold air shirtfronting the lazy summer heat.

Clem walked briskly towards the carpark and a blast of icy wind arrived, sweeping a sudden chill across her bare arms. She breathed it in, hoping for some sort of relief.

It was in that moment that she heard something. The hairs on the back of her neck sprang up.

No. She didn't want to acknowledge it. But she knew what she'd heard. Breezing past her impossibly, like a spirit: her name, Helen's voice. She shook her head in a shiver. She looked around, as if others might have heard it too. It didn't seem so. The rest of the mourners were in a hurry, rushing to their cars before the clouds dumped their load.

Clem scrambled for her keys. *Don't be bloody stupid, Jones—it's just the cold.* A heavy plop on her forearm. The first drop.

Huge, big enough to move itself and trickle down the curve of her arm. Then another, then they were slapping on her head, splotches forming on the pavement at her feet and a blast of wind blowing her hair back. The sound again...someone calling her name.

Get in the car and get a fucking grip, Jones.

As she reached for the car door she took one last look up, the rain slamming onto her eyes, the cloud above dark green at its base, layers of black above. Then a single, warning crack of thunder, like a curtain tearing.

'*Shit!*' Clem struck her head as she threw herself into the car. She swiped at the strands of wet hair that had whipped across her face. Her hands were shaking.

Of course she hadn't heard Helen's voice. It was just the wind. But it didn't feel like 'just' anything. It was as if the planet had roused itself to bring her a message, bidding Clem to...

To what?

But she knew what. It was obvious. There she was, the only one in the chapel to know...to know for sure, with a certainty that took her breath away, that Helen Westley, her dear friend, her second mum and a woman who had *known great enthusiasm* and *dared greatly*, had not jumped to her death.

Helen Westley was pushed off that cliff. Clem knew it.

This near-empty chapel, this pitifully limp service had been judged and overruled with all the power of the weather gods. Helen had lived and loved and contributed and made her days count on this planet. Then violently, shockingly, someone had killed her, and the police, who should have been working overtime to track down her killer, had consigned her to the archives: filed and forgotten under S for suicide.

Clem's head pounded. It was a death that nobody other than the turtle-lovers grieved for, and every other fucker with an axe to grind was pleased about. Helen had become an obstacle in the path of powerful people.

And just like that, the resistance that had come so easily before—
to let things take their course, stand back and not interfere—now
sloughed off Clem's shoulders like burnt skin. She knew, with a
clarity she'd rarely ever felt, that it fell to her to expose the truth
about the death of Helen Westley.

CHAPTER 3

Gripping the steering wheel, eyes staring blankly through sheets of water streaming down the windscreen, her thoughts began to realign, straightening up into logical grooves. The police had moved on, that was clear from her visit the day after they released the name. But there was an obvious list of people with a grudge against Helen—the executives from Marakai Mining charged with driving the mine project ahead; Blair Fullerton, the local mayor, who equated jobs with votes; and Ralph Bennett, the 'Resident President' of a vocal group of financially motivated locals—the Piama Progress Association—all hoping for economic deliverance from their desperate plight, to name a few.

She would have to speak with them, each of them. But what was she to do? Turn up on their doorstep with a notepad and pencil? Demand to know if they had an alibi?

The rain was deafening on the Commodore's roof, horizontal spears against the windows. The car rocked with each gust and she could barely make out what was happening in the car park. A hire car was first out. Maggie perhaps, up from Sydney? Then, turning the Commodore's headlights on, she could see a blue hatchback with the celebrant at the wheel; then the Parks and Wildlife twin-cab ute; a kombi van stacked with four environmentalists crammed across the front seat and who knows how many more lounging on a mattress in the back; and behind that, Brady's multi-coloured Corolla, complete with a very amateurish picture of the white-throated snapping turtle on the bonnet and plastered with 'Abort the Port' stickers.

She needed a reason, a legitimate reason to meet with the people she now understood to be suspects. As each car filed past her, the awful thought began to take hold: she must take Helen's place as campaign leader. It would give her access to company executives, the president of the progress association, the mayor and any other advocacy group that might want WAGSS to roll over and die.

She let her forehead flop down onto the steering wheel. The prospect of such a role filled her with dismay. She had sought to avoid the WAGSS headquarters at Turtle Shores, resisted the sit-ins and the meetings. But this was much, much worse. She would be taking on all of that *and* the leadership.

Lifting her head she saw the headlights flick on from the last of the vehicles left in the carpark—a flash-looking SUV. It reversed out of its space, the Galimore Foundation koala logo emblazoned on the passenger-side door. Helen had told her about the financial sources for the campaign. The Galimore Foundation was the biggest contributor. Without them the campaign would be hamstrung. But foundation funds didn't come without jumping through hoops, the first of which was their fussiness about who they gave the money to, the 'optics' of having a squeaky-clean operation, a presentable leader. Helen had told Clem how much effort she'd put in to building her relationship with Jonathon Galimore—it was why she'd been so successful in getting such generous donations from the foundation.

It was suddenly obvious and immediately urgent, as Jonathon's car passed by and slowed for the exit, that she needed to speak with him, make an impression. She could pull out later if she changed her mind, but this opportunity would not come again.

She thumped her palm down on the horn, three short pips and jumped out of the car, running with the rain like pistons driving into her face. His brake lights were still on. She started yelling and waving. Had he seen her in the mirror?

She made it to the SUV's passenger side, the koala decal eyeing her warily, grabbed the handle and threw herself in, slamming the door behind her. Her hair was plastered to her head, water dripped down her nose and arms and all over the seat.

Jonathon looked across, a soundless O forming in his mouth.

'Hi Jonathon, I'm Clementine Jones. The lawyer that was helping Helen save the turtles,' she said, panting from the run across the carpark. 'Your speech—inspiring! So inspiring.'

\\//

Inspiration turned out to be the right line to take with Jonathon the Great, who was duly impressed by her passion. He made some encouraging remarks, gave a few tips for her submission to the foundation to continue the funding under her leadership and recommended she write to him as soon as possible.

Which was why his email a week later was a slap in the face.

Clementine sat at the kitchen table, facing the rusty old fridge with the backyard and the beach to her left, the morning heat ramping up on its way to uncomfortable but not yet overbearing, the phone at her ear.

'Look, I understand it's a decision of the Foundation Committee'—because, typically, he'd laid the blame at the feet of some faceless non-individual—'but I guess I'd just like to understand the basis for the committee's decision,' she said. Her frustration meter was pushing up into the red zone.

'As I said, Ms Jones, it's just that you didn't fit the criteria.' Jonathon's voice was beginning to sound impatient. He'd given her the company line, now he just wanted to get off the call.

'Yes, you said that, but what exactly are the criteria?'

'Well, there's a number of factors but I don't think—'

'Take me through the factors.'

'Oh, you know, the usual. Experience, relevant knowledge and such.'

'Okay. Well, I'm an experienced leader of people and I know the legislation backwards, as well as every single page of the company's development submission. Every weakness, every angle.'

'Yes, and I'm sure they took that all into account, but the committee also retains a discretion in making these decisions.'

The words hung in the air for a moment as Clem felt her face set into a stony hardness. 'Ah, I see,' she said, through her teeth. 'A discretion. And that would be to filter out unsavoury types, would it?'

'Well, I'm not sure that's how I'd put it, Ms Jones. But this is a private foundation, as you know, and governance is critical. It's very important to ensure foundation funds are in the right hands.'

'Jonathon, I'm a corporate lawyer and a governance professional. I'm a safe pair of hands.' She sensed Jonathon recoiling. He probably wasn't used to aggression. Why would he be, in his cushy nepotistic job?

'Look, I really can't discuss it any further, and I do have some rather important things to attend to...'

'Well then, could you just answer me one question please, Jonathon. Has anyone else put up their hand to lead the campaign?'

Clem had looked at WAGSS' latest accounts. Without the Galimore Foundation, their effectiveness would be severely curtailed. They needed money for mail-outs, advertising, research, travel for meetings and legal fees. All of these things would buy influence and an audience with decision-makers. Without them, WAGSS would be fobbed off.

'Well, I'm not at liberty—'

'I'll take that as a no. Which means the foundation is officially abandoning the white-throated snapping turtle.'

'I can't disclose—'

'Jonathon, you owe it to the people who've put so much into this to give me an answer.'

'There are many other deserving projects...'

There was a long pause as Clem felt the blow: the door slamming on years of dedication from Helen and her team.

'Well. Thank you, at least, for making that clear,' she said. 'But tell me why, Jonathon. For Helen's sake, and for those who are carrying on the fight, tell me why the foundation is throwing away the significant investment it's made in this campaign and into this biological wonder—a cloacal ventilating turtle!—and allowing it to shuffle off into oblivion?'

Crickets.

She sensed it straight away, in the embarrassed pause. She'd been expecting it, but nevertheless it was always a shock to be reminded of this thing she wore, this cloak that covered everything.

'All right,' he said finally. 'If you must know, the foundation can't be associated with an organisation led by the drunk driver who killed a poor little girl's mother.'

A flame had flared inside, her frustration exploding in anger.

'Listen to me, Jonathon'—she was pointing in the air as she spoke—'you can go back to your committee and tell them this is a big mistake. I am capable, experienced and passionate and if anyone can win this fight it's me. Helen literally begged me to be more involved, did you know that?'

'Ms Jones, I really must—'

'And something else you can tell the goddamned committee: I'm preparing the press release now. *Galimore Foundation Fails Turtle,* it'll say—and you can bet your life I'll be including a paragraph on your own arsehole-breathing capabilities too.'

\\//

She was walking the dogs an hour later when the phone rang.

'So how's the turtle wars going? Smashed those fuckers yet?'

Not even a greeting. Yelling down the phone like he had to clear

26

the sound of fifteen chainsaws was Matthew Torrens: ruckman for the Katinga Cats and now champion meat boner at the Earlville Abattoir. He'd been ringing her every week since she left.

'Nope. Think it might be over, mate,' she said, holding the phone away from her ear.

'No way!' he shouted.

'Afraid so. The turtles will have to fend for themselves.' The words didn't come easy. A disrespect to Helen and what she'd stood for. She stopped on the beach path. Sergeant took a seat on her foot.

'Eh? What the fuck? You need some muscle up there? Cos I can be there, Jonesy, just say the word.'

Torrens had been a standover man, very successfully, before his meat-boning career. He'd only recently been released from Loddon prison when he turned up at training, asking for a run. She'd taken him on—at six foot six, built like a heavyweight boxer, who wouldn't? She'd given him extra conditioning sessions to build his fitness. He'd become critical to the team's success and something of a hero around town when they won the drought-breaking grand final.

'No, Torrens. It's not muscle I need. The foundation's pulled the pin, which means no more money to do anything meaningful. And now Helen's gone, there's no leadership, just a bunch of ferals with posters.'

'I got money. How much do you need?' he said.

Clem smiled, 'Yeah, nice of you, mate, but we're talking quite a lot of dough here.' *More than a meat-boner makes.*

'Yeah, well...I probably shouldn't say this on the phone—dunno who might be listening...'

'Hang on, Torrens, hold it right there. I don't want to hear anything untoward.' Meaning 'criminal'.

'Nah, nah, it's all above board, Jonesy...see, I came into some money the other day.'

'Lotto?'

'Let's just say it was an inheritance.'

'You have a rich aunt too?' said Clementine, thinking of Jonathon and just for a second trying to imagine Matthew Torrens in a designer suit. It didn't work, all she could see was his muddied Cats jersey with the parachute-sized shorts, socks bunched around his ankles.

'More like an uncle, actually. Remember I told you about Sinbin?'

Oh dear. Clem recalled Sinbin very well. In the stories Torrens had told her about the colourful characters in his past, Sid 'Sinbin' Schenko had loomed large. A rural drug boss making a fortune corrupting country kids, hiring Torrens as his local muscle in Katinga when he was just fifteen. She even remembered the detail: Sinbin loved cigars, had a collection of blue-tongue lizards and, apparently, thought the world of Torrens. Especially his competence with boltcutters and crowbars.

'Um, not sure that's the sort of money I want.'

'Aw, don't be like that Jonesy. Sid was a good man.'

Clem pinched her forehead together with her fingers, eyes closed.

'Anyway, that's why I'm calling, see—I need to lay low for a while.'

'Hang on, I thought you were going straight?'

'Yeah, I am! This is legit—it was Sid's stash, he earned it and no copper took it off 'im, no court neither, so he can give it to whoever he wants. You should know that, Jonesy, you're a bloody lawyer!'

Clem grimaced. It was no use arguing.

'Sid wanted me to have it—said I was like a son to him,' said Torrens, his voice dropping a few decibels. 'Sat me down one night—this was after he got the big C a few years back, see—he said, *Mattie,* he said, *when I'm gone it's yours.* I thought he meant the land down Tallowbark Creek way at first, but he left that to his ex and their daughter. The Old Cow and the Suckling Pig he called them. Ha! But that's Sid all over, looking after his kid, never mind the mother was a money-grabbing parasite.'

All these characters—she'd heard the names before, it was like a pantomime.

'You still there, Jonesy?'

'Yep. Still here.'

'No one around?'

'Just me and the dogs and the life-giving mangroves.'

'Right,' he said, his voice hushed. 'So then Sinbin says, *Stand under the bloodwood and line up the notch in the mountain, the top of the shed at the back and the dunny. Then dig.* Couldn't believe me ears! I didn't even know there was a stash!' There was a pause and Torrens' voice caught in his throat. 'Yeah well, anyways, he's gone now, old Sid. Cancer got 'im.'

'So sorry, mate. I know how much he meant to you.'

'Yeah.' He let out a long exhale. There was a silence for a moment while they both paid their respects.

'You know what, Jonesy? I told him about how you helped me. I reckon he'd want you to have some of this money for the turtle.'

Oh dear. Clem recoiled at the thought of funding the campaign with the proceeds of crime. 'Um, that's very generous of you, mate'—and it was—'but I couldn't accept it.'

'Fair enough,' he said, philosophically. Torrens might not be fully on board with the concept of dirty money, but he had pride. 'Maybe I'll start me own turtle society. Matty's Butt-Breathers,' guffawing at his own joke. 'Or maybe the Turtle Fart Society. Oh gawd, I could get the Queen onto it. Right up her alley with her Horrible Anus.' He could barely get the words out, snorting with laughter.

'Annus horribilis. It's Latin, you clown,' she said, chuckling.

'Whatever. You shouldn't be quitting. Take a teaspoon of cement and harden up! That's what Sinbin would've said.'

She sighed, kicking at a dried-up coconut husk in the sand. Pocket trotted over to the outer limits of his lead and gave it a sniff, looked up with questioning eyes. *Was she a quitter?* She'd quit Katinga. Now she was quitting Helen after the first setback. *Yes, a quitter for sure.*

'Anyways, what I rang for, Jonesy, was to ask a small favour...'

Here it comes, she thought: *he wants a bloody lawyer—me—to help him launder his wretched cash.*

'...need somewhere to lie low for a bit, you know, just till the heat dies down.'

'You're not suggesting you come up here, are you?'

'Yeah, why not?'

'But it's not even my house.'

'Even better. Less likely they'll find me by connecting me with you.'

'They? Who's they?'

'There's talk...you know, about Sinbin having a stash...plenty of bastards on the prowl.'

'Oh Christ, Torrens.'

'Nah, but that's it see, that's why it'd be great if I could hide up there with you.'

She let out what she thought was an inaudible groan.

'What's wrong?' He sounded hurt, surprised. 'A little holiday in the tropics. No harm in it for ya, is there?'

Ping went her conscience, like an ant bite inside her head. Torrens had helped her out in Katinga, helped her keep her secret, steadied her when she'd wobbled. He'd even organised a homemade bomb to get her out of a sticky situation, despite being on parole at the time.

But harbouring an ex-con in possession of unlawfully obtained monies? She would never have dreamt that she'd be standing here now, underneath a palm tree, contemplating that very thing. And yet, in the wounded tone of Torrens' voice, in the connection they'd

30

built up and the gratitude for what they'd done for each other... Somehow it seemed right.

She felt a wave of realisation. It had changed her. All of it had changed her—the accident, the conviction, the shame, the humiliation of incarceration, the weeks living out of her car, the sanctuary of a dilapidated old cottage in the hills, the small-town jubilation over something as simple as a footy premiership and the country friendships that smouldered and glowed, slow and steady, in a way she hadn't known in the city.

'Jonesy?'

She shuffled her thong across the top of the sand, smoothing where her weight had made an impression and heard herself say, 'Split the food sixty-forty.' *He could damn well pay for his hairy mammoth-sized appetite.*

'Ripper! But I reckon I should put in more than forty, I like a good feed.'

\|/

She reached the end of the walk and turned the dogs back towards the shanty. A regiment of mangrove shoots thrust up through the grey sand to her left, then plains of salted caramel and the shimmering remains of the tide, mirror-still, ankle-deep. A lone pelican stood at the shore's edge inspecting the shallows. And to her right, the shade of sheoaks, pandanus and a frangipani in full flower.

She reflected on what Torrens had said about quitting; did battle with the thought for a moment, but the truth of it was hard to budge.

Something caught her eye in the long grass, fluorescent green but fading in the sun. A large water pistol, shaped like a machine gun and caked with dirty sand. *Bloody plastic everywhere.* She picked it up, brushed off the nozzle and squeezed the trigger. A jet of water cannoned into a tree, Pocket straining to chase it.

Her phone rang again. She stared at the name for a few rings. Rowan again. He'd called her several times. He'd only once asked her when she was coming back but he didn't have to. Each call was a question, a proposal, a request.

'Hello,' she said.

'G'day.'

They did the usual thing. Small talk, how was she, the weather...

'Nice day,' he said. 'Too hot but. Cooler up here at yours.'

Her little cottage was half an hour out of town, up a winding road in a saddle between two ridges. The breezes would hustle and gust through the bush and march across the yard, never allowing the heat to get a grip. But down in the valley at the height of summer, the town of Katinga was canned hell, a vice-like heat trap.

What was he doing up there? Mowing the lawn?

'Oh well, make yourself at home...don't mind me,' she said, recalling his words as she was leaving, asking her not to go, telling her she'd be okay, that he'd help her get through it. She'd kept jamming stuff into the car, still crying. As she rolled out, he'd yelled, 'At least show me where the bloody spare keys are so I can keep an eye on the place!'

Definitely mowing the lawn.

She hadn't told him she might not be coming back. The prospect of the new job in Melbourne had taken hold since she left, spreading and lodging itself in her mind. Wealth, sophistication and, best of all, anonymity among the bustling thousands. She should tell him now, early, spare him the sudden shock.

'Your fridge is empty,' he said.

'Pretty sure there were beers in there when I left. You been cooling off up there often?'

'Forty degrees in Katinga.'

'Are you in the backyard? Try the swim-up bar in the pool.'

32

He chuckled. The cottage was ramshackle at best. That's how come she'd got to know Rowan. A handyman could make a decent living from a place like hers.

'Didn't bring my bathers.'

It was a game and, as much as she knew she should tell him, she wanted to play. She wanted to sneak away from the burden of turtles and mining and Helen. 'Secluded up there, Rowan. No one around for miles.'

'Maybe I could get my daks off and get under the hose. Test the water pressure for you.'

The dogs were slumped in the shade, resting. She hooked the leads on a branch, wandered over into a knot of trees, the ground soft and padded with fallen leaves and a mat of sheoak fronds.

'Well, it is bushfire season. Good preparation,' she said.

She'd only known him in the cooler months, imagined him now in the heat—same work jeans but shirtless maybe, the lean torso, tanned and sweaty from mowing, pants hanging low on those snake-hips. He was so beautiful, Rowan. Inside and out. She felt her skin prickling. She was supposed to be telling him about Melbourne.

She heard his phone thump down on the ground, a rustling of clothing, felt a thrill across her shoulders. Then the phone in his hands again.

'Cooler already.'

'How so?' She wanted him to say it.

'Don't wanna drive home in wet jeans.'

'So you're...?' She put her hand on a pandanus trunk, felt the ridges press into her palm.

'As the day I was born.'

She said nothing, just breathed, felt her heart pound and recalled that one kiss—the night she'd taken him home. How he'd gently drawn her face to his as he lay there, his leg bandaged after the shooting, and his empty living room and the fire crackling in the hearth behind her and his lips, brushing hers at first, then enveloping hers, enveloping everything, all her loneliness and all her grief and all that was lost.

'What are you wearing?' he asked.

'More than I need.'

'Secluded up there too?'

She looked around. They were a long way from any houses. There was no one in sight, Pocket and Sarge scarcely visible from where she was. Her hesitation was enough answer for Rowan.

'Just take one thing off,' he said.

'I'm not sure I—'

'Don't think so much.' She scanned her surroundings again. No one. Just blue sky and jade sea and the leafy grove in which she stood. 'One thing,' he whispered.

The chatter of a wagtail, the calming hum of insects, a shush of foliage in the breeze, the silky moisture behind her knees, around her neck, on her forehead. She took a step behind a tree, slipped off her singlet, felt a rush of cool air against her bare skin and lay down in the supple layers of sheoak carpet.

'What did you take off?' he asked.

'My top.' She heard the sound of running water, the hose. 'What are you doing?'

'Cooling my neck.' He let out a groan of relief. 'Uh, so good.'

She listened to the flow, imagined it running down his chest and continuing on down the valleys and furrows. He had the lean man's muscular stomach. She'd seen it when his shirt rode up that time fixing the shed roof.

'And my back.'

She saw his shoulders, the narrowing to his waist, the curve of his lower back and the water rushing to the cleft between his buttocks. Everything was tensed between her thighs. He kept talking, more words than she'd ever heard him speak, describing the path of the water, the channels and the rivulets, telling the story

34

of his body, the lines and the arcs and the muscled curves. She let him continue while she lay, breathless. He asked her for another item of clothing—a gentle prompt, like the kiss of a feather.

Then another.

And with each one she described to him what lay beneath, feeling her hands touching her body as if they were his.

She lay there afterwards, emptied of herself, looking up into the branches of the sheoak that drooped its shelter around her. A small bird arrived, brown and indistinguishable from the colour of the tree but framed in the perfect blue of the midday sky. She could hear Rowan breathing, a slow exhale as he lay stretched on the grass in her backyard.

She should have told him.

'Rowan.'

'Yeah.'

Say it. She hesitated. *Say it now.* But the words had stalled somewhere deep down. 'I should pay you for mowing the lawns.'

He snorted.

'I should. What's your account number?'

'Is this a scam?' he said, and she could tell he was smiling.

'Yes, it's a scam. Let's have your password as well, while you're at it.' Then followed one of his long pauses—the man never felt the need to fill a silence. Damned if she'd do all the work.

Finally, he spoke, 'Clementine.' Slowly, like he was savouring the word.

'Yeah?'

Another pause.

'What?'

'That's it. That's my password.'

'That's bloody sad, Rowan,' she said. Chiding, playful; whatever she could muster.

'Easier to remember, like that Elvis song.'

'Eh?'

'You're always on my mind.'

They both laughed, at the ridiculous high-schoolness of it. 'So what year were you born, old timer?' she said, through the giggling.

'Classic, not old. I like Johnny Cash too.'

'Good reason to change your password, then—I can't stand country music.'

'Aagh.' He was scornful—but smiling again, she imagined.

'I'll send you a cheque.'

'Nah. Buy me a beer when you get back.' *She must say something.* 'When are you back?'

Say it. Now. Get it out there, for Christ's sake, it will only get worse from here.

Out of the corner of her eye she saw Pocket rolling in something. Something lifeless. A dead water rat! Dropping his shoulder into it, wriggling madly, a big gummy smile of sheer pleasure. She leapt up, grabbed the water pistol and sprayed a jet at his tummy. He jumped to his feet, shying then laughing at her.

'Um, don't know yet. Listen, I better go. Pocket's just rolled in something foul.'

He scanned the yard: nothing obvious. But he had time, plenty of it. He stepped out of the Chrysler, wraparound Ray-Bans reflecting the glare of a relentless sun, and made for the house.

He knocked at the door. Nothing. Birds chirping from the thick bush crowding around the house. A blue-tongue lizard stared up at him from a dried-out patch of lawn. Standing at the front door, waiting, there in the shade...Peaceful. Not like last time he was here—bloody SOGs smashing down the door, yelling and shouting, guns drawn.

Squinting through the side window next to the door, he couldn't see any movement inside. He scanned the yard then reached down, grabbed a rock from the border of an overgrown strip of garden and smashed it through the window. A dozen white cockatoos in a gum tree next to the house took flight, screeching a warning across the bush and into the mountain behind. Noise didn't matter out here. You could shoot a guy in the kneecaps, as Sinbin was known to do, and nobody would hear the shot—or the scream. Nevertheless, he refused to waste a bullet on Sinbin's front door.

He went straight to the obvious places and found nothing there. Then he began to slit cushions, rip the backs off paintings, tap the walls and bash holes wherever the sound rang hollow.

The morning ticked on, the heat built and his irritation grew. Bird calls gave way to the hustle and hum of cicadas. He stomped outside, did a full circumnavigation of the house, banging on the walls with frustration. He stopped at the back of the shed near the dunny, under the long shadows cast by a bloodwood tree. Something out of place. There, near his feet, a slight discolouration. Darker than the rest. He almost stepped into it, and caught himself at the last minute. Crouching down, he scraped at it. The dirt was loose, poorly packed. Definitely a hole, recently dug, then filled in and smoothed over.

He looked up and around as if perhaps the hole-digger might still be around. Walked back to the car.

CHAPTER 4

Clem went straight to the Galimore Foundation website after returning to the shanty. The idea had come to her as she hauled Pocket off the rat carcass. The foundation was a prestigious organisation with some serious heavy-hitters on the board, and powerful men can leave a trail of bodies. She just needed to find that trail, follow it till she got to a decomposing rat—roll in it for all she was worth.

She didn't recognise anyone in the directors' group photograph, just the usual gaggle of grey-haired suits carefully coiffed for the camera—four men seated on a crimson brocade sofa, another male quartet standing behind with a lone woman between them.

She scanned the caption hoping one of the names would ring a bell. Finding a smudge on any of these pillars of society was a long shot, though; likely to require a shitload of research with no guarantee of a result. It would be much easier if they'd been linked to something grubby already. But nothing jumped out at her as she scanned the back row. She moved on to the three amigos seated in front. *John Bester?* Nothing. *William Goh?* Nothing. *Kenneth Borman?*

Kenneth Borman.

Yes! Holy snapping turtles, yes! And he wasn't just a director: *Kenneth Borman, Chairman.*

She sat back in the chair and stared at the shining smiles in the photograph. There he was, seated proudly—navy suit, houndstooth tie, one slender hand draped limp-wristed over the right knee, the left displaying an eye-catching gold watch. *The* Kenneth Borman, Miranda Cato's boss.

Clem knew all about the Cato trial. Sitting in the library at the Dillwynia Correctional Centre, she had devoured every newspaper article she could find. Then she'd asked for, and been granted, access to the online court judgement. She'd pitched it as part of her prison rehab and reintegration program. But Cato was two weeks into her sentence before Clem actually had a chance to meet the woman at the centre of the scandal.

Miranda Cato. Of all the people implicated in a series of legal proceedings brought by the corporate regulator against the big banks for rate-rigging, she was the only one to go down. They'd got her on perjury. If she'd just admitted to participating in the rate-rigging she would have copped a monetary penalty, and probably not even a very big one. But perjury was a different matter. The justice system is very keen to let you know you cannot play fast and loose with it, and then expect to just open your wallet and walk free. Nope, six months for Miranda.

The story was a goldmine for the newspapers—Cato was the stereotypical sexy corporate executive, outrageously wealthy and, being a banker, hated to boot. But it was what Cato had told Clem about her boss as they strolled around the exercise yard that clanged like a cymbal in Clem's head now.

Kenneth Borman. Clem stared at the photograph—bushy eyebrows projecting jauntily at the edges, remnant hair carefully clipped to sit tight around his ears, then a smooth, bare expanse of scalp hovering over that immense financial-genius brain. This man, facing the camera intently and sitting up proud like a rabbit on a ridge, was her target now. She was determined to hit the bullseye with her first shot.

Cato had been relieved to meet Clem—someone else from the corporate world. She unloaded her rage into Clem's sympathetic ear, describing in fine detail just how Kenneth Borman had screwed her over. For Clem, the pointless parading around the exercise yard became her favourite thing: a chance to hear more from Cato—stories of deceit and treachery played out in the glass towers of the financial sector.

She told Clem that Borman, one of the bank's most senior executives, had personally orchestrated a longstanding campaign to rig the benchmark interest rate. As Clem was well aware, that was a very big deal. This was the single number with the most influence on the cost of finance for absolutely everything—mortgages, monthly credit-card interest, the cost of money for every business and every project around Australia, from a shop fit-out to a new city freeway. And it was supposed to be driven by market forces, changing daily with fluctuations in supply and demand—not by Kenneth Borman.

It was Cato, as Borman's 2IC, who made it happen, operating under his protection. Her claim was that they made tens of millions in profit for the bank every quarter by manipulating the seemingly 'natural' fluctuations in this number. When the regulator got wind of it and an investigation commenced, Borman assured Cato there was no evidence—nothing in writing, not a single hook for ASIC to hang its hat on—and all they had to do was 'sit in a room with these bozos and tell 'em there's nothing to see here'. Cato believed him.

But as ASIC's interrogation got closer to the truth, Borman became more agitated. Then an email surfaced in one of the boxes upon boxes of documents handed over to the regulator. Purporting to be sent by Cato, the email instructed her team of senior traders to *take the rate to the cleaners...shake out a couple of mill.*

Cato had learnt the email off by heart, reeling off the words like she was peeling an orange. Borman, she said, had feigned distress, raged at where the email might have come from and 'which of the bastards had sold out'. He promised to take care of it, look after her: he hand-picked her legal team, the finest silk, two juniors and a swathe of solicitors and not a cent from her own pocket. What could possibly go wrong?

Everything, said Cato, absolutely everything, from the very first day in court. But it was only towards the end of the whole nightmare, after the trial had been running a week, that she'd allowed herself to realise what she now saw as obvious: the deck had been stacked against her, she was the patsy in Borman's game, the decoy carcass he'd planted for the hyenas at ASIC. Borman had been right about the lack of evidence against him or anyone else at the bank, and nothing she might now say to accuse him would stick, with her credibility completely undermined by the perjury charge. Even talking to Clem, she was incandescent with rage—it wasn't just the rate Borman had rigged but her life—hauling her up on a gibbet and leaving her dangling.

And now Clementine owned that information. She held onto it like a grenade, ready to pull the clip. She drove in to Barnforth, bought a burner phone, returned to the shanty and tapped in the number. A woman with clipped vowels answered, 'Kenneth Borman's office, June speaking.'

It seemed Borman held enough board roles post-retirement that he could afford his own serviced office and executive assistant. Clem figured the Galimore directorship wouldn't pay much, but it would be like a gleaming halo in his portfolio, helping him get better paying gigs elsewhere.

'Good morning, June, this is Alice Baguley,' said Clem. 'I'd like to speak with Mr Borman please.' She used the name of one of Miranda's Borman-funded legal team. Not the partner—Borman would probably recognise the voice—but the senior associate on the next rung down, who Miranda said had tried to warn her. Not the biggest fish, but a name Borman might recall.

The usual platitudes from June...not in at the moment, can I take a message...

'Yes, please. Could you let him know I rang and ask him to call me?' Clem gave the phone number and spelt out the name. 'And if you could mention I have something he needs to know about from the court proceedings two years ago?'

It was just before dark when the call finally came through. A blocked number. She'd poked about the shanty all day, compulsively checking the phone for missed calls even though it had never left her pocket the whole time. Now she was sitting on the back deck in her cut-off denim shorts, oiled in Aerogard with the twilight fading and the biting insects of Queensland giving her a wide berth. With the Great Sandy Straits silver in the distance, she reached for the tumbler of scotch beside her on the rickety old table and took a swig before accepting the call.

'Hello, Alice speaking,' she said. Professional, unhurried, imagining herself in an air-conditioned office on the thirty-third floor, white shirt crisp on her shoulders, high heels cocked beneath a sleek black chair.

There was a pause, then: 'This is Borman.' Gruff, abrupt. She'd expected as much from Cato's description.

'Thank you for calling back, Mr Borman.'

'And?'

'You may remember me. I was part of the team representing Miranda Cato in her perjury trial a couple of years ago.'

A grunt.

'I wanted to alert you to something.'

'Can't wait,' he said, sarcastic.

'I've come into some information that I feel I may need to report.'

'Report to me?'

'No, Mr Borman, to the authorities.'

Silence. She could almost hear the gears clunking in his brain.

'You may remember an incriminating email, sent from Ms Cato's computer?'

43

'Sent by Cato, you mean...computers don't send things themselves.'

'Of course, you're right Mr Borman, always a human at the keyboard,' said Clem, waiting a beat. 'Which human, though? That's the question.'

A welcome rush of breeze lifted the frayed edge of her shorts and tickled her leg. She gave the silence time to unsettle him.

'Look,' he said. 'I don't have time for riddles, Alison. You said you had something important for me.'

'Alice. The name's Alice.'

Clem took another sip from the tumbler, making sure the clink of ice was audible, making him wait, putting the glass down on the table, feeling the fire in her throat before she continued.

'For fuck's sake, out with it woman.'

She sniffed, gave him another pause. 'I met a man from the bank last week at a bar in Sydney. Knows you. Works in IT. He told me Miranda's swipe access card placed her in a meeting room on the other side of the building at the time that email was sent.' The lie was as liquid and smooth as the whisky.

'What? Oh, for Christ's sake,' he croaked, an indignant toad. 'That's it? That's your important information?'

Shit. Not even rattled. Work to do.

'As a lawyer, Mr Borman, I have a duty to the court...'

'I don't give a flying fuck.'

'...The proceedings were decided largely based on that false evidence.' That part was true.

'Oh, fucking give me a break, sweetheart. The case is long dead.'

'Yes, but I'm not sure that's relevant, Mr Borman, certainly not to the courts. And as it's just the sort of thing that undermines public confidence in the judicial system it's therefore squarely within my duty to report it.' *God, she was delivering a lecture on ethics to a man who had none.*

Borman laughed, but she picked up a nervous edge. '*Ppphht.*

ASIC won't have a bar of this. They nailed a banking executive, at long bloody last, put her behind bars…it was their only decent scalp in ten years of trying! You think they're gonna let this spoil the party?'

This Borman—what a piece of work. The biggest swinging dick she'd taken on so far in her thirty-three years. He wasn't going to go down easy. Clem took a breath, rallied and drew on every ounce of gall she had.

'I'm afraid it won't be up to ASIC, Borman. And once the court overturns Miranda Cato's conviction, ASIC will go after those whose swipe cards *do* put them in the right place.'

No laughter now. A crackling hot silence, snapping in her ear like static. Then his voice again, impatient, angry, snarling, 'Now let me tell you something, Alison…'

'Alice.'

'…I have ways of stopping this sort of thing. Self-righteous little bitches like you—I'll send you into a living hell. You think Cato was the first I've despatched?

He'd flicked to bully mode and it fired a corresponding switch in Clem—a wick of anger sparked and flared into full flame, white hot at its centre but calm and unwavering. 'I think you're getting a bit worked up, Kenneth, and it's completely unnecessary…you can fix this matter quite easily with one simple decision.'

The sun sank lower behind the great sand island of K'gari, the darkness wrapping itself around the sword-like fronds of the backyard pandanus. A cockroach, Queensland-sized, strolled along the edge of the verandah.

'What are you talking about?'

'Something you can do to prevent all this coming to light, Mr Chairman.'

'You're trying to blackmail me? Oh, you're in serious trouble now, girl.'

'The Galimore Foundation withdrew its funding from the

Wildlife Association of the Great Sandy Straits. This organisation is leading the charge to save an endangered freshwater turtle. You need to reverse that decision and release the funds.'

'What? Who is this?'

'Well, you seem to remember me as Alison, so let's run with that shall we?' She could hear his breathing. 'And Borman, you have exactly three days.'

She hung up.

\\/

As Clem scooped half a tin of Pal into the dog bowl the afternoon storm clouds rolled in, eating up the sunshine. She fed Pocket first, then put him inside to stop him sticking his snout into Sergeant's bowl. Sarge was a slow eater for such a big dog and far too polite to shove Pocket out of the way. The two had formed a contented friendship and while Sarge would happily rip the head off the labrador up the street he couldn't get enough of the frisky little blue heeler that had come to play.

The first scouts of the storm front pushed across the backyard, cool puffs breaking through the heat and casting a pleasant chill on her cheeks. She walked back inside and checked the pantry for dinner. Canned tomatoes, pasta, mince in the fridge. She started working on the onions for a bolognaise, her mind drifting back to the phone call. She wasn't confident. Borman was a player, a big, big man. Who was she to unseat him?

Marakai Mining had been in the news again, announcing the first of many environmental approvals. She would have to read up on it, see if there was an angle, a way to drive a wedge. If not, there were plenty more stages to go, plenty of time. But the way the company's media release was worded, it was as if the mine was inevitable, concrete and dump trucks already rumbling into Piama.

She chopped the onions savagely. The world was marching on, trampling all over the turtle and stomping big heavy boots all over Helen.

She was stirring in the tomato paste when she heard a knock on the door. The rain started at exactly the same time, fat drops pinging on the tin roof. No one visited. Had Borman put two and two together? She couldn't think how, but maybe he'd tracked her down and sent someone around to sort her out, buy her silence? *Compel her silence?* She dropped the wooden spoon with a splash into the pot, flicked the light off and picked up the kitchen knife, feeling the heft snug in her hand. Another knock. She stepped slowly into the passageway, peeked around towards the front door. Dark outside.

Barking from the backyard. Sarge. *Of course! Get him in here!* She crept back into the kitchen, opened the back door a crack and the two of them came charging through, Pocket's high-pitched machine-gun yelp and Sarge's thunderous baritone barrelling up the hallway. She followed them, turned the porch light on, peeked behind the curtain beside the front door. A tall, hulking figure, baseball cap, the handle of some sort of large container in his hand. The man saw the curtain move, turned towards it.

Torrens. Thank God. With an esky.

Pocket recognised the scent, stopped barking and began an urgent tail-wagging whimper. Sarge just looked confused, shifting from one massive paw to another, eyes flicking between the door and Pocket, a thick drop of drool hanging from the corner of his mouth.

As she opened the door, Torrens grinned from behind a thick bush of freshly grown beard.

'Saw your light on.'

After Torrens had scooped the last of the bolognaise into his mouth, she hoped he'd take himself off to bed. She'd prepared the shed for him yesterday with a secondhand camp stretcher—he'd said he didn't want the spare room, thankfully. She watched with regret as he pulled two more beers from his esky.

'Oh no, not for me. Two's more than enough,' she said.

'But we're on holidays,' he said planting the cans on the table.

He was wearing a bright yellow T-shirt with a kangaroo in sunglasses, incongruous under the dark expanse of untrimmed beard covering his neck. A man this big made everything look incongruous—the tiny kitchen had surely been built for hobbits.

'You are. I have stuff I need to do.' She hadn't mentioned Helen, or the turtle for that matter.

'Such as?'

'Oh, you know, stuff to keep me going for another day in paradise,' she said, scooping up the plates and making for the kitchen sink.

'Hey, no you don't.' He got up and nudged her aside. There was suddenly no room for her at the sink. 'I invited myself here, dishes are me punishment. Now get yourself a beer and sit down.'

She sat down and cracked her third, watching his back as he washed.

'Saw your photo online,' he said.

'Mmm. Stalking me?'

'With that woman that died.'

'Helen. Helen Westley.' She tried to keep her voice level but was surprised to find it a challenge. For some strange reason Helen's signature came to mind—looping and flourishing across the page. Just like her...until someone ripped the page right out of the book.

'She was your friend, yeah?'

Torrens had heard the twang in her voice. *God, must she be so transparent?*

'More than a friend. She looked after me when I was a kid,

48

five months while Mum was in hospital.' It was painful, talking about Helen. She hadn't had to until now. She cleared her throat and found a reason to get out of the room, grabbing the kitchen garbage bin and marching outside with it half full. She emptied it and stood there a while, listening to the hush of waves expiring on the beach. No moon, and the cloud still clearing. The storm had been short and sharp, raindrops the size of buckets, a few snaps of lightning then a calmness, the lingering smell like gunpowder.

When she came back in Torrens was wiping his hands on the back of his boardshorts, big red things that hung loose and billowy around his knees. 'Reckon I deserve another after that!'

He opened a beer and leaned with his back up against the sink, one hand lodged behind him on the edge of the bench, the other wrapped around the beer, legs thrust straight in front. No room left to swing a cat.

'Heard it was suicide,' he said.

Clem raised her gaze to the window, out into the blackness of the night. She took a big breath, blew it out between pursed lips, focusing on a single pinprick of starlight in a thin veil of cloud.

'You heard wrong,' she said, more to the star than Torrens. 'Someone pushed her off that cliff.'

Saying it out loud for the first time to someone she knew had an immediate galvanising effect—a public declaration pinning her to the argument. But it was also awful, horrifying to hear it articulated. Helen had been murdered.

Torrens looked up sharply. 'What the hell?'

Clem nodded. 'No suicide note, no sign of depression. Nothing.'

'So how come the papers said it was suicide?'

'Because the cops think that.'

'Oh now, don't go telling me the pigs got something wrong.' He held his hand high, eyes closed in mock protest. 'Don't say it, Jonesy, I'm just not having a bar of it.'

'Only one set of tracks up at the quarry.'

49

Torrens took a deep draft of beer and belched loudly, lips thrust out, projecting forward with gusto. 'Up there on her own, hey? An accident then?'

'Helen hated the quarry. She said it was a scar on the landscape. She'd never have gone for a walk there. She loved the river and the beach and K'gari and the state forest. She was always going for hikes in the bush. Never the quarry.'

Torrens folded one arm across his chest, looked across at Clementine sternly. 'You told the police that?'

'Of course. One-eyed bastards jumped on the suicide thing after that.'

'Oh, that's harsh, Jonesy. Bastards they may be, but one-eyed? You gotta count their arsehole too!'

He broke into uncontrollable laughter, shoulders shaking. She couldn't help but join in.

CHAPTER 5

Clem's first purchase with the Galimore Foundation funds after the board reversed the Funding Committee's decision was a large whiteboard. It was propped up in the shanty's sunroom on a stepladder she'd found in the shed. Its white glare looked completely out of place surrounded by Noel's drooping bamboo blinds and grubby grass mats. Ariel and Brady and Gaylene and Mary, along with a few of the more committed WAGSS members, sat in the mismatched sticks of chairs at the table, the dogs banished outside. She'd asked Torrens to come in at two o'clock; make up a reason to end the session. Clem didn't want the ferals overstaying their welcome.

In the first column she'd written a summary of the actions taken to date and they'd been brainstorming the second column, marked *Allies* (the various wildlife advocacy groups, the Galimore Foundation and a major local donor, Andrew Doncaster, were at the top of the list). They'd just moved on to the third column, *Opponents* (she'd been careful not to write Suspects), before finishing up with column four, *Next Steps*. This third column was the whole purpose of this strategy session as far as Clem was concerned, but the meeting had been slow going so far. In hindsight, the idea of extracting valuable intelligence from the protesters seemed a little optimistic.

So far, they had listed Blair 'the Mayor' Fullerton. Jobs meant votes and he was hot for the mine, the port and everything in between. The group had advised that he had a very young, very blonde wife who spent most of her time shopping and sipping champagne in Brisbane, and a pair of teenage kids from his first marriage.

'So, anything more on the mayor before we move on?' she asked, marker pen poised.

'Well, I do know he's wonderfully effective as a politician,' said Mary, a retired librarian who'd lived in the area for forty years. 'Charming, people say—smarmy in my view. But then I've never voted Liberal in my life.'

'I'd agree with that,' said Brady. He had a forty-a-day smoker's voice. 'Helen always got a bit sucked in by him. Time to apply the blowtorch, I reckon.'

Brady was always looking to apply a blowtorch to something. He was bored sitting around in meetings strategising—much preferred to get out there and *take it up to the bastards*. Apparently, Helen's moderate approach had often resulted in arguments.

'He's a bloody silver-tail, got a huge powerboat called *Success*. What a wank,' Brady continued. 'My mate skippers for him sometimes. Reckon we could stage something noisy, maybe something stinky even—right there at the marina, where he keeps it.'

To keep him happy, Clem wrote it down as a 'possible' under Next Steps. The group then added Ralph Bennett, the President of the Piama Progress Association, a retired plumber who lived in the new(ish) estate on the far side of the bay with his wife Selma. Clem had seen him in action at a town meeting—a bull of a man, red-faced, arm-waving and always on the verge of shouting. He and many other members of the residents' association had been cast into something like financial slavery, sudden and wretched poverty after a lifetime spent preparing for a secure and peaceful retirement. There were about thirty of them, all retirees, who'd fallen prey to a rogue financial planner and a catastrophic fall in the share market a few years back. The port would involve acquisition of a number of Piama properties and the retirees were desperate to sell their heavily mortgaged homes at the inflated prices Marakai Mining was throwing around. It was possible, Clem thought, that some of them might be angry enough to have taken matters into their own hands.

Next was the company itself: Marakai Mining. None of the group knew the names of anyone within the company, but Helen had mentioned a key contact: Karene Bickerstaff, Director of Public Relations, and Clem added the name to the whiteboard and wrote next to it: 'likes a drink', which was all she could remember from her conversations with Helen.

It was almost two o'clock and the group seemed drained. She decided to move the discussion on quickly to some more targeted questions.

'So, any of these Opponents violent?'

Looks of surprise all around the table.

'Violent?' said Gaylene from underneath her mane of hair. Gaylene was a sixty-something hobby farmer and always the first one there when you wanted someone to chain themselves to something, provided she wasn't off on one of her caravan holidays with husband Les.

'Well, we need to know what we're up against, don't we?' said Clem.

'They're pensioners, most of 'em. Probably couldn't kill a fly in a paper bag,' said Gaylene.

'I don't know about that. Reckon they could do some damage with their walking sticks,' said Brady, sniggering. 'Crush a few toes with those mobility scooters.'

The meeting was deteriorating. Clem moved on.

'All right, any of our Opponents own a four-wheel drive?' The police had not found any tyre tracks but Clem thought it might be possible to get a four-wheel drive up to the quarry's edge over a rocky section of ground where it would leave no impression.

'What's that got to do with anything?' Brady again, slumped in his chair, holding a piece of celery between his fingers like a cigarette. He was trying to give up. Doing it tough, by the looks.

'Cars can give an insight into personality,' said Clem. 'Useful information for how best to influence people.'

'Oh yes,' said Ariel. 'Like star signs. I read something about that somewhere. Geminis love the little Volkswagen Polos, whereas a lot of Scorpios drive Jeep convertibles—brave and secretive...off the beaten track.'

'Ralph Bennett drives a Landcruiser,' said Brady.

'Surprised he can afford one,' said Clem.

'Looks like it's from the Second World War. Even older than he is,' he barked, fidgeting in his seat. 'When are we going to talk about the next action? I've been thinking about a siege of some sort at council chambers.'

'I wonder what it means if you drive a station wagon.' Ariel's eyes had glazed over. She turned to her notebook and scribbled a note next to the elaborate swirling doodle she'd crafted over the course of the meeting.

'Yeah, we'll talk about our next action in a minute, Brady,' said Clem. 'So does Ralph go off-road much?'

'Wouldn't know,' said Brady. 'Heard you drove a four-wheel drive once, Clem. Prado wasn't it?'

She turned away from the whiteboard, checking his face for signs, trying to hide any on her own. He stared at her, took a pretend drag on his celery cigarette, pinched between his thumb and forefinger now, a reefer grip. He might be off the ciggies but that didn't exclude anything else on the chemical menu. He exhaled and his mouth turned up in a sly smile.

'And?' she said.

Brady rested his celery on the lunch plate like it was an ashtray.

'Was that the car?' Ariel's question hung, unsupported, without need of explanation. Clearly she and Brady had discussed Clem's accident. Why should she be surprised? Of course they would have. Everything came back to that. Why would she be here in this backwater otherwise? She was defined by that mistake. *And how dare she use the word mistake for such a reckless, deadly act?*

'I don't see it's relevant what car I drive,' she said firmly, pivoting back to the whiteboard.

'Hell yeah, it is. Our opponents could use it against you, to undermine the campaign.' Brady was smart enough when he chose to be.

'I think we should bring death into our conversations more,' said Ariel. 'It's so important. I mean how do we appreciate life without death?'—*Oh God,* thought Clem, her felt-tip marker stalling on the whiteboard as she wrote down the make of Ralph's vehicle—'I mean, I think it's also a tribute, like a song of respect for those who've passed.'

Clem blinked hard and turned to face the meeting again. Time to take control.

'Okay, so shall we talk about Helen?' It was fair enough—the group had been devastated, beating themselves up for not having seen the signs, failing to notice that their loved and apparently strong leader was suffering.

'Oh yes. I mean I can feel her presence right now, in this very room.' Ariel had everyone's attention now.

'Well, what does she think our next steps should be?' asked Gaylene impatiently.

'But the thing is,' Ariel went on as if she hadn't heard Gaylene, 'you and Helen both share this amazing experience, Clementine. A truth very few people will ever know.' She turned her eyes towards Clem. 'Perhaps you could share, something...'

'Eh?' said Gaylene, completely confused and obviously not privy to Brady and Ariel's previous discussions. Brady was looking fascinated, like the information might be genuinely useful in some sort of tactical way. Clem felt the marker slipping in her sweaty palm.

'...something of the mystery of what it's like to have life, there before you, and then gone.' Ariel's voice was a whisper now, as if sound might kill the magic.

All eyes were on Clem. Her mind was totally stalled and she could feel her mouth gaping open stupidly when the door burst open. Torrens filled the door frame completely, fully bearded, wielding the green water pistol menacingly—just needed a Ned Kelly bucket helmet with an eye slit to complete the picture.

His voice boomed into the sunroom, shaking the bamboo blinds. 'Righto folks, this is a hold-up. Now off you all go. Come on, hands in the air and no one gets hurt.'

\\/

Council buildings in country towns like Barnforth followed a model. Two-storey Victorian buildings, high-ceilinged, with wide shallow steps along the extent of the street frontage. This one had the year of construction (1879) carved into the stone above the front door.

Clem waited twenty minutes. The group had decided Blair the Mayor must be handled with diplomacy—he'd been known to attack when cornered. They were unaware that Clementine's primary purpose was to expose Helen's killer; nevertheless, it was good advice and Clem thought hard about how to approach him. She decided to present as a better alternative to Helen, someone he could work with; more capable of compromise, perhaps even vaguely corruptible. Who knew, she might unearth something. Might even score an invite onto his boat, she thought, smiling to herself. The door opposite her opened and a woman with an incredible hairdo, a hard-wired bouffant mass, appeared.

'Miss Jones, the mayor will see you now.' The woman bared a set

56

of small pointy teeth and led her into another room that appeared to be her office—carved wooden chairs, coat rack and gilt-framed but slightly faded Tom Roberts print. Then on through another door into a huge semi-circular office, with a dark mahogany desk at one end big enough to play a game of table tennis, long windows from the lofty ceilings to the burgundy carpet—plush and so deep your shoes left a footprint. Outside was a carefully sculpted lawn with manicured hedges and stone bench seats.

Blair Fullerton stood up from behind the ping-pong table and advanced towards her, hand outstretched.

'Good afternoon, Ms Jones, good to see you again.' Round face, grey eyes and a smoothly barbered helmet of greying hair.

He ushered her to the other end of the room where chairs were placed around a dark coffee table in front of a huge fireplace with fake logs. The mantelpiece above displayed a few carefully arranged ornaments.

'Thanks so much for seeing me, Mr Mayor,' she said, smiling with as much tooth as she could muster. 'I know you have a very busy schedule.'

'Never too busy to meet with my constituents, Ms Jones.'

She wasn't a constituent, just passing through. Never mind.

'Oh, call me Clementine, please.'

'My sincerest condolences on the passing of your predecessor.'

The words were as hollow as a paper straw and in his eyes she saw nothing resembling sympathy. What she could see, reflected in the concrete grey, was a fleet of earthmovers and a hundred local voters in hard hats and high-vis shirts.

She repeated the word diplomacy in her head like a mantra; visualised herself stepping onto his boat.

'Yes, a great loss. Something we're all struggling to recover from.' The words were like a mouthful of dry flour.

'I'm sure it will be felt for some time. But now,' he said, clasping his hands together, 'how can I assist you, Ms Jones?'

'Well, although we're still mourning Helen's death, we all agreed she would want us to keep moving forward.'

'Indeed.'

'So, we're about to take the next steps on the campaign but we wanted to speak with you first and keep you in the loop.'

'Well, I appreciate that very much, Ms Jones, transparency and dialogue are fundamental, I always say.'

She forced herself past the management babble and pressed on. 'We're lodging an appeal against the minister's approval for the mine's water management plan. Funding has come through from our supporters and we're preparing for the first stage.'

Fullerton's cheeks fell, then quickly reconvened themselves back to their moon shape.

'Well, I'm disappointed to hear that, given we believe the mine and the port are in the community's best interests. But of course,' he said, holding his palms out wide, like a true believer, 'it's the right of every citizen to call for further scrutiny.'

'Democracy in action, Mr Mayor,' she smiled.

He nodded; smiled back.

'The thing is, councillor, I didn't want to deliver this news without at the same time extending an olive branch. I do believe there may be some scope for further dialogue.'

'Ah, well that sounds promising. What did you have in mind?'

'Well, with legal proceedings under way, it's often an opportune time for parties to come together and explore more practical solutions.'

His eyes lit up. 'WAGSS is prepared to discuss a compromise, then?'

'You could say that, councillor,' she said, in full knowledge she had no authority from either WAGSS or the Galimore Foundation to say any such thing. She hadn't even raised it with either of them. 'I'm inclined to think the best solutions are uncovered outside the courtroom, don't you?'

'I totally agree. So have you anything particular in mind at this stage?'

'Well, it would certainly need to include a sizeable commitment from Marakai Mining, you know, to a mutually agreed conservation program...something sufficiently meaningful to satisfy our membership.'

'I see.'

'The association could then withdraw the legal proceedings...'

'And the port could proceed?'

'As you said, councillor, it's what the community wants.' She forced a smile.

'Well, that is certainly something that ought to be explored.' The grey eyes had a glossy sparkle to them now: polished concrete.

'And I think it would be useful if the council could act as a broker of sorts, at least in the public eye. I'm sure it would be helpful if the community were to see your leadership bringing the parties together.'

His face was aglow with enthusiasm—the opportunity to increase his standing, to be the hero of the day, he was eating it up.

'You know, I'm very pleased to be hearing this type of thinking,' he said. 'Your predecessor was, well, somewhat inflexible.'

'Helen was a passionate advocate.' *Forgive me, Helen. This is all for a greater goal, I promise.*

'And have you considered the sort of monetary contribution that might be sufficient for the association's ends?'

'I'll give that some thought now that we've discussed the concept, councillor. But before we move to that step, there is something else the members are keen to pursue and they'd like to raise it formally before we progress any discussions about a compromise.' She could see he understood the euphemism: this is a precondition. Listen up.

'I'm all ears, Ms Jones. If there's something I can do to help, please let me know.'

'Thank you,' she said, with a slow nod. 'The thing is, a number of us believe the investigation into Ms Westley's death was, quite frankly, lacking.' She watched his face, searching for a sign. Was that a twitch, like a feather tickling the edge of his right eye?

'I'm sure the police have given it their close attention,' he said. Definitely a pained look in his eye. Was it guilt, or just the simple realisation that the deal Clementine was offering might come with an awkward price? Impossible to tell.

'Still, we'd like your help. We're speaking to the Labor Party councillors and the independents,' she lied, 'and it seems they're keen to support WAGSS in calling for an official inquiry.'

'Inquiry?' Fullerton uncrossed his legs and planted his feet firmly on the carpet.

'Yes, a council-led inquiry into the efficacy of local policing in the Rivers Shire.'

'But council has no authority over the Queensland Police Service,' said Fullerton, completely rigid in the deeply upholstered chair.

'No, no,' said Clem. 'I realise council has no jurisdiction, but it doesn't mean the QPS aren't alive to politics, does it? I mean, don't tell me the cops don't know what's good for them, right? The last thing they want is the Police Minister coming down on them because he's under pressure from local government.' She gave Fullerton a knowing look; decided a wink would be over the top. 'And in the spirit of open dialogue, you would be doing them a favour to go see the local officer in charge and let him know the lie of the land. Call it community relations, whatever, but get them to dig deeper, demand they dig deeper, or...'

'Or what?'

'Or else, an inquiry. A public inquiry, with Helen Westley's death a central focus.'

Fullerton's look was blank, all expression vacuumed away. She couldn't tell whether it was actual culpability or a stock defensive routine, well-practised in the heat of politics. Either way, she was sure she'd got under his skin: unnerved him and, at the same time, hung out a most tantalising carrot. If he was the killer, maybe it would scare him into a mistake. If he wasn't, he would go ahead and pressure the police to take up the investigation again.

Win win.

\\/

The view from Ralph Bennett's living room was superb. So much better from a two-storey house than the verandah at the shanty. From here Piama was a canopy of palm trees above a strip of golden beach, the Great Sandy Straits banded in teal and navy and the vast expanse of K'gari's shoreline stretching as far as the eye could see.

She was looking out from the dining room with Ralph the Resident President himself—in checked shirt and brown shorts, smelling of Deep Heat—as he explained how he'd come to the Seascape Avenue subdivision twelve years ago.

'Got in first,' he said, nodding proudly. 'Best block in the whole estate.'

Clem had heard Ralph *got in first* on most things, took his share, staked his claim, bullocked his way to the front of the queue. He'd chosen his home for their first meeting, Ralph's territory marked with Ralph-scent: elephantine leather recliners, a framed fishing photograph of Ralph with a huge tuna hanging from a steely gaff, and instructions to his wife, Selma, to bring tea like she was his personal secretary.

They sat down at the large dining table and Selma laid the cups in front of them, darting back to the kitchen and appearing again with a plate of homemade Anzac biscuits. She smiled sweetly at Clem with her hair fresh out of rollers, soft curls around crinkled eyes.

'Thanks love,' said Ralph lunging for the plate.

'Beautiful view, Mrs Bennett,' said Clem. She wanted to say,

'Shame to bulldoze it for a coal port' but held herself back. Selma turned towards the kitchen and as soon as she was out of the room Ralph started.

'Now. Let me tell you a few things.'

He sounded like Clem's old high school headmaster. It made her feel cheeky, rebellious. She reached for an Anzac and took a bite. Still warm!

'I worked hard all me life, see. Had me own business, raised four kids, made enough for me and Selma to have our little piece of paradise up here. Grandkids can stay for school holidays, teach 'em to fish, get 'em outside and away from them Apples and Blackberries into the sunshine. Selma can have her garden and play bowls once or twice a week. And believe me, we deserve it. Fair dinkum tax-paying Australians all our lives.'

The polite thing to do would be to say 'too right' but Ralph didn't look like he wanted to be interrupted, so she nodded enthusiastically and kept her listening face on, chewing discreetly on the Anzac. Golden syrup crunch, soothing, like home.

'So everything's peachy, just like we planned, until this bloke, this preening rooster come through town: Robert Considine.' He scowled and leaned back in the chair abruptly, arms crossed tight on his chest. Clem could imagine Ralph swinging a gaff straight through Robert Considine's eyeballs.

'Yep, Robert Considine sold us a line. Could make one of those rhyming things out of it. What do they call 'em?'

'Limericks?' said Clem helpfully.

'Yeah, that's it,' he said. 'A limerick. Only it wouldn't be anything I'd recite in front of a lady.' He glowered at her for a moment then looked away. She could tell he did not consider her a 'lady'. More of a 'girly,' probably. She had expected as much and didn't take offence. Ralph came from an era of unconscious patriarchy, as normal and healthy in a man as a bushy moustache or chest hair. She'd already planned to play the part. You never knew what a full-blooded man of the 1940s might let slip to a harmless girly.

She frowned, shook her head in silent agreement with Ralph, damning Robert Considine to hell.

'And bugger me, I got in first again, didn't I,' he said, startled, as if he was still stumped as to how it could have happened. 'Fell for his bullshit hook, line and sinker. Had me eye on a new centre console fishing tinny, 115 horse four-stroke on the back, even showed him a picture of it. Fifty grand's worth. Well, old mate Rob the Dog said I'd earn that in less than twelve months. Take out a loan against this place, invest the cash in shares. So I thought to myself, this joker's backed by the big banks, obviously successful, drives a flash car, and the graphs! Oh! Those pretty graphs—all pointing up and up. And I thought, Selma'd like a trip to visit the youngest in London, I could have my boat…I'll give it a go.' He rested his big plumber's hands on the table, bitterness oozing from his fingertips.

'That slimy bastard,' his hands flew up and thudded down again with a crash. 'Said it'd never happen. *More chance of getting struck by lightning* were his actual words.'

She knew what came next. The share-market collapse, the price of Ralph's shares falling too low to secure the loan, the margin calls from the banks demanding payments from cash that Ralph and Selma did not have. Then, to save them from taking his home, he would have had to sell the shares as the prices were diving to the bottom—not enough to pay out the loan, substantial mortgage against his home and nothing to show for it.

She sat quietly as Ralph continued.

'Banks were on the phone the very next day, the vultures. I didn't even tell Selma. Kept it from her for weeks until I had to sell her car. She cried. Not for the bloody car either…' Ralph blinked. 'For our dreams.' He swallowed hard, his lips coming together in an embarrassed, emasculated line. 'And she cried again when

Lynette—the eldest—started sending us money to pay the bills.'

Clem imagined Selma weeping. 'Ought to be illegal,' she said softly. 'Playing with people's lives like that.'

'Yeah, well, we've got a class action going,' Ralph declared, bristly jowls bouncing like exclamation marks.

'And I understand there's quite a few in the same boat?'

'Yep. You can repeat that tale thirty times over and you'd have the story of Piama.' Ralph picked up his cup, took an angry gulp.

'So,' said Clem after a polite pause, 'the court case? What are the lawyers saying?'

She'd researched the class action against the banks that supplied the margin loan products to Considine's clients—it had been dragging on for five years or more with a series of interlocutory hearings, procedural matters, long and pedantic picking over the documents to be disclosed and those that might be withheld, barristers arguing over timetables…All of it eating up months and years.

She imagined all the pensioners living on mince and canned peas; ageing bones sweltering in their beds, unable to turn on the air conditioning; taking three-minute showers and watching their carefully tended gardens shrivel as they minimised the water bill.

'Ha! Bunch of blood suckers the lot of 'em! Useless as tits on a bull. And we'll be waiting till kingdom come for a decent offer from the banks, with all their carry-on.'

As much as she felt for the Bennetts and the cruel turn their lives had taken, she sensed it was time to take the conversation closer to the end goal. 'So if you could get a satisfactory offer you'd settle?'

'Of course we bloody would!

'Maybe one will come soon?'

'Don't be silly—the parasites have to run up the fees first and the banks are still in combat mode. Could be years away.'

'So how will you and Selma survive till then?'

'Can't keep accepting money from the kids, that's for sure.

Tried selling the house. Couldn't even cover the mortgage. The new port's our best shot. They're offering a shitload more.'

'Enough to clear the mortgage?'

'Yep, and some left over.'

Clem nodded, 'Geez, you'd kill for that I reckon.'

Was that a curl of his lower lip? Ralph Bennett, proud provider to Selma and his kids all his life, the man in front, first in the queue, now accepting money from his daughter to survive, his paradise turned to the pinch and pucker of poverty in the blink of a financial flog's eye—he was motivated, for sure, and now she searched his face for discomfort, for compunction of any type.

He leaned in towards her and spoke slowly, so the girly could understand. 'Listen, this is pretty simple, love, it's you and your reptiles versus people. Right? Real people. Senior citizens who've made their contribution and deserve more than what's been served up to them.'

'Yes,' said Clem. 'I can certainly see your point of view, Mr Bennett, it's a terrible situation'—and it was—'but I guess, well, it is only one perspective isn't it?' She was pushing shit uphill here, but she had to give it something.

'There's only one perspective that counts, sweetheart.'

'But it's just...well...an entire species. To see it obliterated, lost forever...'

Ralph snorted. 'What about your fellow man? Geez, you lawyers are all alike,' he started laughing now, 'reptiles protecting reptiles.' A crumb of Anzac exploded from his nose and he grabbed a handkerchief from the back of his shorts and blew it loudly.

Helen would have persisted: *Humans need no special support, Clementine, we're dominating, relentlessly...we've got to share the planet...be the voice before it's too late.* Clem didn't see the *voice* having any impact whatsoever here in Ralph Bennett's dining room. But still, it seemed she had managed to convince Ralph that she was not a threat, little more than a hippy turtle-lover

65

and certainly no match for his manly arguments. That was an advantage she might be able to use.

'Hey, have you heard the one about the catfish and the lawyer?' he said.

'Ralph, don't!' yelled Selma from the kitchen. Clem knew the joke: it was one of her favourites.

'One's a bottom-dwelling scum-sucker and the other's a fish.' Ralph's whole body was shaking with laughter, holding his eyes pinched between his thumb and forefinger as he laughed.

Clem laughed then helped herself to another Anzac, taking a big bite into its crisp honey-ness. 'Gee these are good,' she said, savouring the sweetness. 'Helen could bake, too, you know. Her brownies were the best.'

Ralph looked uncomfortable. He drained his cup. 'Selma, love, could you get us another?'

'Can I ask you something Mr Bennett?' She put her Anzac down on the plate in front of her. 'Do you think it was suicide?' Eyes trained on his face, every movement, every twitch. As much as she felt for his situation, nothing justified what had been done to Helen.

He didn't flinch, calmly rested his arms across his chest again.

'Cops seem to think so.' The words had a finality to them. Ralph was a man easily satisfied by whatever the cops might say, the blue-collar workers of the justice system. Not like lawyers and other assorted scum-suckers.

'You knew her longer than I did, of course, but she seemed pretty happy to me, that's all.'

'Hmm,' he sniffed. 'Who the hell knows what goes on in women's heads?'

There was a crash from the kitchen as Selma amped up the tea-making.

'The woman is dead, Mr Bennett.'

Ralph was defiant, leaning forward, whispering so Selma

couldn't hear, 'Yeah, well, I didn't know her that well and as far as I'm concerned, she was a waste of air. All that nonsense about scientific turtle studies. I'll tell you what the science says,' he pointed his fat plumber's forefinger at Clem's face. 'We need a mine and a port to give young families jobs and we need to start producing in this country, exporting instead of buying everything from China. That's what'll pay for hospitals and nurses and teachers. It's basic common sense,' he spat, pushing back again into his chair. His face had gone the colour of a good shiraz.

Selma appeared with another cup of tea, which she set down, just a little too firmly, on the table in front of Ralph.

Turning to Clem she said, 'Another cup, dear?' Those nanna eyes would melt your heart.

'No, thank you Mrs Bennett. The Anzacs were delicious.'

Selma smiled, nodded and turned to go, giving Ralph a glare. He glared back at her.

After he'd finished his tea, Ralph saw Clementine to the door. Selma followed them out as they strolled down the driveway and past Ralph's old Landcruiser.

'Enjoy a bit of four-wheel-driving do you, Mr Bennett?'

'Used to. Can't afford the fuel now.'

Clem cast her eyes down to the tyres as she passed by, checking the tread: caked with mud. There were no dirt roads in the township and the highway in and out was bitumen.

'Take her up to the quarry much?'

Ralph turned towards her, slowly, eyes narrowing to slits.

'What's that got to do with anything?'

Clem tried to look casual. 'Just interested to know what folk do around here, other than fishing.'

The police should be taking soil samples. She could ask them to; demand it. She imagined that sergeant—what was her name? Wiseman—her condescending look. Clem wondered whether you could just rake over tyre marks. How long was the track in? Might be a lot of work. She should go up there.

'You don't get it do you, you people? We can't afford to do anything other than put food on the table and pay the bills, never mind fuel for skylarking! We're in bed before dark so we don't have to turn the lights on, for God's sake.'

Ralph had gone that shiraz colour again. He stood near her, too close, imposing his height, his weight and his shock of wiry grey hair on her.

'Sorry Mr Bennett, didn't mean to offend.' She kept walking down the driveway, looking back at the house to check for security cameras. There were none of course. Who would need such things in Piama; or, as Ralph had pointed out, who could afford them? Towards the front, on the concrete landing pad of a driveway, was an aluminium dinghy on a trailer, covered in a tarp.

'I suppose you get out fishing though? Dinghy would run on the smell of an oily rag wouldn't she?' Clem didn't wait for an answer, she knew he did—had seen him out there a few times. 'Do you enjoy fishing too, Mrs Bennett?' asked Clem.

'I used to love it. Haven't been for a long time now, though. My hips...I can't get in and out of the boat like I used to,' she smiled, 'but I love a nice fresh flathead. Lightly seasoned and fried with a bit of lemon, that's how we do it.'

'Me too,' said Clem. 'Delicious.'

A surprised grunt from Ralph.

'So, do you fish, Miss Jones?' asked Selma.

'Never tried it but I'd love to have a go.'

'Well I'll be,' Ralph chuckled. 'The Westley woman was a flaming vegan!' He seemed genuinely delighted to find a greenie who would not only eat meat, but hunt and kill it.

'Well then, you must go out with Ralph!' said Selma.

'Oh no, I wouldn't want to impose.'

'Don't be silly—he'd be pleased to take you, wouldn't you, dear?' She rounded on Ralph like a teacher, both scolding and encouraging.

Ralph harrumphed and raised his hands in submission. 'S'pose it wouldn't hurt. Whiting are running,' he half-smiled. 'Let's hope we don't catch too many catfish, eh?'

CHAPTER 6

The view from Andrew Doncaster's mansion made Ralph's look cheap. Halfway up the mountain just out of Piama, the house could hardly be seen from the road, thick forest crowding around it. Myrtles arched above, shading a layer of palms and leafy vines, a blanket of wet, green ferns covering the ground.

Clem buzzed at the gate, a woman's voice answered and the gate swung wide. She drove in and parked in front of an enormous timber-columned entry portal. Doncaster's housekeeper met her at the door and ushered her to the expansive deck on the top floor. Two other levels of opulence receded beneath them down the steep block, and below that an infinity pool blended seamlessly into the forest. The top of a towering mango tree stood to the right of the deck, so close you could reach out and pluck the plump golden fruit.

Doncaster was sitting in a vast outdoor setting, all supersized cushions and designer throw rugs. He had the thick-necked look of a rugby player and a full head of stiff hair—the kind that tends to stick straight up—once orange, now mostly grey. It came with the fair skin of a redhead and when he smiled two dimples appeared in his squarish cheeks. Definitely in the 'rugged' category. Attractive, if he hadn't been thirty years her senior.

As he greeted her and waved her into a chair, the housekeeper poured them both some water from a jug brimming with sliced oranges and lime.

Doncaster was a self-made man, the son of a Hunter Valley grocer. Most of his money came from property development and he'd built this, his holiday house, after the breakdown of his third marriage. Opposed to the port, he'd donated many thousands of dollars to WAGSS over the last two years. Clementine hoped he was in a mood to write another cheque. The Galimore Foundation grant conditions stipulated that recipients must have at least one other regular and significant source of funds. The WAGSS operating account was down to its last two hundred dollars and she was due to report to the Galimore Foundation by the end of the week. Without a top-up from Doncaster, questions would be asked.

She also wanted to ask him about Helen.

They sipped on the iced water and exchanged condolences.

'I'm sure Helen thanked you many times in the past, Andrew, but I'd like to say it myself, personally, as the new coordinator. The battle to save the turtle only has wings because of you.' Flattery had worked for her before with powerful men, but as soon as she said the words she knew she'd laid it on too thick.

He ignored her and looked out over the view. She felt her nervousness about the funding ratchet up a notch.

'Corker of a day don't you reckon?' He swept one arm before him. 'A bloke could sit here for hours on a day like today.'

Clem doubted that was the case. That was not what property tycoons did with their time.

'Yes, beautiful. And not so hot today, thank goodness.'

In the distance Piama looked very small. Doncaster kept looking out at the view, his view, as if he owned everything within it, including all of Piama. How to win his attention, his interest? Asking for money was not something she'd had to do since primary school fundraising raffles.

'So, I imagine the white-throated turtle is not the only cause you support, Andrew,' she ventured. 'Are you generally focused on environmental matters?'

'Hhhmmm, it's pretty broad really. I kind of go after whatever grabs me at the time.' He smiled at her as he spoke, then turned back to survey his dominion.

'The turtle is certainly something that grabs your attention. I mean, a reptile that breaths under water from, ah, you know where...not something you forget easily,' she smiled hopefully.

'Would you like another water?' He picked up the jug and waved it at her.

He'd ignored her a second time. She'd have to try a more direct approach.

'And tell me, how was it you became involved in the campaign against the port?' she asked, holding out her glass for a top up.

'Well, Helen...She was very enthusiastic, and very convincing,' he paused over thoughts of Helen. 'And the timing was right,' he added. 'I'd been funding a kids' camp for cancer sufferers for the last four years. Construction completed and Helen knocked on the door almost the same day.'

Nothing to do with the extinction of an entire species, then. Just Helen's energy and a timely coincidence.

'You've gotta seize the opportunities—*carpe diem* as they say.'

He spread his arms back and lay them atop of the lounge like wings, displaying his impressive chest and biceps. *Must work out.*

'Timing's the key to so many things, not just in business either... so many other things in life too. I'm not an educated man, Ms Jones. I've had to fight for things, make the most of what comes my way...'

The whiteness of his skin beneath his collar and the pink sun damage on his face made him look like he'd been fighting the elements all his life.

'...and supporting good causes is just as important to me as my business interests.'

'Helen could be quite persuasive as well, I would imagine.'

He looked pensive, as if he was trying to remember, calling up his entire stock of Helen memories. She waited, hoping he might open up: reveal something about his commitment to the cause that she could use as a hook.

'Yes, she was.' He stared into his glass, as if speaking to the orange slices, continuing to avoid eye contact with her.

'So you got to know Helen quite well, I guess.'

'Oh, I wouldn't say that,' he looked up, startled. 'She'd call in to give me updates on the campaign, of course,' he said, casually. Too casually? Forced? Clementine couldn't put her finger on it. 'She was diligent like that.'

It was true, Helen had been diligent but the word grated. It seemed disrespectful of the woman she'd been, diminishing her somehow. Passionate, driven, articulate, kind—any of those words would have been acceptable.

'Yes, she was tireless for the cause,' nodded Clementine. 'Hard to understand why...' She left the sentence ambiguous. She wanted to see if he would take it as a reference to Helen taking her own life.

He gazed out over the lush green canopy again. 'I guess you never can tell, really...what's going on underneath the surface.'

Death. Her death was on his mind. But hey, so what? It was on everybody's mind.

'Did you notice anything with Helen? Any signs?'

'Signs?'

'Yes, you know, depression or anything like that.'

'No. Didn't know her well enough.' He swished his glass again, watching the fruit swirl around for a second before raising it to his lips, throwing his head back to get the last of the water. Then he leaned forward and planted the empty glass on the table with a thud.

'So. Tell me, Ms Jones, what can I do for you?'

Switch flicked, all business.

'Please, call me Clementine. Or Clem, or even Jonesy if you like. That's what the team back in Victoria call me.' He looked like he'd be into some sort of footy—it was worth a chance. It bombed, awkwardly.

She moved on, gave him an update on the campaign.

'Legal proceedings?' he said.

'Yes, we're appealing the minister's decision to approve the water management plan.'

'Not a big fan of legal proceedings.'

'Oh?'

'Well, they're messy aren't they—messy and very public. No fun at all, except for the lawyers.'

She recalled Helen had mentioned that Doncaster was a very private man who deplored publicity. Why hadn't she shut up about the appeal? Her stomach was plummeting. The donation cheque was like a white sail on a boat out to sea, disappearing over the horizon.

'Well, of course if we can apply enough pressure, the developers may seek to settle and we could—'

He cut her off, launching into a diatribe on how the court system sucks money away from what society really needs, like camps for sick kids and a cure for cancer.

This wasn't going to plan, not at all. She managed to swing the conversation away from the legal proceedings and chatted about the coming turtle-hatching season. When she did finally slip the question about a donation, she got a big surprise.

'Yeah. Will ten thousand do it?'

She'd been certain he was going to give her the flick, just like the Galimore Foundation. She scrambled to compose herself. 'Well,' she cleared her throat, using the seconds to think...ten thousand wasn't bad but then he'd once given twenty thousand in a single cheque. *Come on, Jones. Game on.*

'It's a wee bit shy of what we need actually, Andrew.' He

grunted, raised an eyebrow. Clem took it as an invitation.

'Thirty will see us clear for a bit.'

\\//

The moon was up and Piama slept. Clementine Jones and Matthew Torrens had work to do. They did a drive-by first, checking who was up in Seascape Avenue at ten o'clock at night. No one, it seemed, not even on a Friday. Maybe they were all saving on power.

'What makes you think he won't have washed it off? Especially after you put your foot in your mouth asking about the quarry.' Paranoid about anyone recognising him, Torrens wore a very wide-brimmed felt hat with indentations in the crown. He'd bought it in Tamworth on the way up, and with the Ned Kelly beard it made him look like a Canadian Mounty.

'It's a possibility, but I don't think so. Ralph wouldn't credit me with enough intelligence to suspect him. Besides, he's saving on the water bill.'

Torrens pulled up at the community hall carpark at the other end of the street.

'This is bloody déjà vu, this is,' he said, slapping the steering wheel. 'You really are gunna have to invest in a balaclava!'

Clem felt the same way. Only on their last nocturnal adventure they'd been up to serious no-good. Taking a sample of dirt from the tyres was hardly even a crime.

Clem checked the Woolies bag one more time. Sterile pack of tweezers from the Barnforth chemist, ziplock bags, mobile phone set to camera and a small torch. The thick hedging around Ralph's driveway would provide a screen and all she had to do was scrape some dirt into plastic bags, photograph the make and model of tyre and walk back to the car. Easy.

She put on the baseball cap and black hoodie. Can't be too blasé about these things. Torrens reached into his pocket, pulled something out. A flick-knife, flashing in the light from the street lamp outside the carpark.

'Here you go, for old times' sake,' he grinned.

'I don't need a knife, you clown.'

'For protection, not to slash the tyres, although I know how much you like a bit of that action.'

She shook her head, 'You're insufferable.'

'Aw, come on, you're no fun anymore!'

She got out of the car, closed the door as softly as she could, walked briskly down the street. This wouldn't be of any use as evidence in any criminal proceedings, of course, but she could use it to get the police moving. And at least she would know.

The evening was still, the day's heat hanging like a curtain, and to her dismay the midges were still up and about. Must be the full moon or something. They started going for her ankles and behind her knees as soon as she stopped outside Ralph's front yard. She peered up the driveway to the house. Still no lights on and the street was deathly quiet. Not even a single dog unhappy with her presence. A possum scurried up a tree across the road.

She crept up the driveway, keeping to the shadows, her sneakers soundless on the concrete, the car shielding her from the house. Crouching by the rear driver's-side tyre she held the torch between her teeth and opened the first bag, carefully scraped the dirt from the tread. The lab only needed a small amount for testing.

She tiptoed to the front tyre, still shielded from the house, repeated the procedure, the midges feasting on her ankles—pricking, sucking, setting them alight. Her mouth was beginning to ache from gripping the torch. *Next time bring a headlamp.* Two done, two to go. She crept back up to the rear of the car and around to the passenger-side wheel. It felt exposed. Nothing between her and the house, Ralph and Selma sleeping only metres away, the moon threatening to burst from behind a cloud and send shafts of light her way. A curlew gave a heart-rending cry and a flying fox flapped softly overhead. She looked up to see it silhouetted against the moonlight, the perfect batman shape. She liked to keep her eye on the wretched things—carried some sort of killer disease, rabies or Hendra or something.

She scraped and pinched at the dirt on the tyre, sweeping each minute portion into another bag. One to go. Sneaking forward towards the wheel closest to the house.

The porch light flicked on. She froze. It spotlighted her as if on stage. *Shit*—a movement sensor. She snuck back to the other side of the car; scanned the house. Nothing. The whole street still silent. She waited for what seemed like ten minutes but was probably only two, brushing away the midges from the fleshy part of her thighs. The light went off. Everything dark again, eyes adjusting slowly.

She weighed up the situation. Ralph and Selma's bedroom might face the other side of the house. The light could be triggered often, by animals, possums, cats. She wanted to do that fourth tyre. It could be the one that held the best match with dirt from the quarry track. She didn't know if the quarry dirt was distinctive, of course, so the whole procedure could be inconclusive. But being a quarry, she thought it might have unique characteristics.

All these thoughts rushed through her head as she waited. It had been a few minutes since the light had switched off. The coast was clear, the moonlight still weak under a thin layer of cloud. She crept forward, slow, hoping not to trigger the sensor, made it to the hinge on the passenger-side front door. Snap! Light flooding the driveway.

Bugger it. They're not going to wake up. Just get it done. She worked quickly, trickling dirt into the bag, fumbling, spilling some of it, checking nervously for movement in the house. Nothing. Scraping, pinching. Almost done.

Another light. Inside the house this time. She held her breath, watching. A shadow then a form, someone approaching the front door. *Oh God. Where to go?*

She dived under the vehicle just as the front door opened. A pause, then the pad of footsteps down the stairs and along the path. Her heart was pumping so loud she could hear it pulsing in her ears. She rolled further under. The footsteps stopped. Bare feet, less than a metre away from where she lay under the car. Big, lumpy feet. Ralph the Resident President's feet. He didn't move. Then a slight shuffle, his feet wider apart. Then a noise like a tap. She turned her head ever so slightly but she could already smell it. Urine. Splashing onto the concrete and running towards her.

The first customer for Saturday morning arrived in a metallic grey Chrysler with an enormous front grille. It pulled up outside the kiosk and a man wearing a bottle-green polo shirt and jeans got out. Medium build, beer gut, tan deck shoes and wraparound Ray-Bans. He walked over towards the beach, looked across the golden shallows and out into the stripes of aqua and sapphire across to Fraser Island, then stuck his hands in his pockets and walked back to the kiosk, sweeping the multi-coloured plastic ribbons aside at the doorway. He left the Ray-Bans on in the cool darkness within.

The manager, sitting on his vinyl stool behind the cash register nodded at him, flicked him a 'G'day mate'.

'Got any cabins available?' asked the man. He spoke in a languid, easy bass as if the world had never denied him anything he might have wanted.

'Yeah, mate. Deluxe and standard. How many nights you after?'

CHAPTER 7

Marakai Mining's Public Relations Director, Karene Bickerstaff, was pretty much what Clem had expected. Dyed-blonde hair, tied back tight with not a strand out of place, a stiff-collared light blue shirt that sat pertly at her neck and a string of tiny pearls.

Karene picked up her chardonnay and sipped.

'Ew,' she said, plonking it down on the table. 'That's it, I've tried them all now. Every wine in every pub in this godforsaken town. All of them vinegar.'

Clem was disappointed. She needed Karene to sink a couple more glasses, loosen those lips. Helen had said she liked a drop.

'Are you sure you've tried the sav blanc? I had a glass here a week ago and I thought it was drinkable.' Clem was making it up, still hopeful.

'Not that dreadful Yalumba?' Her face pinched like it was caught in a door.

'No, no, something else. I can't recall the name...'

Karene persevered with the chardonnay, which would clearly have to do, and began recounting her day escorting a bevy of state MPs around the proposed mine site.

'It's like hosting a bunch of bored children on a school excursion to see a patch of empty dirt,' she said, holding her head. 'Draining.'

Eventually Clem managed to shift the conversation to Helen.

'Doesn't matter what your politics are—sad, just sad,' said Karene. 'I guess the signs were all there, though.'

'Really?' Clem sat up straighter. Had she finally found someone who'd noticed something?

'Oh yes, you see Marakai Mining are big donors to the Healthy Minds Institute. Big donors.' She closed her eyes and nodded. 'We sponsor the management training program they put on for businesses. The first day is all about understanding the symptoms, day two is how to manage them. That part's a bit of a joke, though—I mean who can afford flexi-time and quiet spaces? The public service perhaps—hardly realistic anywhere else.'

'What symptoms did you see in Helen?'

'Oh you know,' said Karene, flicking a hand in the air. 'She seemed irritable, that sort of thing.' She took another sip. 'It's the little things.'

If Helen was irritable it might well have been Karene that irritated her, thought Clem.

'She certainly took offence at anything I had to say, but you see all I could do was give her the facts: freshwater turtle habitat disturbance will be minimal. We engaged two independent consultants and they both say the same thing.'

'Independent? Hired? Bit of an oxymoron, don't you think?'

'Oh come on, Clementine, you must know the drill, you're a lawyer'—another sip—'Sorry, sorry...*Were* a lawyer. Do you still practise?'

'Yes, but I only have one client—the white-throated snapping turtle.'

Karene chuckled, 'I expect you'd have trouble getting your invoices paid, then. But I guess the Galimore Foundation pays your fees?'

'Nope. I'm pro bono. The foundation pays the law firm handling the appeal and, of course, for the independent scientific study that indicates catastrophic habitat destruction.'

'Like I said, girlfriend, no such thing as independence.'

Surprisingly, Karene had finished the glass of vinegar already.

Great, thought Clem. Time for another. 'How about I get you a glass of that sav blanc?'

'Oh well, what's the harm? I'm out of this hole tomorrow— good reason to celebrate.'

Clem went to the bar, approaching from the side, away from the line of men in filthy jeans and high-vis work shirts. She ordered a soda water for herself and a glass of the house sauvignon blanc— 'Yes, a large one thanks'—flicking through her wine app as she waited. She found what she wanted and committed it to memory as the barman set the glass on the bar. She handed him her credit card to start a tab and carried the two glasses back to the table. Karene was scrolling through her Twitter feed.

'Dear God, Canberra's going mad today,' she said. 'I swear, if there's a spill I bloody hope the leadership goes to someone who understands corporate imperatives. I mean, how the hell is this country going to survive otherwise? Fairy dust?'

Clem put the glasses down on the round table. 'There you go, 2013 Peringel from Margaret River.'

'No! You're kidding me. I didn't see that on the menu.'

'I know the barman. Told me he keeps a few specially,' she lied. 'But only for those that know to ask—wasted on the rest of these philistines.' Clem glanced towards the rowdy bunch at the bar.

Karene took a sip of the stock standard, no-name house wine, closing her eyes as she swallowed.

'Oh my God, you're a magician.' She took another gulp. 'Mmmm,' she said, eyes still closed.

Clem smiled to herself. 'What say we order dinner?' she said, hoping to extend the evening.

'I could go a medium-rare rib fillet with a nice, full-bodied shiraz. Could you conjure one up, maybe?'

'Think I might know the secret code.'

\\/

Karene was drinking the house red like cordial. The rib fillet was more well-done than medium-rare and the chips tasted like they'd been baked for two days, cooled and then blowtorched. Karene didn't seem to care anymore. Now's the time, thought Clem.

'You know I'm totally with you, Karene, on the Federal leadership...you know...about corporate imperatives...'

Karene forked another piece of steak into her mouth.

'Mmmm, well, sadly very few in your environmental circles get it.'

'...get industry moving, revenues flowing, wipe out the deficit,' said Clem.

'Absolutely! Healthcare, education, welfare...nothing happens without taxes and mining royalties.' There was a pause while Karene chewed. 'Gee, you're different from Helen,' she remarked, shaking her head. 'I mean, I don't want to speak ill of the dead, but tree huggers who believe in magic puddings are all too common.'

Clem ignored the slur. 'So I imagine there's a lot riding on the port development—'

'Well, there is a little thing called the share price...'

'And if that gets a lift, there'll be a decent bonus all round, I'd guess.'

'And well-earned too.' Karene plonked her wine glass down clumsily onto the cardboard coaster so the glass toppled and half the remaining wine sloshed over onto the table. Clem quickly had it replaced, with a wave and a wink to the barman.

'So I suppose Scott Stanton-Green will do pretty well out of it.' Clem had researched him: Marakai's Director, Infrastructure and Operations, the senior executive in charge of the port project. His performance plan would be heavily weighted towards port milestones: EIS acceptance, government approvals, construction commencement, on-time completion of each phase. Before Marakai, he'd been at Meatco. There'd been a scandal—brown paper bags to foreign officials in return for contracts. If he'd been involved in that sort of skulduggery who knew what else he might be capable of. Clem had lined up a meeting with him the next day but she hoped Karene would know something.

'Hey, it's been a good night so far, why spoil it by mentioning the Hyphen.'

'Not a fan?'

'Look, I'm used to being the only female around the executive table and I expect a level of boorishness, I'm not precious, but, oh, Clementine, SSG takes it to a new level.'

'I wonder how involved he was in the Meatco scandal...'

'I've heard a few whispers,' she said, leaning towards Clem with her fork in the air. 'None too savoury, either.'

'And?'

'Up to his eyeballs.'

\|/

The door to the donga opened directly into an open-plan area. Clem looked to her left: rows of workstations that stretched down three lengths of shipping-container-width office. The air was chilled and everything was plastic. Grey vinyl floor, grey furniture, large windows and the light of a cloudless summer day drowning the unnecessary glow from the fluorescent light boxes. Coal miners' offices—wouldn't be too worried about saving energy, she supposed.

A woman got up from her desk to show Clem through a door to a meeting room on the right. Table and chairs to seat about ten, a bench just inside the door with a kettle and a tray of coffee mugs, a map rack and satellite photos Blu-tacked to the walls. A television attached high on the far wall, sound muted, was playing the lead-up to the One Day International against the Kiwis, due to start shortly at the Sydney Cricket Ground.

She sat and waited, fully expecting the royal brush-off from

Karene's king of boor. She set herself a goal: make it to five minutes and you never know what might happen.

But how? She couldn't steal the mayor's thunder by mentioning the deal she'd suggested: that had to be a victory for the mayor if she was going to get any further down that road. She had Karene's hearsay on Stanton-Green but nothing substantive. Make it up as you go was not her preferred approach, it made her uneasy, but none of the plans she'd dreamt up on the drive out seemed to stack up.

She waited another two minutes, got up and poured herself a plastic cup of water from the bubbler in the corner, stood looking at the satellite photos. The first couple looked like they might be the mine site area at different zoom levels. The next two followed a winding line of thick trees—Piama Creek, the proposed route for the railway and road. She moved along the row of photographs, the creek widening to become a river until she came to a sharp kink, the one just after Helen's house about a kilometre before the river met the bay. She took a step closer and peered into the photograph. She could make out Turtle Shores' roof and the large WAGSS headquarters shed in the backyard. A lump rose in her throat and she sat back down.

Everything about this room—the maps already prepared and draped neatly on the rack, the fresh new office chairs, the upturned tray of mugs ready to go—all of it screamed inevitability. And the photographs tracing the creek from a satellite in space were like the view from a fighter plane—an armoury in Iraq, a Taliban base in Afghanistan—she almost expected a pilot's voice over the static: 'target locked'. Her stomach sank at the sheer scale of the task that had fallen to Helen and her plucky little band. And what the hell was Clementine going to do about it? What the hell could she do about anything? And who in this metal capsule of an office, this outpost of empire, the spreading dominion of Marakai Mining, even cared the slightest fig that Helen was dead?

85

She closed her eyes, drew a deep breath.

Helen had sat here and not been daunted. She had met the challenge head on.

Clem breathed out to the count of ten, snapped her eyes open, lifted the water to her lips and drained it, crushing the empty cup in her fist. Then the Hyphen walked in.

'Oh for fuck's sake!' he said in a voice way too big for the room.

She jumped. Stanton-Green was glaring at the television, standing there in a chambray shirt, camel moleskins and brown steel-capped boots—huge, out of proportion to his height, which she judged to be just under six foot.

'Finch. First ball! Fucken loser.'

On the screen the Black Caps were getting around the bowler, back-slapping and hooting in their dinner suit uniforms. The camera flicked to Aaron Finch, on the long walk to the boundary, head bowed.

He likes cricket. The boor likes cricket. It was something. A start, at least. She reached across the table and grabbed the remote, flicking the mute switch off. The roar from forty thousand fans filled the little meeting room in the grey donga on this nondescript piece of dirt a thousand kilometres away. The Hyphen barely even glanced at her, eyes glued to the screen. The replay showed Finch pushing forward, an inside edge and the ball cannoning into his leg stump.

He slumped into a chair opposite Clementine, swinging it around towards the television so she was looking at him in profile. A little overweight, not a lot. Tightly curling hair clipped into submission, tiny ears.

'Shit. That just cost me five hundred.'

'You had Finch for top score?'

'Yep.'

'Jesus.' She let out a low whistle. 'One ball, five hundred gone.'

'Still got a thou on Australia for the match,' he growled as Steve

Smith made his way out to the crease, kicking up his heels in a jogging burst, shadow-batting at phantom balls, adjusting his eyes to the light, a gathering wall of concentration.

'Early days, early days,' said Clem. 'Plenty of talent to come, including this guy.'

Stanton-Green was a big punter. And apparently not averse to a bit of corruption—a man who would play the odds, take a risk, *give* in order to *get*...even if it was outside the rules. A plan began to take shape. A conversation she could manoeuvre somehow: risk and return...angling towards payment for favours...you scratch my back...She didn't know the detail, but she had the broad outline.

They sat there while Smith soaked up the rest of the over. During the ad break Clem made some comments about team selections to keep him interested, then Smith and Warner began to crank it up, keeping the strike turning over, boundaries starting to flow, a run a ball for the next six overs. She'd long passed her five-minute success threshold and even though they hadn't spoken a word about the turtle or Helen, Clem could sense the longer she bonded with the Hyphen over the game, the greater the chance she had of learning something.

She made a comment on the field-setting—'not sure why the Kiwis don't put a third man in'—and as if they'd heard it, the commentary team began to express a similar opinion. The Hyphen looked at her properly for the first time. A slightly bewildered look.

Finally Warner was out in the ninth over, playing on to Ferguson, but Smith was well set at the other end and progressing with trademark intensity. She'd been sitting there sharing the cricket with the Hyphen for over half an hour. He'd probably have to go shortly, actually do some work, so when the ads came on she flicked the remote to mute, reached across the table, hand extended and announced herself, 'Clementine Jones,' for all the world like she was meeting him in the Marakai corporate box, beer in hand and a platter of beef bourguignon party pies in front of them.

He gripped her hand. 'Scott Stanton-Green,' he said. 'You're the new turtle woman, then?'

The way he spoke, the cursory question—it seemed he hadn't bothered to look her up, didn't know her past. She found herself wondering if this would always be the first thing she thought of whenever she met someone. Regardless, she kept her game face on—time to front up to the first delivery.

'Yeah,' she said, trying to sound uninterested in all things turtle.

'Hmmph,' he sniffed. 'Bit different to the last one.'

There was something about the way he said it, it was subtle, but it seemed like he'd been offended somehow by Helen, some sort of personal affront. Had he been rebuffed by Helen in some way? Or was she just overthinking it?

'Helen didn't like cricket?'

'Fucked if I know. Barely spent two minutes with her, thank Christ. Looked like she'd be as much fun as a wet sock.'

He said it with a snarl and Clem's suspicion grew. It was a long shot, little more than a possibility. But it got a head of steam up and ran away like a freight train in her head: had the Hyphen offered Helen a bribe? Which she had then refused? This man with a reputation for corruption and a truck-sized drive to win, a big-punter high-stakes edge-of-the-envelope risk-taker? Had Helen refused to play ball? Had she threatened to expose him and his crude offer?

'Yeah, only met her once but she struck me as a bit of a wowser,' said Clem, chumming it up.

'So, you got anything riding on the game?' he asked.

He saw her as a player. Good.

'Shit yeah,' she lied. 'Not in the same league as you, but I've got fifty bucks on the win and twenty for Starc as man of the match.'

'Nice odds for Starc?'

'Yeah. Ten to one. Mortgage could do with a boost,' she grinned. *Yes, Scottie, I'm poor.*

He looked at her carefully. 'Like the horseys?'

'Used to. Had a system on short-priced favourites for a place. Didn't do too bad, built up a kitty over a few years. It's a numbers game, though...I wouldn't know a pony from a platypus.' Her father had bet in accordance with a strict set of rules every weekend, until her mum had put a stop to it and made him cash out. Clem knew the details; she could recite how it worked if she had to, make up a story to go with it.

'Ha! A system. That's nice. Wanna share?'

She recounted the rules, described the slow grind of big punts for small gains. 'Took me three years to make two cents,' she laughed.

'Gave it away, though?' He was testing her, she could feel it, checking to see if she could be trusted. Not that there was anything at stake—there were no witnesses here.

'Yeah, had to—lost my kitty, all of it, in a moment of stupidity. Got drunk one night at the casino and put it all on red. Took me years to get to that point, years, and I lost the heart for it after that. Bloody hell, I could use that dough now, though,' she said shaking her head ruefully. *Hint number two, Scottie-boy.*

'So whaddya do for a crust?'

'This is it,' she said, palms up, holding air for a moment, down again on the table. 'The turtles.'

'Geez, that wouldn't pay much.'

Come clean, Clementine—he'll look you up as soon as you leave here; let him in, let him in. She exhaled a long breath through pursed lips, clenched her teeth tight—the whole performance for this guy...Only it wasn't a performance, and the idea of talking about it here, to this man—it made her feel nauseous.

'Well, I used to be a lawyer but there was another drunken misadventure.' She lowered her eyes, then lifted them back to his face—he was intrigued, intent. 'Killed a woman on the road. Nobody's all that interested in taking me on anymore.' She gave a sour grin. 'Bit of a stench about me.'

'Shiiiit. Criminal lawyer?'

'No, commercial—business clients, contracts, whatever.' She avoided the word 'corporate', it made her sound too sharp.

The Hyphen drummed his fingers on the table in an even gallop. They were big, fat and, like his feet, out of proportion for a man who wasn't that overweight.

'You seem to know about cricket. Fuck the law, you could bloody get on the fucken commentary team for Channel 9. They're looking for females these days,' then he laughed, like it was the greatest joke—that a woman might be paid to speak about sport.

Clem laughed along, tedious as it was. He'd really cracked himself up with his own wit.

'Listen, Jones...'

'Call me Clementine.'

'Clementine then,' he said, nodding. 'I like you. You're a good sort.'

'Thanks Scott.' First-name basis now, and suck, suck, sucking for all she was worth—the only way to go with an ego this size.

'So, what say we cut the crap?'

'I should talk to you about the turtles, though,' she said weakly, trying not to give up too easily but so, so hot for cutting the crap.

'Yeah, yeah. I know all about the bloody turtle with an arsehole for a mouth—I've done my homework,' he said, waving a hand dismissively. 'But why so serious? More to life, yeah?' He leaned in closer, staring intensely at Clementine, weighing up the odds, deciding, about to make his move. 'I've got this gelding, see— Meat the Magic. He's doing well. How about I cut you a share?'

She smiled tentatively, attempting something cautiously gleeful. 'Did you just offer me a share in your racehorse?'

'Well, a share in some of his winnings—and you're in luck, he just happened to score last weekend—I can cut you in. Might help you get through until you can get back into some money.'

'But...' she shook her head, a look of awe and appreciation towards the great man. 'I don't understand...that's just... ridiculously generous.'

'Not really.'

'Why?'

'Cos you can scratch my back too, if you get my drift.'

Clem nodded, every muscle of her body signifying to the Hyphen that she understood the game, the way the ball swung in the air, seamed off the pitch, spun past the bat...smacked into the keeper's gloves. 'Right. So you want the road humps smoothed? For the mine, the port and all the rest of it?'

He nodded.

'You want the turtle stuff to go quiet?

He kept nodding.

She leaned back in the chair. 'This is sounding too easy. What's the catch?'

'No catch.'

'So why the hell didn't Helen go for this?' she said, looking bewildered but feeling sick—she didn't want to sound like she was fishing, but she had to know more. 'What the fuck was wrong with her?'

'Like I said, fucked if I know. Silly bitch wouldn't know her arse from her elbow.' Clem felt a flush of heat rising in her cheeks. 'But you know, it's like so many people,' he said, his face sliding into philosopher mode. 'Virtuous people, self-righteous, stuck-up people: so far from the action they're not even in the game, right?'

She nodded.

'Just...irrelevant. Like a moth in the headlights—next thing they know they're up against the windscreen with their arse through their brain.'

The image was shocking, breathtakingly shocking. Had he been there when Helen died? Watched the killer do the deed? Done it

91

himself? Was he getting a sick thrill out of playing around with the visual?

She forced the image of Helen at the base of the quarry out of her mind, swallowed hard—*finish this Jones, and get the hell out of here.* 'So, maybe we run out of money to pay the lawyers, drop the legal proceedings…sneak in some doubt about the science, leak it to the media? For authenticity, nothing too high profile,' she offered. He was slow-nodding, a smile growing wider. 'A gaffe to a journo to make us look silly…that sort of thing?'

He sniggered. 'Now *that*'—he waved a finger at her, grinning— 'that would be a fucking man of the match performance.'

\|/

The four-wheel drive was facing towards the street, already hooked up to the boat trailer. In the dash to hide underneath it on Friday night, she'd lost her house keys. She scanned the concrete driveway, the grass alongside. Nothing.

Shit. He must have found them.

Ralph appeared at the front door in navy Stubbies and a white terry-towelling bucket hat. He swayed down the stairs with his stiff, heavy gait. Arthritic knees or hips or something, big brown sandals with slabs of rubber underneath. He reminded Clem of her grandfather, although Ralph was a much bigger man. Big enough even in his seventies to overpower a sixty-year-old woman, she thought.

'Good day for it,' she said from the front yard.

'Yes, she's turned out quite nice and the moon's right too. Fish'll be biting like puppies on a shoe I'd reckon.'

The moon. Was this an oblique reference to Friday night?

'You didn't happen to find a set of house keys did you? I've lost mine. Thought I might have left them here when we met the other day.'

'Nah, didn't notice any,' he said, pulling up in the exact place he'd relieved himself the other night, looking concerned. 'Let's have a look.'

He bent down, leaning on the trailer, scouring under the boat, making quite a show of it.

'Ah well, looks like I've left them somewhere else,' she said.

'Bloody nuisance, losing your keys,' he said.

An hour later and they were bobbing about on a turquoise stripe in the Great Sandy Straits. With the gentle breeze the sea tilted and peaked, making a playful chinking noise against the sides of Ralph's tinny.

'Now,' said Ralph, 'when you feel a nibble, like a pecking action'—he demonstrated with his hands—'could be a nice whiting or bream or flathead or something, then you straight away give it a hoik.' Ralph jagged his fishing rod up aggressively. 'And don't let any slack on your line, just start winding before you drop that rod tip. If ya give the fish any slack that's their chance to throw the hook.'

Clementine nodded, practising the jab action.

Ralph caught three fish before Clem finally managed to hook one. She'd had several bites with nothing to show for it but this time, as she jerked the rod in the air, she felt with a sudden thrill the added weight, the full-bodied tug on the line.

'Yep. That's it, you got him, wind it in,' Ralph cried.

Reeling in fast, feeling the unmistakeable flap and urgency of the fish battling in the depths below.

'Ease up!' said Ralph. 'You'll rip the bloody hook out of its mouth.'

The first sight of it in the deep: a flash of white, darting and jerking against the line, then the frantic flip of its tail splashing against the surface.

She swung up, the rod flexing, the fish swinging through the air in an arc, arriving with a plonk in the bottom of the boat, writing and jumping at her feet, glimmering pink on silver, flanks glistening in the sunlight.

'Nice little bream,' said Ralph, reaching for the line and manoeuvring the fish into the bucket.

With a rush of hope she asked, 'Is it big enough to keep?'

'Oh yes, he's well over thirty centimetres, see,' he said, holding a ruler close to the fish. Its little mouth was grabbing at the air, gills desperately cracking open and shut, eyes wide with shock. She felt a pang of regret—that this plucky little creature's struggle to live would end now—but alongside it, the thrill of the catch, something primitive and satisfying, a feeling of connection with the natural world and the cycle of life—a long way from the chilled aisles of a supermarket.

They fished for an hour and she pulled in another one: a whiting this time, without the fight of the bream but slender and elegant, yellow strips highlighting its tubular shape. And they spoke a little, every now and then, Ralph mostly about Selma and how much she used to love fishing.

'But doesn't she love eatin' them though, a nice whiting fried in butter!' He smacked his lips and grinned, a sparkle in his eyes that Clem imagined had been more frequent when he was a younger man.

'Nothing better,' said Clem, trying to sound like she knew all about it. 'Don't know how anyone could be a vegan. Seems to be all the rage, though.' Hanging out the bait, hoping to bring the conversation around to Helen.

'Hmph, bloody vegans. Them and the safety freaks, ruining the country. Kid can't even climb a tree these days without a rubber carpet underneath. In my day...' Ralph launched forth on riding free in the backs of utes, billy carts hurtling down hilly streets, his brother breaking his wrist after colliding with a parked tree. 'Never done 'im any harm. Soft, kids of today, soft.'

By the time they headed back, she'd gained very little by way of information pertinent to Helen's death but had made great strides in building a relationship with Ralph.

Standing there with the water rippling around her ankles as he winched the dinghy up onto the trailer, she watched another boat about fifty metres away, two men aboard. It stopped at a white buoy and the man in the bow began hauling on a green rope, pulling up a rusty brown cage from the shallow waters. A crab pot, she guessed.

'Ever do any crabbing, Ralph?' She'd love a mud crab; maybe Ralph would sling one her way now they'd become mates. It might pay off somehow in other ways, too, she thought.

That was partly why she was so shocked by the story he told next. The implied violence of it.

'Oh yeah. Mad not to here. Got some decent bait now, too, with these fish heads,' he nodded in the direction of the bucket. 'Mind you, I did hear a story once about crab bait.'

'Yeah?'

He continued strapping down the boat on the trailer, speaking from underneath his terry-towelling hat.

'Well, there was a fella, Crabpot Kiernan they called him, old bloke lived up north somewhere in a little shed. I believe it was somewhere near Topper's Inlet but no one ever really knew exactly where—old Crabpot kept the location pretty tight. Had solar panels up there, a generator, chest freezer and not much else, so they reckon.'

Ralph stood with one elbow on the side of the dinghy now, looking dreamily out onto the water.

'Not surprising really. He had a few skeletons best kept in the closet, so to speak. Been inside for a bit from what I heard.' He nodded for emphasis. 'Well, he was a magician with crabs, see. Used to sell 'em to the locals. Turn up with half a dozen. Get twenty bucks each for 'em.'

Clementine was wondering where the story was going when

Ralph swivelled his eyes towards her. She noticed the red veins and the way they protruded—a little like a lizard. He had both elbows on the gunwale now, leaning forward and locking onto her.

'He used what he had in the freezer, eh.'

'For bait?'

'Yeah.'

'What, mullet or something?'

'Nah,' said Ralph, evidently enjoying himself now, 'human flesh.'

Like a punch to the diaphragm, she felt the air going out and nothing coming back in.

He grinned an ugly smirk and cackled, watching her, wanting to see her revulsion, feeding on it.

'Yeah, good one,' she managed, half-heartedly.

'Nah. Fair dinkum,' he said, holding her gaze for an uncomfortable moment.

Suddenly the afternoon sun was burning her face, heat coming up from the boat ramp into her rubber thongs. It was a deliberate scare campaign. He'd planned on telling the story all along, the bastard.

They drove back to his place in silence and she helped him hose the boat down, thanking him for her first fishing experience. Ralph was unnaturally chirpy, having had his little victory.

As she walked towards her car, Ralph followed. She was opening the driver's door to get into the cab when he gripped the edge in his big, meaty hand and leaned into the shaded interior, pulling something from the pocket of his faded Stubbies.

Keys. Her keys.

He held them up between thumb and forefinger, dangling in front of her face.

'Don't forget these, Ms Jones.'

A big lump of anger formed like a fur ball in her throat. She reached up to take the keys and the moment her fingers clasped around them, he swung his other hand up, grabbing hers, pulling her close. Strong. Definitely strong enough to shove a woman over a cliff.

Centimetres from her face, eyes flashing, he growled, 'Don't ever come creeping around my yard again, girl. Don't even think about it. Or mark my words, I'll do more than just piss on ya.'

CHAPTER 8

Clem threw off the sheet, lay there naked on the rickety old bed under the rusted ceiling fan churning and clunking above. The sun had only been up an hour and the sweat was already forming a film across her forehead. Her eyes were drawn to the gap in the grimy curtains. A hook had come off one end and the folds hung down forlornly, letting a shaft of light fall over the old dresser in the corner. So many questions still, not enough light.

Ralph's vindictiveness had infected her mind and she'd barely slept. Was it all just empty threats, or was Ralph Bennett indeed a violent man, incensed enough by the humiliation that had befallen him to throw a woman off a cliff? The menace in the big man's posture at her car door came back to her, the hot spray of his breath on her face. And Crabpot Kiernan—what was all that about, other than to warn her off something Ralph wanted to hide? A shiver ran across her as the fan cooled her skin.

Then there was Stanton-Green. Helen must have been repulsed by him and his crude attempt to buy her off. Perhaps he needed to keep her quiet. Steve Smith had gone on to score one hundred and sixty-four taking the Aussies to a convincing win. The Hyphen would have cashed in his thousand-dollar bet. He said he'd be in touch, through a third party, to get Meat the Magic's winnings to her.

And then, the mayor. Clem needed to know more about him, dig deeper. She'd called in to see Sergeant Wiseman but she was out, so Clem asked the young officer at the front desk, Constable Griffin, how the investigation was going and received a blank look in reply. He said he was pretty sure there were no further steps being taken—suicide, case closed. So Fullerton had done nothing, it appeared. Perhaps she'd gone too easy on him. Maybe it was time to up the ante.

Or maybe it was none of them. Maybe she was wrong about Helen. She forced herself to see the facts through the police's eyes: Helen, on her own, no family, running a lonely and unpopular campaign, taking the blows from powerful people and the community and, perhaps, what hurt the most, battling some dark and potent internal demon that Clementine hadn't taken the time to notice. Was it to do with the years of failed IVF treatments? Perhaps being on her own, without Jim, brought the pain close again? It all gets too much and eventually she walks up to the cliff and ends it. It happens. In fact it was probably commonplace and Clem, of all people, should have been able to spot the signs.

With her self-loathing primed she got up, pulled on a T-shirt, washed her face in the bathroom and went into the sunroom to check her emails. Another one from Burns Crowther, the Melbourne law firm. Their first written offer. She sat there, one finger tapping on her teeth. The offer was right in the zone and she couldn't deny how good it felt to see her worth quantified by such a healthy number. It was a blessed distraction from everything going on in Piama. She let the idea roll through her head. She could hide in Melbourne, get away from everyone, everything. Disappear in the crowds.

She surfed the web for apartments in Melbourne, estimated her annual rental costs. Yes, she could have a very decent living on that money. But still...early days in the negotiation.

She tapped out a response:

Thank you...Perhaps not quite in the ballpark...but I like what the firm is seeking to achieve...I can see real

synergies...Giving the concept serious consideration...
Offer falling a little short of market indications...Could
you reconsider the numbers and get back to me?

She walked out onto the back verandah, looked out across the backyard. K'gari was serene, settling into the day. The straits were getting busy with a light breeze and a playful little chop, aqua and emerald tints all the way across and the palm trees fanning the backyard with cooling whispers. Helen loved this view, she loved this planet...She would not have deliberately removed herself from it. It was impossible. The cops must be wrong.

Torrens was hanging out his washing with Pocket spinning and jumping around his legs. Sarge looked on in wonder, taking a kind of contemplative pleasure in the younger dog's antics. Torrens tousled the fur around Pocket's neck and threw him a stick then whipped around to peg a pair of shorts on the line, while the dog tore off. Sarge plodded after him half-heartedly, then gave it away—far too hot for darting about.

Pocket was fully recovered from his ordeal two months ago, apart from the slightest limp and the scar on his little face. They'd survived a lot together, she and Pocket. What could Ralph or Fullerton or the Hyphen do that the two of them hadn't dealt with before? One of these men may have overpowered Helen but Clementine was half Helen's age, surely able to protect herself.

She wondered if Helen had known she was in danger; that at least one of her opponents was capable of violence. Did she have any warning? Unlikely, thought Clementine. Helen was conducting a peaceful campaign, nothing more—how could she possibly have considered it might lead to her death?

Images scrolled before her. Helen smiling, Helen laughing, Helen raising a cup to her lips, Helen rallying the troops, her confidence inspiring the little group...and then Helen struggling with her attacker at the cliff face, her terror. It was still a shock that sent a shiver across Clem's neck and set the hairs on her arms bristling.

She padded to the shower, the old timber floor creaking beneath her bare feet, and turned on the cold tap. Cool sheets of water flushing the salt sweat from her skin, streaming down her hair, caressing her forehead and carrying the saddest tears she'd ever known from her cheeks over her body and into the swirling current at her feet, trickling away and out to the sea.

\|/

Auction day. Helen's beloved Turtle Shores up for sale to the highest bidder. Clem wished she had the money to buy the place herself. But even with the equity on her cottage in Katinga and the remains of her savings, there wasn't anywhere near enough. And anyway Helen had done something strange. Clem had pretended, out of curiosity, to be an interested buyer. The agent had sent her a statutory declaration that all bidders were required to complete before the auction declaring they'd had no relationship with Helen in the past. When she'd rung to ask about it the agent said it was stipulated in Helen's will. So, for some reason, either Helen wanted a stranger to buy the place or, more likely, she just didn't want someone she knew to buy it. It didn't make sense.

There was a handful of people, perhaps a dozen all up, in the conference room in the Grand Hotel at Barnforth. One was the agent, another the auctioneer; then three couples, an older woman and two middle-aged men, one seated in the front row and the other near Clem in the back row. The auctioneer recited the rules and announced that telephone bidding was permitted and that there was indeed a bidder on the line.

The auction started slowly then heated up, sailing past the reserve, bidders dropping off one by one until only the mystery phone bidder and the man on Clem's right remained. She angled her chair around an inch to get a better look at him. Thick hair, olive skin, the hint of a dimple. The face reminded her of someone but she couldn't place it.

Bids continued to inch upwards and Clem was pleased for Helen. Others valued what she had held precious. The auction continued in twenty-thousand-dollar increments, the two of them duelling it out for another hundred thousand then the auctioneer was calling, 'Once. Twice...' on the telephone bid, waiting for a word from the man to her right. He shrugged.

'...Three times. Sold to our telephone bidder. Congratulations sir.'

People were filing out. Clementine stood outside trying to place the man. It came to her as she fixed her eyes on the mango tree across the road from the hotel, drooping with fruit. Doncaster. A younger, leaner version of him; darker as well, olive complexion instead of the redhead's pink and white. His son? A much younger brother? Either way, she needed to meet him.

She'd left Doncaster's house feeling dissatisfied about something. She put it down to his very neat responses to questions about Helen: hedged and trimmed like there was something hiding behind them. Perhaps this younger Doncaster might be able to shed some light.

She sat in her car opposite the hotel waiting for him to emerge. Half an hour went past. Perhaps he was staying at the Grand? She stepped across the road, through the foyer and scanned the bar area. In the corner, seated in a low armchair with his legs crossed languidly and a near-empty glass of red wine in front of him, the man was scrolling through something on a tablet.

'Care for another? Commiserate?' Clem asked with her coyest smile.

He looked up, surprised, but pleasantly so, as he gave her the once over. An eye for the women, thought Clem.

'I could be persuaded,' he said, and his voice was a lovely velvet. She was convinced he was related to Doncaster, absolute dead ringer. Andrew would be sixtyish, this man maybe a couple of years older than her, mid-thirties. His son, then.

She came back, two glasses of shiraz in hand, sat down breezily as if she did this sort of thing all the time, approaching complete strangers. She didn't, of course, and she had a vaguely queasy feeling at the prospect of making small talk.

She needn't have, as he breezed through the exchange with polished ease. His name was Hamish. He'd come up from Sydney and would be staying the night. She sensed a subtle 'come on' in his manner, like he was open to an offer of overnight company—a lonely sojourner, just passing through. She caught herself checking for any flirtatious element in her demeanour, which was absurd. It wasn't in her makeup, much as she once wished it was, back when she was prancing around Sydney's legal fraternity and her friend Rosemary had hooked up with the most eligible young partner in the firm. Her jealousy was part of the reason she'd drunk so much that awful night, and made the indefensible decision to drive home.

'So, you loved Turtle Shores as much as me by the looks of it?' she said, taking a gulp of wine to mask the obvious nosiness.

'It's a delightful location. Too many midges for me, though.'

'Really? You seemed keen to get hold of it.'

'Hmm. My interest was more connected to the person bidding on the phone,' he grinned and the Doncaster dimple appeared.

'Let me guess—a mission to push the price up on a sworn enemy?' Clem raised one eyebrow.

'You could say that.' He considered her again. 'Oh, what the heck, it'll be public information once it settles,' he said, waving his glass in the air. 'The telephone bidder was an agent employed by my father to bid on his behalf.'

'Sooo, you don't like the agent?'

'No, I don't like my father.' Hamish smiled at her, like it was the most ordinary thing in the world.

'Your father?'

'Yes. Silly old fool lives up on the hill behind Piama. Out in the rainforest like some hippy.' She must have looked startled because he added, 'Oh, I really shouldn't speak like that about him. He's no fool, Big Red. Actually he's one of the smartest businessmen I know.'

'Wow, sounds like an epic falling out—you just cost him, what, an extra hundred grand?'

'A very long and boring story.' He uncrossed his legs and leaned forward to place his glass on the coffee table between them. 'Tell me about you. What's your interest in Turtle Shores?'

'I'm the coordinator of the Save the Turtle campaign. Trying to stop the port development in Piama. I took over from Helen, who owned the house before. I think our biggest individual donor may be your father.'

'Ha! So you know him. And he's won you over with his money! The generous philanthropist act claims another scalp!'

'So you're Hamish Doncaster?'

'One and the same.'

Hamish Doncaster might be the spitting image of his father, but that was where the resemblance ended. He was suave and elegant, with the clipped vowels of fifteen years in a top private school. The son of the son of a grocer.

'Then tell me, Hamish Doncaster, why does your father want Turtle Shores? He's already got that lovely house in the rainforest and an old Queenslander in the scrub wouldn't really seem to fit his tastes.'

'No idea. The place has a wildlife preservation covenant on it. Big Red's a developer. It's a non sequitur. His biggest focus at the moment is some resort up north somewhere, Whitsundays, I think.'

This was news to Clem. Helen had always spoken about wanting to keep Turtle Shores in its natural state as a wildlife habitat but she'd never mentioned a covenant. And what about the stat dec?

Doncaster was no stranger to Helen. Easy, she thought: use one of his companies to buy it.

'I guess he's just keen to keep supporting what Helen started,' she said, more a question than a statement.

Doncaster smiled at her as if she was a child. 'I don't mean to be rude, but since you've been so sweet as to buy me a glass of wine, may I ask your name?'

'Oh! Sorry. No, no, it was rude of me. Clementine Jones,' she announced with her usual embarrassment at meeting someone for the first time, waiting for that moment of recognition.

'Pleased to meet you, Clementine,' he purred in his gorgeous voice.

He'd had his teeth whitened to a perfect glow, she thought as he smiled, and he hadn't recognised her name. It was perhaps even worse when this happened because at some point, he would. He'd find out, and then everything would be doubly awkward. She almost considered telling him now. At the same time she wanted to ask him why he was at war with his father. It seemed nosy and so she decided to leave their respective pasts alone.

They spoke about the turtle campaign mostly. He seemed bemused by his father's support for the cause.

'This Helen, was she attractive?'

'Um, yes. Yes, I would say so.' Clem let Helen's face linger in her memory a moment. 'She had this smile that kind of made you feel good to be alive. It wasn't the looks, though. She was a genuinely good person and she lived this generous life, like everything she did was about contributing—to the planet, to people—and doing that...well, it made her...I don't know, whole.'

Clem wished she could tell everyone this about Helen. She wished she could shout it from the middle of the main street in Barnforth. Just walk out there now and call it out. She wished Helen hadn't been buried as the complete opposite of what she actually was—someone so sad that life was too much for her. She wished the newspapers hadn't made it sound like all she had ever been was a corpse at the base of a cliff.

'Doesn't sound at all like Big Red's type then,' said Hamish.

'Why would you say that?' said Clem, seeing an angle to explore more about Doncaster senior.

'Oh, God, I keep going on about him,' he said, brushing his hand in the air. 'Let's talk about something other than him.'

So they did. He told her about his boutique corporate law firm. Himself and two other partners, handling smaller acquisitions and restructures. Clem relished revisiting the old turf, and Hamish seemed to enjoy reeling her in, dropping hints about the firm's need for top lawyers. She couldn't help but be intrigued. It was another possibility perhaps: a pathway out of the formless swamp her life had slipped into. She found herself gripping hold of the idea, wanting to tease it open. She hadn't said yes to the Melbourne job yet and this was an area of law she knew better. But then, Hamish had no idea who she was or what she'd done. It was silly to be so eager, as if she was normal.

They'd both finished their shiraz and Clem stood up to leave.

'It's been such a pleasure meeting you, Clementine, I didn't expect to have such good company up here in...well...the boonies,' he said, getting up from his chair. 'Are you doing anything for dinner?'

'Oh, yes, sorry. I'm heading over to a friend's place,' she lied.

'That's a shame. Here, take my card. I'd love to meet up again,' he said, handing her a business card.

'Thank you,' she said.

He paused, probably waiting for her to hand him a card in return. But when she didn't, he reached across and shook her hand.

'Oh, and by the way, how about you send me a link for donations to the campaign? We're apolitical at the firm but we do what we like as individuals. I think I might take a fancy to your turtles.' And with a flash of those pearly whites, he released her hand and turned towards the hotel lift.

The man in the grey Chrysler put his binoculars down in the centre console beside him. He was pleased he'd finally tracked the big fella down. But seeing him was a reminder of just what a handful he used to be. And there was a woman too. That was how he'd found him. The coach's stupid mug on the local rag's webpage.

Then there were the dogs. Maybe he should get some help. But then he'd have to share the kitty. Worse—the chance of a cock-up would double. No, he could handle it. He'd have to pick his moment, though, and he'd have to get friendly with the dogs.

He opened a packet of sweet chilli and sour cream chips, cracked the top off a Pepsi, flicked the radio on and pressed the button to ease his seat back. He was glad he'd brought plenty of supplies. Could be a long wait.

CHAPTER 9

The heading on the whiteboard read *Next Group Action*. There followed a number of brainstormed ideas:

- *Commence new petition*
- *Picket Marakai-sponsored events e.g. Barnforth triathlon*
- *Tip manure on the Mayor's driveway*
- *Vacuum clean Council Chambers steps*
- *Meet with Andrew Doncaster (new owner, Turtle Shores): confirm commitment to covenant*

They had settled on all of them, except for Brady's manure idea, which they concluded was apropos of nothing and overly personal. Brady was sulking.

Under the next heading, *Sponsored Actions*, was a list of things that required funding; chiefly the ongoing legal proceedings, and the billboard that was going up on the M1 with a photo of a cute white throat looking bemused under the slogan *Extinction is Forever. Stop the Port.*

'Right. So does anyone know someone with a portable generator? We want these vacuum cleaners actually working. The more noise the better.' The vacuuming idea was to highlight the turtle's biodiversity value as a critical contributor to cleansing the river by eating algae and dead matter, keeping it habitable for other native species.

'Oh yes, and we should scatter soot or something on the steps,' said Brady, perking up.

'Where do we get soot?' asked Gaylene.

They finalised the plan. Brady and Ariel (less concerned than the others about being arrested) would tip a few buckets of dirt on the steps under cover of darkness and the rest of them would arrive around 7 a.m. with their vacuum cleaners and Gaylene's generator from her caravan and, with any luck, the local journo.

'Okay. Let's move on to the action items from last meeting,' said Clem. 'Brady, how did you go with your skipper mate?'

Brady, in a blousy hemp shirt and tie-dyed headband, was hunched forward over the table tapping his celery stick frenetically like he just couldn't shake a chunk of ash off the end.

'Yeah. Spoke to Candles. He said he hadn't done any jobs for Fullerton for a while, but he got a call from him only a week ago— Blair the Mayor's planning a trip next weekend. Some VIP from the mine. Can't remember his name but he was on TV the other day talking up the port.'

Scott Stanton-Green. Had to be.

'So is Candles doing the job, then?'

'Nah. Had to knock it back. It's his kid's eighteenth that day.'

'Ooh, it'd be great if you could get an invite, Clementine,' said Mary.

Clem snorted. 'Not sure I'm the mayor's first choice for social occasions.'

'So would Fullerton take the boat out on his own?' asked Gaylene.

'Candles said he wouldn't. Completely incompetent. Besides, it's too much work,' said Brady.

'What about catering? Could any of us get on board as a galley wench?' asked Clem.

The group concluded they could not, having no contacts in that field. At that point Torrens barged in as arranged, claiming he had a meeting with Jonesy in her professional capacity and could they all kindly leave so he could discuss the kidnapping charges?

Andrew Doncaster's housekeeper had just prepared a prawn and mango salad when she ushered Clem into the living area on the top floor. It was almost 3 p.m. but, as she told Clem, Mr Doncaster had only just arrived back from a business trip to Sydney.

Doncaster entered the room with wet hair, fresh out of the shower and smelling like pine trees. She noticed again how white his skin was near his neckline and on the underside of his arms. He must've had a hell of a childhood in the Australian sun.

'Afternoon, Clementine. You'll share a glass with me over lunch? I need something after dealing with those city slicks.' He uncorked a bottle of something cool and pale gold. 'What a bunch of wankers.'

Doncaster still had so much of the grocer's son about him. And yet Hamish had been expensively schooled, refined and processed… she guessed Doncaster probably saw him as having crossed over to the wanker side.

'I see you were one of those, once,' he said.

He'd had someone look her up. Not surprising if you're handing over thousands of dollars to a stranger.

'Just joking. You wouldn't be up here if you were that big a wanker, wouldn't have coached a footy team. Wrong code, of course…aerial ping-pong.' He laughed as though nobody had ever made that joke. He seemed so much more relaxed than on her first visit.

The salad was the most delicious thing she'd eaten in a very long time; some sort of lime juice and honey dressing, and the mango straight off the tree. The wine was crisp and summery. Oh, to live like this. And a cleaner! No, even better—a housekeeper-cook! It'd be doable on a partner's salary. How many years had Burns Crowther said? Four?

'So? You've come here for a reason. Run out of money already?'

'No, no. The donation was very helpful, thank you. We've been able to pay the bills and get things moving on the appeal and the marketing. No, why I dropped by was because I heard you've bought Turtle Shores.'

He picked up his glass. 'Word gets around quick, eh?' Took a swig, swishing the liquid around his mouth before swallowing. 'Yep, I did. One of my companies, at least,' he said, putting his glass down.

'Good that it's staying in local hands.'

'Yeah,' he said, scooping up a forkful of salad with the juiciest slice of mango and a big luscious prawn glistening in its coating of dressing.

'I hear the land has a wildlife covenant on it. Helen told me she'd seen white throats there once or twice. Too far downstream for them to nest, but it seems like there's feeding grounds there for them.'

'Mmm,' he said, still chewing. 'She showed me a photo.'

'Amazing, to think they're right there, in the river off the backyard.' Clem laid her fork down. 'So the WAGSS group were keen for me to check in with you—confirm you feel the same way about Turtle Shores.'

He spoke and swallowed at the same time, his throat straining with the effort to combine the two operations, 'Blood oath.'

'We're all so keen to see it preserved as it is.'

He wiped his lips with a napkin. 'Oh yeah. Covenant says you can't build anything more than what's already there and the grounds have to stay as is.' He picked up his glass and they clinked a toast, 'Here's to Turtle Shores!'

They finished the lunch and Clem felt peaceful, like at least one part of Helen's legacy, what she stood for, would carry on.

'It'd be nice to put up a plaque or something. For Helen,' she said, contemplating the fine grey swirls in the stone benchtop, like tide marks in the sand. 'Something to honour her efforts.'

Doncaster agreed and they tossed around ideas—something on the river bank or a stone cairn at the front gate.

Clem hadn't drunk much, since she was driving, but Doncaster was really taking the opportunity to unwind. It seemed like the right moment to ask him again.

'You know, Andrew, there's something I can't work out about Helen. I worked so closely with her the last three weeks before she died, and yet, I didn't see a single thing to suggest she was struggling.'

He got up from the kitchen bar and sank into an enormous lounge suite, low and white, behind a coffee table made from a single majestic slice of tree trunk, growth rings pushing out to the edges, telling the stories of hundreds of years. 'Yeah, well, as they say—people don't speak up about these things, do they? Keep it bottled up.'

He went on to tell Clementine about a bloke he'd played league with not long after he'd left high school.

'Seemed fine, old Stevo, always up for a beer after the game, wouldn't have said there was a thing wrong with him. Woke up one Monday morning to find out he'd blown his brains out,' he shook his head, staring across the room. 'You just can't pick it.'

Clem thought for a moment. 'Maybe, but...' she swivelled around on her stool to face him. 'It's just I don't think Helen took her own life.'

'What? Accident then?' He stretched out his thick, sunburnt arm across the back of the lounge suite and rested his glass on his stomach.

Clem shook her head. 'She never went to the quarry. She hated the place. Why would she even have been there?'

'Jesus Christ! What are you saying?' His face crinkled with a look of disbelief.

'I think Helen was murdered, Andrew.'

'Oh, fuck, Clementine, that's a fucking massive thing to put out there. 'Scuse the language, but shit...have you told the cops?'

'Yes.'

'And?'

'They think I'm mad.'

'Well then. Maybe that's your answer.'

'I think they want the easy solution. They're under-resourced and overworked, and there's a convenient explanation served up on a plate.' She paused, searching the floor. 'I just wish they'd look under the plate.'

Andrew's phone buzzed. He picked it up from the table and checked the caller, then lowered it for a moment with an apologetic look towards Clem.

'Sorry, gotta take this.'

The housekeeper saw her out.

\\//

She clicked on the Purchase button and waited. A pop-up declared her order had been successfully placed. She'd declined the overnight delivery option and saved twenty dollars. The package would arrive by Wednesday. Plenty of time before the weekend.

'Shopping, Jonesy?' Torrens towered over her shoulder as he came into the sunroom from the kitchen, lightly dusting a tea towel over a plate. Clem closed the laptop. Now was as good a time as any to ask. He would not be happy. She knew that.

'Yes. Something you might be able to help me with, actually.'

'At your service. Long as it's kosher, of course.'

'I kind of need access to something.'

'Not something behind locked doors I hope.'

She drummed her fingers on the table.

'Aw, come on Jonesy.' He cocked his head to one side, looking reproachful. 'Didn't we already talk about this?'

Yes, they had spoken about it—in Katinga. She was a role model, apparently. An exemplar of a life lived lawfully, dreams achieved through honest work. Clementine found it inconceivable that she, a convicted killer, could ever be seen as someone to emulate. But there had been a moment, in Katinga, when the big man had almost begged her to be the person he wanted her to be. It seemed Torrens had no one else to fill this space in his life. And here she was again, about to involve him in something nefarious. She could justify it in her head. His parole period had been completed; and she would do the risky bits herself; Torrens would be look out and driver, nothing more.

She caught herself. How easily did her mind slide into the planning of a criminal endeavour? She was becoming inured to it, happily project-managing it—delegating tasks, ordering equipment.

'Look,' she said, finally, 'a friend of mine—a good person— died and nobody gives a damn. All I want is some information, that's all.'

He'd clunked the plate down, the tea towel hanging limp by his side. 'Let me guess: you're going to steal it.' He sounded like she'd already let him down.

'No, I'm going to access it.'

She explained the plan, making it as benign as she could, colouring it as a necessary thing for a valid and important purpose. Behind his Ned Kelly beard there was less of his face to see and his eyes drew her attention like magnets. There was a disappointment there now, a hurt that it pained her to see, but she'd long ago decided it wasn't her job to be the embodiment of other people's ideals—they can bloody well grow up and make their own choices.

Besides, there was a murderer out there, killing good people because they stood in the way, and everyone was carelessly ascribing it to mental health issues. Such a wretched lie.

'So, will you help me?'

'Let me ask you something first,' he said and sat down in the chair next to her, smacking the tea towel down on the table like he meant business. Pocket's head bobbed up at her feet, ears spiked. 'I want to know: are you coming back to Katinga?'

She'd sent the email to Burns Crowther two days ago, asking for more money.

'I haven't decided just yet. I kind of thought I'd take some extra time to think about it.'

He sat there, staring, his eyes accusing.

'You mean you're considering walking out on the team.'

'No, no, it's not like that. It's just...well, it's complicated.'

'Seems simple to me—come home to a town that wants you back and a bunch of blokes that reckon you're all right.'

'Ah, mate,' she sighed. 'It's not the team. It's the whole small-town thing. It's a bloody fishbowl and now everyone knows what I did, so I'm the goldfish. Every time they see me they'll be thinking about it—*good old Jonesy...turned out to be a low-life drunken killer, eh*. It's like I'll just be this appalling curiosity, it's...it's impossible.'

'Yeah well, we all done things we're not proud of. Shit! Look at me!' he said, raising his arms and slapping them down on his thighs. 'I mean have you ever wondered why Joey Conti's half-deaf?'

Joey played on a half-forward flank. She wasn't sure she wanted to hear what was coming next.

'I bashed him so hard with the blunt end of a hammer he lost his hearing in one ear. And that was just for the four hundred he owed.' Torrens shook his head, grimacing. 'How hard d'ya think it was for me to turn up that first night at training with Joey there? And not just him. There were others. Sure, they were still scared of me. They wouldn't try anything. But geez, me guts were doin' a fucking dance that day. Felt like I should turn around and leave, just drive off and keep going,' he said miserably. 'But I didn't 'cos you were the first person I spoke to and you said you'd help me. You said I could bring something to the team. Thank Christ I'm a big bastard 'cos I don't think you'd have taken me on otherwise

115

and I wouldn't have blamed you neither.'

It was true. There had been an iciness towards Torrens at the beginning. She hadn't known what it was about and hadn't cared to ask. She just wanted him on the team.

She sat there, silent, the two of them staring at each other. She looked away, embarrassed by his gaze. Pocket got up, walked out through the dog door. It swung back, squeaking on its hinges. Even Pocket didn't want to be around for this.

She was about to lie. A very big lie and her ribs felt heavy in her chest. But it was for Helen, and she was just as important as Joey Conti and Matthew Torrens.

'Yeah.' She nodded. A wattlebird screeched in the backyard. 'You're right, Matt. I'll come back and coach next season.'

'You're not just saying that to shut me up?'

'No, mate.' She lied again. *Fuck.*

He gave her a grin and nodded. 'Righto. Good one. So what are we doing for old mate Helen, then?'

\|/

Her knees were starting to ache from squatting. She stood up, stretched them out. Beside her Ariel hadn't moved, rust-coloured harem pants flapping in the light breeze, eyes glued to the nondescript hollow in the dirt in front of them. The eggs could hatch any day.

It was a clear blue sky but the ground was spongy with moisture. Clem had stupidly worn her white dress thongs, twice as heavy now with a thick pastry of chocolate-red mud plastered beneath and oozing up the sides. Her bare legs were itching from the midges. She scratched her calf again, leaving a burning sensation. Bloody Queensland.

She'd left Torrens watching the second one-dayer against New Zealand. The Kiwis had won the toss and elected to bowl, then she'd had to go. She checked her watch. After two o'clock. She would miss the whole session. The whole of that first golden hour when the ball was new, the bowlers fresh and the batsmen ready to fire, primed to fall. She felt her phone buzz in her back pocket. A text from Torrens.

Warners a weapon smith on fire bring more beer

She sighed, tucked the phone back in her pocket.

Gaylene had been telling them a long story about when she and Les had taken the caravan up to Cape York. Apparently this bit of the Piama River reminded her of that time when they'd camped near a croc-infested creek. Clementine missed the bit where she explained what madness had possessed them to select that particular piece of deadly real estate to set up the camp chairs.

Brady stood back a little, smoking like he'd just got off a ten-hour flight. He'd gone two months, his longest stint. He swung his head sideways with each exhale, careful not to blanket the three women gathered around the hollow.

'So how do we know they're coming out today?' Clem asked.

'We don't,' said Ariel. 'But I'm pretty confident. I felt something stirring this morning during my meditation.'

Clementine stared at the hollow, willing something to move, wondering if she should try meditation, if it might help her sleep. They would be having drinks now at the cricket or celebrating another boundary. Torrens would be eating the leftover tacos. Should have made the food contribution seventy-thirty with the quantities he puts away. She'd made her own guacamole for the second time in less than a month—something of a kitchen-craft record. So many avocados in Queensland, and so cheap. A willie wagtail was chattering in a low, scrubby tree beside the river and she could hear the insistent, four-beat call of a kingfisher.

Her stomach grumbled. 'Did anyone bring anything to eat?' she asked.

117

'Here you go.' Brady passed her an apple from his canvas bag. Clem gave it a quick wipe on her T-shirt. 'Anyone else?' Brady asked.

'Thanks Brady,' said Gaylene. Ariel was silent, transfixed. Gaylene began chomping into her apple like there was no tomorrow, the crunch cracking out across the river.

Clem took a bite and checked her watch. They'd been here almost two hours. Dare she call it? How would that look? The coordinator, the leader, fed up with the inconvenience, impatient with the very creature they sought to save. She didn't have to, thankfully.

'Well, love, I reckon your stirrings must've meant something else entirely,' said Gaylene. 'Sure it wasn't just indigestion?' She stood up, tossed the apple core into a clump of bushes and arched her back into a luxurious stretch. 'Les'll be wondering when I'm gonna be home to make his sandwiches.'

Ariel looked up at Gaylene, disappointment in her face. 'Just a few more minutes.' She turned her gaze back down to the earth, elbows on her knees.

They waited a few more minutes. 'Yeah, time to get going I reckon,' said Brady, picking up his canvas bag and hoisting it over his shoulder.

The sun had gone behind a cloud and Clem's eyes were adjusting to the shaded light when she saw...something. She blinked, looked harder, leaned in closer. Then she heard a gasp from Ariel, saw it again—the slightest ripple in the dirt.

'Oh my God,' said Ariel, in a whisper. 'They're here.'

Gaylene and Brady squatted down to join the tight huddle, all four heads bowed over the hollow. Gaylene squealed as a stubby, leathery looking thumb-shaped thing poked up out of the dirt: a little grey snout flicking dirt to the left and to the right. The ground bulged to its left, then the tip of a flipper, all the way out now and scraping busily, swiping tiny amounts of dirt aside. Then the other one, pushing the dirt back, propelling forward. Above its tiny neck, the edge of the shell appeared, a semicircle plate, like a collar. Clem felt an instant bubble of something in her chest— it was hope and happiness and wonder on a scale she couldn't remember feeling.

As the little fellow heaved himself out of the dirt, another ripple began on the other side of the hollow and a third one just behind it. Within minutes there were three of them thrusting themselves up the side of the hollow, tiny avalanches of dirt slipping down behind them, and two more beginning to emerge, their little eyes taking in the new world as they burst through the surface, their mouths set in a delighted little smile, the flippers going like windscreen wipers.

The shell was intricate. An oval edged with geometric shapes, like stubby triangular shark fins all in a row. It curved and domed across the back, pentagonal plates gathering towards the centre in a sweet ridge, like a baby's tufted hair.

The little family of twelve struggled over the lip of the hollow and scrambled their way down to the river, leaving a feathered trail of flipper prints in the mud. Poised on the river bank for a moment as if savouring the moment; then pushing off and landing in the river with the slightest of splashes. Clem could sense their relief and surprised glee as the water lifted their cumbersome little bodies and they felt the freedom, the brand-new joy of it under their white bellies.

The whole experience had taken around thirty minutes and it had left Clem's heart full, bursting. She bit her lip and took a conscious breath of the hot Queensland air, feeling it fill her lungs. She couldn't explain it but in the half-hour it had taken for the little band of brothers and sisters to bust up from the earth and plunge into the flowing stream, she'd been captivated. Her normal edgy impatience was gone, replaced by a grateful, peaceful bliss.

Clem wished Helen had been there to see it and she understood,

119

for the first time, why Helen had been so committed. The sense of obligation, to save a living creature, so pure and guileless, happily doing its thing on the earth, hoovering up the algae and decay— making this intricately networked planet everything it is in all its abundant, outrageous variety.

She looked across at the others. Brady and Gaylene were smiling, laughing as they watched the little flotilla swimming away. Next to her stood Ariel, hands clasped in front of her chin, a beaming smile on her face and a tear rolling down her cheek.

CHAPTER 10

Checking her emails the next morning there was a reply from Burns Crowther.

> We're delighted you're considering our offer and very much hope we can conclude terms. Attached is a draft press release. Of course, we wouldn't issue any publicity without your prior approval but we think it will help to give you an idea of the sort of market resonance you can hope to achieve here at Burns Crowther.
>
> We also attach a draft contract with a revised offer and would appreciate your confirmation of acceptance at your earliest convenience. In the meantime, please don't hesitate to contact us if you have any concerns or queries about the details of the offer. We are keen to tailor the final arrangement to suit your needs.

The last sentence was code for 'willing to enhance the offer'. She read the press release—'someone of the calibre of...', 'deep knowledge of the requirements for clubs and players alike...', 'match-winning skills...', 'hard-headed negotiator, able to take your contracts to the next level...'—and it made her feel vaguely ill. She opened the draft contract to find they'd upped the offer by forty thousand. Geez, they were keen. They shouldn't have done that, she thought. Too eager. She tapped out a reply, edited it to tone it down.

The dogs were going berserk in the front yard. An outpouring of indignation at the postman who'd dared to stop at the ramshackle wooden mailbox. Rare to have mail at the shanty. She looked out the window. The postie looked calm enough, satisfied with the sturdy fence standing between him and the fangs. The fence was about the only thing Noel kept in a state of good repair around here, for obvious reasons, she thought.

She reread her draft email:

> *Appreciate the adjustment...very encouraging for our future working relationship...we should agree on an allowance for living expenses given I would be moving into the city.*

She hadn't received a city living allowance in Sydney personally, but she knew they were common, at around twenty thousand per annum. The firm would be aware of that too—she need not be so crass as to actually mention the figure.

A slight flutter buzzed in her stomach as she hovered the cursor over the send button—the familiar nerves that came with audacity. But they would expect her to bargain. They'd be surprised if she didn't. She clicked and a notification appeared: *Message sent.*

She began thinking of cars. New cars. The ones in the ads that kept popping up whenever she was online. One of those Fiat Spider whatsits perhaps? White with black trim. Maybe she'd need something less showy, more professional?

She didn't know Melbourne well but an apartment in Fitzroy or Southbank might work. She imagined creamy carpet, modern appliances, extravagant art and a cleaner. *Oh God, a cleaner.* Her thoughts swung back to the damp, draughty old cottage in Katinga with the curling lino and the crumbling cornices and the impossible-to-clean mould. She couldn't afford to renovate it. But in some ways, she hadn't really wanted to. In her mind she'd formed a connection with the previous owner, who she imagined as a widow, with lots of pets. Then the thoughts turned to the yard, the towering mountain gum, the old shed she planned to fix up and have actual chooks in—real live chooks laying fresh, warm eggs.

Pah. A pipe dream. She'd never get around to it.

Pocket came charging through the dog door, tongue flopping to the far corner of his mouth, a certain pride in his gait at having averted the postman invasion. Sarge lumbered in after, squeezing his big shoulders through, approaching her with a substantial dollop of drool making its way south from his jaws.

'Good dogs, good dogs,' she said, patting them both to avoid any jealousies. 'You scared the nasty man away. You showed him!'

She topped up their water bowls and went out to check the mail box.

It was a handwritten envelope, her name and the address in wobbly copperplate. She turned it over in her hand, feeling its soft sheen. The return address:

Mrs E. Lemmon
10 Roberts Road
Katinga VIC 3996

Dear old Mrs Lemmon. Her husband had been a life member of the Katinga Cats football club. After he was wounded in Vietnam, Clem was told, he could no longer play, so he'd just volunteered his heart out till the day he died. He saw the 1954 premiership win as a boy—then nothing since. Mrs Lemmon carried on his memory, turning up to training sessions, manning stalls at club fetes and knitting beanies in Cats red and black.

Clementine went back inside, poured herself a water, snapped out a couple of cubes of ice from the ancient freezer and dropped them in the glass. As she sat at the table she slipped her thumb under the seal and unfolded the pale pink notepaper.

Dear Miss Jones

I hope you're well and not too hot up there—hotter than Hades I expect but not as hot as the inside of an armoured vehicle in Nui Dat! My Tom always said that about Queensland. We've had good rain here and the gardens around Katinga are thriving. You would love my gardenias. I think it's their best year!

There's a young man in my street. His name is Jason Tookley, Bob Tookley's boy. Well he mentioned to me only two weeks ago he wants to play for the Cats this season. So I said, Well son you'll have to have a beanie then. He's not a big chap so perhaps you'll try him out in a pocket or some such. Oh goodness, listen to me now! Telling the coach what position he should play! High time you came home and that won't be soon enough!

Well, anyway, I told this young Jason you were the best thing to happen in Katinga since the war ended. Young lads like him would have been conscripted, like my Tom was. It's funny how the world works. And he agreed. In fact he said he wasn't sure how he'd go with all the training and he'd heard you were a hard taskmaster. Well, I said, that's half the secret isn't it! I believe football is making men out of these youngsters Miss Jones, and it's thanks to you. It's a joy for an old lady to know our town's menfolk are stepping up.

I wasn't going to give young Jason his beanie until he turned up for training three weeks in a row and I told him so. But oh well! I finished it last week and it just seemed a tease to keep it from him. Well, he was so happy to see it, you'd have thought him six years old and getting his first new bicycle for Christmas. It gave me such pleasure to see his face, I can tell you. Next thing I know he's turned up to mow my lawns! You could have knocked me over with a feather. And didn't they need a good mow too! The transformation of the young men in this town. Well, it's all because of you, my dear, though I know you won't hear of it. I'm just thankful I lived to see it.

I'm looking forward to the first training session, cheering the boys on. I expect there'll be a good turn up. In fact I've started another beanie for any other new lads. Do let me know the date. I couldn't bear to miss a minute of it!

Warmest regards

Elspeth Lemmon

Clementine put the letter on the table in front of her, held her head in her hands and scrunched her eyes tight shut.

\\\//

Clem and Torrens drove through the outskirts of Barnforth and past the giant banyan tree near the war memorial. The town was quiet but for the roar of the wind buffeting palm trees into frantic dances, sending scraps of litter swirling across the street. She was wearing her black outfit again, but hadn't been able to find a balaclava in Target—there wasn't much call for them in the middle of a Queensland summer. Knowing there would be serious security at the marina, she'd searched the shanty for boot polish. No luck. So she smeared her face with Vegemite and Torrens had nearly pissed himself laughing. With her hoodie over her head, she hoped all the security cameras would show was a short human, possibly female, possibly black.

Torrens had attempted a bikie disguise with a black skull scarf tied tight around his bearded face and a baseball cap tipped low over his eyes.

They'd picked up the swipe card for the marina from Brady's place earlier on. It was the first time Clem had been there and it

125

was exactly as she had imagined. A tiny hut in the hills, barely holding back the crowding forest, a hammock slung between two trees in the front, free-roaming chooks pecking at the scrub beneath it and a beehive lying on its side with moss greening one leg. And everything crept-upon, draped-upon by creeping tendrils of vine and fern. Brady had said Candles had been happy to help in exchange for a modest bag of weed.

'Why do they call him Candles anyway?' asked Torrens as they drove off.

'No idea. Burns at both ends maybe?'

'What, like a hot curry?' Torrens snorted with laughter.

They parked away from the cameras, dodging a huge branch that had split from its trunk in the gale and crashed to the ground at the entrance to the marina. Torrens was on watch—if anyone turned up or any alarms went off at the office, he was to call her. She'd have time to hide and make her way back to the car. With the high security standards at the marina, Clem had factored in back up as an essential.

Clementine picked her way along the shoreline in the shadows and swiped Candles' access card at the gate while Torrens waited in the car. She hustled quickly past the office, no light on inside but the lawn and pathways around it lit up like a football field, cameras on every pole. Still, she told herself, she'd entered with a valid access card; no alarms and no reason for anyone to scrutinise the CCTV.

She walked towards the boats. The wind screeched in the rigging—a violin-shrill rasping across the wire stays and the whip crack of halyards slapping hard against masts. She pulled the drawstring on her hoodie tight under her chin, licking some stray Vegemite off her fingers, and started down Pier B, making her way along the timbered pontoon as the boats bobbed wildly to her left and right.

Blair Fullerton's boat, the *Success*, was at the very end of the

126

pier just as Candles had said. Boat? More like a ship. An even bigger vessel, a sailing yacht called *Hermes,* too big for the marina berths, was perched behind it at the end of the pier. The blades of its anchor protruded through the opening in its bow and hung ominously above Clementine's head as she stood on the pontoon near the stern of the *Success.* The wind was tearing up the river mouth, sending waves into sharp pinnacles, peaks collapsing, flashing white froth in the moonlight. Fifty feet of powerboat rearing like a horse and smashing to the water, great sausage-shaped fenders along its flanks shunting into the pontoon, screaming rubber shrieks as they squeezed up and down.

She hadn't foreseen this. She watched for a moment, heart rate climbing as she imagined herself attempting to mount this bucking beast. A boat this size heaving and plunging in the slop as if pushed around by a giant invisible thumb. But she was a strong swimmer. She'd trained after school week in, week out for years at her father's bidding, before the boredom drove her nuts and she refused to go anymore. If she went in, surely she'd have no trouble making it to the pontoon?

She took a step closer. The *Success*'s teak duckboard plunged beneath the inky green then sprang back up, water gushing through the slats as it rose high above the surface. She tried to measure the interval between waves, the time between gusts, hoping to find a pattern. Her eyes were swept dry as she watched and counted in the wind. The biggest gusts were followed by the longest breaks...? Wait for the boat to climb up and out, then settle: that was the moment to jump. She steadied herself, one foot forward, one back to push off, rocking like a child waiting to enter the jump-rope circle. A screaming banshee of a gust tore across the marina, flags cracked, the *Success* reared with the waves then crashed down, the weight of its bows sending spray over the pontoon and a great wash of water sloughing across the rising duckboard.

The wind held its breath for a split second and Clem leapt. She was airborne, right leg fully extended just as a trough opened up in the green depths, sucking the duckboard down, her left foot finding nothing, then plunging knee deep in water, foot sliding, right hand flailing for the rail, the wind shrieking with outraged fury. The tip of her fingers touched the cold metal of the rail and slid along the wet surface. She was falling backward, hitting her head on the duckboard, salt water sloshing over her face. The bow flung upwards again, thrusting her under and rolling her right off. She sank, fully clothed and heavy, tried to swim up, reassuring herself it was only a metre or so, darkness above, then her head cracking into something hard. The *Success*—she was under it.

She forced her head down, her butt up. Diving, pulling down with her arms, feeling her feet against the hull, kicking, then heaving against the water with her arms, diving, and with her lungs bursting, turning up towards the surface, her head hitting the hull again. Floundering, unwieldy and slow in the dead weight of her clothing. Lungs burning. *Calm down. Refuse the panic. The clothes will help you sink.* She stopped struggling and allowed gravity to take effect, willing it faster. *Deep enough now? Must be, go across, out from underneath. Air, need air. But which way? Everything black. Which way is up?*

Is this what it feels like? Is this drowning?

Light and froth above, a metre away. She thrust up urgently, kicking her legs like a demon. Head emerging, she gasped a desperate gulp. A wave hit her face, a mix of air and salt water rushing down her throat. The back of her head smashed into something sharp that ripped at her hair. She turned, thrust her hand up, grasping— something rigid but pliant, covered in serrations. A tyre, encrusted with barnacles, on a pylon, behind the *Success,* the duckboard lurching to her right. She hung on, gasping at the air in between waves, the barnacles like sharpened gravel under her hand, sawing through skin.

She thrust her left hand inside the donut, clutching the rim of the tyre, tearing lines in her palm, pulled herself up, kicked with her other leg and shoved her knee in. It lodged firm and she hooked her right elbow over, hugging the tyre with every sinew.

Breathing air. *Oh God, breathing.*

She hauled herself up onto the pontoon, on her hands and knees dragging in hungry breaths.

Cold, wet, bleeding, she made her way back to the car. The mission was over.

\\//

Torrens looked horrified at the blood streaming from her scalp down her neck and her hands, red with saw-toothed lines of open flesh. As they drove back to the shanty, she reached a trembling hand inside her jacket pocket and pulled out a sodden package. She unwrapped it and flicked the switch: a crackle, barely audible, then nothing.

At the shanty, after she'd washed and treated her wounds, she had Torrens take the listening device into the bedroom, door closed, while she went to the other end of the house and switched on the app.

No sound.

'Are you talking?' she called.

'Yeah,' yelled Torrens.

Nothing.

\\//

Operating the laptop was difficult. The bruising in the heel of her hands meant she had to keep them up, away from the keyboard. Stretching her fingers to the top row sent a stinging pain up her elbow.

She found the website she'd used earlier and ordered

replacements, along with two of a different kind—waterproof, which was good, but unfortunately without the ability to transmit to an app—and selected 'express delivery'. They would arrive by Friday, for installation that night. Just in time, hopefully: the *Success*, with Blair the Mayor and the Hyphen aboard, would be heading out the next day.

She clicked open her email. Something from Burns Crowther.

Revised contract attached with additional $20,000 pa city living allowance.

The kettle whistled. Smiling to herself she got up and busted a move there at the kitchen sink. She dropped a tea bag into a cup, so engrossed with her own brilliance she didn't hear Torrens approach behind her and plonk himself down in front of the laptop.

'What the hell?' he said.

She spun around, her mouth dropping and lunged for the laptop lid. Torrens was ready, fending her arm away.

'Hey, get out of my private mail!'

Torrens eyes flicked across the screen, reading the emails, absorbing the contents.

'This is no joke, get away from my computer!' She pulled at his arm. He brushed her off like a fly, eyes tracking down to the bottom of the email thread, her message asking for more money. His mouth was flattening tight under the bush of black beard.

Finally, he spoke. 'Melbourne, hey?' Voice gravelly, eyes set hard. 'Sounds like bloody good money. Twenty grand extra.'

'It's just an offer. I haven't accepted it.'

'You just asked them for more money! Sounds pretty fucking accepted to me.'

'It's what you do when someone offers you a job. You negotiate. Doesn't mean you're going to take it.'

Torrens laid his hand on the trackpad, scrolled down to the earlier emails.

'Says here you're "seriously considering it",' his voice like granite

130

now. 'Oh, and look at the date. Right about when you told me you were coming home to Katinga.'

'Oh God, Matthew, it's complicated.' Weak. Struggling with the deceit; losing the battle.

He slammed his open hand down onto the table. 'You're fucking complicating it!' he yelled. 'You need to come home, you need to do the right thing by the boys. By me, for Christ's sake. How much simpler can it be?' Shouting, standing, throwing the wooden chair back with a screech, a furious blast of red-hot energy filling the room.

She backed away, her hand went up to her neck. The kitchen suddenly seemed too small.

'You just can't understand how hard—'

'Oh, come on. You had a car accident. A woman died. Everyone knows. Get the hell over it.'

She dropped her head. Torrens was stomping a heavy, maddening circle around the kitchen, filling it completely until the cupboards, the ceiling started to close in. The pain in her shredded hands was a pulse, zinging up her arms. She could think of nothing, absolutely nothing to say. The monstrous lie she had fed Torrens to get him to help her was like a beast in the room, a presence of itself.

He took two steps towards her, grabbed her shoulders and twisted her around to face him. In his eyes she could see the rage but there was something else. Disbelief. Betrayal. He dropped his hands from her shoulders and stared at her.

'Funny,' he said. 'It's not the fact you're not coming home...It's actually the lie that's hardest to take.'

Then he turned and stormed out of the room, through the front door, slamming it behind him. She heard the sound of his Nissan Patrol roaring to life, wheels spinning in the dirt. There was a flash of metal as it rocketed up the drive.

It wasn't until later that evening that she got the call. Queensland Police had arrested Matthew Torrens in Barnforth. Drunk and disorderly. Trying to kick a bottle of rum through the pub-door goals, he fell over and passed out in the middle of the road. He resisted arrest when they tried to move him, and was in the lock-up now, about to be charged.

CHAPTER 11

The package arrived the next morning. She went out to get it, casting furtive glances towards Torrens' shed as she slunk back to the shanty.

He hadn't surfaced; or maybe he had and was avoiding her. He had a camp stove in there and a tap just outside the shed. She'd put a loaf of bread and some leftover sausages in his esky yesterday evening after she ushered him into bed. Thought he would want something to soak up the alcohol.

Jesus, he was a wreck.

She had made him a wreck.

The charges were enough to send him back inside, given his record. His whole body crumpled when the cops read them out to him as he sat there, on the bench in the cell, mountainous shoulders shuddering. Then he cried, in his drunkenness and his regret, saliva and tears in his beard, sobs interspersed with great gulps of shame.

She wanted to give him a hug, take him home, tuck him into bed. A big-sister kind of feeling, side by side with the sense that it was all, quite clearly, her fault. She stayed away, giving him space as she signed a form and got him bailed. They drove back to the shanty in silence, his gaze averted, watching out the window or eyes closed, head resting on the door frame.

He was close to going back to prison. Very close. Hanging by a thread. With the grinding monotony of his job at the abattoir, football had held him together, solidified his desire to go straight, given him joy and victory and friendship and respect and hope that this new kind of life might just work out.

She had brought all of that crashing down with her despicable lie.

\\/

Rowan rang again. He'd been doing some reading about the turtle.

'Smaller than I thought,' he said. 'And the breathing thing—it sucks water up its bum, draws the oxygen out through blood vessels.' He was excited about the discovery and clearly had planned to tell Clem all about it. 'They can stay under for days, foraging. Apparently they eat algae and decaying stuff—keeps the river clean for all the other critters.'

He was making an effort, acquainting himself with the turtle, attempting to understand more of her world. It confirmed for her the sense that this was more than a game for Rowan—there was an intention underneath, modest in ambition, unforced, yet serious.

She had to tell him the truth. Secrets, half-truths, dissembling... none of it was fair, all of it was harmful.

So she told him all of it—the Melbourne job, her desire to take up her professional career again, her lie to Torrens, his response when he found out, how close he was to going back to jail.

He said nothing, the wind taken completely from his sails.

'I just...I thought you should know,' she said, forlorn, expecting the worst.

'Yeah.'

There was a long pause and it was loaded with his disappointment, with his shock. She waited for him to echo Torrens: tell her why she must move back to Katinga, fulfil her coaching duties...come back to him, for Christ's sake. She prepared herself.

Nothing. After a silence, she said, 'So, what do you think?'

Rowan let out a long exhale. 'Not gonna lie, I want you back'— so gentle, an ache inside her chest—'The whole town wants you back.'

He sighed and she recognised, in the sound, the memory of his own sorrow—his late wife Kate, weakening, slipping, thinning to nothing. The light in his life dimming with her.

'But I dunno what you should do. I dunno what the hell anyone should or shouldn't do. I mean...'

Another long pause.

'I've known times...times when there's nothing else you can do but go...anywhere, somewhere. Just go.'

It was harder to take than if he'd come right out and told her to come home to Katinga. She could operate in contrarian mode, pushing back, pushing away, rejecting advice, objecting to suggestions—such a familiar pattern, like the ticking of a clock.

But this? She was upended, torn by his selflessness. It was too much.

A raw cord of longing wound tight through the length of her body—longing to know what to do, which way to jump. Longing for Rowan's comfort and longing to avoid him.

They didn't say much after that and the call fizzled out. As for Katinga, she didn't want to think about it. Melbourne was an anonymous substitute, a blanket she could throw over her future and shunt it from her mind.

Clem sat down, aimlessly cruising the internet, an assault of targeted ads for new cars and Melbourne apartment rentals flashing on the screen. She shut the lid and stared at the kitchen table in front of her, getting lost in the scatter of white flecks on the worn-out red laminate.

Rowan was not going to fight her. He could see the similarities— sorrow that you couldn't shake, that simply refused to allow you to just return to normal life.

Clem wanted Helen's killer exposed, wanted to paint his name in blood across the sky, that was number one. And combat on that battleground was about to step up. Before her on the table was the cardboard box. She'd opened it earlier. The two waterproof devices hadn't arrived—delayed until Monday. But the five replacements she'd checked and tested, ready for tonight.

From behind a banksia at the other end of the street, he watched the Commodore wagon turn right out of the driveway. Female driver. No other passengers. Had to be her. What would she be up to this time of the night out here in nowhereville?

The left indicator light came on about two hundred metres up the street. He eased the black BMW out from behind the tree and began to follow, slowing as he passed her driveway, swinging his eyes right. High metal fence, patchy lawn. And she'd shut the gate behind her—likely to be dogs.

An outside light was on in the corner of the house. The driveway was just two tracks, grass growing between, muddy from the rain, extending all the way down the side of the tiny yellow shack. A shed to the right-hand side and next to it, another vehicle, Nissan Patrol. Perhaps a visitor, one she trusts to leave in the house while she's out.

He kept his distance. It was an easy tail. She followed the main road to Barnforth then turned into the marina and parked, swiped herself in. Very strange. He rolled in, lights out, waited, watched for ten minutes until the clock hit 10.30 p.m. Then another vehicle came into the marina carpark. A man—long, skinny legs, boardshorts. He loaded a number of shopping bags and a backpack into one of the trolleys, wheeled it to the gate and swiped himself in. He was wearing a white long-sleeved T-shirt with 'Success' emblazoned across the back.

He waited another half hour. Was she meeting this guy? If it was a regular thing, a weekly rendezvous or something, it might present a good opportunity. He'd have to check the security camera locations in advance.

After another fifteen minutes he called it a night. If it was sex with the Success *bloke, on his boat, she wouldn't leave till the morning. He might as well get some sleep.*

The BMW rolled out of the carpark and headed to the Barnforth Best Western.

CHAPTER 12

Getting on board was a cinch this time. In better weather the *Success* was as docile as a sea slug. It was a simple matter of stepping across to the duckboard, over the transom and across the deck to the sliding door. She was in her black outfit with the Vegemite face paint and latex gloves. She used the key she'd cut from the set Brady had lent her.

The door was heavy, screeching along the tracks. The marina was lit up like a carnival and she hunched down, reaching for the control panel to the left, exactly as Candles had described it to Brady. She punched in the code he'd provided. A red light blinked three times then faded to nothing, alarm deactivated. She waited long enough for someone to walk the length of the pontoon.

Nothing.

Then she heaved the sliding door closed and waited again—all quiet. She flicked on her torch.

The saloon featured a C-shaped sofa curving around a long table. Overhead was a television on an adjustable arm and in the corner a double sink and a slab of granite benchtop, shining chrome rails around the edge. The *Success* was pretty much a penthouse on water.

She took the container from her pocket and picked out one of the devices, no bigger than a ten-cent piece. The first one she stuck behind a light fitting above the table in the saloon, peeling off the backing tape and pressing it on for ten seconds. The second, near a huge barbeque in the rear outdoor lounge area.

Then she went below, down the narrow winding staircase and stuck the third bug on the side of a drinks cabinet at the bottom of the stairs. Two left. One for the master cabin—if she could catch one of them in some sort of philandering it could be useful leverage. She stepped inside to find a king-sized bed with a stylish amount of pillows, mirrored ceiling above. She stuck the device behind the door.

She was in the downstairs dining and lounge area, peeling the plastic off the adhesive strip on the fifth device, when she felt a brief rocking motion. It had been a perfectly calm night, the water as thick as oil in the moonlight, the boat completely still. The wave registered against the hull then faded—probably another boat going by. She placed the tiny device on the underside of the table, counting to ten as she pressed. At five she heard something—a scratching noise...A key, the sliding door above screeching open. *Oh God!* She flicked off her torch, slinking away backwards towards the bow, further from the stairs, soft footfalls like a cat on a cloud.

A light flicked on upstairs. *Shit, the alarm. It's off. They'll notice.* She was in the master cabin again, lush carpet under her feet. To her left a wardrobe and a set of drawers; to her right an ensuite. She opened the wardrobe. Big enough to hide a six-year-old. Just. She closed it, gently clicking it shut. No other option but the ensuite.

Above, in the main living area, footsteps, the clink of a glass, a tap running. Who was it? The mayor? Another break-in? That would be just her luck. But what burglar casually pours themselves a glass of water? The stand-in skipper? She let out a silent groan. If it was, he might be here all night, up early to prepare the boat. He wouldn't sleep in this cabin would he? The master cabin?

She heard thuds, the clink of bottles, the soft click of a fridge door. Unpacking groceries? Then footsteps on the stairs. Heavy, male footsteps. Her mouth dried to a powder. She heard a cupboard opening in the downstairs dining area. More stacking. Her breath so shallow it was barely enough, her legs tingling like a hundred ants crawling across her bare skin.

The master cabin light flicked on. Through the crack in the ensuite door she saw a hand place two fluffy towels on the bed, aqua, folded tight into a pillow shape. A body moving across—male, his back to her. Boardshorts and bare feet, hairy legs, long skinny calves—Longshanks. Captain Longshanks come to prepare the boat for the guests. She held her breath, knowing what would come next, squished herself flatter against the wall.

He moved closer to the bathroom, then flicked the light switch on, bathing the ensuite in light. He was right there, on the other side of the door. She could only see the gleaming white tiles of the shower cubicle to her right. She felt her own hot breath against the back of the door, breathed in the shallowest of breaths, held it.

The sound of something thrown onto the floor—a mat. She caught a glimpse of the edge of it—fluffy and white—then a tanned bare foot smoothing the wrinkles out. The squeak of the toilet lid. A second passed, then the unmistakeable sound and smell. As he flushed she was able to gulp in a big breath, exhale and take another before the noise trickled away. The light switched off. Cabin light off. Footsteps fading up the passageway.

She closed her eyes. *Thank God. Now please, send Captain Longshanks home to his own bed.*

\|/

She was sitting on the closed toilet seat, elbows on knees, when the TV above decks finally went quiet. She got up, and stood behind the door again, she heard his footsteps on the stairs, then a toilet flushing in the main bathroom down the other end of the boat.

Had he gone to another cabin? Was he coming here to sleep? Would he leave?

She had tested the app when he had the TV going in the saloon. She could hear Tom Cruise's voice on *Mission Impossible* loud and clear. She'd wanted to listen in, kill the boredom, but it wasn't safe—Longshanks might hear the echo. She'd spent the next half-hour alternating between sitting on the toilet, standing in front of the mirror, going through the contents of the wardrobe and searching for better hiding places.

She heard his steps. A door opened further up the corridor, then there was a rustling noise, then silence. Just the slow sway and creak of the ropes on the pontoon. Ten minutes went by. She was conscious of how loud her own breathing seemed.

And then snoring. Longshanks was sleeping in another cabin. She crept out from behind the door and poked her head into the passageway. A door was open at the other end. She stepped out of the master cabin and tiptoed closer. She could see his feet on the bed in the moonlight. She moved to the companionway and slowly placed one foot on the first tread. If he woke he would see her, right there. She took a step. The floor creaked. Another, and another, quickly, out of view now, into the saloon. No sound from Longshanks. The alarm looked to be off as she passed the control panel, but the sliding door would wake him. Was there another way out?

She looked around, not daring to turn on her torch, but the moon was higher now, just enough light to see. A bottle of something on the table. Spirits? Suddenly she needed it. She unscrewed the top, took a swig and felt the whisky trace a scalding path down her throat.

Stupid. Why did you do that? Just get out, you idiot!

She clambered up on the leather couch, grimacing with the squeak of the leather, and up onto the ledge in front of the huge windows facing forward onto the deck. She unlocked four catches, opened one of the windows outwards, stepped through outside onto the foredeck. She wouldn't be able to latch it closed. Too bad. She was wearing her latex gloves, nothing to connect her if they did notice anything.

She gently closed the hatch and tiptoed around the side of the boat to the duckboard, then stepped across to the pontoon and got the hell out of there.

\1/

It was late afternoon and, judging by the clouds, the tropics would be letting loose any moment. She'd been lying still on the creaking old bed for only ten minutes since emerging from a cold shower and sweat had already formed in every crease, beneath every fold.

Looking back, thinking through each decision she'd made, each step she'd taken over the last few days up to the moment she broke into Fullerton's boat, and her spell behind the door while Longshanks took a piss, she considered that it had to be one of the most foolhardy capers she'd ever embarked upon in her entire life. Not *the* most foolhardy, but this...This was right up there.

Caper. What a word. It suggested high-school pranks. She realised she'd rationalised it beyond stupidity—innocuous information-gathering, no harm to any property or person—when in fact it was a flagrant criminal break and enter. Not only that, from the moment she turned on the app to listen in and record, she'd be breaking a whole sheaf of state laws. Enough to get her struck off, probably.

It was surprising to consider how far she'd departed from the blameless existence she once led. A pristine life, a shining career in corporate law, an officer of the court, no less. A momentary lapse in judgement had been all it took to bring her down. 'Reckless disregard' the judge had called it. A 'rash and deeply culpable error'. Nine months in jail among thieves and burglars, and now look at her—she was one of them.

Well, it was done now, and no matter how she might recoil from it, there was a sliver of satisfaction in it. She had done something—something audacious—for Helen. And it would move her closer to exposing the killer.

She wondered how the boating party was going. She'd read on a forum that these listening devices didn't transmit well in real time, but each device would record up to five hours of sound. She'd been waiting all day for a chance to hear what got loaded onto the app.

She checked her watch. Four-thirty. Checked the rain radar—dark, thick animated bands closing in on the coast from the west. Another afternoon thunderstorm. They would have come back to the marina by now to avoid it, surely. She picked up her phone from next to the pillow and tapped the app, got up, closed the door and sat on the bed.

The devices were sound-activated so the recording only played when people were speaking or moving about. Device number one, in the light fitting above the saloon table, yielded nothing of interest—clinking plates, compliments about the catering, long silences when it seemed everyone was outside. She could make out four voices though, two of them female. Right towards the end of the recording, the time stamp showing three-fifty in the afternoon, there was a thud followed by scratching noises. Something wrong with the device? Then Blair Fullerton's voice: 'What the hell is this?'

It was so loud she jumped. She could hear breathing. The bug was in front of his face. He must be holding it.

'Not a camera. Maybe a listening device?' he said, talking to someone near him. 'Martin,' he called. 'Did you see anything strange when you came aboard last night?'

Longshanks, Martin, said no, he hadn't seen anything strange.

'Everything locked up, alarm working?' asked Fullerton.

'Um, no actually. I just thought you must've been a bit more

144

relaxed, with the boat being in the marina,' said Longshanks.

'Oh for Christ's sake. If this is what I think it is...' Clem could hear him walking around the saloon. 'Let's have a look at the CCTV.'

Oh shit. She felt a string stretching tight across the back of her neck. She hadn't looked for cameras on board. *So stupid!* And she'd had her torch on. Thank God for the Vegemite. But how had Fullerton found the bug? It must have fallen off the light fitting onto the table.

The recording continued. She could only hear three voices, the mayor, Stanton-Green and Longshanks. The women must have left.

'How many cameras you got?' asked Stanton-Green.

'Just the one. Here. It takes in the back deck and the saloon so I can see anyone coming aboard or inside the saloon.'

There was a pause, then, 'Here we go.' Another long silence, a minute ticking by.

'Can you fast forward until we see some movement?' said the Hyphen.

'Yeah. Hang on.' They were watching, waiting for her figure to appear in the sliding door. A brief silence as Fullerton fast forwarded. Then a click.

'There!' said the mayor.

No sound. Then Stanton-Green's gruff, hard-edged voice: 'Well, fuck me sideways.'

There was a thunderous crack of static and the sound went dead.

Oh no. Oh no. Clem had her head in her hands, her mind rushing over the possibilities. Assume the worst. *What's the worst? Think, Jones.* The camera had captured her entering and fixing the device in the saloon and probably the one on the rear deck. Fullerton had destroyed that device now, as soon as he'd seen the CCTV confirming the break-in. They would try to locate the others and destroy them too. Could they identify her? Her burglary outfit—hoodie, Vegemite—was basic but there was only one camera on the saloon deck. They would see her disappear below decks and come up a long time later when Longshanks was asleep, but she'd hidden the devices well downstairs and they were so tiny. They would search, but even if they found them, she should still have the entire recording up to the moment they were discovered.

She switched the app over to the second device, which she'd located on the rear deck. Lots of party talk including a steady stream of vulgar jokes from Stanton-Green, the chatter and laughing going on and on. They must have spent most of the day out there, apart from a long gap just after they finished lunch. Then just the Hyphen and Blair the Mayor, congratulating themselves, bawdy comments, before the women re-joined. They left around three. The men must have gone inside because the recording jumped forward to the three of them, searching.

'Here it is,' said Longshanks. A repeat of the first time: a scratching noise as Longshanks peeled the device from the surface and a crash of static, then nothing.

The third device, from the drinks cabinet at the bottom of the stairs, had recorded the girls speaking in hushed tones about 'the old gits' and culminating in a giggling pact to 'bloody well enjoy what they could get' anyway even if it did involve having to 'take turns in the bedroom'. The men had located this device and destroyed it in the same way.

Listening to the fourth device in the master cabin it seems 'taking turns' had not been necessary as the 'old gits' had enjoyed a raucous foursome, punctuated with panting, slapping and exhortations to 'go deeper baby'. Useful. The men knew it too. They spent a long time looking for this device, swearing heatedly, before they found it.

The fifth device was from the downstairs dining table, the one she had rushed to stick on when she heard Longshanks entering. It sounded like it had fallen off into the carpet—inaudible at times, muffled as if something was covering it—maybe a cushion over the top or an item of clothing? And then she struck gold. With the time stamp at three-twenty, two voices came through loud and clear: the Hyphen and Blair the Mayor. Longshanks must be upstairs cleaning up or left for the day.

They were talking about the women in fairly disgusting terms; then they got bored with that and there was a silence, the top of a beer bottle hissing open, a slurp and a change in subject that had her ears burning.

'So what've you done about Williams?' said the Hyphen.

Williams? She racked her brain, trying to place the name.

'I met with him last week. Independents in the senate are making noises and the department's being bloody painful, picking over everything. But Brian reckons he can swing it,' said Fullerton.

Brian Williams, Federal Minister for the Environment and, very handily, a relative of Fullerton's. His brother-in-law.

'He bloody better swing it. The amount of dough I've forked out.'

To Williams? To the mayor?

'Speaking of dough...' said Fullerton. Clem could hardly breathe.

'Fuck! You're like a pup on the teet! Hang on.'

She heard footsteps, the creak of the stairs, a pause. She could hear her own heartbeat. Then the footsteps again coming back down the stairs.

'This has to be the last one.' The Hyphen was approaching the table from the stairs, his voice getting louder. 'The syndicate's running out of patience.'

'As always, Scott, I'll do what I can,' said the mayor. 'I can't promise more than that.'

Stanton-Green grunted. 'Make it happen.'

Then there was a rustling. Clem could hardly believe it. Was

Blair Fullerton sitting on his boat counting a wad of cash from a brown paper bag?

The sound stopped. 'Good-oh,' said Fullerton.

The Hyphen belched and she heard the sound of leather hissing as he sat down. 'What about the new turtle woman? Think she's a problem?' he said.

'No. On the contrary I'm quite encouraged. I managed to get her to start considering a deal'—*the bastard, it had been her idea*—'and she seemed open to the concept. Thinks she might be able to swing it with the ferals if Marakai throws in support for a conservation program.'

'Shiiiit,' said the Hyphen, sounding hopeful. 'Now we're getting somewhere. So did you talk dollars?' A donation from Marakai was probably a lot more palatable than sacrificing hard-earned Meat the Magic winnings.

'Not at this stage. I need you to come back to me with an idea. Ballpark will do. I'd like to be prepared for next time I meet with her. I think with the costs of litigation, I might just be able to bring her round to some sort of compromise.'

Oh please, somebody hand me a bucket.

They sat there and finished a beer and went back up the companionway stairs. This must have been the point at which Fullerton made the first discovery, the device in the saloon. She heard the search party come back down the stairs, then nothing. The search was over and they had not found this one—perhaps when it dropped off the underside of the table it landed somewhere obscure. The sound was faint, distant. From the corridor? The devices had a range of ten metres. The men were discussing the intruder.

'Whoever it was looked short and black,' said the mayor.

'Definitely female. The bitch had tits.' The Hyphen's voice was slightly clearer, closer to the device.

'How could you tell with that bloody great hoodie? Could've

been a male. Maybe a kid. Teenager?'

A grunt, then: 'Got tits on the brain.'

'Oh good Lord, don't remind me.'

'Everything, mate. All of it's fucking on there.' The Hyphen punctuated this with a loud belch as if trying to expel the thought.

'Jesus Christ,' groaned Fullerton. 'You think we should call the cops?' He sounded close to frantic. It gladdened Clem's heart.

'Nuh. If they find the bastard and the recordings, we're done.'

'I'm not sure about that. The cops wouldn't release anything, would they?'

The Hyphen grunted. 'Not officially. But it'd leak for sure—there'd be one or two who'd make sure it leaked. Fuck! Whoever has a copy'll be blackmailing us anyway if there's any heat from the cops.'

There was a pause. She could almost hear the cogs turning as she stared at the audio graph on the app: the broad bars of their voices becoming a thin line as the men paused, silently modulating her fate.

'Yeah. You're right—too risky,' said the mayor.

Clem let the relief wash over her, dropped her head to her chest.

'It's a fucking nightmare.' It was the first time she'd heard Fullerton swear. 'Not a word, not a single syllable to anyone about this,' he hissed.

'Ha! Think I've got a death wish or something? I've got a career too, ya donkey.'

CHAPTER 13

The gate was locked, so Clem left the car on the road out the front and climbed over. It was Saturday night, three days after the auction. The *For Sale* sign still stood out front. Didn't they normally whack an *Under Contract* sticker on after an auction? Probably too remote out here to bother.

The two acres of land at Turtle Shores were studded with paperbarks and gums, palms and messy scrub, long grass in big tufts lining the dirt path up to the house. At that time of night the likelihood of a snake was low, but it didn't stop Clem stomping loudly as she made her way up the long driveway, swinging her torch back and forth ahead of her.

The recording had given her more than leverage. It had confirmed to her that corruption was lurking around the port development. And if powerful men were willing to engage in bribery, was it such a big step to have an obstacle like Helen removed?

She had no evidence of that, though. Two men neck-deep in corruption and she had enough to put them in jail. But she hadn't caught them admitting to conspiracy to murder. And the results of the soil test on Ralph's car had come in the mail late on Friday: no match with the quarry. She'd decided to switch her focus from the suspects to Helen herself, and the circumstances of her death. Maybe she could find something at the house to link these crooks to Helen herself.

She walked up the steps to the verandah where the living room looked out over the river, put the surgical gloves on and gently removed the flyscreen. Helen hadn't bothered with locks on the old sash windows. Clem placed her hands in the centre of the glass and pushed up, it didn't budge. She applied more pressure, thrusting upward with a grunt. Bingo.

She shone her torch inside and climbed through, then switched the light on. The house was so isolated, she had no concerns there, and the power was still on, probably for the open homes. They'd sold it furnished but all the nick-nacks and decorative pieces had gone. She stood in the doorway, looking across at the heavy wooden dining table where they'd sat so many times. She recalled the conversations, turned them over, trying to see a sign that she might have missed. The one that kept cropping up was Helen telling her about how she and Jim had both desperately wanted kids, the whole IVF thing.

'It was a form of torture,' Helen had said with downcast eyes. 'With every failure there was grief and I went into a wretched spiral. James couldn't help me. I couldn't help me. It was like I was getting sucked into this emptiness.'

Then she came to the point of the story, or so Clem thought at the time. Helen's way of delivering a lesson, passing something on to Clem. 'Well.' She shrugged. 'You have to live the life you're given. Play the hand you're dealt. And, Clem, even if the cards are shit, at least you're still in the game.' She'd fixed her hazel eyes on Clem. 'So anyway, I only came out of that spiral when I gave it a label: Plan A.' Then she gave her the same look Clem remembered from when her father had dropped her at the door, a little girl lost and scared. 'Because you know, Clem, if there's a Plan A, there's always going to be a Plan B.'

Helen's Plan B had been her career. She'd returned to university at thirty and given it everything she had.

Was the Melbourne job Plan B for Clem—out of Sydney, starting again—or was it a return to Plan A? Same gig, different city. How could she know? She wanted to talk to Helen about it. The fact that she couldn't...She felt like crying.

She ran her hands along the bench where Helen had kept her coffee machine and the row of cookbooks. Helen was everywhere in this place, but nowhere.

She closed her eyes, took a few deep breaths, then stood tall and shook her shoulders out. She'd come for a reason. She'd come to immerse herself in Helen's last moments, find something, anything that might inch her closer to the truth. The police had been so quick to arrive at suicide, it was unlikely they'd done a thorough search of the house. If Helen had been forcibly taken maybe there would be signs of a struggle, however minimal. Something the cleaners wouldn't notice. Or maybe—the thing that Clem had been clinging to all afternoon—maybe Helen had left her some sort of message. Something that would speak to the people who loved her.

And she did cry then, standing there in Helen's home. Silent tears.

She wiped her eyes with her sleeve, started looking around, checking drawers and cupboards first. All of them were empty. The bathrooms were sparkling, the curtains and blinds all hanging straight, not a single one torn or pulled. But of course, the executor would have had any damage repaired for the open homes.

In the bedrooms she got down on her hands and knees and searched under the beds. Nothing but shiny timber floors.

She walked back to the kitchen, stood in the centre. They'd left the fridge, a big stainless-steel thing, wedged open and switched off. Next to it the back door opened out onto the verandah. Half a dozen steps down to the driveway, which curled around the western side of the house and ended near the steps. Helen loved cooking, always had her music up loud, never locked her doors. She wouldn't have heard a car. They could have just strolled up and wandered in, taken her by surprise while she was in the middle of baking her brownies, her back to the door. She would have fought, with her skinny arms, she would have scratched and clawed and screamed. Clem gulped, caught her breath as she imagined Helen's terror. Then there was a shiver along the back of her neck and the hairs on her arms stood up. Standing in the kitchen she could feel something...something to do with this room. Was it just Helen's lingering presence, or something more?

She checked the cupboards again, the oven. Nothing. If Helen had been attacked she might have fallen to the floor. Clem dropped to her hands and knees, trying to put herself in Helen's shoes. What could she grab at if they were dragging her out? She looked around. There was nothing but the cupboard handles. She checked them all again. Nothing. She wheeled around, still on her hands and knees, until she was facing the fridge. She hadn't looked under it.

She pulled out her torch, lay down on her stomach, shone the beam underneath. The light hit something—something small, hardly visible but casting a tiny shadow. Cockroach? No, that would have run from the light. She tried her hand underneath but the gap was small and the gashes on her palms were still sore. She slid around on a different angle to get a better look but it was still just an unidentifiable shape.

She stood up. The fridge was huge: double-doored and heavy. She gave it a shove. On wheels—*Oh thank you, sweet Jesus!*— and gently eased it away from the wall, not wanting to disturb whatever it was underneath. Edging it out and away to the right, the thing became visible. A necklace, one of Helen's beaded things. She crouched down to take a closer look. Not just any necklace, it was her favourite, the one Jim had given her before he'd died, the one she was wearing in the funeral photograph. It was broken, the beads scattered around it. Clem's heart was beating hard. She took out her phone, took a series of photographs from different angles and up close. The cord was torn in the middle, nowhere near the clasp, just a random spot, the edges frayed.

Helen's favourite necklace had snapped in two and she hadn't bothered to retrieve it and get it fixed. It had to be because someone tore it off her neck.

Clem left Turtle Shores, striding up the path, almost running, not caring about snakes or spiders or the dark or any damn thing. She was right—Helen had been taken, forcibly—and now she could prove it to Sergeant Wiseman.

\1/

The next day was Sunday. She rang the station to make sure Wiseman was in but Constable Griffin answered. Clem told him she'd be in to see them with the photos of the necklace.

'You still on about that suicide?'

'Yes I'm still *on* about it. I've got evidence proving Helen was abducted from her home.'

'Case is closed, I'm afraid,' he said officiously. 'She was single anyway.'

'What's that got to do with it?'

'Half of all female murders are at the hands of a partner or an ex. Domestics.'

'How about the other half, then?' Clem scoffed.

He started rabbiting on about murder statistics, like he'd been swatting up on the topic for an exam recently...that morning even.

'So when's the sergeant in?' she interrupted.

'Not till the afternoon shift.'

Clem threw a load of washing on and took the dogs out, heading for the quarry. Plenty of time to check out the actual place of death. In fact she was angry with herself that she hadn't done it previously. She'd been relying on the police, believing they would have been thorough. She should go up there, try to work out how someone could have got Helen to the top without leaving a second set of tracks. She stepped along gingerly, trying not to allow the hot sand to spill over the top of her thongs. Sarge kept to the shady bits beside the path while Pocket skipped around, wherever the scents drew him, his paws hardly touching the ground.

Her phone rang, a number she didn't recognise. It was Selma Bennett. She wanted to know if Clem was up for another fishing trip. Ralph wouldn't call himself, she said. 'Silly old duffer didn't want to admit he enjoyed your company. But he gets lonely going out on his own. I thought if I tell him you asked me, he'd jump at the chance.'

It was remarkable—Ralph such a brute and Selma still loving him.

And the moment the thought entered her head, Griffin's statistics twigged: the birthday card she'd seen on the sideboard at Turtle Shores the last time she was there. Roses on the cover, *all my love*...What if it was from a lover? And the entire row of kisses. Who puts so many kisses on a birthday card? But Clem had been working closely with Helen for weeks and she'd never mentioned anything about a man.

'Of course,' said Clem, dragging herself back to Selma's question. 'I expect his fishing is about all he's got to look forward to these days.'

'That and his cards night. Second Saturday every month.'

Clem recognised the significance straight away. Helen had died on Saturday night the twelfth of November—the second Saturday of November. Ralph Bennett could not afford a hired killer, the tyres on his car did not carry quarry soil in the tread and now Selma, in complete innocence and without any hint of collusion, had confirmed he had an alibi. It was a strangely powerful relief to know she had finally, conclusively eliminated one suspect. It seemed that being a ghoulish old prick who likes to tell horror stories doesn't make you a murderer.

Pocket dashed out from behind a large paperbark, tangling his lead around its feathery trunk and pulling up abruptly at her feet with a surprised yelp.

'Hey, come round this way, knucklehead!' He looked up at her from under his twin black eyepatches—her little double pirate. She released the lead and, without a second glance, he charged off towards a patch of long grass, tugging her forward. So much energy. What was she thinking? She wouldn't be living in any inner-city apartment in Melbourne. She'd have to find a place with a yard for Pocket. Unless she left him with someone, maybe someone in Katinga. Maybe Rowan? Certainly not Torrens. Not now.

Torrens. She'd barely seen him since he'd found out about the Melbourne job. His car was still there, outside the shed during the day, so he must still be around. She wondered what he was doing. He'd been gone when she got back from Barnforth yesterday, the Nissan Patrol he'd bought with Sinbin's money rolling up the driveway about an hour after she'd returned from her night visit to Turtle Shores.

She let Pocket and Sarge off the leash as she left the cottages and beach shacks behind. Pocket leapt ahead, darting his snout in and out of the patchy saltbush scrub. Sarge took it easy.

She had a meeting with the mayor organised for Tuesday. Perhaps she could cancel, fake some illness. So soon after the escapade—she didn't want to give him any reminders about her height or body shape, or even her face-shape under the Vegemite. He wanted to talk numbers with her, map out a plan for coming to a compromise, the greasy creep. Of course, she couldn't take any of the information from the recorded conversations to the police, not yet at least—she didn't want anything connecting her with the mayor or Stanton-Green so close to the break-in and besides, she needed to use it to extract something from them.

She took what seemed to be the most obvious route from Helen's house, trying to recreate the path she might have taken. After the dunes along the dry creek bed came a bracken scrub wasteland, sprinkled with dead and stunted trees, the ground crusted with a thin layer of gravel. She looked back. Her footsteps left a faint but clear impression on the surface. The police had said they had found tracks in the *sand* matching the sandals Helen was wearing when she died. Clem made a mental note to ask them about any tracks in the gravel. Not that they had to tell her anything, but there was no harm in trying.

To the north of the quarry was the thin, sandy track Helen would have used if she'd walked to the top that day. Was this the sand the police had referred to? What about the first section along the creek bed? Clem was panting in the heat. She stopped, took a swig from her water bottle, called Sarge over, cupped her hand and poured some in. His tongue nearly covered her entire hand and the water was gone in two licks. She called Pocket. His little pink scooper was like a teaspoon compared to Sarge's shovel.

Within about twenty metres she was at the top on a plateau of smooth, flat rock the size of three netball courts. There'd be no footprints here—neither Helen's nor the killer's. Clem's back was soaked with sweat, her T-shirt stuck to her shoulder blades. She brushed a trickle from her face and looked across the shimmering dry land to the blue streak of the Great Sandy Straits, and beyond to where K'gari hovered at the edge of the sky. She walked closer to the quarry, stood three metres away from the edge, crisp and brittle where the machines had cut into the face. Was this the spot? The last place Helen had trodden?

She wanted to look over the edge. She wasn't sure why. She got down on her hands and knees, inched her way forward, the warm surface of the rock pressing up into her legs, specks of gravel digging into the cuts on her hands. Half a metre to go. A giddy flush swept over her. She had to see...see what Helen had seen in her final moments.

She lay down, gently lowering herself onto her belly, her head just a few inches from the edge. She caterpillared forward, her fingers gripping the edge of the cliff, stretched her forehead over, then stared down to the rocky floor below.

It was a sheer drop. No jutting ledges. Just the rubble at the base. They'd removed the death tree.

Clem closed her eyes, opened them again. *Helen.* She would have fallen, screaming, fifteen metres or more. The terror of her friend's final moments sent a chill over her skin, the hairs on her forearms standing up and she could not inhale for a moment, her breath catching in her lungs. She imagined Helen's cry as she tumbled, her arms frantically grabbing at air, fingernails scraping at the cliff face.

A wave of nausea pitched through her stomach. For a split second Helen might have felt the tree gore her insides. Then her head, splitting open would have ended it. *Surely, dear God, surely.*

\\/

'Yes, but what about the sand along the creek bed and the gravelly bit here?'

Sergeant Wiseman gave her a blank look.

'Here,' said Clem, pointing at the map. 'She would have gone along here first.'

The sergeant pursed her lips and leaned forward, stabbing a finger at the map. 'She went along here.' Pointing at the boardwalk. The long way, perhaps another twenty minutes longer, tracking the water's edge, scenic and used by pretty much every grey nomad that ever pulled up at the caravan park. There would have been a thousand footprints on the sandy approach and none, of course, on the boards.

'But she could have gone the quicker way. Did you check for footprints there?'

Wiseman blinked hard and sighed. 'We conducted a thorough investigation—'

'Which didn't include checking for footprints along the fastest route from Helen's house to the quarry?'

'As I said, Miss Jones, no stone was left—'

'Bullshit, sergeant. If Helen was intent on suicide, as you have concluded, why would she take the scenic route?'

'Look, there was no sign of a struggle up there, nothing to indicate a second person.'

'I told you, sergeant, I showed you the photographs, the struggle was in the kitchen! She could have been bound before she got to the fucking quarry.'

'Yes, well about that...I need you to provide some more details of your unauthorised entry into Turtle Shores.'

'Oh for fuck's sake! Go ahead, charge me! It'll give me a chance to tell the court and all the reporters in the public gallery how utterly cursory, how hopelessly inept your efforts have been. This is not an investigation, sergeant, it's a lazy, poorly stitched-together grab bag of assumptions and incompetence.'

Clem slammed her hand down on the counter and stormed out.

\\\\/

She stayed in Barnforth for the afternoon, waiting for Karene Bickerstaff to arrive. Time to test how deep Karene's loathing of the Hyphen actually was. The drama of the morning was wearing off and she was beginning to feel tired, drained with disappointment and frustration.

They met at her unit in the best hotel in town (a 'third-world dive' according to Karene) and they were two deep into the pinot grigio Karene had brought from Sydney, an antipasto platter half-eaten, when Clementine mentioned she might have some dirt on Scott Stanton-Green.

Karene nearly choked on a strip of prosciutto. Earlier she'd been complaining about his behaviour. Talking over the top of her at the board meeting, pretending to be an expert in all things media and ignoring her advice, red-penning her latest media release as if she was a schoolchild.

'What's the beast done now?' she said.

'Well, I can't be sure yet. I have a source that hinted at something...'

'Oh darling don't be coy—tell me what you have on the monster, please, before I die of curiosity,' said Karene, her eyes hungry for gossip.

'I need you to tell me what you would do with it.'

Clementine wanted to understand the value of her prized information. Would it be enough to scare Stanton-Green? Get him to dob in his mate, the mayor, for Helen's death rather than have his deeds exposed? Assuming it wasn't Stanton-Green himself who'd had her killed. Either way, she wanted to test the potential of the information—and the manner in which the Hyphen's rivals might leverage it—to unsettle the man.

'What I would do with it? Well, it entirely depends on the flavour of the sauce, doesn't it? I mean if it's like the Meatco thing, you know, brown paper bags and so on, I might be compelled, reluctantly of course, to throw poor Scottie-baby under the bus! I mean, I'm the chief custodian of this company's reputation,' she declared. 'We can't have a hyphen sullying it!'

'And something else? A spicier-flavoured sauce, perhaps?'

'Oh God, I'm going to die. SSG and sexual misadventures! It doesn't get much better. And actually, now you mention it,' her eyes were wide open, as if she was understanding a profound truth for the first time, 'bonus schmonus. I think it probably wouldn't matter what flavour it is—I would gladly throw him under a fully loaded Sherman tank.'

Hamish Doncaster was passing through, so he said. (*Who passes through Barnforth?*) She'd agreed to a coffee with him before her meeting with the mayor. As she approached the coffee shop, she could see him sitting at a table by the window, looking out of place in his white designer shirt and brogues while locals in shorts and thongs, high-vis and work boots, queued for bacon and egg rolls.

He stood up to welcome her to the table, moving aside the plastic tray of vinegar and sauce bottles.

'Clementine, good to see you again.' Air-kiss, both sides. The most distinctive product of a decade's private schooling on show: European manners.

His greeting. Kisses. It jumped out at her, surprising in its force—could Hamish Doncaster be the giver of the birthday card? It would explain both the oddities about Hamish: the golden boy's repeated presence in this backwater and his rabid bidding for Turtle Shores—perhaps the romance had become obsessive somehow, attaching itself to Helen's home? It seemed a stretch. But all Clem knew was there had been a greeting card, possibly from a lover. As a subtle waft of expensive aftershave blew across the gap between Hamish's moisturised throat and her face, a host of formless suspicions gathered in her head.

'So, I looked you up,' he said as they sat down.

The familiar sinking feeling. How quickly her thoughts switched back to herself. 'And you still wanted to meet for coffee?'

'Of course—I'm intrigued!'

It was like Helen had said, she'd become a curiosity.

'I want to know why on earth you're not still practising law after doing so well at Crozier Dickens and then I want you to give me one good reason why I shouldn't offer you a position in my firm. But first,' he said, waving his finger at her, 'I want the full brief, no detail too small, on how on earth you came to be coaching a team of meathead footballers out in the sticks.'

Clem swallowed her discomfort. She told him about herself—a few snippets, enough to satisfy for now, and Hamish was too polished to press—then changed the subject.

'So, tell me about you, Hamish.' He was mid to late thirties, she estimated. Helen would have had over twenty years on him.

'What would you like to know?'

'Well, how about we start with your marital status.'

'Oooh, businesslike...to the point...I like that,' he said. 'Currently married but recently separated...'

'Sorry to hear that. But didn't I see a photo of you online with your wife only last month?' A fundraiser: Hamish, olive-skinned, dimples, resplendent in black tie and a stunning brunette with her arm linked through his.

'Yes. *Very* recent. Sadly, my wife is an accountant,' he said, 'and I've found myself on the wrong side of the ledger. She rather likes to draw nice neat lines under things...in fact, I'm soon to be "off balance sheet"—divorce papers on their way.'

The coins were dropping into the slot without so much as a clang—he could be Helen's lover, someone who needed to keep their relationship a secret, tried to do so...but failed. Helen was attractive, experienced; and Hamish came across as someone up for experimentation, keen to taste the many flavours of life...an older woman could have been a delicacy or a conquest or both.

Her suspect list was blowing out again. It was both encouraging and disappointing.

162

She wished she could ask if his wife had discovered his infidelity but instead she said, 'I don't mean to be insensitive, but you don't sound too upset about it.'

'Yes, one could be down in the mouth, I suppose, but I'm actually finding it...well, liberating. I mean I'm living in a trendy apartment, I stay up late listening to *my* music, *my* opera...loud...I can travel whenever I please, and to hell with the exhausting, goddamn life-sapping budget she insisted on. And, to prove my point, here I am, meeting interesting women without so much as a pinch of guilt.' He flashed a full smile. *Yes, he was very easy on the eye.*

Should she flirt back? It felt weird even to consider it. Rule number one when she was released from prison was No Relationships, not even a friendship. Hiding in her little sanctuary in the hills behind Katinga, her shame locked tight, buried deep so she never had to speak of it, never had to parry the well-meaning questions or endure the looks, avert her eyes from the loaded glances as they imagined her at the scene: the woman, the blood, the smell of death, the reek of alcohol on her breath.

Well, there was Rowan of course. She'd broken the rule with him.

She took a gulp of coffee. Black and bitter.

This was different, though. This would be a pretence—she wouldn't *actually* let Hamish get close.

'It's you that's interesting.' She gave him a single raised eyebrow. *That's it, that's the best you can do Jones?* It was like prising open a rusty padlock. 'I mean why? Why is a man like you even here, in downtown Barnforth?'

'Well, let's see...I had the good fortune to meet a captivating young lawyer who's courageously throwing herself against corporations and power. It seems so hopeless...and yet so enchanting...I find it irresistible.'

Or perhaps he's keen to make sure she's not poking around in

Helen's story, thought Clem, unimpressed by the show.

'I thought you said you were passing through on your way to somewhere else?' she said.

'Oh yes, I'm passing through...passing through on my way to new adventures, new life, new loves.'

She snorted out a giggle. It was just too silly, she couldn't possibly play this game. He was laughing too, dimples on demand, apparently thrilled that Clementine found him humorous.

'Please, tell me—what lures a man who loves opera to Barnforth? Really?'

'If you must know, Madam Interrogator, I'm here to see His Redness. He has graced me with an appointment this afternoon.'

'Surprising...I kind of got the impression you might not be on speaking terms.'

'Whatever made you think that? It's the only time I get to use my Japanese sword collection!' he laughed.

She regarded him for a moment, tapping a single finger on the table. 'I'm not sure how to take you, Hamish Doncaster. I've met your father twice now, and both times he was an absolute gentleman.' She imagined that Hamish might be embarrassed about his father—the grocer's son with his crude inflexions and liberal use of expletives, but she was still struggling to understand what would drive someone to be so gratuitously hostile as Hamish had been at the auction.

'He is, isn't he? That's why he's so effective. Let me guess, he told you about the kids' cancer camp?'

'Yes, he mentioned it.'

'Did he tell you it's on a piece of prime real estate in the Blue Mountains?'

'Not in so many words, but I got the impression it's surrounded by bush, great views...peaceful for the kids and their families.'

'Oh, don't get me wrong, it's a great concept and a wonderful place for sick kids, just...not for long. He plans to sell the operating rights to a hotel-management firm as soon as he can. He'll make a motza, and then: hasta la vista kids. Meantime, he's getting government-subsidised rent until the right buyers come along.'

Clem searched his face. Why was he so eager for her to understand his father's shortcomings? Perhaps he regretted telling her what he'd done at the auction and needed to cover his tracks, provide a justification for what must have seemed spiteful to a stranger he'd only just met. There was something hollow about it, though. Something forced.

Hamish explained how his father had made him a director of certain of his companies and then sacked him as soon as he realised his son, not cut from the same ruthless cloth, refused to support his schemes. She didn't buy it, not entirely; perhaps Hamish had a couple of schemes of his own that clashed with his father's plans. Hamish had already accumulated enough wealth by that stage, he said, most of it from the property portfolio his father had set up for him before they fell out. His talk was light, chatty, referring to his father as he might a disagreeable pet.

'So I've made my first donation to the campaign,' he said brightly, 'and I expect you to reciprocate by sending me your CV.'

Was this his first donation, or was he one of Helen's regulars? In more ways than one. He struck Clementine as smart, even cunning, with the kind of charm that would open doors and the looks to turn heads, including maybe Helen's. (In which case, Clem found herself wanting to give Helen a high five for being such a hot cougar.) But why was he in Piama again? Was there something he needed from his father?

He probably didn't donate personally, he'd have used a company. She made a note to check the WAGSS books for donations anyway. The Doncaster donors. She couldn't shake the feeling that one of them was lying.

\I/

The smooth white curve of the windowsill in Fullerton's office seemed to accentuate the knife-edge in her stomach. All she'd achieved thus far was to confirm her suspicion that Helen was murdered. She'd eliminated Ralph but added Hamish. It was time to corner Blair the Mayor.

She would play her cards carefully. She held the ace, two aces in fact, but she was aware that the chance of forcing a favourable outcome was still low.

The executive assistant with the bouffant ushered her in with the same shark-like smile as the first meeting and proceeded to make a self-important show of placing glasses of water on the coffee table. Fullerton nodded obsequiously to the old dragon—some sort of weird power inversion going on that Clem could only guess at. With the assistant safely out of the room, the small talk ended. Clementine sat with her hands palm down in her lap, her feet planted firmly in the cushioned burgundy carpet.

'Well, Ms Jones, let's get down to it, shall we? I'm interested to hear where you're at with the concept of a compromise.'

'Yes, well it's only hypothetical at this stage but I've tested the idea with key stakeholders'—she hadn't—'and it seems there's a fairly solid consensus on what might work. All on a theoretical basis of course: *if we were to consider an offer, what might we be prepared to request?*'

'And?'

'So, in broad terms, we spoke about a ten-year commitment. During that period, the mine would fund a monitoring program across the three known white-throat habitats throughout the state to get clear visibility of the total population, Piama being the largest of these. Combined with that would be a significant commitment to fox and feral cat eradication in turtle habitats across Queensland. In addition, there would need to be an amount allocated for research. And we're thinking the Galimore Foundation could administer this fund and select the research that will have the greatest impact.' She was mildly surprised—the string of hastily made-up rubbish coming from her mouth sounded almost feasible.

'Good, good, I see,' he said, nodding solemnly. 'And do you have any kind of budget for these measures. Ballpark numbers?'

Even though this was all her own creation, without any authority or input from the Foundation or WAGSS, the fact remained that this was where the campaign might end up in any event—failing in the bid to stop the port and desperately trying to get money to save the turtle.

If minister Williams managed to shepherd the proposal through the department it all came down to the WAGSS legal challenge, the outcome of which would always be a coin toss. A deal might be the best option. Time to shoot for the stars.

'Five million per annum for the ten-year period,' she said confidently.

The mayor's face turned a delicate shade of peach. The number was clearly well beyond anything he and the company had anticipated.

'That's...' He cleared his throat. 'Well...let's call that a starting point...the parties would of course need to meet somewhere in the middle, one suspects.'

She was warming to the task as his discomfort grew. Despite his concern about the number, on the audio recording the mayor had openly shown his enthusiasm for a deal and she could sense, sitting in front of him, how valuable to his public image it might be: honest broker, grand poobah deal-maker, saviour of the port and the community's only hope for economic deliverance. Time to go harder.

'Oh, and I should have mentioned an additional two million per annum if numbers in the Piama region drop below current levels. As you would expect, it will be situation critical if that happens and the need for funding will be acute.'

'Oh, Ms Jones, we should keep this in perspective, you speak as if this is a bottomless pit—'

'Fifty million is less than 0.5% of one year's revenues for the syndicate members. If anything, we should be asking for more.'

'Oh, I don't think that's quite right.'

'Oh, I think it is. On a global basis, syndicate members turned over a combined total of more than two billion last financial year and before you say it, I know profit and cashflows would be a better measure than revenue but you can't tell me those numbers aren't healthy.'

'Well, perhaps, but the mine's profits are likely to be negligible for the first two years of operation at Piama, not to mention the three years of construction activity before that. And I think the concept of a penalty for a drop in turtle numbers might need to be reconsidered—it suggests the syndicate is somehow underwriting the turtle population regardless of other factors.'

'But councillor,' she remonstrated, palms uplifted, 'that's pretty much what the company's EPBC Act submission said: *The EIS demonstrates no substantial reduction in turtle population.*'

But he wasn't listening. He was staring at her hands, fixated, his face darkening. She glanced down and stifled a gasp. The jagged cuts from her first failed mission to the *Success* were healing but the raised scabs stood out like black-red strings across her palms. *He knew.* She dropped her hands back on her lap instantly, pretended nothing had happened. His eyes locked on hers, blanketed with cold.

It dawned on her: the latex surgical gloves. They were transparent, he'd managed to make out the wounds from the security-camera footage.

'Your hands look very sore, Ms Jones.' The tone was clipped, icy.

'Hah, yes. I had a fall walking the dogs. Nothing to worry about.'

He nodded, his gaze searching, creeping under her skin. And in his reaction, in the chill of his stare...she could see the possibility: this man, his ambition, his attachment to power—he could want something enough to kill. Forget being arrested for burglary. She had just become his next target.

'Well, this is an interesting conundrum. I'm unsure what to make of you.' He grinned, a lip-curling kind of sneer. 'You come here offering what sounds like a compromise—an expensive compromise, but still, something to start the conversation—and meanwhile, you've been breaking and entering.'

Was there any point denying it? She had to give it a shot. 'I don't know what you're talking about.'

'Oh, it's perfectly clear, Ms Jones. I have video footage of someone trespassing on my boat wearing surgical gloves which, on a second viewing and in the torchlight were quite transparent.' *Why hadn't she thought of this?* 'And a large amount of my wife's jewellery missing.'

What a snake. Denying the jewellery would be tantamount to an admission that she'd been there.

Her mind was scrambling to collect itself, her heart racing. It felt like she was slipping, falling off the knife edge she'd set up for herself by coming here.

Get a grip, Clementine.

She gave a half-smile and clasped her hands together. A demonstration of strength—*they may be cut and bruised, but I still hold the aces and he knows it.*

'Well, Mr Mayor, I'm glad you enjoyed the show. The home video must have been fun to watch. I didn't get any visuals, of course, but I certainly enjoyed the audio.'

'So tell me, why shouldn't I call the police and turn you in? Break and enter, theft...should be enough to see you locked up again, I expect.'

He wouldn't go to the police anyway, he'd made that clear

onboard the *Success*. She needed to stick a knife in. 'We both know that's not going to happen. And I don't think your wife will be pleased if you suddenly decide to lift her jewellery from home just to make a point. No, what we should be talking about,' said Clem, easing the blade against his throat, 'is the joyous sounds of the master cabin. Now *that* was a show!'

Ace number one had been played. A vein was pulsing in his neck, a rope-like thing stretching down to his shirt collar.

'Ms Jones, whatever you have has been obtained illegally,' he said. She could see the nerves flutter in the corner of his lip. 'It can't be used against me. And you'll be going to prison regardless.'

Her heart thudded against her ribs but her anger, her rage at what she thought this man had done to Helen, was taking over the fear. She wanted to jab something sharp into his face.

She shook her head and let out a long, disapproving sigh as if she was disappointed in his lack of intelligence.

'Oh come on man, don't pretend you don't understand the impact of this. The media don't care if the information is illegal. You know the damage will be done and your career will be over, at least for the foreseeable future. No doubt your marriage too.'

His teeth began grinding, the strain rippling across his jaw. Time to strike hard. *For Helen.*

'Councillor. I also know about the other thing,' she whispered as if it was a secret between them. 'The bribes, Blair. The bribes you've been receiving from the syndicate, from your mate Slippery Scottie the Meatco man. And it seems you're branching out as a bagman too, distributing the largesse in Canberra via your brother-in-law.'

She let the words sink in: stones falling through his concrete eyes, down through his spine.

'And let's face it, Blair, you're not going to the police. Like you said, and I hope you don't mind me quoting you: *Not a word, not a single syllable to anyone about this.* Ring a bell, does it?' Christ, it felt good to mimic him. Like throwing an egg and seeing the yolk run down his cheek.

He was twitching, then suddenly lunged forward in his seat. She tensed, rocked back, anticipating his hands around her throat, but he stood up and stormed to the window, gripping the back of his neck as he looked out.

She quietly eased her way up out of the chair, keeping her eyes on him and found the house keys in her bag, held them firmly, longest key out. If he was going to do something crazy, she would do what she'd been longing to do for the last two minutes and fork out his eyeball.

He swung around, his hands in tight fists by his side, spoke through his teeth. 'What is it you want exactly, Ms Jones? I mean what is this bizarre little performance all about? Is it the turtle or is there something else going on here?'

She breathed, a long slow breath in through her nostrils, the first decent air since she'd stupidly let him get a look at her hands. She wanted the inconceivable, of course. She wanted him to confess to Helen's murder.

But in fact, here she was, no closer to nailing Fullerton than she'd been when she walked in—absent a confession, which was highly unlikely. Why would he confess?

It was the weak part of her strategy. Now her cards were on the table and the two of them, herself and Fullerton, were locked in an impasse. She'd suspected this was where they would end up; hoped she was wrong.

'What I want, Mr Fullerton, is for you to tell me who it was that killed Helen Westley.'

His mouth dropped open in disbelief.

'I know you were involved.' She didn't, but at this point he seemed the most likely candidate. Or, alternatively, he was the Hyphen's accomplice, and she fancied the odds there. Especially if she could divide and conquer, split him away from Stanton-Green.

She was pretty sure he'd drop his boating buddy like a stone if it might save himself.

'I suppose there would have been a paid killer hired to do the actual deed. You can tell me who that person was,' she said, taking a step towards him, 'and, you can tell me who did the hiring.'

'You are insane. Certifiably insane. Ms Westley died of...she killed herself.'

'Oh come on, Blair. Let's not play games. Let's do a deal together. You and me,' she gave him a fully charged false smile. 'I know it's not the one you originally had in mind but it's going to be good for you: you give up whoever killed Helen and I let you off the hook. But I must hear from you by tomorrow or else I'm going to share your little boat show—broadcast it as far and wide as I can.'

She had no intention of letting him off the hook, of course. It wouldn't be her choice anyway. Once she had a name, the police would finally do their job.

His lips drew down in a thin curve, pinched above and below. In his eyes was a slow ticking. He was making his assessment, forming his strategy as she watched.

She ran through the possibilities: if it wasn't him but he knew who it was, he might agree to tell her everything. Or he might tip off the killer, who would probably contract the hitman again to get rid of her. If he didn't know who'd done it then he was in deep shit anyway, exposed to public release of the audio from the *Success*. If shit didn't stick, then nothing did. In this scenario he might even accuse someone, anyone, just to silence her.

If it was him, of course, he would probably just have her killed.

Two out of the four possibilities ended with Clementine's death. She'd played her aces. She still didn't know who had killed Helen, and she now had a fifty-fifty chance of being murdered herself. Maybe she should have folded early.

The man watched a grey Chrysler 300C—a beast of a thing, huge front grille—ease out from the corner behind her as she pulled away from the council chambers. He slipped his BMW in behind.

Moving slow, this Chrysler joker—a gap opening between him and the Commodore. Another car, a white hatchback, pulled out from the cross street and slipped in front of the Chrysler. Something not right. It was the speed—deliberately slow. As if the Chrysler driver was making sure the hatchback got between him and the Commodore.

He followed, keeping his eye on both the Chrysler and the target, backing right off. If this guy was some sort of pro, he'd pick a tail easily.

He closed the gap as they approached Piama along the hundred-kilometre per hour straight stretch and overtook, glancing left as he passed. Tinted windows, couldn't see a thing.

He took the first right in Piama instead of the route to the target's home. He knew these streets well by now. Then he took a left and parked in the cross street closest to the target's home, jumped out of the car pulling a baseball cap down hard and low on his head, walking quickly, eyes scanning left and right underneath dark sunglasses.

As he got closer, he kept himself obscured behind one of three gigantic fig trees on the corner. He watched as two hundred metres up the street, the Commodore turned into the driveway. She got out and opened the gate, drove through and closed it. As the target's Commodore disappeared behind the shack, the Chrysler approached the driveway, a long way behind, slowing momentarily then continuing on down the street.

Completely hidden behind the fig tree, he waited for the car to go by, memorising the plates. 1ZH607. Victorian.

CHAPTER 15

Torrens' Patrol was parked on an angle in the driveway like he'd rushed in or just couldn't be bothered straightening up. She drove down past it into the backyard, rolling carefully over the rain-softened ground and turned in behind the shed so the Commodore would not be visible from the road. She'd driven in a state of high tension all the way, nervously checking in her rear-view mirror, but seeing nothing unusual. There was a white hatchback with an old man at the wheel, and a big charcoal grey sedan on the main road out of Barnforth but she lost sight of it once they hit Piama.

The dogs bounded up to her as she opened the car door, Pocket poking his nose in then backing up to let her out, his tail wagging at top speed. She gave his ears a tousle and he reached around to get a few reciprocating licks in. Sarge, so polite, stood back, waiting for the crumbs and grinning with black rubbery lips. She went over to him, stroked the muscles through his neck and down to his shoulders, her hand tracing his size and power. She'd thrown a dangerous ultimatum at Fullerton; now she felt a thimbleful of her fear ebb away.

Helen didn't have a dog. What if she had? Would things have been different?

She looked around the corner of the shed—no sign of anyone on the road. She knocked on the door, making it clang and wobble in the frame, heard movement from within.

'Torrens. It's me.'

175

'Yeah, yeah. Hang on.'

The door squeaked open. Torrens hardly looked at her, turning his back and walking inside. She followed him in. He'd shaved off his beard and looked five years younger. Inside he had a camp stretcher, a fold-out table with a gas stove and a pot, an esky, his duffel bag on a chair in the corner, a pair of shorts folded on top. There was a football lying under a bench. Otherwise, the shed was clean and tidy.

'I'm heading out tomorrow. Get out of your hair,' he said, leaning against the wall near the cobweb-cloaked window.

'Oh,' she said, her heart sinking. 'I was kind of hoping you might stay for a bit longer.'

'Gotta get going, things to do.'

'Back to work?' she said hopefully.

'Nah, I quit the job. Don't need it now.'

He'd been so pleased with that job. More than pleased—proud, determined. She remembered how he'd bought her dinner and a beer to celebrate his first pay, the only honest money he'd earnt in his entire life to that point.

'So what've you got on the go then?'

He shrugged his shoulders, bent down, rummaged around in the esky, pulled out a bottle of water and slowly unscrewed the cap, avoiding her eyes as he took a gulp.

This was not good, not good at all.

'Got anything stronger in that esky?' she asked.

'Sorry, knocked off the last beer earlier on.'

She nodded, nudged her toe at the corner of a rubber mat on the floor, looked up. 'Come up to the house?'

'Nah. Reckon I'll head up to the pub shortly.'

This was all her fault. This cold lack of interest, this miserable void. She had collapsed whatever it was they had, a beautiful friendship, into this hollow, airless cave.

'Matty. I need to talk to you,' she said softly. 'I need to

176

apologise. I mean I do apologise. I'm sorry. I'm just so...' Her arms raised halfway and flopped by her sides again. 'So sorry. About everything.'

Torrens screwed the cap back on the water, slowly, blinked twice, searching her face. Blinked again with ferocity.

'I've hurt you. I know that. I lied to you and I used you,' she shook her head, scarcely able to understand how she'd got to this point. 'I've...well, I've ruined everything.'

Torrens said nothing but when she looked at him she thought his eyes were glistening. A big man with a soft heart.

Her apology was genuine, more than he could know, but she had come here inside his shed to get something. She wanted his expertise and experience, a second perspective on her precarious position from someone who knew about these things. And, she admitted to herself as he stood there in the backlight in his footy shorts, huge tree-trunk thigh muscles, shoulders the width of a single bed...She wanted the security, the comfort of facing whatever was coming with a man like Torrens at her side.

All of this was true. But now, standing in the cloistered heat of the shed, an ocean of distrust floating between them, she didn't want anything from him. Nothing at all. She just wanted to go back to how it was before. Before she'd betrayed him. Just for tonight at least. Pleading with him was not the answer, so she picked up the footy, handballed it to herself a couple of times.

'Skip the pub, come up to the house for dinner,' she said.

He looked up at her, a slight change in his expression. He wanted to, she could see that. It was pride or mistrust or both that were stopping him. She couldn't blame him. But he was going tomorrow—she must not waste this moment.

'Listen mate'—using her coach's voice—'I've got two T-bone steaks and a six-pack inside and I'm not letting you leave until you've eaten your forty per cent.' She handballed the footy to him.

He caught it.

177

The man in the black BMW eased himself back in the seat. He'd been promised the call to proceed could come through at any minute. He'd need to pick his moment, there'd be no rushing into it, especially with Chrysler-man hanging around. Whether that was a problem or an advantage he couldn't tell yet.

He could see the Chrysler near the corner at the intersection of The Esplanade. He'd parked in the next cross street, further behind a row of scraggly banksias. He watched. Through the leaves and the yellow pincushion flowers he could just see the driver's door and front tyre. He set up his motion-activated video camera on the dashboard and wished he'd brought more than a packet of barbecue chips and a Coke. This might take some time.

CHAPTER 16

The steak sizzled and spat in the pan. Clem gave it a pat with the back of the spatula. Somewhere approaching medium. She scooped it out and sat it on a plate to rest, began piling lettuce, chopped tomato and spring onion next to it, with a few slices of avocado, a splash of Greek dressing and a dollop of last night's leftover potato salad.

She got out another plate and made a bigger salad with two large scoops of the leftovers, took a sip of red wine and stood watching the other steak for a few more minutes. Torrens liked his twice dead.

Her thoughts kept hovering back to the meeting with Fullerton. He would have to be weighing up his options. Getting rid of her would be one of them, but she was clinging to the notion that two deceased WAGSS coordinators within a month of each other would not be his favoured scenario. It was a slim hope. Killing her was probably a safer bet.

She flipped Torrens' steak again, took another swig. To be thinking like this, assessing the likelihood of being murdered, it felt as if she wasn't in her own body, as if she was trapped inside some unconscionably violent video game.

She plated Torrens' piece of rubber and sat down at the table, under the old-fashioned oyster light, speckled with deceased mosquitos, the big man opposite.

'Here you go.'

His eyes lit up. 'Now that's better than the Katinga Arms and that's sayin' something,' he said, sawing into the slab.

Torrens was one of those sunny souls, unable to maintain rage with any stamina. It made it hard to imagine his days as a standover man. What Clem could imagine was an impressionable fifteen-year-old, a child looking for a father figure, finding it in Sinbin Schenko.

As if he'd read her thoughts he said, 'Sinbin could cook too. So many things in common, you two.' He jammed in a mouthful of meat and waved the empty fork at her. 'In some ways, you're the new Sinbin.'

'That's a backhanded compliment, if ever I heard one.'

They ate in silence for a while, then Torrens sat back in his chair. He took in Clem's face as she looked up. 'Did I ever tell you about when I went and saw Sinbin after I got out of the slammer? You know, when he was crook?'

'Don't think so.' Clem took a discreet sip of wine.

'I went there to tell him I was going straight.' There was a long pause as Torrens seemed to gather himself to tell the story. 'Sick to the stomach thinking about it, cos here he was with the cancer and everything, and me bailing. But man, when I got there, God he was so sick—skin and bone, bald as a bandicoot, no eyebrows, not even his stupid moustache to poke fun at. I bloody cried at the sight of him, right then and there.'

She placed the glass down gently on the table.

'Sinbin told me to stop embarrassing myself. Ha ha,' he chuckled softly. 'But yeah, in the bed he was just so...small...nothing left. The bastard cancer took it all. Even his voice—used to be he had this booming foghorn set of lungs on 'im and now it just sounded like he was choking and it was all he could do to get the words out.'

Torrens was staring at the table, distant, like he wasn't in the kitchen, he was sitting by Sinbin's bed and Clem was looking down at them both from the ceiling.

'Yeah well. Sinbin knew he was on the way out, not long for this world. I'd been there a while, hadn't said nothing to him about my plans yet, in fact I was bloody feeling like I couldn't do it, like I'd be letting him down when he needed me most. And then, all of a sudden, he looked me in the eye and said, *It's time.* Just that, Jonesy, nothing more, just those two words. Then he fucking closed his eyes! I'm sitting there—no idea what the hell he meant. Thought it might be the morphine—he'd said a few loopy things—but I was shittin' myself that he was gonna say it's time for me to take over or something, you know, take over the business. So then next minute, he opens his eyes again,' Torrens widened his eyes, re-enacting the scene, 'and says, *Time you made a name for yourself, Matt. Make your own life.*'

'Those were his actual words, Jonesy, his actual words,' he said, staring into space like he still couldn't believe it. 'And I was so honoured, fucking honoured, to receive them, even though I was feeling sick to my gut about what he might say next. Last thing I wanted was to take over Sinbin's operation—or start me own for that matter. I'm no leader, Jonesy, never wanted to be the boss of anything. And besides, after being inside...man, I wanted out, I just wanted out. Didn't want nothing more of that life. It was fucking scary in there, Jonesy, really fucking scary. A man my size and I was scared! Soft, eh? But on the outside, in the country, I was a big fish in a small pond, see. And all these city thugs, the bikie heavies and their goons—they were everywhere. Organised, and everywhere. Any one of 'em could've taken me out with a shiv for no other reason than the signal it would send—showing the rest of the mugs inside how even a big man like me could go down, so don't try it on fuckers, don't even think about it.'

It was real. She'd been inside too; she knew what it was like. But she'd never known this brand of fear, the fear that Torrens described—being the biggest, the most obvious target in a shooting gallery wholly composed of violent men.

'Anyway, old Sinbin must've known what I was thinking because he laughed then—thought it was funny that he'd scared me, the mongrel,' Torrens chuckled, shook his head. 'See, he knew me. Knew me since I was fifteen and loved me like a son, and so he did the opposite, the exact opposite to pushing me into shoes he knew wouldn't fit. I remember his words: *Go straight lad. Do some schooling. Get a job. Buy a house. Find a nice girl. Have a family. In that order, mind*, and then he waved his scarecrow finger at me and smiled.'

Torrens put his cutlery down on the table, cleared his throat, sat for moment. Then he got up, went to the sink and tore off a sheet of paper towel, dabbed his eyes and stood there, his back to her, head lowered, leaning his hands on the sink. The air outside had cooled to that serene kind of mild. A curlew howled into the night. He turned back towards the table.

'But for Sinbin to say it—to tell me to go and do what I wanted most, what I'd always wanted, if I'm honest...For old Sinbin to say them words. Well. I could've lay down and died with him there and then, a happy man. A happy man.'

Clem was silent, staring at the fridge; speckled rust blots creeping up from the bottom like a rash. Silence seemed the only thing. Torrens' loyalty, his love, was too big for the kitchen. She'd not experienced anything like it, the way it consumed the space around her, enveloping her.

She swallowed, found her voice. 'I'm glad you didn't. Kind of like having you around.'

'Yeah well, I got a grand final win under me belt now!' he grinned. 'Wouldn't have missed that for quids!' He came back to the table and made another attack on his dinner. 'Did I ever tell you about that first time I turned up at training? Remember that day, Jonesy?'

'I was there,' she said, smiling.

'Yeah, but you don't really know what was going on in my head, eh? See it wasn't just Joey Conti I'd smacked around. There was others too, or their cousins or mates…Broken arms, holding their head under water, faces into concrete…all of that,' he said, his face grim, volume lowered as if speaking of it somehow repeated the offence.

Clem always found it hard to imagine that much violence in Torrens.

'So I'm there, waiting for training to finish, sitting in my ute, the guys are streaming out to the carpark laughing and joking… until they saw me, and just like that'—he clicked his fingers—'all of the chatter dried up and they're making a beeline for their cars, trying not to look my way, pretending I wasn't there. I felt like walking away, driving off and not coming back. Actually, that's not true—at first I just wanted to smash their smug little coward faces in.'

'Jesus, Torrens.'

'Yeah nah, but that's how it was right? Been living that way for years, just came naturally. But it was like Sinbin gave me the okay to start a new chapter. So, I waited until you came out—this coach lady everybody was talking about—and there you were, tiny little thing next to all the blokes, backpack over your shoulder, and you were on a beeline too, weren't ya? Ha ha, avoiding everyone, heading straight for your car, ya bloody hermit!'

'Yep, sooner I could get away the better,' said Clem.

'But I was nervous as all hell. You've got no idea. I mean I didn't know how you might take it, me just rocking up like that. But there was no two ways of going about it, so I walked up and asked you straight if I could join and you said, was I willing to put in the hard work to get fit?'

'Did I?'

'Yeah!' he shouted gleefully. 'Here I was, years inside, right, with nothing but weights and shit—that's all I did, worked out. Mate, I came out solid as a fucking wrecking ball and here's this jumped-up midget of a sheila saying was I gonna work hard to get fit!'

She laughed. 'I told you to do three laps of the oval if I remember rightly.'

'And I said I didn't have me running shoes...'

'And I said, "Well, do it in bare feet then!"'

'So I did it—the three laps—and you had your flaming stopwatch on, so I was friggin' pushing hard, going for it—and man, I was muscle fit but I was no way running fit, me lungs were on fire after the first lap.' He nodded. 'But there you were, with your fucking stopwatch, and me running like me whole future depended on it!'

Clem took another sip, smiled wryly from behind the glass. 'I didn't even have it on.'

'What?'

'I didn't have the stopwatch on.'

'No way!' he said, eyes wide, fork suspended in the air.

'What did you think? Six foot six and built like a brick shithouse—no specialist ruckman in the team—you think I gave a rat's how fast you could run?'

Torrens dropped the fork. 'Oh you mongrel!' he said, indignant but unable to smother a laugh. 'And you put me through that?'

'Yep. I was going to get you into shape regardless of how quick you were. But I knew I couldn't do anything if you weren't willing and determined enough.' She sat back in her chair, her gaze fixed on him. 'That's what I was measuring, mate: your ticker, not your bloody duck-paced running.' She paused, hands resting on the edge of the shaky red table in the poky little kitchen. 'Turns out you've got the heart of a lion.'

Torrens was still. There were tears welling in his eyes again. In her eyes too, for that matter. This bloody lump of a man. He'd come to her for so much more than just footy. And they'd worked together. She'd given up her time to do extra conditioning sessions. He'd landed the first honest paid job of his life. And later, when

184

she needed him, he'd helped her out. They'd been a little team of two for a while there, battling their separate demons together. She realised now that for him it was not just the premiership but the respect of the rest of the team, the whole town, that had changed him, cleared his self-doubt, his disgust at what he'd done for so many years, the person he'd been. But now, after all that, after everything the Cats had achieved and everything the two of them had faced down together—she was selling out. It made her ache inside.

Torrens put his knife and fork down, rested his hands on his thighs. 'Jonesy. This Melbourne thing. I can't...well it's just...'

He looked like he'd been smacked in the guts with a cricket bat. But it wasn't a muscled bikie or some other crim, it was her, Clementine Jones...Jonesy, wielding the bat.

\|/

They washed up together. Torrens cracked another beer and they went outside on the deck. The moon was up now and shining a white pathway across the Great Sandy Straits right up to the backyard. They reminisced about the premiership game and the after-party antics she'd missed, with the whole town packed into the Arms, flowing out onto the street, filling the steps in front of the post office, players sleeping in the front bar, Dave, the publican not bothering to kick them out, throwing blankets over them. The town had buzzed and hummed, flitted and soared in the clear skies above the paddocks and hadn't come down for weeks.

It was like old times with Torrens, only it wasn't. They were skirting around the thing that had come between them.

They went back inside and Torrens boiled the kettle, said it was time to get back into the training routine—'You should know better than offering me another, Jonesy. Three light beers a week, tops,' he said earnestly, fumbling around in the cupboard for mugs.

185

She was pretty sure he'd put away a six-pack of heavies so far this afternoon.

They sat with steaming cups of tea and, in the silence, the fear she'd felt in the mayor's office made its way to the surface. It was time to tell him.

She put her mug down, her hands in her lap and began retelling it all: the audio recording, the meeting, the look on Fullerton's face when he saw the cuts on her hands, her accusation, his denial, her ultimatum. Or was it a threat? A threat to a killer. *Good one, Jones.* Torrens closed his eyes. He shook his head, sighed, but said nothing.

'So, what do you reckon then?' A queasiness churned in her stomach.

'Well.' He leaned back, scratched the back of his head like he was assessing the tread on a set of tyres. 'I'd say you're squarely in the shit, Jonesy.'

'Yeah?' Her voice was squeaky.

'Ah-huh. Don't have to be a bloody genius to guess this mayor bloke needs you silenced.'

Clem had been clinging to the hope that perhaps she'd misread the situation. Still, she refused to take his comment at face value. 'Silenced? That's a bit extreme isn't it?'

'He's the killer, right? Or he's part of a plot to kill?' he snorted. 'You know it. You fucking told him you know it. And, as if that wasn't enough, you went and threatened him, you bloody numbat!' He waved his hand up once, let it flop.

'So what do I do? I mean, in your professional opinion,' she added hastily. 'Not asking for help or anything.'

'Only one thing you can do.'

She waited, hoping for a miracle.

'Get out of town. Hide. I know just the place. Little country town, starts with K.'

'But he'd follow me there.'

186

'Don't stay at your place, then. Stay with me or some other place out of town.'

'Melbourne would be better.'

He frowned. 'Yeah, could be. But big cities are good places for crims too. Plenty of connections there, people to sniff you out, little hidden-away places for doing the deed.'

And then, like a tree crashing through the ceiling, the thought entered her head and she wished it would crash straight back out. Had Torrens *done the deed*? She'd only seen his potential—from that first moment in the carpark when he rocked up and asked if he could join training. She'd never asked about his background, never found out what he'd been inside for—or what he hadn't been inside for but should've been. But now for the first time since they'd met, she wondered if Matthew Torrens might himself have taken a life. She grabbed at her mug, took a hasty swig of tea and hoped the thought didn't show on her face. She put the mug back down heavily.

'Yeah well, I can't go. House-sitting contract doesn't end for a few days yet,' she said.

'Tell him you've got a family emergency. Your mum's sick or something.'

It wasn't the real reason she couldn't go. Helen was the reason. People can't go round pushing other people off cliffs, good people, loving people who shelter little children with broken hearts and scared, empty eyes; worthy people who live decent lives, making a contribution, sharing their wisdom, caring for their neighbours and their planet and...and everything Helen was. Especially those in authority—men elected to represent an entire region of good people—their misdeeds should be doubly punished. And even if Fullerton wasn't responsible for Helen's death, he was like a seagull perched on the mast of a ship, shitting on the deck below, defecating on democracy. He had to be taken down, not run away from. And Clem was the only person who cared enough to shake the mast.

Torrens downed the last of his tea. Times gone by he would have taken more of an interest, begged her to head to safe harbours. Their relationship had been tainted by her lie. But he sat there, regarding her, turning something over in his head. What was he thinking? Could he be considering helping? Did he have an idea? A tiny seed of hope began to form.

The breeze had died. A green frog in the downpipe on the far end of the deck gave a series of honking croaks, then fell silent.

'If I help you out,' said Torrens, 'will you come back and coach the Cats?'

It was relief and heartache in one sentence. She groped around inside her head for a moment, searching for an exit. There was none. She knew, as deeply as she knew she must fight for Helen, that she could not lie to Torrens this time. She must never lie to him again.

It was eleven at night when the motion sensor woke him.

The door on the Chrysler down the street was open, a dark form stepping out onto the grassy verge, standing there for a moment.

Short, maybe about the same height as him at five foot six. Not enough light to make out the features.

His fingers tensed around the wheel as he watched the man walk over to a tree, further from the glow of the single street light into the darkness, unzip his pants and adopt the stance.

He needed to know who this other watcher was, why he was watching and whether it could be to his advantage. Maybe this bloke would even do his job for him, who knew? It had been known to happen: two hits hired for the same target.

He opened his door, making sure the latch didn't snap, and stepped out, keeping his feet to the grassy patches.

It was still hot. Not a breath of air, just the scratchy crackle of crickets. His shirt was wet under the armpits, stuck to his back.

Fucking Queensland.

He waited for the man to turn and go back to his car so the street light would light up his face. He had one of those bright lens cameras that would function okay without the flash—just needed to be fifty metres closer.

He crept to the edge of the banksias, moving quickly, hoping the man's bladder was full. For as long as Chrysler-guy's back was towards him, he would not be detected.

189

He took up a position behind another shrub where he had a fairly clear view.

Full all right—chock-a-block. Like him, Chrysler guy had been sitting there all afternoon and all night, watching. It was another fifteen seconds before he zipped up. As he swung back towards the car, his pale face under the light, the watcher squeezed the silent shutter.

CHAPTER 17

It was just gone eleven when Torrens said goodnight. Clementine watched him through the window, worried he might drive off or do something stupid. He walked down the steps from the front verandah and ignored the path to the shed, heading towards the fence.

He wasn't getting in his car. That was good. But why was he jumping the fence? She followed his path as he picked his way through the bush in the vacant block next door. He seemed to be taking care to conceal himself from the street. Then he stopped behind a tree and looked up towards Parks Avenue, the street that came down the hill to a T-intersection with The Esplanade near the shanty. She couldn't see what he was looking at: the shed obscured her vision. She hurried down to the spare bedroom at the far end of the house to get a better angle. A street light, the street, the fig trees on the corner of Parks Avenue, no movement, nothing. There might be a parked car somewhere up behind the fig trees— something metallic—yes, probably a car.

She looked back towards the vacant block. Torrens had disappeared.

\\\//

She checked her phone when she heard the shed door bang shut. Seven-thirty in the morning. A magpie started up, close and loud,

191

perhaps sitting on the guttering above her window. It paused, then began another riff before flapping away. In the quiet she counted the urgent break of tiny waves on the foreshore.

She lay there in bed, her mind swelling with last night. The final argument with Torrens. He didn't understand about Helen—that her life counted. All he could think about was the team, the boys, the town. He'd begged her to give it away. She'd refused to 'sweep Helen under the carpet like something dirty'. He'd insisted she leave it to the police.

If only they would lift a finger, she would gladly have let them pursue this. But they weren't interested. The cops out here in Hicksville had no concept of what was at stake for men like Stanton-Green—the making of his career as an executive, set up for life if he pulled the development off, job of his choice in mining... infrastructure...Not to mention his supersized bonus. And the mayor? Well, they hadn't seen the violence and the cunning in that man's eyes like she had. Then there was Hamish Doncaster. What was up there? Had he been screwing Helen? His wife's earning the big money, she's his honey pot—she gets wind of an affair... he gets rid of Helen. Or Helen didn't want the secrecy anymore, threatened to tell his wife? Or maybe Helen had simply become one of Constable Griffin's intimate-partner violence stats...?

She got up, looked out the bedroom window in her singlet. It was a wind-blown, overcast kind of a morning. The tide was making its way in but the Great Sandy Straits were washed of colour. Gulls tooled about on the gusts above. She watched them soar and drift, cut and rise again.

There was no noise from the front yard but she imagined Torrens would be leaving any moment. She felt as grey as the sky.

He hadn't suggested she was wrong about any of these men, just told her it wasn't her job, she should leave it to the cops.

No one seemed to get it. A woman had died, violently, and no one seemed to want to know. The conversation had ended badly,

'I'm not going to just let it slide,' she'd shouted at Torrens. 'Helen took it up to the bastards and so will I.'

She needed air, crashed out through the sliding door, stood on the back deck, leaning on the railing. The wind blustered across the Straits, the water agitated and wary, a grey-green slurry of sand in the curve of the waves as they peaked and toppled, spreading white froth right up to the backyard.

She wanted Torrens to go. It was her job to fight for Helen, not his. And she didn't want to hurt him again. In fact the best thing that could happen now would be to shut her friends, good people like Rowan and Torrens, out of her life. Stop hurting them. Cut them loose, push them out if necessary, before things got worse. They would never understand that her life was simply worth less since that split-second two years ago when she took someone else's.

She could no longer hear the waves, the wind, just a fierce silence closing her in tight, and the creeping, relentless heat sending its tentacles into the day.

\|/

Clem was barely out of the shower when she heard the knock on the door. Pocket rushed through the dog door, yelping his high-pitched welcome bark. She threw on a T-shirt and a pair of shorts, padding up the hall with wet hair. She could see Torrens' form in the frosted glass. As she opened the door he burst in, waving his mobile phone around, striding past her, yelling, 'It's him! It's him!'

'What? Who?'

'That motherfucker Membrey!'

'Never heard of him.'

'Here,' he said thrusting the phone at her, pacing across the lounge room, shoulders tensed in a knot.

It was a photograph—the dark of night, a streetlight, a man, shortish, pot belly, his face turned side on. He was opening the door of a late model sedan—big with a huge front grille—a fig tree off to the side. Parks Avenue.

'I can't believe it, I cannot believe it! Fucking Membrey.' Torrens was pacing across the lounge room.

A tingling panic began in her hands as she gripped his phone. 'This looks like the grey car I saw the other day coming back from Barnforth. Am I being followed?'

'Oh yeah, you're being followed all right. But not by this bloke, he's following me. The guy coming after you is worse.'

'Okay, now I'm really confused,' she said, handing him the phone back. 'Here, Torrens. Sit down. Tell me what's going on.'

He kept pacing, gripping his hair, running his hand over the back of his neck. 'Fuck. *Fuck*. The bastard. He's fucking not getting any of it. Not a cent.'

'Okay, this Membrey guy's after your money?'

'Yes! The fucking parasite!'

'So he knows about Sinbin's stash?'

'Oh, he knows. Wouldn't have known where to look, but he's probably guessed I've got it,' he stopped pacing, eyes flashing, pointed his finger at Clem. 'Over my dead fucking body is he getting one single cent. That's what I promised Sinbin and that's how it's gonna be.'

'So who is this guy?'

'Just the crookedest cop you'd ever meet. He's so bent he could be the S-bend in your crapper. Detective Declan Membrey. The Snout. He was on the take from Sinbin for bloody years, then the day he gets the sniff of a promotion he sells us out. Twenty SOGgies surrounding the house, automatics, the lot. Turned the place fucking upside down. It was only bloody lucky we didn't all go down that day.'

'So he's a cop?'

'Was. Sinbin should've let me break the fucker's neck when I had the chance.' He shook his head as if in disbelief, then pulled up

194

short in the middle of the room. 'I wanted to squeeze his throat so hard I squished the living breath out of him while he watched me.'

And there it was—that question again. But this time she knew the answer: Matthew Torrens, her friend, her big-hearted friend, had killed. She swallowed, blinked. A shiver ran across the back of her neck, she shook it out.

Torrens glanced at her. 'Oh Jesus. I didn't mean to say that,' he said, his arms waving up then slapping down onto his thighs. 'I'm sorry. It's, it's just...you know, the past...this prick is bringing it all back,' he slumped into the couch, his head in his hands. 'Oh God.'

'Hey,' she said, sitting down next to him. 'We've all got our pasts, right? All of us.'

He let out a dry moan, the air getting caught in his throat. They sat for a bit.

'Jonesy,' he said, voice raspy, 'I need to tell you about the other guy.'

'What other guy?'

He swallowed, his jaw hardening, 'Warwick Jackson.'

'Okay. Who's Warwick Jackson?'

'He's your tail.'

'What?'

After she lost sight of him last night, Torrens explained, he'd gone along the beach and cut back up the hill. He'd seen a car parked in Parks Avenue—looked like it had been there all afternoon—and after Clem's brush with the mayor, he'd gone to check it out. When he'd got to a high-enough point he'd walked along Juniper Street towards Parks. There was another car parked there: a black BMW.

'Right, so this is the guy I saw coming back from Barnforth?'

'Dunno. Might have been. Got a copper mate to check the rego. Fake number, but the name's an alias that Jackson's used before.'

'And this Jackson, you said he's worse than Membrey?'

Torrens was on his feet again, pacing and she didn't like the length of this pause. The light was streaming in through the window, the sun having broken through the cloud and edged around the corner of the house. A thousand dust motes ducked and dived.

He turned and looked her in the eye. 'He's a hitman, Jonesy. A hired killer.'

It felt like a wall—concrete blocks coming at her, smacking her in the face, laying her flat. Her head was thumping and she couldn't speak.

This is the person who killed Helen.

This man is after me now.

I am being pursued by a hitman.

She was staring at the flying dust motes, her eyes picking one, following it up and around then down out of the light beam.

'It's all right Jonesy. He's not gonna get ya. I'm here.'

She'd heard Torrens but the words hadn't registered. The mayor or the Hyphen—or both—or Hamish had used a hitman to kill Helen.

'I reckon we should...'

Torrens was sitting down again, making a plan. He was going to help her. Something about setting Membrey up. She couldn't think, couldn't follow.

He sat down next to her and she felt his hand on her shoulder, as big as a baseball mitt, heavy yet gentle. She'd felt the comfort of having this giant as her protector before. But again, she was drawing him into criminal circles, away from his promise to Sinbin and all the hard work he'd done.

She sat there on the dirty old couch with him, her eyes searching the sunlight. And she knew.

Helen would have agreed.

She could not accept Torrens' help.

\//

196

It was after eight o'clock. She followed him into the kitchen. He was stooped over, searching through the meagre offerings in the fridge. She gently pushed the door closed. 'No you don't,' she said.

'Eh? Man's gotta eat,' he grunted.

'Eat on the road. You're not staying,' she said, her words sounding so much stronger than she felt inside.

'What?'

'I'm not joking.' Her stomach did a flip and left an emptiness as she thought of what it meant—facing it, whatever it was, on her own.

'Ha! You're hilarious when you're trying to look mean,' he laughed, opening the fridge again, brushing her arm aside.

'I'm serious. I want you to leave, Torrens.' She wasn't getting through but she couldn't seem to come up with anything. She knew why—it was fear. Not the adrenaline-filled rush of imminent danger but the drawn-out, spun-tight terror of what was to come.

'Yeah? Well you know where you can shove that.'

She pushed hard on the fridge door, her stomach churning. She knew what she was doing was right, she was absolutely positive, but it didn't make it any easier.

He slowly stood up, his full six foot six. 'What are you doing?'

'You need to get out of here. You can't be involved in whatever's coming.'

He snorted. 'Don't make me laugh, Jonesy. You think you can handle these guys on your own?'

She nodded.

'Oh for fuck's sake. Don't be an idiot.'

'It doesn't matter. You can't be here. You just said a few moments ago you wanted to kill this guy.'

'Membrey? *Pfft*, who bloody wouldn't?'

'You were fucking serious. I heard you,' she said. The wind was freshening outside and the wooden chimes had begun their clacking and jangling on the back verandah. She could hear the waves of the incoming tide—must be breaking onto the lawn almost.

'Of course I was fucking serious, Jonesy! You think he's gonna leave me standing after he gets his hands on the money?'

'Matthew, listen to me,' she said soberly. 'I've never asked you about your past, why you were in prison, and I don't expect you to ever tell me. In fact, I don't want to know. But one thing I do know is you're not going back there. Certainly not on my behalf.'

'Oh, come on, Jonesy, this is the Snout we're talking about! No one's going to prison and there'll be no one happier than the cops if he disappears and never shows his face on the planet again.'

'No. No, I don't care who he is. You can't be killing people, Torrens. Oh God, I can't believe we're even having this conversation.'

'Oh get real, why do you think I'm hiding here? That guy'll kill me as soon as look at me.'

'Which is exactly why you have to leave. Get out of here, head to Darwin or...or Perth or something.'

'Oh for fuck's sake. This is fairyland. Come here, have a look for yourself.' He stormed out to the lounge room, stood in front of the wall near the window, beckoning her over. She stood next to him hidden behind the curtain, moving across just far enough so she could see out.

'Look up behind the trees in Parks Avenue,' he said.

She saw a glint behind a thicket of trees. She looked harder. Was it a car? She pulled back behind the wall, catching her breath. Fuck. Fuck. *Fuck.*

'See? There's no leaving here for me—Membrey's waiting for me to leave. Surprised he hasn't made a move already. Sitting there waiting for the right opportunity, the bastard. And I'm gone if I don't get him first. Simple as that.'

She closed her eyes, one hand to her face. Her mind had gone to mush, nothing would line up. How they had arrived at this point seemed a blur and now Torrens was actually contemplating killing a man.

She pushed away the thought and instantly, a wave of guilty reprieve flooded into its place, unbidden. He would have left today, walked away from her, possibly forever. He was staying. Maybe it wasn't because of any concern for her—maybe it was because he had no option. But it didn't matter. In that moment, she didn't care if he thought of her as a liar, a coward, a traitor and everything else, all she felt was an unstoppable tide of relief.

She would not be alone.

Warwick Jackson hung up the phone. Finally, the go-ahead. Hanging around this dump was a kind of slow death in itself. And the risk in coming back here was borderline crazy, only weeks after the first job. Sure, he'd charged twice his usual, but no money could ever make it worth being caught.

He'd had time to consider the lie of the land over the past days, plenty of time. She had no routine, though. That made it awkward. As much as he wanted to get the thing done and get out of here, it was all in the timing—he'd have to pick his moment and take the opportunity when it came.

He had no idea what this clown in the Chrysler was up to. He'd checked him out with his contacts. Disgraced cop. If he got in the way, well, it wouldn't be the end of the world, bastard probably deserved it. In fact, it might pay to wait just a bit longer—this guy might make a move. With a bit of luck he'd do the job for him. The customer would be none the wiser. As long as the target was dead, Jackson would be paid.

CHAPTER 18

Torrens said he couldn't think if he didn't eat something. He made himself some toast while she kept an eye on the street. Now that she knew Membrey was there, she couldn't take her eyes away. She and Torrens discussed the situation. She'd given the mayor a deadline—a name by today or else she'd talk to the press. If Fullerton was behind Helen's death, Torrens was certain Jackson would have received instructions to dispose of her before that deadline came around. Membrey, on the other hand, needed Torrens alive, at least until he got his hands on the money.

They brainstormed ideas. The element of surprise seemed to be their best weapon but as they sketched out a plan, Clem just couldn't see it working, too many things that could go wrong, and the clincher: they were up against armed men. She kept coming back to it, Torrens trying to reassure her, the discussion getting more and more heated.

'Listen to what I'm saying: I've got it covered. All right?' said Torrens, thumping the chair with frustration.

'Yeah well it won't be bloody all right when we're lying on the ground, with...'

'Farkenhell, will you let it go, Jonesy!' he shouted over the top of her.

'...holes through our heads,' she shouted, louder.

'For fuck's sake, Jonesy. Here. Here it is.' He reached around to the back of his shorts under the baggy black AC/DC T-shirt, a wildness in his eyes. 'This is why it will be fucking all right.' She watched as his hand emerged.

A gun. Short. Squarish. Black.

Clem's jaw dropped, waves of disbelief rippling across her face. 'A gun? A freaking gun. Here in this house.'

Torrens was already shoving the thing back in his pants.

'And you didn't think to mention it?'

'Yeah right. I'm gunna ask your permission. Get real, Jonesy. Sinbin's stash is hot property. So just relax, everything's going to be fine...no one's gunna have a hole in them except the Snout.'

'But you can't just shoot someone,' she spluttered. 'And not here. I'm bloody house-sitting for Noel—looking after the place, for Christ's sake, and you're planning a fucking shootout in the kitchen!'

Torrens proceeded to ignore her, making a start on the preparations for the plan they'd discussed.

'You gunna help or what?' he said, glancing at her over his shoulder.

'Jesus Christ, Torrens.'

He kept working. She sighed a long, bewildered breath, shook her head. What could she do? She couldn't stop him. She couldn't make him leave, walk out into Membrey's sights. She watched him for a moment longer then took a step in front of him, forcing him to stop and pay attention.

'Okay. Here's the thing. I don't approve of guns, okay? I hate guns. And once this is over, I never want to see one anywhere near me or my house or my car or my dog or any bloody thing close to me. Right?'

They stood, squared off and bristling. 'Suits me,' he said, and there was an awkward pause, their eyes locked on each other defiantly, before he stepped around her and got on with the preparations.

They worked in silence in the lounge room for a while before Clem spoke again. 'So where have you hidden the money, then?'

'As if I'd tell you,' he muttered under his breath.

He didn't trust her. It hurt. He noticed.

'Look, if Membrey gets hold of you it's best you don't know,' he added.

She watched him leave the room. God, he was still making an effort to be kind. She didn't deserve anything from him, least of all trust. And the fact remained, she was not returning to Katinga.

She couldn't bear it—him not knowing, still hoping. He had come clean on the gun—it was her turn. Staying silent was a lie in itself.

She followed him into the kitchen. The gulls were still wheeling and screaming over the rising tide and the smell of the sea pungent through the open back door.

'Torrens.'

'Yeah,' he said, sitting at the table, polishing off the last of the toast.

'I've made up my mind. I'm going to Melbourne.'

He stared at the table, swallowed the last mouthful, got up abruptly and threw his plate in the sink with a crash.

Declan Membrey took off his Ray-Bans and picked up the binoculars, watching as she reversed up the driveway in her clapped-out Commodore wagon and headed up the street. He was getting sick of watching, waiting, sick of the shitbox cabin at the caravan park, sick of the local radio station with the mind-numbing complaints about the shortage of council bins and the one-sided raving about the port. Oh, and the turtle. A fucking turtle that breaths out its arse. Unbelievable.

  He'd have to find an opportunity soon, he couldn't take the waiting anymore. But he'd always been careful and picking the right moment had served him well. Like when he withheld telling old Sinbin about the raid. A masterstroke, as it turned out. The promotion had allowed him more influence, greater knowledge from his position further up the tree—and the ability to command a higher fee. Sinbin never saw it that way, of course, but there were bigger fish seeking his services after that, in the city where the real networks are. Sinbin's shitty little operation could go fuck itself.

  As for Matthew Torrens, well, Membrey had seen him in action; knew what he was capable of. He wouldn't even have considered this caper if it weren't for something as significant as Sinbin's stash. Over a million, so they said. He'd believe it when he saw it. But even half that was worth it. He needed that money these days.

  And about a minute after the Commodore had cleared out up

the road there he was, the big fella himself, closing the front door behind him like he finally learned some manners, the oaf.

Something odd about how he moved across the verandah though. Hold the phone! Hold the fucking phone—his arm's in a sling. And, as he took the steps down—limping...Bingo!

Taking on a fully fit Matthew Torrens was dangerous. Injured, he might still be a handful but the odds got a lot better. And with the girl out of the way, there would be less complications.

He watched as the big man stood at the mailbox, looked inside, took out a piece of junk mail—why do they even bother out here?—and limped back up the path to the house. Hadn't even looked up the street, the dumb prick. Sharp as a bloody bowling ball.

Okay. This is it. Opportunities like this don't come twice.

Membrey waited until Torrens had shut the front door, then got out of the car and walked briskly across the road. He made his way down through the bush block, sand creeping over the top of his deck shoes and working its way down to his toes. When he got to the beach he turned left towards the house, stopping before the trees thinned out about ten metres from the backyard. The tide was right up to the grass and still coming in, highest tide he'd seen since he'd arrived in this hole.

The house was quiet, no movement on the back verandah. Both the back door and the sliding door to the main bedroom were open, just the flyscreens closed. The dogs were stretched out under the shade of the sheoak in the corner of the yard closest to him, over by the lemon tree. He'd fed them on and off the last few days, whenever the house was empty. The big dopey one was surprisingly placid but Membrey went carefully with him, not attempting to pat him over the fence until they'd become well and truly acquainted. The little mongrel blue heeler had been a bit nervy at first. Probably mistreated as a pup.

He waited a few seconds longer. Still no movement. He squeezed his left arm in towards his chest, felt the bulk of the

Beretta, walked the few steps over to the yard, whistling softly, and threw a Schmacko at the heeler's head. The clever little thing snapped his head round, caught it before it fell to the ground. The mastiff raised his enormous lump of a head, looking over to see what all the activity was about. Membrey threw another treat his way. The dog levered himself up, lumbered over to it. Both of them chewing, Membrey slipped through the gate, stopping briefly to give them his usual pat. Routine and treats. It never failed—dogs or women.

He made his way towards the house, hugging the lemon tree and the shrubs near the fence line. As he stepped up onto the verandah he waited, listening. The sound of a television from deep inside. Had to be the lounge room. The wind had picked up. Too quiet. Something missing? He strained his ears, looked up the verandah—couldn't put his finger on it.

Beyond the kitchen through the passageway that led to the lounge he could see two legs stretched out, big boots. The big fella was on the couch. Even better. He drew his weapon, pushed open the flyscreen door.

\\//

Movement from the Chrysler in Parks Avenue. Jackson flicked off the stereo, picked up the binoculars and watched as Membrey disappeared into the bush block next door to the house. He turned the key in the ignition, drove the BMW to the end of the street, cautious in case Membrey came back to his car. He stopped, looked right down the hill, checked with the binoculars again. He could see her yellow shack from here. No movement and he couldn't see the Commodore. Fuck, had she left? He'd missed it.

He turned right, drove slowly down the hill past the Chrysler parked near the fig trees, kept going to the end of Parks Avenue, slowing at the T-intersection with The Esplanade. He checked the *bush block straight ahead of him. No sign of Membrey, turned left up the street, eyes trained on the little yellow shack as he passed. A little bit further along and he was passing the other bush block on the far side and moving up the rise at the end of the street. As he came over the crest he saw the Commodore. Just sitting there, parked, only two hundred metres from the shack. What the fuck? He drove closer. No one inside.*

He pulled up in front of it, took something from the glove box and got out.

\\//

She heard the creak of the chair. Torrens standing up in the lounge room. Every nerve in her body was on high alert, she felt her sweaty grip slipping on the green plastic. From her position in the bedroom she imagined him there, facing the passageway that entered into the kitchen, just one thin wall between him and Membrey. As soon as Membrey moved towards the lounge Torrens would have a clear shot from three metres. She recalled Torrens' ferocity as he'd laid out the plan: 'The fucker won't even know what hit him.'

She tried to put the thought out of her head. Maybe it wouldn't work out like that. Maybe Membrey would surrender. She looked down the back verandah at Pocket, standing near the sheoak licking his lips and looking up expectantly while Sarge chewed on something. She began counting to ten, as they'd planned.

She got to three and a sudden thought turned her blood cold. They'd guessed Membrey might have been cultivating the dogs by giving them treats, but what if these ones were poisoned?

Shit, the count. She began again at five, trying to focus, staring at her little Pocket with his pirate-patch eyes. He'd already swallowed whatever it was, the little guts-ache. *Oh God, Pocket.*

On seven Sarge turned his great mass in a semicircle and started walking across the lawn towards the back verandah, up the steps

207

towards the back door where Membrey had just entered. Fuck. They hadn't thought of that either.

\\/

Membrey surveyed the tiny kitchen. Washing-up stacked in the dishrack, chairs snug around the red Formica table, the faintest smell of toast in the air and the unmistakeable voice of Kerri-Anne Kennerley from the lounge room. The boots and legs on the couch hadn't moved. He crept towards the passageway and froze. There, in the reflection on the glass door of the cabinet facing into the lounge, the giant form of Matthew Torrens standing in the middle of the room. No sling, gun poised.

A set-up. An ambush.

Had Torrens seen his reflection too? Either way, he'd lost the element of surprise. No advantage now.

He began to back away, keeping his gun on the passageway. A floorboard creaked and in the glass he saw Torrens take off, lunging towards the passageway. In the same instant there was a guttural growl from behind. From the corner of his eye, standing there at the door, eyes wide with menace, lips flared, wet black gums, enormous fangs—the fucking mastiff!

Torrens emerged. Membrey adjusted his aim, an almighty volcano of noise erupting from the screen door behind him. He got a shot away, the big man flung backwards a split second before Membrey felt a huge weight barrelling into the back of his legs. A piercing crush on his thigh, high up, the force sending him falling to the ground face down.

He tried to swivel, couldn't get his gun around, trying to push it away with his other hand, its choppers fixed like giant hooks into his flesh. The woman running into the kitchen, something green in her hands, spraying his face. An instant of cold, then burning in his eyes, and his own voice screaming in his ears.

208

As Clem rushed into the kitchen she aimed the water pistol over the top of Sarge's shoulder and fired. A jet of methylated spirits speared into Membrey's face, into his eyes, splashing across his cheeks. Torrens was in the passageway getting to his knees, gripping his shoulder. Sarge, huge slobbering lips, his fangs lodged deep in Membrey's thigh and buttock. She watched in horror as the dog heaved upward, neck and shoulder muscles straining, began shaking Membrey, left and right, the shrieks louder with each swing.

'Sarge! No!' she yelled, grabbing at his collar. 'Sarge!'

Torrens was there now, grabbing Membrey's gun, standing over him, yelling something. Pocket had come in through the dog door, barking frantically.

She heaved against Sarge's collar. He allowed her to pull him back, a growling thunder emerging from his belly, morphing into an outraged, full-throated bark.

'Good boy, Sarge, good boy,' she said as she hauled him, skidding on the lino, into the laundry and shut the door. Pocket was skirting the edges of the room, still barking. She grabbed him, opened the laundry door a crack and shoved him in.

There was a bloody mess on Torrens' bare shoulder, spreading out across his singlet and under his arm.

'Oh my God, Torrens.'

'Flesh wound,' he grunted, not taking his eyes off Membrey. 'Lucky shot, Snout. Last bit of luck you'll have in your lifetime,' he said. 'By the way, did ya notice you're missing a piece of your bum?'

Membrey was groaning on the floor, blood streaming from his backside and thigh, a patch of his shorts torn away. His eyes were screwed shut, his face contorted.

'Water...please...my eyes. Oh fuck...I'm blind. Please. Water.'

Jackson was crouched beside the Commodore when he heard the gunshot. He withdrew his hand from under the front grille and ducked behind the car. Waited.

What the hell was going on?

Checking all around first, he darted across the street to the vacant bush block, hiding behind trees, slowly working his way forward until he had a view of the shack. No movement. He scanned the area. So isolated out here at the arse end of town. No one would have heard the shot.

He went back to his car and grabbed the silencer, just to be sure. Moved back to his position, waited again, maybe five minutes more, weighing up the situation. He'd heard only one shot between the three of them—the target, the big guy and the ex-cop. More than likely one of them injured or dead. Probably the ex-cop—there'd have been two shots if he was in control. So, the big guy and the target were in there. Neither of them expecting company, both of them distracted dealing with the clown in the Chrysler.

It was an advantage. A moment. A good time to get the job done and get out of this hole.

He ran across through the bush, zig-zagging from tree to tree towards the house. Paused again. Looked for the dogs. Must be out the back.

He ran to the fence, vaulted over and into the front yard, then the five metres to the shack, pressing his back against the fibro wall. Dogs barking—the smaller one frenetic, the big one booming—from the back of the house, maybe inside somewhere? He checked the silencer was screwed on tight and crept along the front of the house in a half-crouch, gun pointing down, then took the three steps up onto the front verandah and peered through the window. Nothing. He tried the front flyscreen door. It was open. He pushed on it gently, arms out front, two-handed grip on the gun, stepping inside. He could hear the dogs' claws scratching. Good—locked in a room somewhere.

He'd taken two steps into the lounge when he heard the sound of an outboard engine from the beach behind the house and then something else—a long groan from the next room. He crept towards the passageway, a smear of blood on the floor ahead. A glass cabinet with a pair of deck shoes, legs, reflected in the door— someone laid out in the kitchen. He swung out of the line of the reflection, back pressed to the wall separating the lounge from the kitchen, then flung himself around through the passageway, gun raised. On the floor, back propped against the wall, gagged, hands and legs bound, the ex-cop, Membrey. Face as white as a sheet, blood everywhere, eyes red-rimmed and weeping.

Jackson kept the gun trained on his chest. Membrey was staring at him, wide-eyed. There was a note taped to the wall near his head. Jackson approached and bent down closer to read it.

Hello Warwick Jackson, I'm Declan Membrey. I'm a squealer and I know everything about you and I know who you work for. I've been paid to tell all.

Jackson stood for a moment, the dogs throwing themselves at the laundry door, howling their protest. In the distance, the sound of the outboard engine was getting fainter. He shrugged and raised his gun. What a shit show. Membrey tried to say something through the gag, his face twisted in fear, bound hands up in front of his face, pleading.

Jackson took a step closer and fired. A single shot, straight between the eyes, Membrey's head slumped on his chest. Another straight down through the top of his head just to be sure. Then Jackson bent down, ripped the blood-spattered note off the wall and stuck it into his pocket.

CHAPTER 19

Clementine looked back at the shanty as they sped away, the roar of the outboard and the pounding of the dinghy across the waves was deafening. A figure appeared on the back verandah. Jackson. Was Membrey dead? They'd as good as killed him. A blast of spray pummelled her back, soaking through her T-shirt and sending a shudder through her body.

Torrens sat beside her as the bow bashed up and down on the chop. He was clutching a tea towel against his shoulder and grimacing.

In the stern, Ralph Bennett gripped the outboard tiller, his face wet with spray and his eyes shining. The crusty old bugger seemed to be enjoying himself, squinting at the sea, his wiry hair standing straight on his head in the wind. He'd been surprised when she rang. Then he registered the terror in her voice and hadn't asked questions. Just said he'd get the boat in the water straight away.

With the tide so high he'd been able to bring the tinny in close, almost to the backyard, and they were safely aboard and already twenty metres from shore when she heard the two gunshots.

Well clear now, she asked Ralph to slow up so she could hear herself speak, called an ambulance then tapped in the number for Sergeant Wiseman.

'An intruder...yes...Then another man. We heard gunshots... No, we're on Ralph Bennett's boat. We managed to get out...'

She hung up. Wiseman was on her way to the shanty but it was a thirty-minute drive from Barnforth.

Ralph opened the throttle again. The bow reared high in the air then eased down again as they picked up speed. More bone-shuddering thumps across the chop. She gripped the gunwale to brace herself. A southerly was tearing up the channel, battering the angry waves, crumbling the peaks to fuming white froth. Her back was wet through. The wind was warm but she felt cold with shock, shivering. She thought about Pocket and Sarge. They had taken the safest option by locking them in the laundry. If they couldn't get to Jackson, he would have no reason to hurt them. She hoped. Surely he'd have the sense to leave the door shut.

She looked at Torrens sitting next to her, his hair wet and dripping, the salt water washing pink streams of blood down his arm. He wouldn't let her tend to the wound, told her to stop fussing. Ralph was taking them to the marina in Barnforth. From there they could get a cab to the hospital—Torrens was already refusing an ambulance.

What if Jackson was there, waiting for them? He would know they were in the boat, perhaps he'd guess they would head to the marina. She tried to force her brain to think of alternative options. Everything was foggy, slow. She couldn't project beyond the current plan.

Ralph was gesturing to her, pointing over her right shoulder. She swivelled on the seat, turning her face, feeling the punch of the wind on her cheeks. Someone waving at them from a large yacht, white hull. It was anchored to the south of the point that stretched out from Piama towards K'gari. Ralph leaned forward towards Clem, his hand cupped in front of his mouth.

'Doncaster,' he yelled over the sound of the outboard.

She looked over at the yacht again. Yes—Andrew Doncaster. And he seemed to be beckoning them over. What the hell would he want?

Ralph leaned forward again. 'Still twenty minutes to the marina. Let's get the big fella onto the yacht. They'll have a first-aid kit at any rate,' he yelled.

She looked across at Torrens, his face was pale and he hadn't said a word for a while. He looked smaller, as if the pain had diminished him. Perhaps he would be better off on the big boat. She tried to get her brain thinking straight but everything was muddled.

Ralph swung to port heading for Doncaster's yacht. As they came inside the lee of the point, the wind disappeared and the sea was calm. She felt relieved, safer somehow without the pounding, as they sped across the sheltered bay to Doncaster's boat.

'What are we doing?' yelled Torrens.

'Gunna get you on the big boat, get you bandaged up,' yelled Clem.

'Nah, fuck that. Just keep going,' he said. Then he spoke into Clementine's ear so Ralph couldn't hear, 'The less people know about me and why I have a fucking gunshot wound the better.'

'You look bad. You're losing blood,' she said.

'No,' he said, insistent. 'Just keep going,' he yelled at Ralph. But Ralph, waving him away, was having none of it. Ralph Bennett, President of the Piama Progress Association, was in command of this vessel.

Torrens spoke to Clementine again, 'I'm fine, I'm going to the hospital and I'm not getting on that boat.'

Ralph slowed as they approached the stern. Torrens grabbed a dirty old towel from the bottom of the boat, threw it over his shoulder, covering the wound, wincing through his teeth as the salty fabric touched raw flesh.

'Ahoy there,' yelled Doncaster, smiling from the cockpit. He was dressed in white shorts and a navy polo shirt, his eyes concealed behind mirrored aviators. His pale face was covered in zinc cream.

'Hello,' she called as the wake overtook the dinghy, shunting the stern up and forward towards his boat in a last sigh of momentum. 'What's up?'

She recognised the yacht now. It was the *Hermes*—the one that had been moored behind Fullerton's boat in the marina.

'Saw you out there, got some good news for you. Come aboard, have a drink,' he said, grinning and beckoning. He couldn't see Torrens' arm under the towel.

Torrens still looked bad. But it was her that Jackson was after, she thought—not Torrens. He would actually make it to the hospital better without her tagging along like a moving target.

She swivelled back around on her seat, facing Ralph, 'You go on, get him in,' she said, nodding at Torrens. 'I'll make my own way back.'

Doncaster heard her. 'We're heading back in ourselves in a moment, we can give you a lift then,' said Doncaster.

'No worries, Clem. We'll catch you later,' said Torrens, before Ralph could comment.

Ralph manoeuvred the boat alongside and she took hold of Doncaster's outstretched hand as she stepped across onto the duckboard. A businessman's hand—dry and warm. After the tinny, it didn't feel like being on a boat; so big it was hardly even rocking. She watched Ralph and Torrens speeding off towards the point, towards Barnforth and suddenly felt very alone as the shock of the morning's events washed over her.

'Geez, you're all wet,' said Doncaster. 'Looks like a rough trip.' He ushered her towards the cabin, past a man in bare feet and cargo shorts standing on the deck. Thirties, thinning sun-bleached hair and the tanned, leathery look of a sailor or a fisherman.

'This is Damien, my skipper.'

'G'day,' said Damien reaching across to shake her hand and opening the door into the cabin for her.

'I'll get you a towel,' said Doncaster and went below.

She stood next to the expansive cream leather lounge inside

the cabin, not wanting to sit down in her wet shorts. The air conditioning was blasting. She heard Doncaster's voice downstairs. Was there someone else on board? No, it sounded more like a phone call. Finally he came back up with the towels.

'Sorry about that, got a transaction happening in Sydney,' he said. 'I've got a beer on the go but there's a chardy in the fridge... or would you prefer something hot?' He handed her the towels.

'Thanks, I'll have a cup of tea.'

She spread a towel on the lounge and sat down, hugging the other around her shoulders while Doncaster switched the kettle on and found a mug.

Everything about being here felt wrong. A man was probably lying dead in her kitchen, shot by Helen's murderer. He had been there, the killer, looking for Clementine—there inside the shanty. She shivered. The police would not have arrived yet and Jackson would be long gone by the time they got there. She wanted to be with Torrens, make sure he got to the hospital. She needed to speak to Wiseman again.

'So, how's it going with the turtle campaign?' asked Doncaster.

The campaign seemed like something she'd done in another life. 'Yeah, um, things are going well,' she said, trying to focus.

'Good, good,' he said, taking a swig on his Peroni. 'That's why I called you over, actually,' he poured her tea and brought it over with the milk, sat down opposite her. 'It seems to me we need a burst of activity before the department makes its decision. So I've decided to make another donation. Fifty thousand.'

Clementine nearly dropped her mug of tea. 'Fifty thousand?'

He nodded, but she struggled to process the information. It was crazy—here on this luxurious boat talking about a turtle while Torrens bled and Membrey lay dead in her kitchen. But fifty thousand. *Shit.*

'That's just...so generous...my goodness...I mean, thank you,' she mumbled.

Doncaster smiled and his dimples appeared. She tried to concentrate—such a large sum of money; how encouraging it would be for the WAGSS stalwarts; what she could achieve with the funds—but her thoughts kept wandering. Why was he doing this? She just wanted to get off this boat, talk to Wiseman, check on Torrens.

'Might take me a few days to get it organised and into the WAGSS account but I'll get my accountant onto it first thing tomorrow,' he said.

He was chattier than normal, and something about his manner was odd. She couldn't work it out. What was it?

'Yeah,' he continued, 'I've thought a lot about it since we last spoke'—he blinked twice. She felt her uneasiness growing—'and, you know, I kept thinking how much it meant to Helen.'

It was then that it came to her...this huge donation, this sudden generosity—it was as if it had only just occurred to Doncaster, just at that moment as he'd seen her in Ralph's boat.

She sat, her mind lurching, not really hearing what Doncaster was saying. She needed some space, time to think.

'Um...excuse me...bathroom?'

'Yes, yes. Damien, show Clementine where it is would you?'

Damien took her below. The space: it was like the Tardis—bigger than Fullerton's whole boat. He showed her down a corridor towards the bow and opened a door to the left. She stepped inside, thanking him, and latched the door closed.

It was hot and stuffy in the toilet, no air conditioning. Shower, vanity unit, everything white and pristine apart from the timber trim. She sat, elbows on knees, the warmth welcome on her back, forcing herself to think.

It was too early to ring Torrens, too soon to try Wiseman again, but at least she could just breathe for a few minutes, collect her thoughts. What the hell was up with Doncaster?

She heard the engines start—a low, pulsing chug from the stern.

Then a loud rumbling noise, a chain grinding. Was it the anchor coming up? Doncaster had said they would be heading back to Barnforth soon. *Good.*

She pulled out her phone, unlocked the screen, checking to make sure it was still on silent. A couple of texts, both from Hamish Doncaster.

You made an impact on the old man. Intrigued to hear we'd met. And! You'll never guess...found out the randy old bugger was seeing your friend Helen! Ha!

Clem felt the hairs on the back of her neck stand up. She rushed on to the second text.

Btw, spoke with a mate who's still inside the business. Big Red's resort plans: not Whitsundays, Turtle Shores! Thinks he can bust the covenant. Call me.

She read the messages a second time. The truth of it all, what it meant—it formed a solid mass behind her eyes. Doncaster had a relationship with Helen. He'd bought Helen's home to develop—level the trees, pour concrete over the river banks. He believed he could contest the covenant or buy his way out of it, or something. Beautiful Turtle Shores, prime waterfront, spread across three acres. The realisation was taking her down like steel boots, she felt sick, her hands began to shake.

Her thoughts were racing now, lining up in sequence: Doncaster had tried to win Helen over, groomed her with sex and whatever else—probably made an offer for Turtle Shores. Helen would've refused the offer, ended the relationship. Then she must have instructed her lawyers to set up the covenant. Even changed her will to include that silly stat dec—easily circumvented, but specifically designed for Doncaster, an attempt to keep him away from the auction.

And unbidden, from within Clem's sorrow, came frustration and rage. *Helen! Why didn't you tell me what was going on? I could have helped...we could have dealt with it together. So*

218

stupid. She squeezed her eyes shut, took a long breath.

No. Not stupid. Embarrassed. Mortified. Ashamed. Alone. And just as fast as it had ignited, the rage was snuffed out.

She sat there on Andrew Doncaster's toilet and forced herself to read the texts a third time. She recalled the conversation as she sat at his kitchen bench, drinking his wine, eating his prawn salad, telling him how she thought Helen had been murdered. He was probably already contemplating getting rid of her right then—as soon as she'd opened her big mouth. And now he knew she'd met Hamish. Whatever plan he'd already hatched would have been accelerated, so he'd be rid of her before she heard about the resort.

Her heart began to pound. She tried Hamish's number. No answer. Her mind was filling with fear. The phone call Doncaster had made earlier—was it to Jackson's handler? Jackson could be coming here, to the boat, already on his way. It would be easier to kill her if she was on board, captive—they could dump her body at sea.

Her hands were trembling as each piece fell into place. Her throat felt swollen, she couldn't swallow.

Get off the boat. Get off the boat before Jackson gets here.

She heard someone calling. Doncaster.

'You all right down there?'

'Yes, all good thanks,' she called, her voice thready and feeble.

'Okay. We're going to head for the marina,' he yelled. Then movement in the corridor. Was he listening outside the toilet? She couldn't risk a phone call. She sent a text message to Sergeant Wiseman:

Doncaster hired Helen's killer. He's going to kill me. I'm on board his boat in the bay near the point. Hurry!

It sounded ridiculous. She could imagine Wiseman rolling her eyes. She copied the text to Torrens and Hamish.

She was sweating profusely in the cubicle. She stood up, turned on the tap, splashed some water over her face, glared at the face in the mirror. It didn't look like her: taut-skinned and panicky. *Pull yourself together. Think!*

The boat was already moving. On its way out to sea, she assumed. Jackson was probably stealing a boat from the marina now. Torrens' phone was probably on silent or he hadn't heard the text over the outboard. Who the hell knew what Hamish was up to. And even if Wiseman took her seriously, would she send someone? She had a single constable, and a town to police.

Clem had to assume Jackson was on his way out to the *Hermes* and no one would make it in time. She could rush upstairs and dive into the sea. They would chase her, pull her back on board. What if Doncaster had a gun? Would he shoot her dead in the water? He's waiting for Jackson though, isn't he? Perhaps he doesn't have one—men like Doncaster don't have guns do they? Damien might, but not on board, surely?

She looked above her. There was a perspex hatch opening out onto the foredeck. She could climb out, but she'd be in full view of Damien seated at the helm in the pilot house. She crouched down, looked through the vent at the base of the door. No sign of any movement in the corridor. Her hands were trembling as she unlatched the door, opened it a crack. No one there. She slipped out and up into the master cabin in the bow, closed the door behind her, looked around, hoping for a hatch that opened to somewhere discreet. There were two small ones above the bed but they would open directly onto the deck in front of Damien.

She opened the door, moved quickly down the corridor, checking the other two cabins. Neither had hatches opening anywhere other than in full view of Damien.

A droplet of sweat trickled down the side of her face. She was conscious of the seconds ticking by. Doncaster would wonder what she was doing down here. She peeked out into the corridor, noticed a small, low door leading aft. She crept towards it, edging sideways around the far side of the stairs that led up to the saloon, the noise of the engine building as she got closer. She levered up the arm on the door and pushed it open. A deafening noise and before her a huge engine, in fact an entire engine room. She stepped over the raised threshold and stooped under the doorway, closing the door behind her.

The space was about the size of a small home office with a walkway all the way around the engine, which sat squarely in the centre. To her left was a storage area with a big open box of tools, a scuba tank in a frame affixed to the wall and a wetsuit hanging above a plastic crate full of goggles and flippers. In the corner was a broom and a boat hook or something, partly obscured by the wetsuit.

Her thoughts were coming fast now. She should disable the engine so they couldn't come after her, then make a dash for it. But how? She knew nothing about engines. She looked around the room, staring at pipes and metal bits—no idea what function any of them performed. Was there an off-switch? But that wouldn't stop them following her—they'd just switch it back on. She needed to do the kind of damage that would stop the bastard in its tracks. She did a full circle around the engine and found herself staring at two glass cylinders filled with a yellowy-green fluid, swirling inside. Fuel? Perhaps she could stop the supply to the engine. She had to try something.

She went to the toolbox, grabbed a spanner the length of her forearm and steadied herself in front of the closest of the cylinders. Feeling the rock of the waves and picking her moment, Clem took an almighty swing, smashing with all her might. There was a low *thwack* but the cylinder remained intact. She swung again, losing her balance with the tilt of the boat into a wave, the spanner slipping ineffectually off the rounded surface. She steadied and swung again. The edge of the spanner crunched into the glass—a tiny crack opened up. Another blow, grunting with the effort. The crack opened wider and fluid began spraying out in fine jets. It smelled like fuel but there was no change to the rhythm of the engine—thundering on relentlessly. She swung hard into the second cylinder as the stream of fuel from the first one collected on the floor, smashing at it again, and again, swinging like a woman possessed. Another crack appeared, one more full-bodied blow and fuel was squirting from the second cylinder...everywhere, all over her clothing, running down her legs—but the engine still roared on. *What the hell?*

She stared at the thing for a second. There must be fuel already in the engine but it had to run out at some stage. In any case, she couldn't wait any longer. Doncaster would come looking for her. He would tie her up, lock her in—as good as dead while she waited for Jackson to arrive. She had to make her move.

She took a step towards the door just as a wave lurched the boat sideways, her foot slipping on the fuel. She fell face first onto the toolbox, her arm flinging out wide and knocking over the boathook as the pain shot through her temple.

Only it wasn't a boat hook.

There, on the floor right beside her on the end of a length of something metallic, was a circle of thick barbed prongs sharpened to a needle point. A spear gun.

She scrambled to her feet, slipping again in the fuel, steadied herself on the toolbox and grabbed hold of the gun. She'd seen them before, there should be a rubber sling to pull back but this one was just a fully enclosed barrel. She looked it over, trying to work it out. There was a switch on the trigger pointing to the word *Safe* and a lever at the base. Was it hydraulic? Was this how to prime the spear? She cranked the lever twice, felt the pressure building, kept cranking until it was too tight to budge. She had no idea if she'd actually loaded the thing but either way, she could do some damage if she needed to—poke out an eye; scare the shit out of them. Just holding the barrel with the fearsome spikes at the tip gave her a burst of strength.

She took off her T-shirt, loosened the belt on her shorts, checked the safety lock was still on and thrust the loaded gun down behind her back, inside the belt. Then she pressed herself against the wall, the spear upright behind her with the deadly tip above her head and the trigger side-on below her butt. She breathed in and tightened the belt as tight as it would go. Fuel was still spraying everywhere, bubbling and frothing inside the cylinders. She kicked off her thongs and dropped her T-shirt, then opened the door. She stepped out carefully into the corridor, the gun secured to her body behind her back.

She stood in her bra and shorts, concealed at the base of the stairs for a moment, the fuel stench filling her nostrils. The boat was moving forward and the bucking motion was getting worse. They must have pulled out from behind the point into the rougher water. The longer she waited, the further from shore she'd be. She inhaled two deep, shuddering breaths and took off, bounding up the stairs.

Doncaster was sitting on the lounge with another Peroni in front of him. He yelled as she ran past, knocking over the bottle as he scrambled out of the narrow space behind the table. She was through the door in a flash and onto the back deck. Damien was at the helm in the pilot house on the next level up. She made straight for the side closest to shore with Doncaster right behind her, shouting, the throttle on the engine easing as Damien turned to see what was happening. She clambered up onto the safety rail and pushed off, diving high and wide, Doncaster's hand snatching at her foot and slipping straight off. She hit the water hard, the spear gun pushing up and sliding sideways but the trigger still secure under her belt. She breaststroked twice under the water, kicked her legs and with her left hand edged the spear straight as she surfaced, then struck out for the shore, arms high, kicking like fury.

She heard the boat engine roar into reverse and flicked her

head up as she breathed to her right, glancing towards the sound. *Hermes* was backing up towards her. *Shit. Go harder.* Right arm, left arm, more from her legs. She could hear the engines throbbing, *Hermes'* hulking white hull looming to her right. She kept an eye on it, turning her head sideways and back with every lift of her right arm. Damien was up high at the helm, Doncaster at the stern, yelling, stepping out onto the duckboard with something long in his hand. A boat hook? Not a gun, thank God.

She reached around for the spear gun, trying to free it from her belt. Too late. *Hermes* was only a few metres away, the turbulence from the propeller churning the water against her. She had an image of her legs mangled in the blades. Hot panic flushed through her body. She spun onto her back, kicked hard, taking desperate gulps at the air as her arms flayed wildly.

The boat was close enough now to see the rage in Doncaster's eyes. Damien was manoeuvring the boat close, the engines roaring, so close she could almost touch it, a violent rush of water swirling and shunting against her legs.

Then the engine noise dropped to idle with the boat right above her, the stern plunging up and down in the waves. Doncaster reached out with the boathook, almost overbalancing on the rocking boat. Clem knocked it away, spluttering on a mouthful of salt water.

Doncaster reached again and the hook lodged under her belt. She grabbed the shaft, wrenched at it, jerking it towards her just as *Hermes* dropped into a trough. Doncaster wobbled on the duckboard, eyes widening, arms flailing, then toppled into the water with a howl. She rolled onto her stomach and struck out for the shore again, her lungs heaving.

Glancing under her arm behind her she could see Doncaster swimming awkwardly towards the ladder at the back of the boat. *Really* awkwardly—almost a non-swimmer.

Five strokes, and she looked again on the next breath. He was

224

climbing up the ladder and the boat was moving forward and turning towards her. *Why the fuck hadn't the engines cut out?*

They would get her eventually. She needed to conserve her strength and prepare for the struggle. She reached for her belt, she would only get one chance with the spear gun. She needed it now.

She watched as *Hermes* came around in a semi-circle, turning towards her, bow up, lunging forward on the back of the waves. Clem sucked in air, trying to get her breath. The belt buckle had worked its way to the side, she groped for it. The engine was drowning out all sound. She fumbled with the buckle, her fingers would not do her bidding. The boat only fifteen metres away now. Then a splutter, as if the engine coughed. Had she misheard it? No. Another splutter, clearly, the engine struggling now. Then it spluttered away to nothing.

No fuel—finally!

Ten metres away, the bow subsided into the water with a sigh and the bay fell quiet. Just the waves splashing against her, the sound of her breathing, the shouts from *Hermes*.

\\//

As he strode down the pontoon, a small tinny was arriving at the far end, its single occupant seated at the stern—slightly built, not much more than a boy. Jackson broke into a run, approaching just as the young man was picking up a rope from the bottom of the boat, the engine idling and the boat gliding towards the pontoon.

'G'day mate,' said Jackson. 'Here, I'll give you a hand.'

'Thanks!' said the boatman, throwing the rope.

Jackson caught it, waited a moment and stepped into the tinny as it bumped alongside, the man looking confused.

'Hey!' he said, rising up from his seat.

Jackson lunged at him. There was a surprised yell as the man tumbled over the gunwale and splashed into the water.

225

She was out of practice—there was no pool in Katinga. She couldn't seem to get a decent rhythm going and the shore was still hundreds of metres away. Beneath her, bottomless depths: a vast green expanse darkening to black. She tried to regulate her breathing. A shape flashed to her right. Shark? No, just her hair flipping forward as she swam. Again. Was she sure? Yes, just her hair.

Every now and then she took a glance under her arm as she swung it high. Somebody was moving on the foredeck of *Hermes*. She looked again four strokes later—something swinging on a crane. An inflatable dinghy. Clementine picked up her pace but she knew that wasn't going to help her against the speed of an outboard motor. She steadied herself again, stopped, felt for the belt buckle, taking her time and easing the tongue out of its hole. She pulled the belt loose, reaching for the spear gun and edging the trigger out from underneath, with the waves rolling and shunting her. She found the safety switch and flicked it off, then began kicking, on her back towards shore, her eyes on *Hermes* as they lowered the dinghy into the water.

A minute or so later she heard the outboard engine fire, then the inflatable screaming towards her, Damien the driver. She clutched the spear-gun trigger in her natural right hand, steadying the barrel with her left. Only one shot. Damien would have her or the gun in his grasp before she could reload. Should she aim for the dinghy? Would the barbs be enough to pierce the sides? Would it sink? Or should she aim for Damien?

Not yet. Not yet. Let him get closer.

The slap of rubber against the waves, a plume of froth from the outboard motor and the thing was upon her. She lifted the spear gun out of the water and took aim, the ring of barbed prongs

226

pointing straight for his chest. He yelled, spun the dinghy around and sped off before she could get her shot away, roaring around in a tight circle, turning back to face her.

'What the fuck are you doing?' he yelled.

'Don't come any closer!' Clem shrieked, kicking her feet to orient herself towards the dinghy, ready to shoot if he moved closer.

He would know about spear guns. He'd be keeping the dinghy just out of range.

'Listen to me,' he yelled. 'Put the gun away. You can't win this, I'll follow you to shore and get you anyway.'

She looked towards the shore. As she turned her head, he swung the boat towards her, full throttle. She was off balance, trying to wrestle the gun through the force of the water. She got it around, far enough, squeezed the trigger. A loud *ppphhht* and the spear exploded out of the nozzle, a flash of silver through the air and then punching into the dinghy with a smack and a loud woosh.

Damien was shouting obscenities as the whole side of the dinghy shrivelled. The shaft had buried deep and ripped a hole the size of a coffee mug right on the waterline. He grabbed for a bucket, began feverishly bailing water out.

Clementine tugged on the gun, hoping to retrieve the spear on the end of its string and reload but the barbs were doing their job, the jagged edges lodged tight in the torn flap of canvas.

The stricken flank of the dinghy was completely collapsed now and the water rushing in. The whole thing was tilting, the outboard lurching sideways towards the sea. Damien gave up on bailing, clambered onto the inflated side, straddling it like a horse. The boat seemed to want to float but it was severely crippled, the engine struggling to propel the misshapen mass, half of it dragging under water.

This was her moment to flee.

She ditched the gun and struck out for shore as fast as she could, counted twenty strokes, looked back quickly. Damien crouched over the outboard, making his way in reverse back to *Hermes*.

\|/

Every muscle in her body was burning, her breath coming in great wheezing rasps. She'd been swimming for close to half an hour. Almost there. Only metres from the shore.

Then she heard the high-pitched buzz of an outboard. She stopped, checked behind her. A tinny in the distance, white spray spearing from its front. It was near the point, coming from Barnforth, zooming across the bay in her direction—a single person onboard. She gasped, salt water burning her throat, then kicked hard for shore.

Another minute and she could see the bottom. Then it was under her feet and she scrambled up, wading through waist-deep water. The tinny was still a long way off but gaining fast as her feet sank into the sludgy sand. Knee-deep now, but she could barely lift her legs: stumbling, splashing face-first into the green then recovering; pushing forward on her hands and knees, then finally, out of the water and reeling up the beach.

She crossed the muddy flats, mangrove shoots like rubbery spears sprouting up through the grey, and headed for the track leading towards Piama. Onto the dry sand now, crumbling and scorching hot beneath her feet, the mangroves giving way to gum trees and palms. From a small rise along the track she glanced over her shoulder, panting hard, and saw the tinny roaring straight through the shallows and up onto the sand, coming to an abrupt halt on the beach. A man scrambled to his feet and leapt over the side. He had long pants and shoes—not dressed for boating.

Jackson! Running up the beach, following her footprints. Still quite a distance between them.

With the loose stones bruising her soles, she ran to the first house, pounded on the door, yelling, 'Help!'

An elderly woman emerged clutching at her throat in shock as she opened it. Clem must have looked a sight—bedraggled and terror-struck in her bra and shorts.

'I need to get to the police urgently,' Clem gasped. 'Please, help me.'

The woman stood there, white hair wispy around her face, an apron tied about her waist, barely taller than she was wide.

'Please. Your car keys. A man with a gun will be here any second.'

The woman turned and hobbled up the hallway as fast as stumpy arthritic limbs could take her. 'I'll have to come with you, dear,' she called in a broad Scottish accent. 'George won't be pleased if I just hand over my keys to a total stranger.'

She came back down the hallway with a set of keys and her spectacles, closing the front door behind her.

'Can I drive?' said Clem, holding out her hand.

'Nae lass,' she said, frowning. 'You're in no fit state.'

Clem glanced up the road as the woman creaked out to the car. 'I'm so sorry but we have to hurry! He's coming up the beach now!'

'Good Lord!' The woman was puffing as Clem grabbed under her elbow and herded her along to the rusty old hatchback parked under a decrepit carport. Clem kept her eyes on the end of the street. Movement on the track behind.

'I can see him. Please, ma'am, you have to let me drive,' she begged.

'Wheesht,' she said crossly. 'Ma'am, my arse. It's Mrs Henderson to you.'

Clem flung open the driver's door. Mrs Henderson plonked herself in and cranked the key while Clem raced around to the passenger side and dived in. The engine revved sharply and the car vaulted backwards, Mrs Henderson's ample bosom bouncing against the steering wheel. On the street now and Mrs Henderson pushed the gear lever into drive. In Clem's side mirror, the man, Jackson, running onto the end of the street, slowing, steadying, raising a gun.

'Duck!' yelled Clem, pushing Mrs Henderson's head down. They heard the sound of the gunshot, the glass exploded in the rear windscreen. Mrs Henderson gave a yelp, eyes like saucers and stepped down hard on the accelerator, tyres screeching as the car leapt forward. Another shot. Clem looked over her shoulder. Jackson was taking aim again. She scrunched her eyes closed as the crack sounded but they were speeding up the road now, Mrs Henderson hunched forward, gripping the wheel, glasses perched on the end of her nose.

Clem looked back again. Jackson, standing with his hands by his side, gun lowered, the rolling flurry of the Great Sandy Straits surrounding his figure in a stripe of brilliant blue, the salted green of the mangroves mocking him along the shore.

CHAPTER 20

Clementine watched one of the junior constables unspool a reel of blue and white police tape around the perimeter of the yard. Both of the Barnforth police vehicles were here and backup from Wallyamba had just arrived. The shanty looked unsettled, discomforted by the presence of a dead body in the kitchen and the authorities descending upon it like flies.

She reached across to tousle the silky fur around Pocket's ears and felt a painful twang in her shoulder. By her estimate, she'd probably swum close to a kilometre in choppy seas. Every muscle felt heavy and stiff and she kept noticing her teeth were clamped tight. She forced her jaw to relax, put a wall between her mind and the future.

Gunning down the main road to Barnforth, Mrs Henderson and Clem had flagged down the second police car, lights flashing, sirens blaring on its way to the shanty. The old lady pulled over and Clem ran out into the middle of the road, waving her arms. They left the hatchback by the side of the road and travelled in the back seat of the police car. Clementine held Mrs Henderson's shaking hand all the way.

Clem sat now, her back against the pandanus in the backyard, Pocket stretched out beside her, his head on her thigh. When she'd arrived he'd been distressed, barking and crying frantically from the laundry.

As she sat now, tracing the scar that ran from his ear to his chin, she could sense his fatigue, but he would not allow his eyes to close.

Through the laundry window she'd seen Sarge's tan and gold shape, still with Membrey's blood spattered on his chest. He seemed subdued, as if the crisis had drained him and weariness had set in. He'd been locked in the laundry, inexplicably from his perspective, as Clem and Torrens ran off, leaving him with the tantalising smell of the attacker's blood in the kitchen just the other side of the door, then a second person and more gunshots. He'd whimpered when he heard her talking to the police officers in the backyard. She wanted to pat him, hug him but they wouldn't let her near until forensics came.

Noel would be home soon. She thought about how to let him know his house-sitter had turned his sleepy little shack into a crime scene, his gentle pet into a vicious attack dog.

Mrs Henderson was so shaken up she couldn't stop talking, her Scottish accent becoming increasingly broad until eventually her husband arrived. A small man wearing sandals and long socks over spindly white legs, he had reached out and put his arm around her shoulders. She melted into him, mid-sentence, collapsing in noisy, wet sobs.

Clem watched Mr Henderson lead his wife to his car. Mrs Lemmon came to mind, back in Katinga, knitting her beanies. Clem was about to make her sad, too. It was better though—to cut the ties quick before she hurt them even more.

She looked up at the blue sky. Not a cloud in sight and the wind abating. *Jesus Christ, Helen. This is too much.*

And she was so...not hungry, but empty. She hadn't eaten, couldn't eat. Her mouth was dry, her tongue still felt swollen with salt. The paramedics had given her a bottle of water. She took another sip, poured a dribble on Pocket's snout. He opened his lips to the side, scooped at the water with his tongue.

Sergeant Wiseman came walking across the yard with Constable

Griffin in tow, towering over his boss. 'So, care to tell us what happened here?' She squinted in the late morning sun, one thumb hooked over her heavily laden belt.

Wiseman had described the scene inside to Clem earlier. Two shots to the head, point blank range, dead, instantly. Clem's stomach had turned upside down and she'd dry retched behind the pandanus. Now she stood up. The police had given her a T-shirt from the bedroom but she was still in the same shorts, dry and crusty with salt. She tensed. This was the moment Wiseman would finally come round and start heading in the right direction. *Don't stuff it up, Jones.*

'Yes,' she said, not sure where to start. Safest to focus on the action, probably. 'This guy, the dead guy, he came in through the back door. He had a gun.'

'D'ya know him?' Wiseman was shorter than Clem, maybe just on five foot, tiny but fit, a little pocket rocket with a voice that made it clear she'd brook no bullshit.

'No, never seen him before.'

'What, a stranger? With a gun, for no reason?'

'Yes, a stranger and yes, he had a gun. Fucked if I know what his reason was...I mean, sorry, I'm so strung out...I don't know why. I didn't have a chance to ask him. He fired a shot and it hit my friend. That's when—'

'Right, so a complete stranger enters your home for no reason and takes a shot at your friend?'

'Correct.'

Wiseman tipped her mouth down, flicked her eyebrows up. 'And then what?'

'Torrens went down and Sarge burst in—'

'Sarge?'

'The bull-mastiff. Sarge. Short for Sergeant,' said Clem.

Sergeant Wiseman flinched slightly, as if the name was a personal insult. 'Go on,' she said, rocking back on her heels.

'Well, Sarge burst through the dog door and latched onto the guy's leg. He went down and I splashed metho on the guy's face. Then we were able to get the gun off him.'

'Metho?'

'I didn't have a weapon.' She didn't want to mention the water pistol or anything that indicated the whole thing was staged.

Wiseman looked at Clem, her eyes searching for something. 'And who is "we"?'

Wiseman knew it was Torrens. Of course she knew. 'Deliberately obtuse' must be one of the techniques they train them in at cop school.

'Matthew Torrens. You know him. You arrested him recently.' Stupid cow can shove it up her arse. *Oh settle down, Jones.* Exhaustion and irritability went hand in hand for her, she knew that, but she had to fight it, try to be civil. 'He was the one who was shot. He went to Barnforth Hospital to get checked out.'

'Right, I think I'm getting the picture now. A complete stranger enters your home for no reason and shoots at your friend, who just happens to be a convicted felon. Don't suppose it was him that put the two holes in this bloke's head?'

Clem felt a flush of anger and protectiveness.

'No, he did not. And you're out of touch, sergeant. Matthew Torrens has done his time,' she snapped.

'And so at this point you rang an ambulance for the wounded intruder?'

'No. There was another man, we saw him coming. He had a gun, too, so we ran out the back and flagged down a guy in a boat.' She missed out the phone call to Ralph and the note they'd stuck on the wall.

'So who tied up this first guy, then?'

'Don't know. Must have been the second guy.'

'A second man with a gun, also unknown to you?'

'Correct.'

'A boat? You got away in a boat. Sounds a bit James Bond.'

'We live on a waterway, sergeant, there's lots of boats pass our backyard. We called the ambulance once we got away from the shore. You can check it out,' said Clem, defensively. 'That was just before I rang you.'

Constable Griffin scribbled a note in his pad, flicked over to another page.

'Still, pretty lucky a boat just happened to be going by,' said Wiseman, deadpan.

'Yeah. Guess we were due a bit of luck after being shot at.' Double-deadpan.

'So the dead guy. Who is he?'

'Like I said, never seen him before.' That was true enough.

'Any ideas why these random armed strangers just waltzed into your house?'

The constable was eyeing Clementine off as well now, pen poised.

'Not the first guy, no. I'm hoping you can tell me what the hell he was after. But the second guy, he's after me because I know he killed Helen Westley.'

The words crashed through Wiseman's ice-cold surface like a rock. *She wasn't expecting that.* Clem let the rock sink right to the bottom. Griffin checked across at his boss, looking just as shocked.

'What makes you think that?' said Wiseman.

'His name's Warwick Jackson and he's a hitman—a paid assassin. Andrew Doncaster hired him to kill Helen and now that I know, they're after me.'

Wiseman almost rolled her eyes. This was not going well. The terror of being shot at, the exhausting swim, had left Clem tetchy, belligerent. Just when the police should be coming around to her way of thinking, she was pushing them away. She needed Wiseman on board, needed the full extent of police resources mobilised, looking for Helen's killer. Bloody hell, she needed their protection, for Christ's sake. Jackson would almost certainly be back for her.

'Listen, Clementine, I know you've had a bad day, a really bad day, but...'

'Don't make it worse by patronising me,' Clem snapped angrily. She was losing it, the threads starting to tear—fatigue, shock, desperation, it was about to tip her over the edge. She could cry. She might cry. *Don't cry. Don't cry in front of the cops.* Clem looked away, stared at the sea, sucking the strength of it through her nostrils deep into her lungs.

Wiseman lowered her eyes, sighed. 'Look, how about we talk through all these details at the station?' There was a hint of softness in her voice. 'You can fill me in on all this stuff, okay, everything you've found out. I need to understand it.'

Clem turned to face her with a tiny skerrick of hope in her heart, the tension in her jaw letting go. Someone on this planet wanted to know the truth about Helen. Someone was going to listen, and it was the officer in charge, Wiseman, the one person who could do something. She could have hugged her right there and then.

'Yes. Yes, that would be great. Thank you,' said Clem, her energy returning.

'Good. I'll take you back to the station as soon as forensics turn up. You okay to hang here for a bit till then?'

Clem nodded, smiling for the first time that day. 'No pressing engagements. But how about something to eat? You guys got some donuts, maybe?'

\\\//

The air conditioner in the police interview room was turned to full-clanking noise. They'd given her the oldest, most threadbare shirt she owned, the one she used for mucking about around the house, the one with the curry stain on the front. The embarrassment was one thing, but it was more the feeling of being out of control of her life: strangers selecting her clothing, telling her where she could go and where she must sit that got to her.

Wiseman had been helpful and thorough, making sure she got all the detail. She was smart, too, immediately understanding the implications of Helen's attempt to protect Turtle Shores with a covenant. Constable Griffin had shown her a number of photographs and thankfully Clem had managed to pick out Warwick Jackson from the line-up.

Then the two cops had left to go and type up her statement. She sat there in the empty room at the grey laminate table. Despite the chill and the smothering glare of the fluorescent light it was a relief to be on her own. She spread her elbows across the table and let her head fall onto her hands, closed her eyes. *So tired.* But now, finally, the police would take over. One man dead and the shooter on the loose. She wouldn't have to put herself in danger anymore.

Slumped on the table, she imagined Wiseman and Griffin arriving at the quarry and finding Helen's body. She was looking over the edge of the cliff again, the sheer drop, Helen's body at the bottom staring up from the tree. She pushed the image aside; thought about her last moments. No one was there with Helen when she died. She was alone. Had Jackson interfered with her, assaulted her sexually before he pushed her over? She'd never thought to ask. A tear rolled down her cheek onto the table and she didn't have the will to stop it.

The door opened. Griffin entered still carrying the folder with the photographs. Clem sat up, rubbed at her face, wiped the tear off the table.

'Okay, Ms Jones,' said Griffin sitting down and opening the folder. 'If you could just have a read through your statement and make sure we've typed it up correctly, thanks?' He pulled out a document fastened with a paperclip and pushed it across the desk.

'Okay, but can I ask you something first?'

'Sure,' said Griffin. He'd taken the customer-service classes seriously at cop school, she could tell.

'Was Helen sexually assaulted before her death?'

'There were no signs of any sexual assault,' he said.

It was good news, but she wanted to make sure of it. 'But you did check, right?'

'If she'd been assaulted, that would have pointed to something other than suicide—so yes, we checked.'

Clem was relieved. It sounded like the truth. But the lack of diligence in the investigation, the weeks of distrust, had left their mark. 'So she was clothed? When you found her?'

'Yes, she was,' said Griffin. 'Well, except for the sandals obviously.'

'Sandals?' Helen only ever wore toe sandals with a strap across the heel. Wiseman entered the room, striding over to the chair opposite Clem. She was frowning, her mouth set in a tense line and her eyes locking on Clem as she sat, sending her a searing gaze. Clem was startled. She'd been wholly onside—had something changed?

'Yeah, they must have come off on impact,' said Griffin. 'Took us a while to find one of them. It was a long way away from the body.'

Clem took her eyes off Wiseman, looked back at Griffin. 'And they were the toe sandals, right? With the strap at the back?'

Even though he didn't seem to notice the change in her demeanour, he looked uncomfortable now that Wiseman was back in the room. He could see where Clem was headed and seemed to be questioning whether he'd given up too much detail to a civilian. Griffin tapped the document in front of her. 'If you could read through the statement please, Ms Jones?'

She could tell from his expression she was right. 'How on earth did they come off?'

'The constable told you—impact,' snapped Wiseman. She hadn't taken her eyes off Clem. What was it? Something was wrong.

Whatever it was, Clem didn't want to get Wiseman offside. She was impressive. Stubborn at first, but switched on: clearly good at her job. If anyone was going to nail Doncaster, it would be her.

Clem lowered her voice and tried for a helpful tone. 'But being so far away from her body—couldn't the killer have thrown them over the edge? Whoever it was that pushed her?' Her mind was racing with this new information. She knew it was important. Somehow it was important that the sandals were off, one of them flung so far away they couldn't find it. Yes, flung. It could not have been the impact. But why would Jackson do that?

There was a silence in the room for a moment. Griffin looked like he might say something but then thought better of it—he'd said too much already. Wiseman was boring a hole in Clem's head with an icy stare.

'Ms Jones, you've been telling us how to do our job now for weeks. But you know what your job is?' Clem looked at her blankly. 'Your job is to tell the truth.'

Oh God, she'd found a hole, a lie in her story.

'Isn't there something more you need to tell us?' Wiseman spoke slowly, deliberately, each syllable loaded.

'Ah, no,' said Clem, all the confidence suddenly absent from her voice.

Wiseman scowled. 'How about the fact that Ralph Bennett didn't just happen to be passing by? That you had time to ring him and ask him to come and collect you?' All the muscles in Clem's throat tightened, her tongue felt huge in the back of her mouth. 'I've just been speaking with him. He rang us to make sure you're okay.'

Clem felt like she was falling—on the lip of the quarry with Wiseman at the top watching as she toppled backwards. Everything she had fought for was slipping away. She swallowed, tried to think of something to say, nothing came.

'So why couldn't you call an ambulance at that point, with

Membrey on the ground, bleeding heavily from a dog bite? And if you had time to call Mr Bennett, perhaps you also had time to tie the guy up.'

Wiseman's challenge was clear and pointed. It triggered a kick of adrenaline and Clem felt the zing coursing through her body. *Grab hold of the ledge and hang on, Jones.*

'Yeah, well...' She cleared her throat, stalling for think time. 'The bleeding...it didn't look that bad, and he had the gun, he was crazy, attacking us. We had to tie him up first. By the time we'd done that, the second guy showed up out front. We ran out and I called Ralph at the same time.'

'So the second guy—Jackson, you say?—he didn't just run after you and shoot?'

'No, he couldn't get in...the door was locked.' They would see there was no forced entry, but it didn't matter, she just needed to keep them engaged, get them back on track for now.

'And what else haven't you told us, Ms Jones? How about not knowing the first guy, why he was there with a gun? Huh?'

'Yeah, no. No idea.' She shrugged feebly.

Wiseman looked at her with contempt and shook her head. Both cops left the room again and came back with a revised version of the statement. Clem read through it under the sergeant's disgusted gaze while a clock ticked behind her. The phone call to Ralph was in there, the lie about the locked front door. She had said nothing about Torrens' gun and the water pistol though.

'Yes, all good,' she said.

The room prickled with silence. Griffin reached for a non-existent pen in his top pocket. He looked crestfallen—probably still stinging from his earlier stuff-up—as if this was a further sign of his lack of professionalism.

'Ah, sarge, you got a pen?'

Wiseman's eyes were locked on Clem. She had a pen in her top pocket but didn't move to retrieve it. Despite the air conditioning the room smelled of sweaty bodies from one or probably all of them. Clem had the perverse sense that Wiseman was quite happy about it.

'So, before you sign, let's just confirm,' said Wiseman, slow, measured, like she thought there was still a chance of getting more information. 'You know nothing about the dead man?'

'No. Like I said, sergeant, I've given you everything.'

'And the shooter doesn't know you or Torrens?'

'We've been through this. Torrens recognised him as Jackson.'

'Let's just hope your story lines up with what Torrens has to say then, eh? Wouldn't want to find any more holes in it.'

She emphasised, *your story*, as if it was a fairytale, a magic beanstalk and a unicorn rolled into one. Slowly, deliberately, Wiseman took the pen from her top pocket and placed it on the table, two fingers holding it there, clamped. Griffin looked on expectantly, eyes widening as Wiseman pressed down hard on the pen, not moving, her knuckles white with the force. The show of power was enough to send a crack through Clem's crumbling calm.

'Look, sergeant, I'm the victim here. Isn't being shot at enough, or do I actually have to get killed to prove that?'

'Oh heavens no, we wouldn't want you to go to those lengths,' she scoffed. There was a long, tense pause. Finally, she released her fingers, held them suspended for a second then flicked the pen with her finger so it skidded across the table. Clem lunged at it before it toppled over the edge, she missed and bent reflexively, scrambling around on the floor to pick it up.

Something pinged in Clem's head then, like a guitar string snapping. Her shoulders ached from the swim, she was squeezed out and limp like a dishcloth, and it felt like Wiseman had just slapped her, but she had no strength to respond. She imagined lying down with a cup of tea and falling asleep to the sound of the waves. But she needed that one thing, just one thing first: to know that Helen's murder investigation had finally begun.

'So, you're going to interview Doncaster now?' she said.

'Spoken to him. Rock-solid alibi,' said Wiseman.

'Oh for fuck's sake, sergeant. He hired a hitman to do it for him. Of course he has an alibi.'

'He was in Sydney,' she said without emotion, completely cold. 'Oh, and by the way, he tells us you jumped off his boat of your own accord, got spooked by something—he had no idea what—and then you proceeded to smash up his property. What was it constable?'

'Fuel filters and an inflatable dinghy, sarge.'

'Yes, that's right. Put a bloody great hole in the dinghy with a spear gun. Quite some damage, wasn't it constable?'

'Yes, sarge. Very nice dinghy, too: rigid inflatable, powder-coated aluminium hull, teak-finish deck. Even had a depth sounder.'

Wiseman gave Clementine the shadow of a smile and Clem felt her mouth sag.

'But you're after Jackson, right?'

'We're after the shooter, yes. A man's been killed and an old lady's been shot at—we've got everyone on it.' Wiseman spoke as if Clementine was holding them up.

'*I* was shot at, sergeant. It was me he wanted to hit, because I know he killed Helen.'

'Yes, you said that in your statement. We have forensics on your house and Mrs Henderson's car, there's road blocks in and out of Piama and extra officers coming up from Brisbane to help. We're doing everything we can.'

'But I told you, he's travelling by boat. A roadblock at Piama won't help if he comes ashore at Benton Bay or Jug Point or...any little beach.'

'Yep, exactly. The Great Sandy Straits are over seventy kilometres long and I can't count the number of bays and coves and inlets—he could come ashore anywhere. We simply can't monitor all of that coastline.'

'What about a chopper? Police boats?'

She chuckled, shook her head. 'This is Piama Beach not *Miami Vice*, Ms Jones.'

The realisation was arriving in Clem's head like an unwelcome guest—her lie had ruined everything. Jackson was going to slip the net and Doncaster wasn't even on their radar. And Helen? She had assumed this would now be a murder investigation. But was it?

'Sergeant Wiseman, are you investigating the death of Helen Westley?' she said with as much force as she could muster.

'The coroner ruled there were no suspicious circumstances around her death. You've made some allegations which we are understandably cautious about, given your propensity to play with the truth. And right now we have a shooting—an *actual* murder investigation—on our hands. That is our priority.'

She had got precisely nowhere. She'd been shot at, Torrens had a bullet hole in his shoulder, their friendship was in tatters and Helen was still a suicide statistic. Everything she'd been through, everything she'd sacrificed had achieved exactly nothing. Clem dropped her head, her mind stumbling at the multiple roadblocks. One thought made its way through and presented itself. It was not a plan, hardly even an idea, but it might help. Slowly she pulled out her mobile phone from her shorts pocket, held it in her lap under the table and switched on the camera. The room was quiet. She signed her name on the statement.

'Can I go now then, sergeant?' she said wearily.

'Yes. Griffin will see you out.' And before Wiseman could blink, Clem darted her hand across the table, grabbed the image of Jackson from the open folder and pulled it across the table onto her lap.

'Hey, what do you think you're doing. They're police documents,' cried Wiseman, standing up abruptly. Griffin erupted from his chair, knocking it sideways, and stormed around the table towards her.

Clem lined up the camera and clicked just as Griffin reached out to grab the photograph. Then she sat back in the chair, pocketing her phone.

'Just want to remember who tried to kill me, sergeant—the man who killed my friend, Helen. Nothing illegal about having a photograph. I expect you'll have this photo all over the news tonight anyway.'

Wiseman's mouth dropped open. Griffin looked confused. Clementine made for the door. She slammed it open, banging it against the wall, and walked out.

CHAPTER 21

The Commodore smelled musty. So much rain, so much damp heat. How do you get the smell out? Domestos? Bicarb? Anything but one of those sickening cardboard cologne things you hang off the mirror.

Pine plantations lined up either side of the road—their tidy rows an affront in this chaos. No order, no justice anywhere except these stupid rows of trees.

Clem's thoughts remained mushy with fatigue and disappointment. She was hungry, too. It was two o'clock in the afternoon and she still hadn't eaten anything since breakfast. She pulled into the last service station on the crumbling concrete fringe of Barnforth and ordered a yellowish sausage roll from the pie oven, looking over her shoulder every few seconds as she waited.

Stupid. Jackson wouldn't be anywhere near Piama or Barnforth. He'd be lying low, laughing at the cops somewhere. *Wake up, Jones.*

Back in the car she switched on the stereo, set her LOUD playlist on shuffle and hit the road again, gripping the greasy paper bag with one hand and steering with the other as the Hilltop Hoods thumped out 'Hard Road'. She screwed up the paper bag and threw it on the floor. Cee Lo Green came on and she wound the window down, shouting the chorus to the pine trees, every one of them, individually: 'Fuck you-oo-oo—WISEMAN!' her hair flying back off her face as she sped along the hundred-k stretch

245

towards Piama. A stream of humidity rushed inside the car and she wound the window up.

The fuzziness in her head was beginning to clear. She breathed sharply—three hard breaths, like a sprinter at the start line. Alert, stomach satisfied, pelting down the straight road as the pine plantations gave way to a crowded mess of gum trees and scrubby undergrowth.

Jackson was on the loose and dangerous. She had his photograph but she didn't know what good that would do. At least the cops were looking for him. It was Doncaster that enraged her though. It was as if he was a figure skater, skimming across the surface with a sparkling white toothy smile, and getting away with it. Wealth without consequence. Power and privilege like a screen around him. She had nothing substantive on him and as much as she hated to admit it, neither did Wiseman. And what was worse, he was going to get his slimy hands on Helen's land, her sanctuary. Turn it into some sort of theme park, desecrate Turtle Shores with concrete and artificial light and fairy floss and noise.

The land. There's a contract on foot—he's going to own the land. *Come on, Jones, think!* This is why Helen wanted you on board in the first place. *You're a lawyer, for Christ's sake.*

An idea started to form in her head, the legal elements lining up, like planks in a tower, rickety but gaining height. She wrenched the wheel left, pulled onto the gravel shoulder in a cloud of dust and a fishtail flourish, picked up her phone. Scrolling through her contacts, she tapped one and pressed the call button, waited as it rang.

'Clementine, what a delight to hear from you. How are you?'

Hamish Doncaster always sounded like he was lying on a banana lounge with a cocktail in his hand.

'Yeah, had better days. Did you see my text message?' He hadn't. She filled him in, the summarised version she'd given to the cops. He punctuated the story with shocked gasps and outrage at his father's role in all this.

246

'Oh my God, this is insane,' he said at last.

'Yep, a real life Loony Tunes. So tell me, do you know who the executor is for Helen's estate?'

'What? No. Why would I know? And what's that got to do with anything?'

'You bid at the auction, didn't you? You would have reviewed the contract beforehand.'

'*Pfft*. I was never going to buy, why would I look at the contract? I dealt with the agent and signed the stupid stat dec as I walked in, that was it.' She heard liquid being sucked up a straw. He had a cocktail. He had a friggin' cocktail.

'So the agent never mentioned the executor's name?'

'No. Why do you ask?'

There was a pause while Clem collected all her rage and funnelled it down into one simple imperative. 'He can't get Helen's land.'

'What? You mean my father? You're referring to my father?'

'Yes. We've got to stop your father getting his hands on Helen's land.'

'Oh dear. You've had a rough day, Clementine, and you're probably exhausted. Let me spell it out for you: he has a binding contract, the executor is obliged to complete, the transaction will settle and he will be the owner of that parcel of land.'

'I think I might have an avenue—'

'But Clementine, don't be foolish. Whoever the executor may be, he can't just pull out of the contract. Big Red will simply commence proceedings against him for specific performance and the court will agree and the land will be transferred to him. Doesn't the thing settle tomorrow anyway?'

'Yes, but I think there's a chance the contract could be validly rescinded.'

'Oh dear. Oh dearie, dearie me. You can't be serious.'

'Hear me out—'

'No, no, no. I don't care what crazy theory you're working on, you're talking about my father. You cannot take on His Redness. The last person who did that is now bankrupt and living in a disused fridge somewhere in Dubbo. Anyway, didn't you just say he hired someone to kill Helen? Not to mention you.'

'Forget that, focus on the transaction, the sale of Turtle Shores. That's all I care about right now. Your father participated in the auction fraudulently.'

'You don't mean that silly little statutory declaration? Surely not?'

'Yes,' she said, starting a Google search for Queensland courts on her iPad.

'But you know that's just a sideshow. The seller will still be bound.'

'Maybe, maybe not. Where are you, anyway? A resort somewhere?'

'Port Douglas. Why don't you come up?'

She ignored him. 'Here we go,' she said, typing in Helen's name and then selecting Deceased in the party field.

'He would have used one of his companies anyway,' said Hamish.

'He'll be the beneficial owner. The stat dec applied to the legal owner *and* the beneficial owner. It's misleading and deceptive, Hamish, and anyway, if someone or some entity was acting as his agent, we might still be able to sheet it home to him as principal.'

'Holy snapping subpoenas, Batman. You might be onto something there,' he said sarcastically. 'But what damage has the vendor suffered? Let me think...' She imagined him in his poolside outfit: black budgie smugglers, tanned abs, designer sunglasses... perhaps a white Panama hat—the whole box and dice. 'Oh yes, perfect! You could argue on behalf of the possums—as interested third parties, Your Honour—that they'll be disadvantaged if he concretes the place over.'

'I'm not saying it's watertight, smartarse, I'm just saying we might have a chance.'

'But it's all a pipe dream. Imagine the legal fees. His Redness will be literally throwing money at it. What executor would allow the estate to be whittled away to nothing like that? God, there won't be any estate left by the time my father's finished with them.' He drew a sharp breath. 'And can you please just stop saying "we"?'

'Yeah, yeah. It was the royal "we". Don't worry, you won't be receiving any instructions to act.'

'My dear Clementine—Charlie's Angel, Arya of Winterfell—you must let this slide. There is absolutely no point in taking on a legal battle with my father. I know this, you know this. You will be squashed like a pea, you will be roadkill. What you must do is get your barge pole out and push away. Get as far from his vile vessel as you can.'

Clementine was hardly listening at all now as the search result came up on her screen. 'Margaret Jeppeson,' she said.

'What? Who...'

'I have no idea. But I'm going to find out.'

\|/

The plastic ribbon of crime-scene tape had gone and the yellow fibro shanty looked different—a cold prickliness about it, as if it no longer trusted her.

Torrens' Patrol was in the driveway and the shed door hung open. Pocket trotted over as she got out of the car, tongue lolling. He seemed nervous and the tail wag was faltering. 'Come here, boy,' she said, fondling his ears with both hands. 'You're okay. We're all okay.' Sarge came over looking lost. She gave him a pat and a cuddle. 'You're a brave, brave boy.'

She shut the car door and peeked in the back window of Torrens' Patrol, cupping her face against the glass to neutralise the reflection. It was packed, ready to go. Esky, camp stove, duffel bag.

She poked her head in the shed. Silent and empty but for his footy, sitting forlorn under the bench in the shadows. She picked it up, flipped it twice from hand to hand, smoothed down the tiny tear near the lace. Bouncing it as she walked up the front path, it hit the pavement close to the point, yoyo-ing back into her hands. She liked the certainty of it and the comforting slap as it hit her palms. Memories of Katinga flooded in. The boys, Clancy, Wakely, each of them. She thought of the nine-strong Flood family; Bob Nicholls from the IGA and his man of the match award. Mrs Lemmon and her beanies and her Tom, 'smiling down from heaven'.

And Rowan. *Oh God, Rowan,* who'd saved her life when she didn't feel like it was worth saving. Who'd slipped, effortlessly, seamlessly, under her skin.

She stopped on the path. He was the one person to whom she'd told everything, weeping, distraught, his arms around her. Rowan was the one person in the world who knew her. And still he wanted her.

As if on cue, her phone rang. Rowan's name lit the screen.

He'd seen the news, shooting death in Piama, recognised the shanty...Yes, she was okay...Yes, it was linked to Helen...No, nothing to do with her. *Then why the shanty?* Well, okay, yes it was linked to her...

'You've found something and they're after you.'

She assured him the police were onto it...no, there was no police guard for her...it was all hands on deck to find the killer... no, nothing he could do...

There was a long pause. She watched a pale-headed rosella land on the roof of the shanty, its mate arriving just after— the brilliant yellow, the breathtaking violet.

Then his voice, distant. 'You can't pursue this. You have to leave it to the police.'

'I am leaving it to the police.'

'Yeah but, I mean…' He searched for the right words. 'You need to look after yourself…*really* look after yourself.'

It was not how she thought of herself—something to protect, safeguard. Not since the accident.

'Yep.' It was a brush-off and he picked it.

'No, I mean it. You…you've got to…' he fumbled for words. The rosellas spun around to face the yard with a quick glance at her and a nod, then took flight in a burst of colour, disappearing together into the bush next door.

'I have to go now,' she said.

'Wait. No.'

She sighed.

'I want to tell you something.'

A wave of exhaustion washed over her—nothing left in the tank. 'I don't think this is the time,' she said.

'No. It is the time. If there's one thing I've learnt it's to say the stuff you need to say when you have the chance.'

'It's okay, Rowan, really, it's okay.' *Oh God, how to end this?*

'I'm not good with words. But Clem, I've thought about it a lot and I was going to tell you when you got back, and…'

'No, no. Rowan, don't, it's going to be all right,' she said softly. She simply couldn't deal with this. Not now.

'…I need to tell you.' She closed her eyes for what was coming. 'I didn't…I wasn't looking for anything.' He paused, struggling to summons the courage or inspiration or something. 'But somehow when you arrived…' He cleared his throat. 'I'm just gonna say it, Clem…you arrived and it was like the rising sun on a clear blue day.'

Beautiful. Terrifying. Just his breathing and the waves collapsing on the beach in the backyard.

'And suddenly I felt like…I felt like I could live again. Like really live. Something I hadn't felt since Kate.' The breeze sweeping across her shoulders and rustling through the branches of the palm tree and Rowan's voice speaking these impossible things. 'And I can hardly believe I'm saying this, but it seemed then, with you, like anything was possible again. I mean it, Clem, anything...even love.'

Her hand began to tremble on the phone.

'I know this is a lot. I never intended to say it over the phone. But there's a time and a moment and if you miss it, it's gone, and I learned that lesson once.' His voice cracked the slightest bit. 'And oh God, you make me do crazy things, you make me say crazy things.'

He'd driven five hours to save her. He'd gone and spoken these words—words that he'd prepared and crafted and lovingly packaged up for her like a gift for her return.

'You don't have to say anything,' he said.

'I can't say anything. I'll cry,' she whispered.

'Oh. Sorry. I mean, no. I'm not sorry. Just...just be careful, okay?'

'I will,' she said. She could not find the strength to say anything more.

\\/

She stood outside for a long while, hugging the football to her chest, then wiped her eyes and took the steps up to the verandah. The flyscreen door slammed shut behind her as she entered the lounge room, stuffy with heat. In the kitchen, Torrens was at the sink, his back to her, filling a bottle of water from the tap. He had a sling around his neck but both arms free.

'Hey mate,' she said. 'How's the shoulder?'

'Yeah, I'll live,' he said, without turning around.

'Not bothering with the sling?'

'Nah. Pain in the arse.' He spoke to the sink, couldn't bear to look at her.

There was an uncomfortable silence, just the sound of the running water. Pocket came into the kitchen, sniffed the spot where Membrey had lain. It was scrubbed clean.

'Did the cops...?' she said, pointing at the floor.

He turned to face her, following her hand, shook his head and took an aggressive swig at the bottle of water.

'Oh geez, Torrens, you didn't have to clean up. You're injured.'

'I enjoyed it,' he said coldly. 'Membrey bled, a lot.'

She felt slightly ill. This side of Torrens was still a shock. He turned back to the sink and began filling another water bottle. Definitely leaving. Preparing for the long road trip. At least it wasn't bourbon.

'Hey, Torrens, nothing wrong with your legs, how about a kick?' she said, handpassing the ball to herself. The words hung in the air, flat and leaden. He didn't even give her the courtesy of an answer.

Pocket was sitting at Torrens' feet, looking up, hoping for a scrap. Her fluffy friend would be the only one left once Torrens had gone. She felt like crying again.

'When are you heading off then?' she said at last.

'Now.'

Finally, he turned around, leaned against the sink, drying his hands on the hand towel. The width of him nearly blocked all the light from the window.

'Come with me,' he said.

Asking her. Proud, but still asking. A lump formed in her throat. She couldn't speak.

'Coach...' He didn't go on with the sentence. Just the word was enough. Loaded. He stood to his full height, threw the towel onto the bench. 'You're everything that's any good in Katinga. There's nothin' there without you.'

He wore a black singlet and his shoulder was heavily dressed with white tape. The navy blue sling hung like a sash across his chest.

'I mean. I just…' He looked away, his face in profile, turned his gaze back on her, every inch of his skin preparing for the words that he wished he didn't have to say. 'I just…Well…Can you just come home, Jonesy?'

Oh God. Don't. Don't fucking cry, Jones.

She pulled out a chair and sat down, quietly, as if to pretend she wasn't there. She slipped her legs under the table. Pocket gave up, turned on his heel and barged out through the dog door. The flap swung on the hinges, squeaking.

Her mind was clicking over. Messy, unfocused thoughts. The kind of thinking she hated, flashes of emotionally charged reason, dis-reason because it's not reason, un-reason. She could go. With Torrens. Noel would be home in two days. Sarge would be fine. She picked at the aluminium edge on the table. She was still holding the football in her other hand, the leather warm in her palm. Torrens reached out and grabbed it, his huge mitt instantly shrinking the ball to the size of an orange.

'Ha. Getting slow Jonesy,' he grinned, taking two steps back, his backside up against the flyscreen door, 'You need to get back into training.' He dropped the ball neatly onto his boot, kicked a tiny little high floater, spinning end on end, just missing the ceiling light. She reached up and caught it cleanly, smiling, despite herself.

She imagined herself at training, the sweet slap of leather on leather, the smack of the physical contest, skin on skin, the inky sky and the stars as the men jogged their warm-down lap. She could be their coach again. They would defend their trophy with everything they had. And win or lose, she would be there to celebrate or console, it didn't really matter which—it was only the quest that mattered.

But what about Helen? Didn't she matter? The silence was growing. She must give him a response.

'I need a drink of water is what I need.'

He smiled, grabbed a glass from the overhead cupboard, tap

full bore, placed it gently before her on the table. Then he rushed outside, came back with a lemon from the tree, cut off a slice and dropped it into her glass with a splash. Big grin.

God, the hope in his eyes. *Oh Christ.*

'I heard from Dad,' he said. 'He's coming back from the Territory, got a job in Earlville.'

'That's great news.' She was speaking to the table, unwilling to risk tears if she looked at him. *Rude. Gutless. Pull yourself together.* 'Excellent, bloody excellent news, mate.'

'He asked me when training's starting.'

She nodded. There was some sort of emptiness in her chest, breathing didn't seem to fill it.

'Jackson's going to slip the net,' she said. 'Doncaster's going to get off.'

His smile faded.

She stared at the floor. 'Helen's nothing but a statistic. Doncaster's building a resort at Turtle Shores, on her sanctuary. He killed her. Now he's going to screw what's left of her.'

\1/

After Torrens left she lay on the bed for a while, the rusty fan busting its guts against the heat. The air in the shanty felt stale. They hadn't said anything more until she tried to give him the footy back as he walked to his car. He waved her off; said he wouldn't be needing it.

'Aren't you going back to Katinga?'

'Dunno,' he'd said and wouldn't tell her any more. If he wasn't taking the footy he wasn't returning to the new life he'd begun. With Membrey gone, it should have been so different. He should have been going to work, buying a place in Katinga, taking his mum on a trip to Hawaii.

Her phone rang. Brady.

'You all set for the working bee this arvo?' he said, in his raspy smoker's voice. She'd forgotten about the working bee. They'd planned to make new banners and posters for their next protest in Noosa. Gaylene was hosting it at her house.

'Mate, I can't make it, sorry. There's been a bit of trouble. A bloke died today, here in my kitchen.'

'What? Man, that's terrible.'

'Yeah. It's been a nightmare. I'm just not up to the working bee today.'

'Who was it?'

'You wouldn't know him. A visitor. He wasn't from round here. Listen, there's more bad news. Doncaster's going to turn Turtle Shores into a bloody resort.'

'Oh fucking hell, no way! If the mine doesn't kill off the turtles a resort sure will! What the fuck's wrong with him? The bastard's supposed to be supporting us!'

'Yeah, I know. It's...I don't even know how to describe it. It's just shocking. We'll have to get ourselves organised with a new strategy for him now. And get some new donors. That's why Noosa's important. We need some wealthy holidaymakers on board. Can you look after the working bee for me? Make sure we get everything we need done?'

'Bloody working bee. I just want to go over and cut his lily-white throat.'

'Fuck's sake, Brady, just cool it for now. We need to meet next week and sort out a plan. It'll be all about that covenant. We'll need the lawyers to get onto it. So get ready for Noosa—we're gonna need that money.'

Brady was disappointed. A legal campaign sounded insufferably tame.

She ate a can of tuna at the kitchen table, trying to work through the angles. How had Jackson got Helen up to the top of the cliff? Why had he removed her sandals before he'd thrown her over? The

256

police had failed to do a proper search for tracks so no one could be sure she hadn't been marched up there at gunpoint. But what were the alternatives? Were there any alternatives?

She opened the fridge, crouched down and took out a can of Coke from the bottom shelf. Stayed down there for a while, letting the cold air envelope her, wake her up.

It came to her quickly. She wondered why she hadn't thought of it before.

She rang Wiseman. She was investigating a shooting, a murder, *if you don't mind.* A myriad of details to cover, not enough staff, most of them manning roadblocks, the homicide guys from Brisbane hadn't arrived yet...She didn't have time to go chasing theories about a suicide.

Clem hung up, pacing the kitchen.

Jackson was on the loose but he wouldn't come anywhere near Piama or Barnforth. Not with all the roadblocks. But she needed to get to the airport. It was an hour away from Piama, less than twenty minutes from Barnforth. Could she risk it? He'd be keeping his distance, surely.

She took the small cardboard box from the dresser in the bedroom and put it in the front zip pocket of her backpack. Then she turned her laptop on. While it was powering up she gazed out the sliding door into the backyard. An older couple strolled along the track between the yard and the beach, hand in hand. No one she knew—grey nomads from the caravan park, most likely. Pocket was up and giving them the usual over-the-top reaction, running up and down, barking himself stupid. Sarge raised his big head, blinked, lowered it again into the thick grass— the dog equivalent of an eye-roll. Pocket was a great little dog: smart, obedient and easy to train. But with Sarge you got a sense of worldly wisdom that meant he'd only engage if there was a real threat.

She stuck her head out the door and called him over.

257

Pocket got there first. 'No, not you noisy. The other one.' She shooed him away and let Sarge inside, closing the sliding door behind him, and went to get his lead.

She printed off a copy of the sneaky photograph she'd taken in the interview room, then she did a search on the laptop, found the image she was after and printed that off too. She typed in the name *Margaret Jeppeson*. It took a moment but then there it was, on the screen in front of her—a LinkedIn profile. A photograph of a woman with an immaculate silver bob and a job title displayed in the text underneath:

Press Secretary and Head of Media, Office of the Premier,
New South Wales

It was Helen's friend. Margaret Jeppeson, the executor of Helen's will, was Maggie from the funeral: 'Noosa Darling' herself.

\|/

Clem was tense throughout the drive to the airport, but it was uneventful. Sarge stuck his head out the window for most of it, his gums ballooning like parachutes in the wind. Pocket, much aggrieved at being left behind, had whined at the door. But the last time she'd had them both in the car it had been Circus Oz in a shoebox.

She drove past the airport and followed the *General Aviation* sign as the road skirted all the way past the airfield, around the back of some hills and then cut back in on the other side of the runway. She passed a number of hangars and other big sheds on industrial paddocks, and a tiny takeaway shop on the corner. She parked the car in the shade and left Sarge tied to the tow ball with a thin piece of string. The tug on his collar was enough to persuade him to stay put and settle himself in the long grass near the bowl of water she'd left. He'd bust through the string easily enough if she needed him.

She entered the hangar, stood at the counter and rang the bell, waited for the aircraft noise from the runway to subside and rang it again. There were a couple of notices taped to the counter, along with a cardboard box full of pencils and a grubby notepad. A helicopter sat dormant in the shadows at the other end of the hangar and another stood outside on the tarmac, shiny in the sun. To the right was a Colorbond office the size of a garden shed with one grimy louvre window. The office door opened and a man walked over briskly.

'Sorry to keep you,' he said, smiling.

'No problem.' Clem smiled back.

'How can I help you?'

She reached into her backpack, pulled out Jackson's photograph and placed it on the counter.

'I'm looking for this fellow, wondered if you might know him?'

The man looked at the photograph, squinting. 'Ummm, I don't think...Why do you ask?'

'I found his wallet. He bought a cake from me at the school fete and left it behind,' she lied. 'I didn't realise it was there until I was packing up but it had a little helicopter key ring inside it. I just thought maybe he might be a pilot.'

He looked at her, sceptical, apparently weighing up the privacy implications. 'Oh, right. Wasn't there a drivers licence or a credit card in it?'

'Well, that's the thing, there was a drivers licence, that's where I got this photo, but his name and address were blacked out with Texta, which was odd. And there was a fair bit of cash, so...'

'I guess you could hand it in to the cops, though?' said the man, obviously uncomfortable.

'Oh yeah, first place I went to, but the station was closed. I heard they've got their hands full with a murder, not to mention the usual protesters and druggies and whatnot. Anyway, this guy said he was moving to Sydney, so I thought I might be able to return it to him before he left.' Clem put on what she hoped was a concerned-citizen look, tugging at the back of her neck and grimacing with the burden of it.

'Wouldn't he go see the cops though? See if someone had handed it in?'

'Hmmm, not sure he would actually. See I think maybe that's the reason he's tampered with his licence...you know, lying low or something. I don't know, I sort of got the feeling when he said he was going interstate...the way he said it...well I just thought he might be trying to avoid the cops, if you know what I mean.'

The guy hesitated and she didn't blame him. This was sounding thinner and thinner.

Did he think she *was* the police? Did he think if the guy wanted a low profile then she should respect that? Maybe he just felt the man shouldn't be assisted in whatever criminal activity he was engaged in. Too many reasons for him not to help her. Time to give him a reason.

'This was in the wallet too,' she reached into the front zip of her backpack, pulled out the printout from Noel's printer. It was a photograph of a young boy, the words 'In loving memory' across the top, dates at the base—a six-year-old's funeral program.

'I saw this and I just thought, man, what if this is the only photo he has of his son or something. I mean, I wouldn't know, of course, but still, if it was me, I'd want it back.'

She hoped the manager guy had kids, hoped he knew someone who'd lost a child. She bit her lip as he stared at the picture of the boy—blue eyes, red fireman's hat, messy dark hair above a cheeky grin. The man sighed and his eyes darted another quick look at Clementine and then he picked up the photograph of Jackson again.

'Yeah...might be the guy who hired the R44 a few weeks back, now I come to think of it.'

The GPS he'd fixed to her front grille was transmitting perfectly. She'd been into Barnforth cop shop, then she'd gone home and the movement alert had pinged on his phone again just before three. Since then he'd tracked her on the app as she headed north-west up the main road from Piama and taken the turn-off that led due west.

It was an opportunity, perhaps his last. It was risky, after all the cock-ups, but the client wouldn't pay until the job was done. He should have insisted on more money up front; it'd been a while since he'd had any decent cashflow.

And now it was turning into a clusterfuck, a complete and utter disaster. But the job had to be done. If nothing else, his reputation was on the line.

He headed north on the highway from the safe house, keeping an eye on her track. He was about fifteen minutes behind. She took the turn towards the airport. Wouldn't be a bad option for her, flying interstate, he thought. This road would also take her to the highway south to Brisbane which might be easier for him than the airport. Small country terminal, it wouldn't be straightforward, but there was still a chance he could hustle her into the car, take her out bush and dispose of her there. Just needed the right set of circumstances.

He took the stolen Hilux up to 119 kph, less than ten per cent over the speed limit—didn't want to attract any more heat from the cops.

After the first airport turn-off, where she kept going, he started getting nervous. He watched to see if she took the second one but she sailed straight past that too. Okay, so she was heading south on the highway to Brisbane.

He watched as the blip on the screen went straight past the highway turn-off and followed the road around to the other side of the airfield and...

Fucking bitch!

She wasn't going to Brisbane and she wasn't flying out, she was going to the fucking helicopter company! He stepped on the accelerator and roared the Hilux up to 180.

CHAPTER 22

Clem made the excuse of going outside to check on the dog while the manager went into the office to look at his records. She made a call to the police station.

'Jackson hired a helicopter...Turners Aviation...other side of the airport.'

'What? When?'

'The manager's checking now, but he said a few weeks ago. Seems to line up.'

'Shit a brick,' said Wiseman under her breath.

At least she was quick on the uptake, Clem thought. She could see the manager walking back to the counter, a large hard-covered ledger in his hand. She started making her way back in. 'And the sandals—I reckon he took them off her feet so he could make the tracks himself...had Helen tied up or unconscious or whatever in the chopper, walked around the rocky plateau to the bottom, then put them on himself for the walk up in the sand.' There was a long pause at the other end of the line. 'You still there, sergeant?'

'Yes. Yes. Ah, Clementine...this is...bloody hell...have you confirmed the date?'

The manager had the book open on the counter—'Just a sec.' He was pointing at an entry dated 12 November, a date etched forever in Clementine's memory. She swallowed hard, turned away and walked out of earshot. 'Same day Helen died. It's him, Wiseman, it's him.'

'Fuck. Fucking hell.' Wiseman let out a groan. 'Yeah...well... that changes things, I think.'

'Yeah, it does, doesn't it?' Clem detected the note of remorse in her voice—this was not the time to dig the boot in. 'Look, just get out here, will you?'

Wiseman was out the door and on her way before the call had even ended. Clem heard her tell Griffin to hold the fort and brief the Brisbane cops when they arrived.

'Okay, here you go,' said the manager. 'His name's Peter Anderson and I've got a mobile number for him if you want to write it down.'

'That's great, thank you.' She typed the fake name and number into her phone, feeling fresh hope, a lightness and a tremendous burst of energy now that Wiseman was on her way, now that something would finally be done for Helen. 'My brother always wanted to be a helicopter pilot,' she said. 'So once you have your licence, you can just hire a helicopter?'

'Yeah, some mobs won't do it—they'll only charter with their pool of pilots. We're okay with it if they've got a clean record. Especially if it's just for one person, not some sort of joy ride or party thing.'

She felt a chill down her spine. He'd hired it for one person but Helen had been there too. Forced at gunpoint? Drugged and carried on?

She chatted with the guy—his name was Mike—for a while longer about the cost of pilot training, the best way of going about it, until she heard the sound of car tyres on gravel. Too soon for Wiseman, surely? She turned and saw a white ute roll past the wide-open hangar doors into the carpark. She turned back to Mike, continuing the conversation. She heard a car door open and then the barking started—that low, throaty boom. Sarge's danger bark. He must have recognised the driver's smell.

A spark fired in the back of her brain. It took a microsecond for the realisation to kick in. 'Oh God, quick,' she said, fumbling as she scooped up the photograph and the helicopter hire record on the counter, shoving them in her backpack. 'We have to hide!' She rushed around to his side of the counter.

'What the?' said Mike as she grabbed his arm.

'Now! The guy in the photograph. He's here. He's a killer.'

'Piss off,' he said, shrugging her arm away. Oh God, the story she'd told, why would Mike believe her now?

'No, no, I mean it. Quick!' she was pleading, terror in her eyes, pulling at his arm.

Mike pushed her off again. 'Go and hide if you want but it's my place, I've done nothing wrong and I'm not hiding,' he said, his legs spread wide and his arms primed away from his body, like a boxer, ready for the bell.

The sound of footsteps crunching on the gravel outside. *Oh shit. Oh shit.*

'Then...then just act natural,' she said, backing away towards the office. 'Tell him I've gone up the street for a burger. And whatever you do, don't tell him you told me his name!' She ran full pelt for the office and shut the door behind her, heart pumping.

How did Jackson know she was here? She'd told no one where she was going; she was sure she hadn't been followed.

She peered through the open window. Mike was standing at the counter looking confused. *Do something Mike, anything but just stand there, please.* She saw a man's shadow approaching the hangar. Mike seemed to pull himself together, picked up a pen from the box, leaned on the counter, began writing something on the notepad as the shadow became a human form, silhouetted in the wide hangar doorway.

She ducked her head down even though she knew she couldn't be seen from outside the office. Sarge was going off outside, but he must have stayed where he was. She checked around her. A second door, on the other side of the office, leading outside to the carpark. She had to contact Wiseman, warn her. She pulled out her phone, turned it to silent, found the contact and typed:

Jackson is here. He's seen my car. Danger!

She peeked out the window again. They were talking. She could just hear their voices. Jackson was saying something about *the chick driving the Commodore wagon*. Mike pointed in the direction of the takeaway shop. She couldn't see their facial expressions. Sarge had stopped barking.

She tapped in another text, her thoughts darting all over the shop. How good a liar was Mike? If Mike said she'd gone up the street, would Jackson leave and wait for her somewhere?

She pressed send on the second text to Wiseman: *I'm in the office 2 the right. He doesn't know I'm here. Sarge is out front. The hangar manager...Mike...is talking to him at front counter. Be careful!*

She checked the time. Wiseman ought to be here any minute. A roll of sweat trickled down her forehead and onto the side of her face. Her shirt stuck to her back. She started scrolling through her contacts for Constable Griffin's number. As she got to the Gs she heard the sound of a car out front and looked out. A police vehicle rolled into view.

Oh God. Did she get the text?

She watched as Jackson turned, saw the car, yelled at Mike, 'Fucking liar!' It took him three steps to get around the counter, whipping a gun out from the back of his trousers.

'Hey, hey, hold on, mate.' Mike threw his hands skyward.

Jackson grabbed his wrist and twisted his arm behind his back, gun levelled at his temple. 'Don't give me any trouble, *mate*. You're dead meat if you do.'

He positioned Mike between him and the door, began walking him backwards towards the choppers, his eyes on the doorway facing the carpark.

'Where's the keys to the R44?' he snapped as they passed the office.

'In the ignition,' said Mike, his voice shaky.

'Fuel?'

'Half a tank.'

Clem's hands were trembling on the phone. Should she rush out, warn Wiseman? Too late—Wiseman appeared in the doorway.

'Keep your hands away from the gun, sergeant, or this guy cops it,' Jackson yelled. Mike's eyes were bulging, his face white as chalk.

Wiseman stopped, frozen, her arms held out from her body, away from her gun. She looked tiny.

'Not a good idea, Jackson,' she said, without flinching. 'Gonna get you in worse trouble.'

Clem's heart leapt at the sound of her voice—no more ruffled than if she'd sprung a teenager breaking into a lolly shop.

'Just keep your hands clear—that's it, out wide—and no one gets hurt,' Jackson snarled.

'I can't let you do this, you know that,' said Wiseman. 'Let the man go and put the gun down. You've got so much to lose doing something stupid like this.'

'Shut up!' yelled Jackson.

'His name's Mike.' She had got the text. Why hadn't she waited for back up? *Trying to make up for her mistake?* 'Got a family, Mike?'

'Yeah. Wife, two little boys,' said Mike, voice trembling, barely audible.

'Hear that Jackson? Judge'll go for those victim statements. That's years on your sentence, maybe a couple for each kid.'

'Shut the fuck up!' he yelled.

'Bet you're ropeable things have got so out of hand. Shooting at old ladies...embarrassing,' said Wiseman. 'But you can reel it in now...save yourself even more embarrassment. Put the gun down.'

God, she was ice cool. *C'mon Wiseman, you've got this.*

'You know we'll find you. We'll track you down. Come on Jackson, there's better options than this.' Wiseman took two steps forward.

'Stand back!' yelled Jackson, continuing to back away past the chopper inside the hangar and towards the one on the tarmac.

'Let's talk it through. Just hold up there, Jackson, and we can talk it through.' She took two more steps.

So gutsy.

He kept moving backwards, tucked behind Mike with the gun pressed up hard on the manager's head.

'All right. Let me lay out the facts, then. Where are you going to land?' Another two steps forward, her hand hovering over the holster on her hip. *Moving closer for the shot.* 'You think you can just take off and disappear? Air traffic control are already on it.'

God, Clem hoped so.

'You'll be tracked to within a millimetre. Wherever you land, there'll be a SOG team waiting for you.'

Was she bluffing? Maybe they could lock in on it. Clem ducked down, started typing a text to Griffin. Her fingers fumbling over the screen, her breath coming shallow and short as she typed. *Jackson's here at Turners Aviation hangar. Gun and hostage. Wiseman in danger. Get air traffic control to track R44. And get here. Fast!*

She pressed send and began to stand up again. As her eyes rose above the window ledge, she caught movement from the carpark—Sarge, moving slowly but purposefully towards the hangar. He'd broken the string. He must've heard the raised voices, knew Clem was in there. The switch had been flicked. She couldn't breathe.

Sarge paused, listened. His flanks twitching, eyes bright, on high alert. Then he extended his throat, head pushing forward, letting out a single growl as he set off at a canter, his shape appearing in the doorway, picking up speed, gums drawn back, top and bottom fangs like icepicks, galloping now, straight for Jackson. Clem threw open the office door, then everything happened at once. Jackson swung his gun towards the dog; Mike seized the moment and twisted himself out of Jackson's grip with a loud grunt, jerking Jackson's gun arm as a shot rang out. Wiseman drew her gun and took aim at Jackson. Another shot. Sarge shying at the sound, his claws skidding on the concrete just outside the office as Clem lunged for his collar, screaming his name. Two more shots, and then Wiseman was falling backwards, a look of surprise on her face and a crimson flower spreading across the front of her shirt, collapsing to the floor. Her head hit the concrete and bounced. Her cap came off and rolled to one side.

Clem screamed. Jackson was on the floor, pushing himself up on one knee, injured, turning his body. Mike was laid out halfway to the counter, then he was crawling, scrambling to his feet, running out the back of the hangar and disappearing to the right.

Wiseman's eyes...

Like the woman in the car crash, her head on the steering wheel, blood in her hair...the eyes...vacant.

Jackson swung his gun hand towards her. Clem felt the surge of adrenaline, the backs of her hands prickling and her heart racing as she tugged Sarge into the office and slammed the door behind them. She raced to open the door that led outside and ran, yelling at Sarge to come. She sprinted for the car, the dog right behind her, flinging open the back door of the Commodore.

'Get in, Sarge!'

She saw the hesitation in his eyes. He slowed, stopped halfway to the car, then turned back towards the hangar, planting his front paws wide, standing guard. He wasn't going to move. He was too big to lift.

She jumped into the back seat, yelling, 'Sarge, *come!*' He glanced over his shoulder at her, took one last look back at the hangar and then swivelled and launched himself into the car as she scrambled into the driver's seat and took off, the back door still swinging open and Jackson appearing in her rearview mirror, gripping his leg. A shot hit the back of the car as she spun the tyres in a tight one-eighty, now pointing towards the carpark exit. She slammed her foot down on the accelerator as another shot shattered the rear window.

She was away now, and in the mirror she saw Jackson moving painfully, dragging his leg, towards the white ute.

\\//

Wiseman. Fuck. Oh fuck. Ambulance. Searching for her phone as she reached ninety k's down the narrow road. Where the hell? *Shit!* She'd dropped it on the floor of the office when she grabbed for Sarge's collar.

Griffin will be on his way. He'll be there soon. But Wiseman was dead. No: Wiseman wasn't dead, she had to think that. Griffin would be there. Mike would call an ambulance. She forced herself to switch her mind to her own situation.

Where to? The terminal? Lots of people there. No, there'd be no one there at this time of the day, the daily flight from Sydney was hours away. *Police station?* No one there. Not a fucking soul in this two-cop backwater. She would pass Griffin coming from Barnforth, though. The relief. Then the switch flicked to horror as it dawned on her. In her panic, she'd turned left out of the carpark, back onto the road she'd come in on. The road from Piama. Griffin would be coming from the other direction, from Barnforth. Griffin would arrive at the hangar and Jackson would be long gone.

How badly hurt was he? Would he flee or would he chase her? She'd have at least a kilometre head start by the time he got going, maybe more if his leg was really bad. But how did he know she was at the hangar? *Think, Jones!*

GPS tracker. He'd stuck one on the car somewhere. Of course, why not? He'd had plenty of opportunity.

Where to go? Around the hills and back towards Barnforth to the shopping centre? Lots of people. He could still get her and she'd be putting others at risk. Drive to Noosa? Or better still, Gympie—there'd be a police station there. She checked the fuel gauge. Half-full, more than enough.

She tried to think herself into Jackson's situation. He knows that I know he killed Helen. He's been paid to kill me. That's two reasons to hunt me down, two reasons to finish me. But no one knows Doncaster hired him. There was probably a middle man, a handler of some kind—so maybe Jackson doesn't even know who his client is. It would be smart to ensure there was nothing connecting them. Was that something Jackson, a professional, might consider worth protecting? He had to have future clients that trusted him to never give them away.

But she didn't know. How could she know? This criminal world, it might as well be another planet.

The Commodore hurtled towards the first bend around the hills, the wind roared through the open back door. Sarge was sticking to the other side of the seat: his back pressed against the passenger's side, he was tentatively raising his nose towards the open door and into the airflow, mouth open. She geared down and braked hard for the first bend, the car juddering as it slowed, Sarge thudding into the back of the front seat, then she slammed her right hand down on the wheel, and the car jumped sideways, slamming the door shut. She pushed down on the accelerator for the short stretch to the next bend.

She could take the highway and head south, to Gympie or Noosa and a proper police station. But the fact would remain: there would be nothing to tie Doncaster to Helen's death. He'd get away with it. The wrongness of that wrenched at her thoughts. The rich man exchanging other people's lives for more riches. Sitting on his money pile above the law and secretly screwing over ordinary mortals, beautiful people like Helen.

Clem had to forge the connection, bridge the gap between Doncaster and Jackson.

She thought through it all again. Jackson could track her, follow her. That meant she could lead him to wherever she wanted him to be. The GPS was like an invisible rope between them. The idea struck her, like a piece of four by two to the back of the head. What if she led Jackson to Doncaster? Might that throw them off? Force the two of them into error? Jackson might not follow her, precisely to avoid the connection with his client. But then at least he'd be off her tail. Win win.

She threw the car around a corner and into another straight, then patted the front zip section in her backpack. It was still there. There could yet be a way to nail Doncaster.

Her palms were sweating on the wheel, her heart raced with each corner, holding her breath as she concentrated into it, then inhaling sharply. She geared down for another bend, braked, accelerated, the chassis swinging wide and the wheels screeching. *Slow it down, Jones. You crash, Jackson catches up, you die.* The sun was glaring. Her sunglasses had fallen off at some point in the chaos so she flipped the visor down, sat taller in the seat, slipping her head into the shade.

She cleared the last of the bends, passed the big green sign—intersection two hundred metres up ahead. Turn right for Gympie and Noosa and Brisbane and any kind of civilisation. Straight ahead to the Piama dead end.

She blinked hard, swallowed, planted her foot down and roared past.

\|/

He lifted his leg up onto the running board, groaning. The bitch cop had got him in the kneecap. He'd never felt so much pain in his life. He stopped, panting, sweat dripping from his face, waiting for the burning to ease, then forced his leg bent and up into the cab, screaming in pain as he manoeuvred it down into the footwell.

He'd shot a cop. 'A fucking cop!' he roared to the dirty windscreen.

Now he really needed that money. That and his fake passport were the only things that could save him now.

He got the Hilux into drive and used his left leg to work the accelerator, checking the tracking app as he got onto the road. He was doing around a hundred k's when he felt a thump, then the vibration started. A slight shudder in the wheel. Oh, you're kidding, you're fucking kidding—flat tyre.

You've got her on the GPS. Just take it easy and keep driving, it might last the distance.

He dropped back to sixty. In the hills, he was down to a crawl, trying to keep the tyre on the wheel. Then, as he pulled out onto the straight stretch he heard the flapping. Strips of tyre whipping around, probably inside the wheel housing. Brakes, suspension, who knew.

He kept driving, looking out for another unoccupied car.

How had things gone so bad on this job?

He swore to God it was going to be his last. His very last.

CHAPTER 23

Clem pulled up at the gate and pressed the buzzer. The green creeper that hung in lustrous strands over the edge of the concrete wall made her think of tentacles, tendrils and how would she get out of here once she was in. A cockatoo shrieked somewhere far away and Sarge shifted from one paw to the other on the back seat, still anxious.

Doncaster's voice: 'Yes?'

Good, the maid wasn't in. 'Hello. It's Clementine Jones. Can I come in please?' There was a long silence. She'd dived off his yacht, destroyed his dinghy with a spear gun. He knew that she knew.

The intercom clicked: 'You've got a nerve.' Then a clunk. He'd hung up. He was referring to the inflatable, still pretending he's got nothing to do with Helen's death. *Fucking jerk must think I'm stupid—or he's untouchable. Or both.*

She buzzed again, checking her rear-view mirror, expecting Jackson to arrive at any moment. There was no response. She held the buzzer down, let it loose, pressed it again, counting to five before releasing her finger.

'What on earth do you want?'

'I think we should talk, Andrew. I need to explain,' she said, leaning across the open car window to speak into the intercom. 'And I have some information for you. It's about the resort.'

She could almost hear the cogs ticking over.

'What are you gonna do? Crash your car into my house, take

274

out a garden bed?' he growled.

'I'm sorry about your dinghy. I really am. It was all a bit crazy, I had a lot going on.' *Oh Lord, this ridiculous, make-believe dance.* 'I'll leave the car out on the road if you like.'

A pause. Would he be calling someone? Jackson's middle man? Not if he knew Jackson had a GPS tracker on her car. But he probably wouldn't know about that. He'd have gone out of his way to avoid knowing any details: to maintain the clear air between him and the hired help.

'I can help you with the covenant,' she said. 'I have inside information. It'll help you with the resort.' The lies were so fluent. So much practice.

Another pause. Then: 'Leave the car outside. Walk in and don't bring anything with you, no bags.'

'Got it,' she said, with the smallest of fist pumps behind the wheel.

The buzzer sounded and the heavy iron gate began to roll sideways. She took something no bigger than a ten cent piece from the front pocket of her bag and stuffed it in her pocket. She left the windows halfway down for Sarge and got out of the car, walking through the gate as it closed behind her. Sarge gave a couple of woofs towards her back.

'It's all right, mate. I'll be back soon. Just wait there for me.' His eyes flickered left and right. Not sure about all this, not sure at all. The gate began rumbling back.

There was a cool damp in the air as she walked across the covered timber walkway. Full gloss green crowded across from both sides, narrowing the path and forming a complete canopy above her head. She could smell the mist and the musty earth, the rotting foliage deep down. Birds called in languid bursts; in the quiet in between, she heard her sneakers creaking on the timber, felt the sweat turning to salt on her back. She imagined Helen walking up this path—first to seek donations, later to enjoy an

275

evening meal, a night of intimacy with a man who'd professed interest in her cause, and in her. *You would have given him all of yourself, of course, free and generous.*

Oh, Helen.

She rang the doorbell and waited on the slate portico, blackened timber columns keeping guard. She felt a tremor in her fingers. What was she getting into here, at this fortress? Jackson would have seen her car here on the app. He'd be deciding whether to follow. Wiseman? Had the ambulance arrived? *But she's dead, you saw that she was dead.* She gulped, gripped her fists, tried to focus.

This was for Wiseman too, now. Wiseman and Helen.

The door was frosted glass, surrounded by more glass in timber frames. She could see Doncaster coming down the staircase. He'd want to check her out before he opened the door: she waved her hands to signify she'd brought nothing with her.

The door opened. There he was in his pale, redheaded glory, a touch of sunburn on his muscled neck. He seemed bigger, stronger than before. His mouth was set in a hard line as he ushered her silently inside. There didn't seem to be a way to make the situation less awkward so she just nodded and kept her head down.

'Come this way.' He led her across the tiled foyer onto a vast deck surrounding the bluest of infinity pools and looking straight out into the raw cool of the forest.

Damn, outside. This was not ideal. She flicked the switch on the listening device in her pocket. She hoped it worked as well as the last one. This was one of the waterproof ones that had been held up in the mail. She headed for the outdoor table, a heavy teak job. She turned to face him as he made his way out, a grim look on his face, took her hand out of her pocket and leaned back on the table, her fingers slipping underneath and pressing up, holding it there ten seconds before gently releasing the pressure. The device stuck firm.

'Thank you for seeing me, Andrew,' she said, 'Um, I don't quite know where to start.'

He stood just outside the door, keeping his distance. Out of range?

'How about the part where you smashed up the fuel filters on my boat? Or the bit where you stole my spear gun? Or, no—the masterstroke—the mess you made of my inflatable?' he said, his sneer mocking her.

He killed Helen. He knows I know. She gave him a slow nod, her eyes ice cold, and walked around the table towards the pool with her back to him. *So follow me out here you bastard, around about near the table would be good.* She said nothing, just stood there, staring at the forest. Its magnificence, the broad sensation of its life-filled green, the sort of thing Helen would have delighted in and fought to save.

He would have known that. He would have taken Helen out among the trees then swum with her in this very pool. Luring her. Clem hated him. From deep down in her gut, she hated him.

Doncaster took a few steps closer to the table. *Good.*

'You're not going to apologise?' he said, coy.

She stood there, still with her back to him. The neat geometry of the blue pool tiles should have soothed her. But her blood boiled with an intensity that made every nerve in her body jangle.

She heard him take a few more steps. *Come on, get a little closer, you pig.*

'You know you're quite an intriguing figure, standing there.' She heard him take another few steps towards her and stiffened. 'With your silence and all.'

She turned around slowly. 'You know, you're quite intriguing yourself. In the way repellent creatures sometimes are.'

He thrust his hands in his pockets, rocked back on his heels, eyebrows raised. It was water off a duck's back. He didn't care what she said. He knew she had nothing to link him to Jackson and without that, she couldn't touch him.

'I've been wondering what Helen was thinking—how she was ever attracted to a man like you.'

There was a look of mild surprise as he registered that Clem knew about the relationship. Then he quickly regathered his cool.

'I generally find women are aroused by powerful men.'

She supressed the urge to punch him. It was close to admitting a relationship with Helen but not quite. It signified that he was being cautious, though, despite his confidence in her inability to link him to the murder. He was wary, careful. Did he think she might be wearing a wire?

'I'd like to know, specifically, what it was Andrew. Why you fucked her and then killed her. We can speak freely can't we? I have nothing with me. My phone is where I lost it earlier today. It's just me.' She stared at him, saw the flicker in his eyes. Yes, she was sure—he thought she was recording him.

The idea came to her and she was surprised at her lack of hesitation. She didn't baulk as she undid the top button on her shorts, 'You can make sure if you like. There's nothing here, no wire, no recording device. This is not some form of entrapment.'

His eyes widened, his gaze dropping to her hands and what was underneath, the tanned flesh of her stomach, the top of her underpants as she unzipped her fly. He did not try to stop her.

'I actually want to know. I want to speak freely with you, Andrew, and I'd like you to feel equally relaxed about it.' She kept going. Her shorts fell to the ground. She pulled her singlet up over her head and let it flop to the deck. Standing there in just her underwear, she felt a shiver. Andrew Doncaster, thirty years her senior, muscled, powerful, perhaps the wealthiest man she had ever met, owner of everything in the world he wanted to own. And he was standing there, looking at her. She felt possessed of a wicked power, something she'd never used in this way: something hidden inside her own body and suddenly released.

'Do I have to go further?' she said. His eyes darted over her body, he seemed to be arguing with himself, tempted but uncertain—teetering on the edge.

'Perhaps this to reassure you?' she removed her bra, unclipping the hooks and letting the straps slide from her shoulders. It fell to the ground beside her singlet. She felt the sun on her back, warm and welcome, she felt the absolute authority of her body over this man. She felt simultaneously outrageous and composed as she turned slowly so he could inspect her.

He shifted his feet, widening his stance as if his balance was unsure. Shook his head with the slightest of movements, disbelieving. 'You're very convincing.' He would not stoop to demand she take off the last of her clothing.

'Good,' she nodded. 'Then tell me, please—tell me about Helen.' She reached for her bra, began putting it back on. He looked disappointed.

Pathetic. What did he expect? She'd stripped off for one reason only; the purpose had been accomplished. It both amused and enraged her that he thought she might have other ideas.

'What do you want to know?' he said.

'Well. I already know why you murdered Helen, so how about you tell me when you made the decision to do it?'

His mouth dropped open. 'What the fuck?'

'Oh come on, Andrew. I know about the resort, and I know about your affair. I just want to know the background. How you came to decide on it.'

'You're crazy. Why are you asking me these questions?'

'Because I want to know. I want to understand...power, I guess,' she said, hoping to appeal to the thing that counted most for Andrew Doncaster. 'Like when, for instance. Was it before you lured her up here? Did you always have it as a Plan B to kill her if she said no to your offer to buy Turtle Shores? Or did you just decide when she turned you down?'

279

The alternative close: pick one, arsehole, and condemn yourself.

Doncaster was considering her, calculating. Assessing his position, and what she was likely to do. And something else... something else was coming to the surface.

Yes, that was it: the urge to brag. A smug leaning back and thrusting of his hips forward, hands in his pockets, looking down at her. He wanted to boast about it. *Come on, put it out there, motherfucker.*

He shrugged as if accepting she was powerless here. Then, standing right next to the table, a metre from the listening device, the great, the untouchable Andrew Doncaster began to talk.

'Strategy always comes first,' he said, smirking. 'But Helen was pretty good in the sack. It became more difficult to execute as time went on.' He spoke as if it wasn't him he was talking about but some other player on a grand stage. Someone he'd delegated a task to. 'She had this way about her, with her eyes and that smile. Definitely a turn-on, even beyond her obvious...physical gifts.'

Clementine had put her shorts and singlet back on. They felt like armour. She sat on the arm of a timber sun lounge with one leg bent up so her foot perched on the edge of the cushion, trying to look casual.

'So, yes, there was a strategy from the start and if she hadn't been so stubborn, the rest wouldn't have been necessary.'

'Stubborn?'

'Yes, stubborn. The resort will be fucking great for this community, jobs-wise. And the happiness it will bring to families all over Australia...to see this beautiful place. I mean not everyone can afford Fraser Island, right? World Heritage my arse,' he snorted. 'Just means you only get to appreciate it if you can afford a weekend in a high-end resort and a four-wheel-drive tour. It's the most elitist piece of bullshit I've ever come across. My father, my mother—they could never experience it.'

'So not important to preserve it for its own sake? Only valuable to the extent humans get to colonise it?'

'Oh Christ, don't start with that self-righteous horseshit. You sound like Helen,' he said, his face looking like he'd eaten a lemon.

Watch it, Jones. Don't get him worked up, just get to the decision to kill.

She wondered about Jackson. Maybe he'd decided not to come here, too dangerous. *Don't count your chickens.*

'Fair point. I was getting pretty sick of the dogma too, towards the end.'

He looked wrong-footed: suddenly unsure of her, as if she was a sand blow drifting before his eyes.

'I mean, I'm leading the show now but it's only because there's nothing better to do in this shithole. I'll be leaving soon anyway, thank God,' she said.

It seemed to settle him, she saw his shoulders relax a little.

'So you made an offer for Turtle Shores and she knocked it back?'

'I made a very generous offer and she wasn't interested. The woman had no concept of planning for her senior years. I mean, I even offered to have my accountant organise a self-managed super fund for her, you know, look after her, and it wasn't like she was set up. I mean, she was getting a part-pension, for Christ's sake! Never ceases to amaze me how some people will not help themselves.'

Not Helen. Not a woman he'd been intimate with. Not even a woman: just a faceless pensioner. Clementine breathed deep, exhaling her abhorrence, willing him on to the next step. It was quiet. A breeze shuffled and clacked the palm fronds against each other. Hosts of small birds were chattering in the forest all around the pool; every now and then a whipbird cracked out a request.

'So, where do you go from that?'

'Well, I had no choice.'

'But do you just call someone?' She was conscious there had

been no clear admission, she needed to keep him going.

'It's not that different to hiring a tradie, really. There are people who arrange these things.' So close, but not quite.

'Did you have sex with her afterwards?'

'Oh, fuck me! Charming. You hire a contractor to kill someone, then have sex with them? No, I did not. I respected Helen.'

She didn't want to breathe at all in case she mucked something up. The man had said it. And he'd said it in such a way as to congratulate himself for being a gentleman about it. She felt her hands trembling with the shock. This man had also ordered her own death. For all she knew, the killer was waiting for her just outside somewhere, or on his way. Her mouth was bone dry and her skin crawled with a prickling heat.

'And me? You've made arrangements for me too, haven't you?'

'No hard feelings, Clementine—it's just business.' He had the audacity to grin and wink at her. He was relaxed now, the unassailable greatness like a force field: all his wealth and his forest lair and his women and his 'tradies'.

'Who's the middle man?'

'Some low-life in Sydney. Calls himself Jerry.'

'How do you find these people?'

A shrug. 'Networks.'

'And the killer?'

'Never met him. Closest I got was after you jumped overboard and he gave chase in that tinny,' he looked amused. 'Like a Roadrunner cartoon.'

'He shot at me.'

'Yeah, well, that's the general idea, sweetheart.'

Sweetheart? Are you kidding me? That alone is worth taking you down, you dinosaur.

'And an old lady. He shot at an old lady,' said Clem.

'Every project I've ever done, there's always someone complaining.' He waved a hand in the air. 'I put up a shopping centre, the corner store has a whinge. I build a casino, the social workers moan about gambling. Jesus! No one would do anything if there wasn't some sort of downside. It's not a perfect world—get over it.'

It was done. 'On the record' done. She had the hit, the middle man, the intent, the context, everything. Now she only had to get out of there with the recording.

'Hhhmm. Yes, I totally understand. Whingers, all of us,' she said. 'But speaking of projects, the resort won't be going ahead.'

'Really?' He raised an eyebrow.

'You're not getting Helen's land.'

He laughed. 'Bollocks. The settlement's going through tomorrow.'

'The stat dec you signed, the false declaration you gave about never having any relationship with Helen.'

'Oh that,' he sniggered. 'Any decent lawyer would tell you it wasn't worth the paper it was written on.'

'Can I borrow your phone for a moment, please? There's someone I think you should speak to.'

'What?'

'I lost my phone earlier today. There's someone who has some important information to give you about Turtle Shores.'

He stared at her for a second then shrugged, took out a phone from his pocket—cheap, probably a burner, the one he'd used to contact Jerry.

'What's the number?' he asked.

She recited the number, thanking the gods that it was so similar to her own. Doncaster put the phone on speaker.

It rang and kept on ringing. *Pick up, now. Please pick up.* Finally, she heard the click and the distinctive sing-song voice she remembered from the funeral.

'Maggie Jeppeson'

'Hello, Maggie, it's Clementine. I have you on speaker and I'm here with Andrew Doncaster.'

'Oh, fabulous, just the man I want to speak to,' she chirped.

'Andrew, this is Maggie Jeppeson,' said Clem. 'She's the executor of Helen's estate and Press Secretary and Head of Media for the Premier of New South Wales.'

Andrew frowned, his jaw clamping into a square.

'Hello, Andrew,' said Maggie, warmly. 'How fortunate that we get to speak first before you hear from the lawyers. I much prefer the personal touch.'

Doncaster shot a look at Clementine. 'You have something to tell me?'

'Yes, I do, rather. You see Helen was a dear friend of mine, a very dear friend. I didn't see as much of her after she moved to Piama—God only knows why there, of all places—but anyway she made a particular point of seeing me a few weeks back. She wanted to tell me she'd just ended a relationship and it had prompted her to think about what was important to her—'

'Look I'm sure you ladies find this fascinating but I'm afraid I have a short attention span for chick flicks.'

'Ha! Yes, she mentioned your short attention span,' said Maggie. 'It was a feature of the sex, too, she said. Lots of *early arrivals*.' Maggie laughed.

Clem was intent on Doncaster. The muscles in his face clenched, sending a shimmer across his jaw.

'Anyway, the long and the short of it is—excuse the pun, darling—Helen told me nothing mattered but that her land remained as a wildlife sanctuary. Forever. They were her express words to me. So, in short, Andrew, you won't be getting your grubby hands on it.'

'Oh, fuck me. This is ridiculous,' said Doncaster, looking like he'd swallowed a turd. 'Let me spell it out to you. There's a binding contract, it's settling tomorrow and there's nothing you can do about it.'

'Well, you see, I can and I will,' said Maggie. 'You told some naughty fibs when you entered into this contract.'

'*Pfft*,' he snorted, looking relieved. 'The statutory declaration? Lawyers'll make short work of that. So if that's all you've got, then I think this call is over, and I'll see you in court.'

'Well, no, actually, Andrew, I haven't finished yet. I don't really give a fig what the lawyers might have to say about it—that's just the context for the real game. I intend to have some fun with this because the thing is, Mr Doncaster, I know you killed Helen, which puts a very different *spin* on everything.'

Doncaster's Adam's apple bobbed in his throat and his hands clenched into white-knuckled fists.

'What utter rubbish. There is nothing to connect me with Helen's death. Nothing.'

Clementine cut in, 'That's where you're wrong, Andrew. There's plenty. In fact, I expect the police around here shortly,' she lied.

'Utter nonsense! Totally false!'

'Spare us the performance, darling,' said Maggie. 'It doesn't matter what the courts do to you because I've got enough to hang, draw and quarter you in the most brutal court of all: the court of public opinion, which I rule, you understand, *sweetheart*. Yes, Queen Maggie presides over that domain. Ha! Do you think the public actually need you to be convicted before they are convinced deep down, in the very depths of their dark hearts, that you are indeed a murderer, darling? Look at poor Lindy Chamberlain!' She didn't draw a breath. 'Your name, Andrew, will stink to high heaven. No government or council will ever approve another development or project or anything that has the taint of your hands on it ever again. I shall see to that.'

Maggie was good. Doncaster's white, white face was turning a vivid pink. It was exhilarating to watch.

Clem stood there. Maggie was quiet. They both knew this was the moment.

'So,' said Clem. 'This can all go away, of course. Well, at least the bit we control. We can't stop the police from arresting you but I'm sure you'll muster up a posse of top-notch defence lawyers and possibly even weasel your way out of the charges. But the publicity campaign—that will be permanent.' Clem paused for effect. 'Or… we can make it go away. It's your choice, Andrew.'

'You scheming bitch!' he snarled, eyes blazing at Clementine.

'Yes, I knew you'd be impressed,' said Clem, trying to hide her nerves as she launched into the final piece, the piece that would save Turtle Shores, Helen's legacy. 'Now, all you have to do is sign a deed mutually terminating the contract for the sale of Helen's land. Maggie's lawyer is drafting it as we speak and it'll be with you today. Sound like a plan?'

He hung up the call, enraged, just as a loud buzz came from the intercom unit near the door and a red light started to flash. Clem's heart began thumping wildly. Doncaster threw the phone onto a chair, stormed over to the device and pressed the button. '*Who is it?*' he shouted.

There was a crackle of static as the person at the gate pressed the button. Then the voice she'd heard in the hangar.

'My mate Jerry sent me.'

Time stood still for the briefest of seconds. An involuntary whimper escaped from Clem's mouth as everything inside her turned ice cold.

She spun around and made for the steps leading down into the garden but Doncaster was already moving. He caught her as she ran along the pool deck. She screamed, stumbled, and fell into the pool, taking him with her. In the tangle of legs and arms she slipped out of his grasp, kicked out for the side of the pool. Gripping the paving stones around the edge, she heaved herself up and out of the water. Halfway out, swinging one leg up, she felt his fingers wrap around her ankle, jerking her back, and then she was going down, the inside of her arm and her face scraping the edge of the pavers on the way.

She held her breath, trying to push him away, hitting out at his arms. She wasn't strong enough; he had her wrist now—she writhed and tugged, her lungs burning, pushed her head up to the surface, sucked in a desperate gulp of air. He shoved her to the steps and up, his vice-like grip locked onto her arm. Dripping and wet, he pushed her across the deck. Blood trickled from her arm and dropped onto the tiles.

He shoved Clementine over to the intercom and onto the ground, forcing her to lie on her stomach, put his sodden shoe on the back of her head and jammed her face into the deck as he pressed the button.

'Are you there?' said Doncaster, panting, the water streaming from his clothes and forming a puddle at his feet. No response. 'Fuck!' He pressed the intercom again. Nothing. 'The dickhead's pissed off. For fuck's sake!' he yelled, thumping his open palm into the wall, his foot stomping on her head, grinding it into the timber, sending shooting pains through her scalp.

It was all on the recording device. The bloody waterproof, non-transmitting recording device—useless unless she survived to tell someone where to find it.

He puffed a couple more breaths, one hand leaning on the wall. Then he stood, his foot still on Clementine's head. She could see from the corner of her eye he was removing the belt from his shorts, one of those ratchet-style ones, no tongue or holes. Then he leaned down, grabbed one of her wrists, twisted it behind her back and took his foot off her head.

'Right. Get onto your knees. Keep your face to the wall. Don't try anything.'

She pushed herself up onto her knees with her free hand. He wrapped the belt around her neck, tightened it, the ratchet clicking over like a child's toy. She was on all fours, leashed like a dog.

'Is this really necessary?'

'Shut up,' he said, jerking her upwards. One hand holding her wrist, the other keeping tension on the belt.

Come on, Jones, think of something.

'You know your mate, Jerry's mate, shot a cop just before he came here?' she said.

'You must be fucking insane if you think I'd believe anything you say.' He shoved her down onto a heavy wooden seat and began to strap the belt through the slats at the back, tightening it again against her neck.

'I was there, at the helicopter hangar. Pretty sure Sergeant Wiseman is dead. This place will be crawling with cops the minute Maggie tells them I'm here.'

288

Maggie didn't know to call the police but the rest of it was true.

'You expect me to believe any of this? The police have got nothing connecting me with Helen's death. If they had, why haven't they been here already?' he scowled. 'No, all that's happened is you and your friend have made some wild allegations. And if they ever get published or broadcast, there'll be a defamation case slapped on you both before you can blink. So what if you were here? We had a meeting about the fucking turtle. You won't be killed here. This guy'll take you somewhere else for that.'

'This is a bad move, Doncaster. My blood is all over your deck. Didn't you notice? They'll pin my death on you as well as Helen's.'

'So you tripped over and there was some blood. It means nothing.'

He didn't know about the recording, of course. But even if the police had a search warrant, would they think to look under the table? She could almost see it from where she sat. About five metres away. If she could get to it. If she could stick it in her pocket...she gulped...at least they'd find it on her dead body.

He came back around in front of her then, backing away a step to pick up his phone. Her arms were free, she could undo the belt and run, but the moment she moved an inch he'd be onto her.

He typed in a number. Clem could hear it ringing as he held it to his ear.

'Jerry?...Yes...Tell your man the package is ready for collection.'

\v/

They'd been waiting there barely a minute, her neck still strapped to the back of the seat, Doncaster pacing nervously in front of her, when she first heard the sound. She could only just make it out—faint, rhythmic, human. She looked across at Doncaster for his reaction. He didn't break stride.

I must be hearing things.

She had an acid burn in her stomach and her face throbbed. She wanted to scream at the humiliation—Doncaster scowling at her as she sat, wet through and tethered like an animal, waiting for the butcher to arrive. She wiped some blood from her face into the chair. *Let them find my blood here.* If Doncaster didn't get done for Helen, then at least he might go down for her.

She was numb, her throat dry. She tried to force the chaotic mash of her thoughts into some sort of logical thread. Would the police know to come here? If they spoke to Maggie, she would tell them she was here. But why would they call Maggie? And Clem hadn't told her anything about Jackson anyway. Would the police conclude, on their own, that Jackson might have followed Clem here to Doncaster's? They must see now that Jackson shot Wiseman because Clem had connected him with the helicopter outfit? They would see they needed to follow her to get Jackson, even though they had nothing on Doncaster...wouldn't they?

But they didn't know she was here, no one knew she was here except Jackson.

The thought of Wiseman was like a punch in the guts. The crimson blossoming on her crisp, blue shirt. The look of surprise on her face, the awful crack of her head on the concrete floor, and the bounce...her police cap falling, rolling away. Clem felt a physical pain inside her chest.

Jackson hadn't bothered with a second shot. Dead? Or... perhaps...it was possible...conceivable...just badly injured and no longer a threat. Jackson might have baulked at finishing off a cop in cold blood...rather than self-defence. Clem was convincing herself. Perhaps she was alive? *Please let her be alive.*

She heard the noise from the direction of the road again, strained to catch the sound when the intercom buzzed and she jumped. Doncaster let out a *ha!* of relief and rushed to the control unit near the door. Clem could scarcely breathe as she watched him hold the button down and speak into it.

'Yes. Hello.'

Clem closed her eyes, sent out a silent prayer. The tick of static then a voice...No. Not Jackson's voice. And in the background—chanting, definitely chanting.

'Good morning, Mr Doncaster.' A hoarse smoker's voice.

Brady!

'This is Brady Gallagher of the Wildlife Association of the Great Sandy Straits. We're staging a protest today to demand the wildlife sanctuary at Turtle Shores be preserved, and to oppose any form of development on that land.'

Oh, praise be! Brady, you angel!

Doncaster's face fell. In the background, the chanting was loud and clear, 'Save the sanc-choo-ary. Save the sanc-choo-ary.' There were a lot of voices. As many as she'd heard at any previous protest—maybe thirty of them? They were supposed to be at the working bee. Brady had rallied them here instead. That must be why Jackson had disappeared. He saw them rolling up, the whole convoy of them, and decided to clear out.

'What the fuck is this?' Doncaster shouted into the intercom. 'I didn't authorise this. Fuck the hell off!'

'Yeah, guess you can shove that one. Public road, mate,' said Brady. She could have cheered. 'We got media out here, a camera crew. We'd like to invite you to come out and discuss the issue.'

If there really was a reporter he would have named the organisation. And the camera crew—that was probably Gaylene's smartphone. Bloody idiot, Brady. What the hell was the point without media? *But, oh Brady, you bloody beauty!*

'There won't be any discussion. You can send a letter. I'm asking you to leave now.'

Clem's thoughts were beginning to arrange themselves again after the tsunami of relief. Jackson had cleared out as soon as the protesters had arrived. He wouldn't be coming back as long as there were thirty-odd witnesses out there. She reached around to the back of her neck and began undoing the belt.

'Hey, leave that!' shouted Doncaster, leaping away from the intercom and lunging at her.

Clem thrust out her foot and kicked hard into his groin. He let out a high-pitched yelp, doubled over, dropped to his knees. She had the belt off in a second. Doncaster was struggling to move but he grabbed at her foot as she sprung up onto the seat, his nails raking across her ankle. Clem ran to the table as he wobbled to his feet, groaning. She had her fingers underneath the listening device and it came loose as he stumbled towards her, one hand on his crotch, the other grabbing at the back of her shirt. Clem spun around, crashed her arm down hard on his forearm and pushed past him, running for the door. She swung it closed in his face and ran across the foyer, flinging open the heavy wooden front door and pelting up the wooden walkway, shouting with all the air in her lungs.

'Brady! Help!'

She heard Brady shushing the crowd, the chanting subsiding as she reached the fence, hitting her palm on the button and the great, rumbling gate began its slow slide along the track.

'Clementine! What are you doing in there?' said Brady, his face appearing at the gate. Ariel beside him, mouth agape.

Clem couldn't speak and as soon as the opening was wide enough, squeezed herself through. She was still wet from the pool, a strand of hair across her face, her face and arm bloodied.

'Give me your phone, quick!'

\1/

Constable Griffin was first on the scene at Doncaster's, leading another car with a contingent of cops who'd finally arrived from Brisbane. He exploded out of the vehicle without waiting for the city blokes, pale and bristling, every inch of his height enraged and shocked by the discovery of Sergeant Wiseman lying in a pool of her own blood.

Clem found out later that Mike the helicopter guy had tried to resuscitate her. Griffin had taken over the chest pumps as soon as he got there but when the paramedics arrived, it didn't take them long to call it. Sergeant Wiseman had lost her grip on life moments after being shot.

They brought Doncaster out in handcuffs. Brady and the protesters gave him merry hell, jeering and chanting, banging angry tambourines in his face and Brady, going one step too far as usual, crowding in close and swiping his finger across his neck, yelling:

'It'll be your white throat that's extinct now ya bastard!'

Clementine sat on the ground in front of Doncaster's house, Sarge by her side. He kept nuzzling her face, going for a lick here and there whenever the opportunity presented. When she couldn't resist a second longer, she buried her head in his shoulder, her arm around his neck and let out a long, exhausted sob.

CHAPTER 25

Clem packed up the shanty the next day. Sarge could sense something was going on. He lumbered around next to Pocket all morning, never leaving his side, and after the car was packed and Pocket was sitting waiting on the back seat, he started whimpering.

'You'll be okay, mate. Noel's back tomorrow morning and Ralph'll be around tonight to feed you.' She gave him a hug and stroked his silky golden fur, then led him into the backyard and closed the gate. As she rolled down the driveway, the howling began—head high in the air, mouth pursed, folds of skin hanging loose and forsaken from his neck, and a sound of loss and longing pitching high into the wind and the sky and out to sea.

Sitting in the living room at Seascape Avenue—the solid dining table between them, the vinyl recliners at the far end of the room and Selma hovering—she told Ralph everything. There had been no time when she'd made the desperate rescue call the previous day.

'What, so you thought I'd killed the turtle whisperer?' he said, offended.

'Well, the way you carry on, dear, it's hardly surprising,' said Selma, laying a plate of Anzacs in front of them.

Ralph sniggered. 'There's plenty of people would've done it, and not just over the port. She was a flaming vegan, for Christ's sake! I've known butchers who'd have done it as soon as blink.'

'Oh Ralph, please!' exclaimed Selma. She went down the hall and came back a few moments later with a letter in her hand.

'Here, Miss Jones, you're a lawyer. Can you help us with this?'

Clem took the letter. It was on Salamander Bridge letterhead, the plaintiff law firm handling the class action against the banks on behalf of the Piama residents who'd fallen prey to dodgy financial advice.

'It's an offer,' said Clem, scanning it.

'I know it's a bloody offer. We're not stupid,' said Ralph. 'Selma, why'd you bring it out? I said we'd handle it.'

'Let her look at it. I want to know what she thinks,' said Selma. 'I think we should accept it, Miss Jones, Ralph thinks we should keep fighting.'

Clem read it all. The banks were offering a sizeable sum—compensation for the catastrophic losses suffered as a result of their failure to properly assess the customers lining up to buy their margin loan products. She put the letter down on the table and leaned back in her chair. 'Well, looks like the firm has spent a lot of time putting the package together and of course they're recommending acceptance, which means they think it's a better bet than litigating further. But then, they'll be taking their share so they're not entirely disinterested in the outcome. I don't know the case, of course, but from a personal perspective, I guess it might depend on how it stacks up for you? I mean for your future.'

'Well, Ralph thinks the mortgage will be pretty much cleared. There'd be a tiny bit left but we'd manage.'

'So you could keep the house?'

'Yeah, but I don't get my Robert-Considine-sold-us-a-line fishing boat,' said Ralph, scowling.

'Don't listen to him, dear, he's just a grumpy old man.'

Clem smiled and glanced out across the backyard to the straits, flickering in the sunshine. This was good, this was great. 'You must've kissed one of those ugly catfishes, hey Ralph? Looks like one of those scum-sucking bottom-dwellers turned into a lovely big mackerel.'

CHAPTER 26

She stood in the meeting room on the forty-third floor staring out the floor-to-ceiling windows at the Yarra River, which, from this angle, looked like an industrial canal—brown and dead straight. The sleek white furniture and the clean silence made the room feel like a cocoon.

Her black suit felt too small. She'd put on weight. Her feet pinched in the new heels. She'd thrown out all her shoes bar her sneakers when she was released from prison over a year ago. And the stockings—she hadn't remembered nylon being so scratchy and claustrophobic.

It was cold in the air conditioning. The Queensland summer had messed with her body's thermostat. She rubbed her hands on her arms, trying to get the blood flowing, but it wasn't just the air conditioning. She always felt the cold when she was nervous.

Since signing the contract, she'd amused herself imagining the trappings of her new life: slick car, trendy new digs...and the cleaner, the blessed cleaner. Fortnightly to start with, then weekly once she'd got her finances back on track.

But now she was about to pick up the threads of her old career and shit was getting real. Standing this high above the river with nothing but glass in front of her, it felt like a platform diving event at the Olympics. Like she'd put her name down for a double somersault with one and a half twist and hadn't done any training at all. Would she be good enough? Could she handle the pressure?

Had she lost her edge, being out of it for so long? And most of all, what would the staff think of her? The partners wanted her on the team—for them, she represented new clients, increased revenue on the back of her celebrity. But what about the others, the secretaries and paralegals, the solicitors? To them she was no more a celebrity than any other thoughtless drunk who'd wiped someone out on the roads. Someone's mother, someone's wife, someone's daughter or sister: dead because she was too careless to get a cab.

Why had she thought this would be any different from the streets of Katinga?

She poured a glass of water from the silver jug. A single slice of lemon slid over the lip and plunged to the bottom before surfacing. It reminded her of that last day with Torrens at the shanty, although this was an elegant sliver—nothing like the chunky wedge he'd so eagerly dropped into her glass. She hadn't heard from him. Wasn't sure where he was. She'd tried his number a few times but he never picked up.

The police had deployed a mass of officers across south-east Queensland and northern New South Wales like it was the Golan Heights. Jackson was intercepted two days later near Eddies Flat and charged with three counts of murder: Emma Wiseman, Declan Membrey and Helen Westley.

Clem had gone to the grave site. The dirt was still piled in a gently curving mound, yet to subside. Stopping at Turtle Shores on the way, she'd picked up two paperbark branches. She made a wooden cross tying them together with string and pushed the longer branch into the soil at Helen's head. At the base of the cross she laid a bouquet of frangipani—white, glossy five-petalled blossoms, golden at their centre.

Then she'd stood there and wept softly.

\|/

The door to the meeting room swung open behind her and the managing partner, Gary Swan walked in, hand thrust out. 'Ah, Clementine, so glad to finally have you here. Welcome, welcome.'

Gary had been the one to recruit her, the one she'd been emailing. He was a nice guy, warm and cheery. He asked about her trip and traversed the small talk with the easy style of a man schooled in the arts of civility.

'So, we have a few things lined up for you today,' he said, clasping his hands together enthusiastically. 'Some of the partners from the sports and media division will be meeting with you, along with the head of our corporate team, but I thought I'd show you your office first and do a stroll around the floor to meet some of the team. HR and IT will look after you from there, and then you and I will meet at the end of the day so I can fill you in a little more on firm strategy. Sound okay?'

He held open the door for her and led her down a corridor, striding purposefully past an open-plan area with people dotted about in large, airy cubicles. Clem avoided eye contact as they each looked up from their desks in a kind of Mexican wave of bobbing heads. Gary walked her into a windowed office on the far side of the floor, the sun streaming through the blinds onto a faux-walnut desk with a slimline monitor. She put her laptop bag down on the desk and walked over to the window.

'You can see the MCG over there,' said Gary, smiling. 'We wanted you to feel at home.'

She felt a single thump of her heart, blinked. She should say something, but nothing would come. Finally, she turned around.

'Um, could you just excuse me for a moment, Gary, and maybe just show me where the bathroom is?'

'Yes, of course. Sorry, should have showed you on the way here.'

Gary took her out to the lift lobby and pointed to the bathrooms at the far end.

She went inside, put her handbag down and leaned on the

wash basin, exhaling as much of the tension as would come out in one breath. The sink was one of those long, trough-style affairs, ultra-modern and spotlessly clean. She looked up and regarded herself in the mirror. Her hair was carefully styled. She couldn't afford highlights yet, but she'd had it cut and conditioned and it was gleaming. She was wearing make-up for the first time in months. Her eyes looked strange and there was too much lip-liner, too thick, clown-like. She hung her head again. Caffeine rattled around her veins, sending a buzz to her fingertips. Other than that, she felt completely empty.

Her phone pinged, a text from the kennels. They'd said they would send a message to let her know how Pocket settled in.

Doing fine, enjoying the yard and a walk.

Of course they would say that, whether he was happy or not. She felt a pang. Top of her list for accommodation was finding somewhere with a yard big enough for an energetic little blue heeler cross who'd never lived anywhere but the country and the seaside. Pocket was no city dog, and he was used to her being there pretty much all of the time. With law-firm hours she'd be lucky to get home before eight now. So much for the inner-city apartment living with the stylish commute, strolling past manicured parks and groovy hole-in-the-wall coffee shops. A long, rattling journey fighting for a seat on public transport, more like it.

There was another message she hadn't noticed, from Rowan.

Changed my password: cleMEntine. Capitals harder to hack and you get more of ME

How incredibly corny. She looked up into the mirror and there was the slightest of smiles on her face.

The phone pinged again. John Wakely, Katinga Cats Club President. She opened up the message. A video clip, downloading slowly in the bathroom fortress, stalled on the still shot at the beginning: the Cats players—all of them lined up in three disorderly rows. She pressed play. There they stood in their training gear—odd socks, grubby T-shirts—shuffling about with that restless energy of young men, some of them still teenagers. Todd Wakely's hair was growing back and Clancy was there. Not dressed for training, but it brought a smile to her face to see him out of the wheelchair. Torrens was conspicuously absent. It made the team look unbalanced—too many runners and ground-level players, not enough height. The captain, Sellingham, was tossing a ball around in his hands.

'You're late for training, Jonesy,' grinning as he spoke to the camera. 'That'll be twenty push-ups and an extra lap around the oval.'

A bunch of them jeered and someone yelled, 'Dose of your own medicine, Jonesy!'

The front row all dropped to the ground and started doing push-ups, grunting and competing with each other for form and pace—all rehearsed, obviously—the rest of them laughing and jostling each other.

Then a tiny old lady shuffled into the shot from stage right. Fluffy white hair and a summer frock in yellow and orange flowers, white ankle socks and white plimsolls so small they were probably a child's size. Mrs Lemmon.

Sellingham welcomed her and turned her round to face the camera. 'That's the camera over there, Mrs L,' he said, pointing.

'Ah yes. Thank you, Benjamin.' She nodded and stared with her permanent smile. A second or two passed.

'So the camera's rolling now, Mrs L,' said Sellingham. 'Away you go.'

'Oh yes,' she said, still smiling. 'Well, they did tell me to say something, Miss Jones, and I can't think what it was now, but anyway we need you to come and get started on the training. These boys got fat over the summer'—laughter, Mrs Lemmon chuckling—'and I know it might sound rude of me to say it, but you're not setting a very good example for them.' And with her voice ringing as loud and stern as she could manage, 'It's high time you got yourself back home.'

It was like being scolded by a budgerigar.

Mrs Lemmon stood there smiling and blinking, as if she knew there had been something else she was supposed to say, until Sellingham leaned down. She only came up to his bottom rib. 'Tell her about the garden, Mrs L.'

'Oh yes, that's right, thank you, Benjamin,' she said. 'We went up to your cottage last week, Miss Jones. I took some tea and scones and the boys mowed the lawns and tidied up the garden for you. I'm afraid you've had a wombat in the backyard. He made a bit of a mess,' she tittered. 'But you've got some lovely pink clematis in flower out the front. Clematis for Clementine.' She was beaming, so pleased she'd remembered the last bit.

The video ended with the whole team shouting the Cats war cry. Clem could feel a heartsickness rising within. She closed her eyes, stayed there in the bathroom another few minutes. Then she took a few deep breaths and headed back out to the office where Gary was waiting for her.

'Gary,' she said. He smiled. She reached out with one hand to the walnut desk to steady herself, her face grim, and watched as his smile faded.

'I'm sorry Gary, I'm not sure this is going to work.'

ACKNOWLEDGEMENTS

A book is a solitary thing until you get towards the end of it all and so many people come together to help it on its way. And the help that is given at that point is expert help, not the bumbling efforts of the author.

Thanks to my agent, Gaby Naher of Leftbank Literary—there's no better first reader for precision insights and masterful suggestions. To senior editor Mandy Brett of Text Publishing for the second round of artful recommendations and thoughtful edits, and an editing process that was supremely professional.

I fell in love with the cover design and thought 'take it straight to the pool room' as soon as I saw it. It's not only apt for the story but it's breathtakingly beautiful. Thank you Imogen Stubbs at Text Publishing.

To my publicist Madeleine Rebbechi, a most talented professional who has worked so hard in difficult circumstances to bring *White Throat* to the reading public.

To Text Publishing generally, thank you for your support and for keeping on publishing Aussie stories, no matter the challenges.

To Dean, as always, my consultant in all things dangerous, outrageous, fast, mechanical, electrical. All of the adventurous parts of this novel are inspired by the man himself who has, in most cases, personal experience of them. Thanks too, my darling for your unending support of all my endeavours and for your courteous silence while I'm working, despite the degree of suffering it causes to be quiet for such lengths of time.

Also to my family and friends who keep supporting me, giving me so much confidence and courage to continue. I love youse all.